BARBARA DELINSKY

Dream Man

HQN™

Recycling programs
for this product may
not exist in your area.

ISBN-13: 978-0-373-77425-8

DREAM MAN

Copyright © 2009 by Harlequin Books S.A.

The publisher acknowledges the copyright holder of the
individual works as follows:

THE DREAM COMES TRUE
Copyright © 1990 by Barbara Delinsky

MONTANA MAN
Copyright © 1989 by Barbara Delinsky

www.HQNBooks.com

Printed in U.S.A.

CONTENTS

THE DREAM COMES TRUE

CHAPTER ONE

EIGHT PEOPLE SAT AROUND the large table in the boardroom at Gordon Hale's bank. They comprised the Crosslyn Rise consortium, the men and women who were financing the conversion of Crosslyn Rise from an elegant, singly owned estate to an exclusive condominium community. Of the eight, seven seemed perfectly content with the way the early-morning meeting was going. Only Nina Stone was frustrated.

Nina hated meetings, particularly the kind where people sat at large tables and hashed things out ad nauseam. Discussion was part of the democratic process, she knew, and as a member of the consortium, with a goodly portion of her own savings at stake, she appreciated having a say in what was happening at Crosslyn Rise. So she had smilingly endured all of the meetings that had come in the months before. But this one was different. This discussion was right up her alley. She was the expert here. If her fellow investors weren't willing to take her professional advice now that the time had finally come for her to give it, she didn't know why in the world she was wasting her time.

Nina's business was real estate. She was the broker of record for Crosslyn Rise, the one who would be in charge of selling the units and finding tenants for the retail space. It was mid-May, nearly eight months since ground had been broken, and the project was finally ready to be marketed.

"I still think," she said for the third time in thirty minutes, "that pricing in the mid-fives is shooting low. Given location alone, we can ask six or seven. What other complex is forty minutes from Boston, tucked into trees and meadows, and opening onto the ocean? What other complex offers a health club, a catering service, meeting rooms and even guest rooms to rent out for visiting friends and relatives? What other complex offers both a marina and shops?"

"None," Carter Malloy conceded, "at least, not in this area." Carter was the architect for the project and the unofficial leader of the consortium. As of the previous fall, he was married to Jessica Crosslyn, who sat close by his side. Jessica's family had been the original owners of the Rise. "But the real estate market is lousy. The last thing we want is to overprice the units, then have them sit empty for years."

"They won't sit empty," Nina insisted. "Trust me. I know the market. They'll sell."

Jessica wasn't convinced. "Didn't you tell me that things weren't selling in the upper end of the market?"

"Uh-huh, but that was well over a year ago, when you were thinking of selling the Rise intact, to a single buyer. Selling something in the multiple millions was tough then. It's eased up, even more so in the range we're talking." She sent her most confident glance around the table. "As your broker, I'd recommend pricing from high sixes to mid sevens, depending on the size of the unit. Based on other sales I've made in the past few months, I'm sure we can get it."

"What kind of sales were those?" came the quiet voice of John Sawyer from the opposite end of the table.

Nina homed in on him as she'd been doing, it seemed, for a good part of the past hour. Of all those in the room, he disturbed her the most, and it wasn't his overgrown-schoolboy look—round wire-rimmed glasses, slightly shaggy brown hair, corduroy blazer with elbow patches and open-necked plaid shirt—that did it. It was the fact that he was sticking his nose in where it didn't belong.

He was a bookseller, not a businessman. He knew nothing about real estate, and though she had to admit that he usually stayed in the background, he wasn't staying in the background today. In his annoyingly laid-back and contemplative way, he was questioning nearly everything she said.

"Three of those sales were in the eights, one in the nines, and another well over the million mark," she told him.

"For properties like ours?" he challenged softly.

She didn't blink. "No. The properties were very different, but the point is that, A, this community is in demand, and, B, there is money around to be spent."

"But by what kinds of people?" he countered in the slow way he had of speaking. "Of course, the superwealthy can spend it, but the superwealthy aren't the ones who'll be moving here. They won't want condo living when they can have ten-acre estates of their own. I thought we were aiming at the middle-aged adult whose children are newly grown and out of the house and who now wants something less demanding. That kind of person doesn't have seven or eight hundred thousand dollars to toss around. He's still feeling his way out from under college tuitions."

"That's one way of looking at it," Nina acknowledged. "Another way is that he now has money to spend that he hasn't had before, precisely because he no longer has those tuitions to shoulder. And he'll be willing to spend it. As he sees it, he's sacrificed a whole lot to raise his family. Now he's ready to do things for himself. That's why the concept of Crosslyn Rise is so perfect. It appeals to the person who is still totally functional, the person who is at the height of his career and isn't about to wait for retirement to pamper himself. He has the money. He'll spend it."

"What about the shopkeepers?" John asked.

"What about them?"

"They don't have it to spend. If you set the price of the

condos so high, the rental space will have to be accordingly high, which will rule out the majority of the local merchants."

"Not necessarily."

"You'll give them special deals?"

"The rental space doesn't have to be that high."

"It can't be anywhere *near* that high—"

Her eyes flashed. "Or you won't move in?"

"I won't be *able* to move in," he said calmly.

With a glance at his watch, Gideon Lowe, the builder for the project, suddenly sat forward. "I don't know about you guys, but it's already nine. I'm losin' the best part of my day." He slanted a grin from Nina to John. "How about you two stay on here and bicker for a while, then give us a report on what you decide at the meeting next week?"

Nina didn't appreciate the suggestion, particularly since she suspected that Gideon's rush was more to see his wife than his men. She couldn't blame him, she supposed; he'd been married less than a month and was clearly in love. His wife, Christine, was doing the decorating for Crosslyn Rise. Nina liked her a lot.

Still, this was business. Nina didn't like the idea of staying on to bicker with John Sawyer when she wanted an immediate decision from the group. Keeping her voice as pleasant as possible, given the frustration she was feeling, she said, "I think this is something for the committee as a whole to decide. Mr. Sawyer is only one man—"

"One man," Carter interrupted, "who is probably in a better position than any of the rest of us to discuss the money issues you're talking about. He's our potential shopkeeper."

Jessica agreed. "Maybe Gideon is right. If the two of you toss ideas back and forth and come up with some kind of compromise before next week, you'll save us all some time. We're running a little short now. Carter has an appointment at nine-thirty in Boston, I have one in Cambridge." Murmurs of agreement came from around the table, along with the scuffing of chair legs on the highly polished oak floor.

"But I wanted to go to the printer with the brochure," Nina said, barely curbing her impatience as she stood along with the others. "I need the price information for that."

Carter snapped his briefcase shut. "We'll make the final decision next week." To John, he said, "You'll meet with Nina?"

Nina looked at John. The fact that he was still seated didn't surprise her at all. The consortium had met no less than a dozen times since its formation, and in all that time, not once had she seen him in a rush. He spoke slowly. He moved slowly. If she didn't know better, she'd have thought that he didn't have a thing in life to do but mosey along when the mood hit and water the geraniums in the window box outside the small Victorian that housed his bookstore.

But she did know better. She knew that John Sawyer ran that bookstore with the help of only one other person, a middle-aged woman named Minna Larken, who manned the till during the hours when John was with his son. Nina also knew that the boy was four, that he had severe sight and hearing problems and that her heart went out to both father and son. But that didn't make her any less impatient. She had work to do, a name to build and money to make, and John Sawyer's slow and easygoing manner made her itchy.

Typically, in response to Carter's query, John was a minute in answering. Finally he said, "I think we could find a time to meet."

Forcing a smile, Nina ruffled the back of her dark boy-short hair and said in a way that she hoped sounded sweet but apologetic, "Wow, this week is a tough one. I have showings one after another today and tomorrow, then a seminar Thursday through Sunday."

"That leaves Monday," Carter said buoyantly. "Monday's perfect." Putting an arm around Jessica's waist, he ushered her from the room.

"Carter?" Nina called, but he didn't answer. "Jessica?"

"I'll talk with you later," Jessica called over her shoulder, then was gone, as were all of the others except John. Feeling thwarted, Nina sent him a helpless look.

With measured movements, he sat back in his chair. "If it's any consolation, I don't like the idea of this any more than you do."

She didn't know whether to be insulted. "Why not?"

"Because you're always in a rush. You make me nervous."

She *was* insulted, which was why she set aside her normal tact and said, "Then we're even, because you're so slow, you make *me* nervous." But it looked as though the group would be expecting some sort of decision from John and her, and she couldn't afford to let them down. There were some important people among them. Impressing important people was one way to guarantee future work.

Hiking her bag from the floor to the table, she fished out her appointment book. "So, when will it be? Do you want to make it sometime next Monday, say late morning?"

John laced his fingers before him. "Next Monday is bad for me. I'll be in Boston all day."

"Okay." She flipped back a page, then several more. The seminar would be morning to night, and draining. No way could she handle a meeting with John on any of those days. "I could squeeze something in between three-thirty and four tomorrow afternoon."

He considered that, then shook his head. "I work then."

"So do I," she said quickly, "but the point is to fudge a little here and there." She ran a glossy fingernail down the page. "My last showing is at seven, but then I have a meeting—" She cut herself off, mumbled, "Forget that," and turned back one more page. "How about later today?"

When he didn't answer, she looked up. Only then did he ask, "How much later?"

She studied her book. "I have appointments through seven. We could meet after that."

He freed one of his hands to rub the side of his nose, under his glasses. When the glasses had stopped bobbing and his fingers were laced again, he said, "No good. I'm with my son then."

"What time does he go to bed?"

"Seven-thirty, eight."

"We could meet then. Can you get a sitter?"

"I can, but I won't. I have work to do in the store."

"But if you don't have a sitter—"

"I live on the second floor of the house. If I'm downstairs in the store and he cries, I can hear it."

She sighed. "Okay. What time will you finish your work?" It occurred to her that she would rather meet with John later that day, even if it meant cutting into the precious little time she had to herself, than having the meeting hanging over her head all week.

"Nine or ten."

"We could meet then. I'll come over."

He eyed her warily. "Isn't that a little late for a meeting?"

"Not if there's no other time, and it looks like there isn't."

His wariness persisted. "Don't you ever stop?"

"Sure. When I go to bed, which is usually sometime around one or two in the morning. So—" she wanted to get it settled and leave "—are we on for nine, or would you rather make it ten?"

"And you work all day long?"

"Seven days a week," she said with pride, because pride was what she felt. Of six brokers in her office, her sales figures had been the highest for three years running. Granted, she didn't have a husband or children to slow her down, but the fact remained that she worked hard.

"When do you relax?"

"I don't need to relax."

"Everyone needs to relax."

"Not me. I get pleasure in working." She held her pen poised over the appointment book. "Nine, or ten?"

He studied her in silence for a minute. "Nine. Any later and I won't be thinking straight. Unlike you, I'm human."

His voice was as unruffled as ever. She searched his face for derision, but given the distance down the table and the fact of the glasses shielding his eyes, she came up short. "I'm human," she said quietly, if a bit defensively. "I just like to make the most of every minute." By way of punctuation, she snapped the appointment book shut, returned it to her bag and hung the bag on her shoulder. "I'll see you at nine," she said on her way out the door.

There was no sound behind her, but then, she hadn't expected there would be. John Sawyer would have needed at least thirty seconds to muster a response, but she'd been gone in fifteen. By the time the next fifteen had passed, her thoughts were three miles down the road in her office.

WITHIN FIFTEEN MINUTES, after stops at the post office and the dry cleaner, she was there herself. Crown Realty occupied the bottom floor of a small office building on the edge of town. The brainchild of Martin Crown, the firm was an independent one. It had the advantage over some of the larger franchises in its ties to the community; the Crown family had been on the North Shore for generations. Over and above two local restaurants and a shopping mall, the family assets included the weekly newspaper that made its way as far as Boston. In that weekly newspaper were real estate ads that would have cost an arm and a leg elsewhere. The money saved was tallied into profits, and profits were what interested Nina Stone the most.

Nina had plans for the future. She was going to have her

own firm, have her own staff, have money in the bank, stability and security. She'd known this for ten years, the first four of which she'd spent in New York. Four years had taught her that as tough as she was, New York was tougher. So she'd moved to the North Shore of Massachusetts, where the living was easier and the market was hot. For six years, she'd doggedly worked her way up in the world of real estate. Now the end was in sight. With one more year like the ones behind her and a respectable return on her investment in Crosslyn Rise, she'd have enough money to go out on her own.

Having a solid name, a successful business and scads of money meant independence, and independence meant the world to Nina.

"Hi, Chrissie," she called with a smile as she strode through the reception area. "Any calls?"

"Pink slips are on your desk," was the receptionist's reply.

Depositing her bag, Nina snatched them up, glanced through even as she rearranged them in order of importance, then settled into her chair and reached for the phone. The first and most urgent call was from a lawyer whose client was to pass papers on a piece of property that morning. At his request, the meeting was put off for an hour, which meant that Nina had to shift two other appointments. Then she returned calls to a seller with a decision on pricing, an accountant trying to negotiate his way into prime business space and a potential buyer who had heard a rumor that the price of the house she was waiting for was about to drop.

Nina was on the phone chasing down that rumor when a young woman appeared at her door. Lee Stockland, with her frizzy brown hair, her conservative skirts, blouses and single strand of pearls, and the ten extra pounds she'd been trying to lose forever, was a colleague. She was also a good friend, one of the best Nina had. Their personalities complemented each other.

Nina waved her in, then held up a finger and spoke into the phone.

"Charlie Dunn, please."

"I'm sorry, Mr. Dunn's not in the office."

"This is Nina Stone at Crown Realty. It's urgent that I speak with him." She glanced at her watch. "I'll be here for another forty-five minutes. If he comes in during that time, would you have him call me?"

"Certainly."

"Thanks." She hung up and turned to Lee. "Maisie Stewart heard that 23 Hammond dropped to eight-fifty." She swiveled in her chair. "It wasn't in the computer last night. Have you seen anything today?"

"Nope."

Nina brought up the proper screen, punched in the listing she wanted and saw that Lee was right. She sat back in her chair. "If word of mouth beat this computer, I'll be furious. Charlie knows the rules. Any change is supposed to be entered here."

"Charlie isn't exactly a computer person."

Nina tossed a glance skyward. "Do tell. He claims you can't teach an old dog new tricks, but I don't agree with that for a minute. What you make up your mind to do, you do." With barely a breath, she said, "So, what did the Millers think of the house?"

Lee took the chair by Nina's desk. "They weren't thrilled to see me rather than you, but I think they liked it. Especially her, and that's what counts."

Nina nodded. "I know him. He'll see every little flaw and be tallying up how much it will cost to fix each one. Then he'll balance the amount against the price of the house and go back and forth, back and forth until someone else's bid is accepted and it's too late. Then we'll start right back at the beginning again." She sighed, suddenly sheepish, and fiddled with her earring. "Thanks,

Lee. Jason is a pain in the butt. I really appreciate your taking them out."

"You appreciate it?" Lee laughed. "I'm the one who appreciates it. If it weren't for the clients you give me, I'd be twiddling my thumbs all day."

Nina couldn't argue with that. As brokers went, Lee was an able technician. Given a client, she did fine. But she didn't know the meaning of the word 'hustle,' and hustling was the name of the game. Nina hustled. When she wasn't showing a potential buyer a piece of property, she was meeting with a seller, or phoning potential others with offers of appraisals, or organizing mailings to keep her name and her business in the forefront of the community's mind.

Lee didn't have the drive for that, and while once upon a time Nina had scolded her friend, she didn't any longer. Lee was perfectly happy to work less, to earn less, in essence to serve as Nina's assistant, and Nina was grateful for the help. "You're a lifesaver," she said. "The Millers insisted on going early this morning. I couldn't be two places at once."

"Speaking of which," she gave a pointed look at Nina's bright red linen dress, "I take it that's your power outfit. How did it go at the bank?"

Nina's mouth drew down at the corners. "Don't ask."

"Not good?"

"Slow. Sl-ow." She began to pull folders from her bag. "Let me tell you, working with so many people is a real hassle. To get one decision made is a major ordeal."

"Did they like the brochure?"

"I think so, but I never got a final judgment on it, because they got hung up discussing the pricing of the units."

"What did they decide on that?"

Nina's phone buzzed. *"Nothing,"* she cried, letting her frustration show. "They want me to meet with this one guy—" She picked up the phone. "Nina Stone."

"Ms. Stone, my name is Carl Anderson. I was given your name by Peter Serretti, who worked with you on your new computer system."

Nina remembered Peter clearly. He had indeed worked with her, far more closely than she had wanted. Long after she learned to operate the system, she'd been plagued by phone calls from Peter asking her out. So now his friend was calling. She was immediately on her guard.

"Of course, I remember Mr. Serretti. What can I do for you, Mr. Anderson?"

"I'm actually calling from New York. My wife and I are both in education. We'll be moving to Boston in August. We were thinking of buying something on the North Shore. Pete said you were the one to talk with."

Nina felt an immediate lightening of her mood. "I'm sure I am," she said with a smile for Lee, who had settled into her chair to wait. "What kind of place are you looking for?"

"A condo. Two to three bedrooms. We have no children, but have a dog and two cars."

Nina was making notes. "Price range?"

"Two-fifty, three hundred tops." He rushed on apologetically. "We just can't handle anything more than that. When we visited Pete, we were impressed with the North Shore. If I'm totally out of my league, tell me."

"You're not, not at all." Crosslyn Rise was out of the question, both in terms of price and availability, but there were other options. "There's an older three-bedroom condo on the market for two-ninety-five, and several more updated two-bedrooms in the same range. But there's a new complex that you should probably see. It's in Salem, near the harbor, and it's beautiful. About half of the units have been sold, but there are still some wonderful three-bedroom ones that would fall within your range." She described the units, at times reading directly from the promotional packet that Lee had smoothly slipped her.

Carl seemed pleased. "We thought we'd drive up Friday and spend Saturday and Sunday looking. Would that be all right?"

"Uh, unfortunately, I'll be at a seminar all weekend—" her eyes met Lee's "—but one of my associates could certainly show you as much as you'd like to see." She frowned when, with a helpless look, Lee gave a quick shake of her head.

"Pete recommended you," Carl insisted. "He said you knew what you were talking about. I had an awful time with a broker here when we bought the place we're in now. She messed up the Purchase and Sales agreement, and we nearly lost the place."

Nina loved hearing stories like that. "I don't mess up Purchase and Sales agreements."

"That's what Pete said."

"Is this weekend the only time you can come?"

"This is the only weekend my wife and I are both free."

"Then let me suggest this. I'll go through all the listings, come up with everything I think might be worth seeing, and my associate will do the showing." Lee was still looking helpless. "You and I can talk first thing Monday morning when I'm back in the office. I'll be able to handle things from there."

Carl Anderson seemed satisfied with that. After taking note of his address and phone number, plus additional information regarding what he wanted, Nina hung up the phone. Her eyes quickly met Lee's. "Problem?"

"I can't work this weekend," Lee said timidly.

"Oh, Lee. You said you could. I've been counting on you to cover for me while I'm away."

"I can for Thursday and Friday, but—" she hesitated for a split second before blurting out "—Tom wants to go to the Vineyard. I've never been to the Vineyard. He's already made reservations for the ferry and the hotel, and he's talking about lying on the beach and browsing through the shops and eating at terrific restaurants—" She caught her breath and let out a soft, "How could I say no?"

Nina felt a surge of frustration that had nothing to do with work. "You can't. You never can, to Tom. But it's always last minute to a dinner or a movie or a weekend away. Why doesn't he call sooner?"

"He just doesn't plan his life that way. He likes spontaneity."

"Baloney. He just can't make any kind of commitment. He goes here, goes there, calls you when he gets the urge. He uses you, Lee."

"But I like him."

"You're too good for him."

"I'm not," Lee said flatly. "I'm twenty-eight, and I've never been married. I'm not cute like you, or petite, or blue eyed. I can't wear clothes like you do or polish my nails like you do. I'm not aggressive, and I'll never earn much money, so I'm not much of a bargain. But Tom is good to me."

Nina died a little inside. Each time she heard a woman use those words, no matter how innocent they were, she thought of her mother. So many times Maria Stone had said the same—*but he's good to me*—and for all the men who'd been "good" to her, she had ended up with nothing. Nina ached at the thought of that happening again, particularly to someone she cared about, like Lee.

Coming forward on the desk, she said with force, "You're not a lost cause, Lee. You're attractive and smart and warm. You're the one who taught me how to cook, and arrange flowers, and save bundles by shopping in the stores *you* found. You have lots to offer a man, lots more than me. You don't need to stoop to the level of a Tom Brody. If you want male company, there are plenty of other men around."

"Fine for you to say. You attract them like flies, then you swat them away."

"I do not."

"You're not interested in a relationship."

"I'm not interested in marriage, and I'm not interested in being kept, but I date. If an interesting guy comes along and asks me to dinner, I go."

"When you have time."

"Is there anything wrong with that?" Nina asked more gently. They'd had the discussion before. "Work means a lot to me. It's my future. At this point in my life, the investment I make in it means a whole lot more than the investment I might make in a man." Under her breath, she muttered, "Heaven only knows the return stands to be better."

Lee heard the low muttering and sighed. "Speak for yourself. Those of us who aren't so independent are looking all over for Mr. Right, but I think all the Mr. Rights are taken."

"Just wait. Give all those Mr. Rights a chance to divorce their first wives, then they'll be yours for the taking. I'm told they're far better husbands the second time around."

"I want Tom first. I think I have a chance with him, Nina. I really do."

But Nina knew more about Tom Brody than she let on. She had seen him in action against her boss years before, when he'd tried to renege on an agreement that was signed and sealed. "He's not right for you, Lee. He's a huckster with his eye out for the fast lane. When he hooks onto it, he'll be long gone. What you need is someone softer, slower, less driven." The image that popped unbidden into her mind made her snort. "You need a guy like John Sawyer."

"Who's John Sawyer?"

"A member of my consortium. He's invested in the Rise, but he's not a businessman, at least, not in the strictest sense of the word. He sells books. He's a thinker."

Lee arched an interested brow. "Married?"

"His wife died. He has a little boy who's four."

Lee's interest waned. "Oh. I'm no good with kids. I don't think I want to get into that. Forget John Sawyer."

Nina's thoughts flipped back to the meeting earlier that morning, then ahead to the one to come later that night. "I wish I could. The man might prove to be the biggest thorn in my side since Throckmorton Malone." Throckmorton Malone was a perennial house-shopper. He found a house he liked, put down a deposit, started bickering with either the builder or the owner or the owner's agent about the smallest, most insignificant details, then pulled out of the deal after handfuls of others who might have been interested had been turned away.

"No one could be that big a thorn."

Nina sighed. "Maybe. Still, this one could give me gray hair. He thinks we're pricing the units too high. He thinks he knows the market. Worst of all, the rest of the group thinks he knows what he's talking about, so they're making me meet separately with him to try to come to some sort of compromise."

"That's not so bad. You can convince him to see things your way."

"Yeah, but he's so—" she made a face as she searched for the word, finally exploding into a scornful "—*blah.* He's so calm and casual and unhurried about everything. He has all the time in the world to mull over every little thing. What ought to take five minutes will take fifty with him. Just looking at him frustrates me."

Lee showed a hint of renewed interest. "He's good-looking?"

"Not to *my* way of thinking. He's too bookish. I mean, we're talking thin and pale. Drab. Boring."

"Is he tall?"

Nina had to think about that, then think some more. "I don't know. I don't think so. Funny, I've never really noticed. He's that kind of guy, blink and you miss him." She frowned. "Mostly when I see him he's sitting down. Everyone else get up to leave, he stays in his seat. He doesn't move quickly. Ever." She sighed. "And I have to meet with him at nine o'clock tonight. Who knows how long he'll drag out the meeting." She grimaced. "Could be he'll put me to sleep."

"That'd be novel." They both knew Nina rarely slept. She had too much energy to slow down for long.

With a glance at her watch, Nina was out of her chair. "I'm meeting with the Selwyns at the Traynor cape in five minutes. Gotta run."

"About this weekend—" Lee began.

"Not to worry," Nina assured her. Taking a file from the corner of the desk, she slipped it into her bag. "I'll get someone else to cover."

"I'm really sorry. I hate letting you down."

Turning to her, Nina said in earnest, "You're not letting me down, at least not about filling in here. You have a right to a life, and if you haven't been to the Vineyard, you *have* to go. I just wish you weren't going with Tom."

"I'll be fine. Really."

"Famous last words," Nina said softly, gave Lee a last pleading look, then murmured, "Gotta run."

CHAPTER TWO

NINA'S DAY WAS BUSY enough to prevent her from giving the impending meeting with John much thought until she returned to her office at seven, with all other appointments behind her and two hours to fill before nine. Filling them wasn't the problem. She had more than enough paperwork to do, and if she finished that, there were phone calls to make. But the urgency wasn't the same as it would have been at the height of the workday. So her mind wandered.

She thought about Crosslyn Rise, and how pretty the first of the units, nestled in among trees at the duck pond, were beginning to look. She thought about the brochure she had so painstakingly put together with the artist who'd drawn pictures of the Rise, and the printer, and the fact that she felt it should already be in circulation. She thought about the pricing, the arguments both ways, her own conviction and John's. She thought about his slow, slow way of thinking and talking and her own preference for working more quickly. The more she thought about those things, the more frustrated she grew. By the time she finally got into her car and drove to The Leaf Turner, she was spoiling for a fight.

The house stood close to the center of town and was a small white Victorian, set in relief against the night by the glow of a street lamp that stood nearby. The second floor was dark, the first floor lit. Walking to the front door as though it were the middle of the day and she were out shopping for a book, she turned the brass knob and let herself in.

"Hello?" she called, closing the door behind her. When there was no response, she called again, in a more commanding tone this time, "Hello?"

"Be right there," came a distant voice, followed after a time by the leisurely pad of rubber-soled shoes on the back stairs, which was followed, in turn, by John's appearance. At least, it was the appearance of someone she assumed to be John. His face was partially hidden behind the carton he was carrying, a carton that looked to be heavy from the way he carefully lowered it to the ground. When he straightened, he looked her in the eye and said in that slow, quiet way of his, "You're right on time."

For a minute, she didn't speak. The man who had emerged from behind the carton had John's voice and features, but that was the extent of the similarity to the man with whom she served on the Crosslyn Rise consortium. This John's face wasn't pale, but flushed with activity and shadowed with a distinct end-of-the-day beard. This John's face slightly shaggy brown hair was clustered into spikes on his forehead, which glistened with sweat. As she watched, he mopped a trickle of that sweat from his temple, displaying a forearm that was leanly muscular and spattered with hair.

"I aim to please," she said lightly, but she couldn't take her eyes from him.

This time he ran the back of his hand over his upper lip. "I'm short of space up here, so the courier service puts deliveries in the basement. I've been carting books around, trying to get things organized. If I'd realized I was going to build up a sweat, I'd have showered and changed."

"No problem." She was still wearing the red dress she'd had on since dawn. "It's the end of the day. Besides," she added in an attempt to set the tone for their meeting, "we won't be long enough to make it worth the effort. I'm sure we can hash out our differences in no time."

He responded to the suggestion with a nonchalant twitch of his lips. "I don't know about that, but you're welcome to try." Leaning over, he slit the carton open with a single-edged blade, set the blade back on the counter and pulled the flaps up. "Go ahead. I'm listening."

He was wearing the same plaid shirt he'd been wearing that morning, only he'd paired it with jeans. They fit his lean hips so familiarly that his shoulders looked broad. She hadn't expected that. She had thought he'd be spindly under his corduroy blazer. She had also thought he'd be weak, but from the looks of the carton he'd been carrying— and the fact that, though sweaty, he wasn't winded in the least—she'd been wrong. She could see strength in his forearms, in his shoulders, in the denim-sheathed legs that straddled the box as he began to unload it.

Straightening with an armful of books, he looked at her. "I'm listening," he said again, and the mild derision in his eyes wasn't to be mistaken. Only when she saw it, though, did she realize something else.

"You're not wearing your glasses." She'd never seen him without them before, had simply assumed they were a constant.

"They get in the way sometimes."

"Don't you need them to see?"

"When I'm reading. Or driving. Or thinking of doing either." Turning away, he hunkered down by a low riser near the cash register and began to stack the books, turning one right, then one left, alternating until his arms were empty. When he was finished and stood, she realized yet another thing. Though he wasn't tall by the standards of men like Carter Malloy and Gideon Lowe, in relation to her own five foot two, he was long. She guessed him to be just shy of six feet.

"Something wrong?" he asked with maddening calm. She felt a warm flush creep up from her neck, all the more disconcerting because she wasn't normally one to blush. Rarely did things take her by surprise the way John Sawyer's physical presence had. "No, no. It's just that you look so different. I'm not sure that if I'd walked in here cold, I'd have connected you with the man at the bank."

He considered that for a minute, then shrugged. "Different circumstances. That's all. I'm still the same guy you're gonna have to give a slew of damn good reasons to before I'll agree that those condominiums should be priced out of sight."

His words stiffened her spine, counteracting any softening she'd felt. "Out of sight? A million dollars would be out of sight. Not six hundred thousand."

"You were arguing for six-fifty to seven-fifty."

"The local market supports that."

He held her gaze without a blink. "Are there any other condominiums—not single-family homes, but condominiums—selling in that range around here?"

She didn't have to check her listings. At any given time, she knew the market like the back of her hand. "No, but only because there haven't been any built that would qualify. Crosslyn Rise does. It's spectacular."

He rubbed the bridge of his nose. "Is that reason to price it so high that no one will be able to enjoy it?"

"Plenty of people will be able to enjoy it."

"Not at that price, and if the condos don't sell, you can kiss the shops goodbye. No merchant—least of all me—wants to open up in a ghost town."

"It wouldn't be a ghost town," Nina scoffed, but softly. He'd raised a good point, namely the connection between sales of the condos and success in renting out the shops. Granted, the shops would hardly be relying on the residents alone; none would survive without the patronage of the public, for which purpose public access had been carefully planned. But the public wouldn't be coming to shop if the rest of the place looked deserted.

Returning to his carton, John bent over and filled his arms a second time with books.

Helpless to look away, Nina noticed the way his dark hair fell across his neck, the way the plaid shirt—darkened in random dots of sweat—stretched across his back, the way his fingers closed around book after book. Those fingers were long and blunt tipped. Rather than being delicate, as she'd have assumed a bookworm's to be, they looked as sturdy as the rest of him. She had the sudden impression that his laid-back manner hid a forbidding toughness. If so, she could be in for trouble.

Wanting to avoid that, she gave a little. "Okay. We could set a limit at seven. The smaller units could be in the low sixes, the larger ones closer to six-ninety-five."

John gathered books into his arms until he couldn't hold any more, then moved to the riser and arranged a second pile beside the first.

"John?"

"You're still a hundred grand too high. There's no need to price gouge."

"There's need to make a profit. That's the name of the game."

"Maybe your game," he said complacently, and returned for a third load.

"And not yours? I don't believe that for a minute. You put your own good money into the consortium, and from what I hear, there isn't a whole lot more where that came from."

One book was stacked on another. He neither broke the rhythm nor looked up from his work.

"The only reason," she said slowly, hoping that maybe a man who spoke slowly needed to hear slowly in order to comprehend, "why a man stakes the bulk of his savings on a single project is if he feels he has a solid chance of getting a good return."

John straightened with the last of the books. "Exactly."

She waited for him to go on. When he simply turned and began arranging a third pile by the first two, she moved closer. "The higher we price these units, the greater your return will be. The difference of a hundred-thousand over two dozen condos is two-and-a-half million dollars. That spells a substantial increase in our profit." She frowned. "My Lord, how many of those books do you have?"

"Twenty-five."

"And you really think you'll sell twenty-five at 22.95 a pop? I could believe five, maybe ten or twelve in a community this size. But twenty-five? How can you be so optimistic about books and so pessimistic about condos?"

Taking his time, he finished stacking the books. When he was done, he stood, wiped his palms on his thighs and gave her a patronizing look. "I can be lavish with books because the publishers make it well worth my while. When they're trying to push something, they offer generous deals and incentives. They're pushing this book like there's no tomorrow."

"It stinks."

He shrugged. "Sorry, but that's the way the publishing world works."

"Not the deals. The book. It stinks."

"You've read it?"

For the first time, she had caught him off guard, if the surprised arch of one brow meant something. "Yes, I've read it."

"When? I thought you worked all the time."

"I never said that."

"Sure sounded it from the way you were standing at the bank this morning struggling to squeeze in a single meeting with me."

"This week's worse than most because of the seminar. It's four intensive days—"

"Of what?"

"Classes on commercial real estate transactions. In the past year or two, I've been doing more with stores and office buildings. I've been wanting to take this seminar for six months, but this is the first time it's been offered at a time and place I could handle."

He gave her a long look. "Funny, I assumed you could handle most anything."

"I can," she said without flinching. "But it's a matter of priorities. Let me rephrase what I said. This is the first time the seminar's been offered at a time and place that work into my schedule without totally screwing up everything else."

He gave that brief thought. "So, when do you read?"

"At night. Late."

"When you can't sleep because you've got yourself wound up about everything you should be doing but can't because no one else is awake to do it with you?"

She was about to summarily deny the suggestion when she realized how right he was. Not that she intended to tell him that. "When I can't sleep, it's because I'm not tired."

The look in his eye was doubtful, but he let her claim ride. "And you didn't like this book?"

"I thought it was self-indulgent. Just because an author writes one book that wins the Pulitzer Prize doesn't mean that everything else that author writes is gold, but you'd have thought that from the hype the book was given. So I blame the author for her arrogance and the publisher for his cowardice."

"Cowardice?"

"In not standing up to the author and sending her back to rewrite it. The book *stinks*."

John pondered that. After a minute, he said, "It'll make the bestselling lists."

"Probably."

"And I won't lose a cent."

Given deals and incentives and bestselling status, he was probably right, she mused.

"Out of curiosity, if nothing else," he went on leisurely, "people will buy the book. No one will be broken by 22.95. Readers may be angry, like you are. They may feel gypped. They may even tell their friends not to buy the book, and I may, indeed, have two of these stacks standing here three months from today, just as they are now. But one disappointing book won't hurt my business." His eyes took on a meaningful cast. "At Crosslyn Rise, on the other hand, a thirty-three percent sell rate will hurt and hurt bad."

Nina shook her head. "The analogy's no good. You're comparing apples and oranges—sweet apples and moldy oranges, at that. Crosslyn Rise is quality. This book isn't. No one who buys into the Rise will ever say that it wasn't worth the money. In fact, some of the sales will probably come about by word of mouth, people who buy and are so excited that they spread the excitement."

"People who are stretched tight financially may not be able to feel much excitement."

"People who are stretched tight financially have no business even looking at the Rise, much less buying into it."

John's eyes hardened. "You're tough."

"I'm realistic. The Rise isn't for first-time home owners. It isn't for twenty-five-year-olds who've just gotten married and have twenty thousand to put down on a mortgage that they'll then pay off each month by painstakingly pooling their salaries." She held up a hand, lest he think her a snob. "Listen, I have properties that are less expensive, and I have clients who are looking for that. But those clients aren't looking for Crosslyn Rise, or if they are, they should be awakened to the rude realities of life."

"Which are?"

"Everything costs. *Everything.* If you don't have money in your pocket to pay for what you want or think you need, the cost comes out of your hide and is ten times more painful."

Her words hung in the air. Even more, her tone. It was

hard and angry, everything Nina was accused of being from time to time by one detractor or another whose path she crossed. Now she held her breath, waiting for John Sawyer to accuse her of the same.

He didn't say a word. Instead, after studying her for what seemed an infinite stretch, he turned away, bent and swept up the empty carton, and forcibly collapsed it as he walked from the room.

She waited for him to return. Gnawing on her lower lip, she kept her eyes on the door through which he'd gone. His footsteps told her that he'd taken a flight of stairs, leading her to guess he'd returned to the basement, but all was still. She shifted her bag from the left shoulder to the right, shifted her weight from the right foot to the left, finally glanced at her watch. It was after nine-thirty, getting later and later, and they hadn't reached any sort of agreement on Crosslyn Rise.

"John?" she called. When the only thing to greet her was silence, she let out a frustrated sigh. Wasted time drove her nuts, and this meeting spelled wasted time in capital letters. She and John Sawyer had some very basic differences. He was relaxed and easygoing, she was driven. Neither of them was going to change—not that change was called for. All that was called for was some sort of compromise recommendation for the pricing of the units at Crosslyn Rise.

At the sound of a quiet creaking over her head, she looked up. He must have gone upstairs, she realized, probably to check on his son, and she couldn't begrudge him that. It would have been nice if he'd said something, formally excused himself, told her he'd be back shortly, rather than just walking out. She hadn't associated relaxed and easygoing with rude before, nor had she associated rude with John. Slow, mulish, even naive, perhaps. But not rude.

He didn't like her. That explained it, she guessed. The hardness that came to his eyes from time to time when he looked at her spoke clearly of disapproval, which was all the more reason why she should finish her business and leave. She wasn't a glutton for punishment. If he didn't like her, fine. All they needed was to come up with a simple decision, and she'd be gone.

The creaking came again from upstairs, this time more steadily. Soon after, she heard footsteps on the back stairs, but they went on longer than they should have. It didn't take a genius to figure out that he'd gone on down to the basement, and in the wake of that realization, she realized something else. She didn't like John Sawyer any more than he liked her.

Annoyed, she stalked toward the back room, turned a corner until she saw the stairs and called out an impatient, "I haven't got much time, John. Do you think you could come up here and talk this out with me?"

"Be right up," he called nonchalantly. She could well have been the cleaning lady, for all the attention he was giving her.

Spinning on her heel, she returned to the main room of the shop, where, for the first time, she took a good look around. The bookstore took up the entire front portion of the house. Working around tall windows, a fireplace that looked frequently used, a sofa and several large wing chairs, bookshelves meandered through what had once been a living room, parlor and dining room. The overall space wasn't huge, as stores went, but what it lacked in size, it made up for in coziness.

Antsy, Nina began to prowl. Passing a section of reference books, she wandered past one of history books, another of fiction classics, another of humor. As she wandered, her pace slowed. That always happened to her in bookstores and libraries. Whether she intended to or not, she relaxed. Books pacified her. They were nonjudgmental, nondemanding. They could be picked up or put down with no strings attached, and they were always there.

At the shelves holding recent biographies, she stopped, lifted one, read the inside of its jacket. She liked biographies, as was evidenced by the pile of them on her night shelf, waiting to be read. Tempted by this one but knowing that she didn't dare buy another until she'd made some headway with the pile, she replaced the book and moved toward the front of the store. At the cookbooks, she stopped. One, standing face front, caught her eye, a collection of recipes put together by a local women's group. She took it from the shelf and began to thumb through.

"Don't tell me you cook."

Nina's head flew up to find John's expression as wry as his voice, but neither of those things held her attention for long. What struck her most was the surprise she felt—again—at the way he looked. Tall, strong, strangely masculine. She hadn't expected any of those things, much less her awareness of them. The relaxation she'd felt moments before vanished. "Yes, I cook."

He turned to put down another carton where the first had been. Looking back at her, his eyes were shuttered. "You work, you read, you cook. Any other surprises?"

At least they were even, she mused. He surprised her in not being a total wimp, she surprised him in being a businesswoman who cooked. She still didn't understand his dislike for her, but there was no point in pursuing it. Their personal feelings for each other didn't matter. If Crosslyn Rise was the only thing they had in common, so be it.

"It's getting late," she said with studied patience as she watched him bend in half and slash the new carton open. "Do you think you could take a break from that for a few minutes so that we can settle the matter of pricing?"

Straightening slowly, he slipped the blade back onto the counter. In measured cadence, he said, "I've been listening to everything you've said. You're not swaying me."

"Maybe you're not listening with an open mind."

He gave the possibility consideration before claiming, "My mind is always open."

"Okay," she said in an upbeat, "why don't you run *your* arguments by me again?"

He arched a casual brow. "Would it do any good?"

"It might."

After studying her for several long moments, he bent to open the box and began to unload books.

"John," she protested.

"I'm getting my thoughts in order. Give me a minute."

Tempering her impatience, she gave him that. During its course, he carried half a dozen books to one shelf, half a dozen to another. She was beginning to wonder whether he was deliberately dragging out the time, when he came to face her. His skin wore the remnants of a moist sheen, but his eyes were clear.

"I believe," he said slowly and quietly, "that we should keep the pricing down on those units because, one—" he held up a long, straight finger "—we stand a good chance of selling out that way, which in turn will make the shops more appealing both to shopkeepers and to the general public—" he held up a second finger, "two, we'd attract a better balance of buyers, and three, the profit will be more than respectable." He dropped his hand and turned back to the box of books.

"Is that it?"

"That's enough." Hunkering down, he started to fill his arms. "Didn't I win you over?"

"Not quite."

With a sidelong glance, he shot back her own words. "Maybe you're not listening with an open mind."

"I always have an open mind."

"If that were true, you'd have already given in. My arguments make sense."

"Mine are stronger."

"Yours have to do with profit, and profit alone."

She wanted to pull her hair out. "But profit is what this project is *about*!"

"Right, and you could blow it all by getting greedy. The entire project will be jeopardized if we overprice the goods."

"Okay," she said with a sigh, "if the units aren't snapped up in six months or so, we can reduce the price."

He shook his head. "That smacks of defeat, and it'll taint the whole thing. The longer those units sit empty, the worse it'll be." He sighed patiently. "Look, the duck pond will be completed six months before the pine grove, and the meadow six months after that. If we don't sell the duck pond first thing, there's no way the pine grove will sell, and if the pine grove doesn't sell, forget the meadow."

"Okay," Nina said, trying her absolute best to be reasonable, "how about this. How about we price the duck pond in the sixes, then move up into the sevens as we move toward the meadow."

"How about we price the duck pond in the fives, then move up into the sixes as we move toward the meadow." He reached for more books.

Bowing her head, she squeezed her eyes shut and pressed two fingers to her brow. "This isn't going to work."

"It'd work just fine if you'd listen to reason."

Her head came up, eyes open and beseeching. "But I'm the *expert* here. Pricing property is what I do for a living! If I was off the wall, I wouldn't be as successful as I am!"

Arms filled with books, John straightened and gave her a look that was shockingly intense. "You're successful because you push with such force and persistence that you wear people down. But you're barking up the wrong tree when it comes to me. I'm not the type to be worn down."

Nina stared up at him, stunned by the vehemence of his attack and its personal nature. She couldn't believe what she'd heard, couldn't believe the anger that had come from the quiet, contemplative, laid-back bookseller. Swallowing something strangely akin to hurt, she said, "Why do you dislike me? Have I done something to offend you?"

"Your whole *manner* offends me."

"Because I work hard and earn good money? Because I know what I want and fight for it? Or because I'm a woman?" She took a step back. "That's it, isn't it? I'm a strong woman, and you feel threatened."

"I'm not—"

"Don't feel singled out or anything," she said quickly, and held up a hand. "You're not alone. I threaten lots of men. I make them feel like they're not fast enough or smart enough or insightful enough. They want to put me in my place, but they can't."

John's look was disparaging. "I wouldn't presume to know where your place is, and I doubt you do, either. You want to wear the pants in the family, but you're so busy trying to get them to fit that you blow the family part. How old are you?"

"It doesn't matter."

"It does. You should be home having babies."

She stared at him in disbelief, opened her mouth, closed it again. Finally she sputtered out, "Who are you to tell me something like that? You don't know anything about me. You have no idea what makes me tick. And even if you did, these are the 1990s. Women don't stay home and have babies—"

"Some do."

"And some work. It's a personal choice, one for *me* to make."

"Clearly you have."

"Clearly, and if you were any kind of a man, you'd respect that choice." She was suddenly feeling tired. Hitching her bag to the other shoulder, she headed for the door. "I think we've reached a stalemate here. I'll call Carter tomorrow and let him know. There's no way you and I can work together. No way."

"Chicken."

She stopped in her tracks, then turned. "No. I'm being practical. My standing here arguing with you is an exercise in futility. My arguments won't change your mind, any more than yours will change mind. We're deadlocked. So we'll have to do what I wanted to do from the start, let the whole committee hear the arguments and take a vote. And we'll chalk up this time to—to—client development."

"What does that mean?"

"That some day when you're selling this house and you want the bitchiest broker to get the most money for you, you'll give me a call." With that, she tugged open the door and swept out into the night. She was down the wood steps and well along the front walk before she heard her name called.

"Nina?"

"Save it for the bank," she called back without turning, raised a hand in a wave of dismissal and rounded her car.

"Wait, Nina."

She looked up to find John eyeing her over the top of the car.

"Maybe we should try again," he said.

"It'd be a waste of time." Opening the door, she slid behind the wheel.

He leaned down to talk through the open window. "Why don't you give me some time to think."

With one hand on the wheel and one on the ignition, she said, "Buddy, you could think till the cows come home and you wouldn't see things my way."

"Maybe we could meet halfway, you'd come down a little, I'd come up."

That was the only thing that made any sense, she knew, but the idea of meeting John Sawyer again didn't appeal to her in the least. "Why don't you suggest that next Tuesday at the meeting?"

"They're expecting a recommendation from us."

"We can recommend that the consortium take a vote." She started the car.

"Look," he said, raising his voice so that its even timbre carried over the hum of the engine. "It doesn't matter so much to me if they think we couldn't come to some kind of consensus. Hell, I'm just a bookseller who's trying to make a little money by investing in real estate on the side. But you're supposed to be the master of the hard sell. I'd think you'd want to impress those guys at that table in any way you can."

She did. No doubt about it. Staring out the front window into the darkness with both hands on the wheel, she said, "If we can agree right now to go with figures halfway between what you want and what I want, we've got our consensus."

"I think we ought to discuss it."

"That's the only solution."

"I still think we ought to discuss it."

Earlier, she had thought him mulish. She thought it again now. John had to be one of the most stubborn men she had met in years. Turning her head only enough to meet his gaze, she said, "That sounds just fine, only there's one small problem. We went through the whole week this morning, and the only time we both had free was tonight. Now tonight's gone. So what do you suggest?"

"We find another time."

She shook her head. "Bad week."

"Then the weekend."

"I told you. I have a seminar. It runs from nine to five every day, and I'll have to allow an hour before and after for travel."

"So you'll be home by six. We can meet then."

Again she shook her head. "I'm moving a week from Monday. Every night after the seminar is reserved for packing. I have to get it done."

"I'll help you pack."

Like hell he would. Eyes forward, she set her chin. "No."

"Why not?"

"Because I can do it myself."

"Of course you can," he said indulgently. "But I can help. I'm not the scrawny weakling you imagined I'd be."

Her eyes shot to his. "I never said—"

"But you thought. So you were wrong. And I can help you pack."

"You can *not*. I don't want your help. I don't *need* your help."

He was silent then, his expression a mystery in the dark. Finally, sounding even-tempered and calm, the John she'd known from the bank, he said, "Tuesday morning before the meeting. I'll meet you at Easy Over at seven-thirty. We'll talk over breakfast." Before she could say a word, he gave the side of the car a tap and was off.

"John!" she called after him, but she might just as well have saved her breath. He didn't move quickly, but he moved smoothly, covering the distance to the house and disappearing inside without a glance behind.

CHAPTER THREE

NINA PREPARED CAREFULLY for breakfast Tuesday morning. After wading through her wardrobe and discarding anything red, purple or lime green, she chose a beige suit that was as reserved as anything she owned. That wasn't to call it conservative. The blazer was nipped in at the waist over a skirt that was short and scalloped, exposing a whisper of thigh with every move. In an attempt to tone that down, she left the matching, low-cut gauzy blouse in her closet in favor of a higher necked silk. With a single strand of pearls around her neck and pearl studs at her ears, she felt she looked as traditional as it was possible for Nina Stone to look.

Her goal was to impress John Sawyer—not in any sort of romantic way, because she *certainly* didn't think of John that way, but in a business way. Normally she dressed in the bright, chic, slightly funky style that had become her trademark; clients came to her because they saw someone who was one step ahead of the eight ball. Somehow she didn't think that was where John Sawyer wanted to be, but she wanted him to be on her side when it came to marketing Crosslyn Rise, so it behooved her to impress him.

She arrived at Easy Over, a light-breakfast and lunch place not far from the bank, at seven-thirty on the dot. When she saw no sign of John, she took a table, ordered a pot of coffee and waited. He arrived five minutes later, wearing loose khaki pants, another plaid shirt, a slouchy brown blazer and glasses. Looking slightly sleepy, he slid into a chair.

"Sorry," he murmured. "Had a little trouble getting out." His eyes fastened on the coffeepot. "Is that fresh?"

She nodded, lifted the pot and filled the cup waiting by his place. "Anything serious?"

"Nah." He took a sip of coffee, then a second before setting down the cup, sitting back in his chair and catching her eye. "That's better. I didn't have time for any at home."

"What happened?"

He took another drink, a more leisurely one this time as though he were just then settling in to being his normal slow self. "My son isn't wild about the sitter. He didn't want me to leave."

"I thought kids nowadays were used to sitters. Don't you have one every day?"

"He likes the afternoon ones. They're high school girls with lots of energy and enthusiasm. For morning meetings at the bank, I have to use someone else. She's kind enough, and responsible, but she doesn't relate so well with him."

"He must be very attached to you."

"I'm all he has."

Nina thought about the boy's mother, wondered how she had died and whether the child remembered her. She wasn't about to ask John any of those things, though. They weren't her business.

"What'll it be, folks?" the waitress asked, flipping the paper on her pad and readying a pen.

Nina didn't have to look at the menu. She'd been at Easy Over enough to know what was good. "I'll have Ronnie's Special. Make the eggs soft-boiled, the bacon crisp and the wheat toast dry. And I'll have a large TJ with that." She watched the waitress note everything, then turned expectant eyes toward John.

He hadn't opened the menu either, but he seemed

thoughtful for a minute. "Make that two," he paused, "only I want my eggs scrambled, my sausages moist and my rye toast with butter."

"Juice?" the waitress prompted.

"OJ. Large." Still writing, the waitress ambled off. John turned placid eyes on Nina. "For a little girl, you eat a whole lotta food."

"I have to. I rarely make it to lunch, and dinner won't be until eight or nine tonight."

"That's not healthy."

She shrugged. "Can't be helped. I'm into my busiest season. If I don't make the most of it, it'll be gone, and then where will I be?" With the reminder, she pulled up the folder that had been waiting against the leg of her chair, set it down in front of her and opened it up. "I spent awhile yesterday working with figures." She lifted the first sheet from the folder, but before she could pass it to him, he held up a hand.

"Not yet."

"Not yet?"

"Not before breakfast." He settled more comfortably in his seat. "I can't deal with business before breakfast."

"But this is a *business* breakfast. That means we eat while we talk."

His gaze touched the clean white Formica surface before him. "We haven't got any food yet. Let's wait on business."

Nina wanted to say that if they did that, they would not only be wasting good time, but if she had to go past Plan A to Plan B or C, they might well run *out* of time before they reached an agreement. She wanted to say that first thing in the morning was the *best* time to discuss business, while they were the freshest. She wanted to say that they were due at the bank at eight-thirty, which, given John's tardiness and the time they'd already spent in chitchat and ordering, left them not much more than forty-five minutes.

She didn't say any of those things, because John's eye

stopped her. She saw something in them, something strong enough to penetrate his glasses, something with a quiet but forceful command. She also saw that his eyes were amber, then looked more carefully and didn't see it at all. She remembered it. It must have registered on her subconscious the last time she'd seen him.

Carefully, with her heart beating a hair faster than it had been moments before, she set down the paper, sat back in her chair, crossed her hands in her lap and wondered what they would talk about in the time before their food arrived. There were a million things she could ask him, things she was curious about, like his wife and his son and his interest in books. Only none of that was her business.

She was used to talking. She *always* talked. Her role in life was to keep things moving, to win people over, to make sales. But she didn't know what to say to John.

She was beginning to feel awkward—and annoyed at that—when he asked, "Did you get your packing done?"

Relieved, she nodded. "Most of it."

"I trust you had other people to help you."

"No."

He arched a questioning brow and shook his head.

She shook her head right back.

"No stream of admirers dying to show off their muscles?"

His tone was deferential, his expression benign. Still she had the feeling that somewhere inside he harbored a grudge. "No stream of admirers. No men at all. Why would you think that there were?"

"You're an attractive woman. You must have men all over you."

"I'm an *independent* woman. I couldn't bear to have men all over me. I told you I didn't need anyone's help."

"You told me you didn't need *my* help."

"Then you took it too personally. I didn't—don't—need anyone's help. When I do, I hire it and pay for it. By check," she tacked on, just so he didn't think she was trading her body for something. Men tended to think that way, and she hated it. The few men—precious few men— she'd been with in her thirty-one years had known that she gave because she felt affection and attraction, and because she knew they wouldn't demand anything more. They never did. She was as free as a bird, and glad of it.

"Where are you moving to?"

"Sycamore Street."

His brow flickered into a frown. "I go down Sycamore all the time. I don't remember seeing any For Sale signs— or were you able to get an inside scoop and snatch something up before it hit the open market?"

There it was again, the deferential tone, the benign look, the little dig underneath. Looking him straight in those amber eyes of his, she said, "I'm not buying. I'm renting the second floor of a duplex, and, yes, I snatched it up before it hit the market. That's one of the perks of being a broker, and it's perfectly legal."

She had been direct enough to issue a challenge and expected him to meet it. Instead, he simply looked surprised. "You're renting? I'd have thought a successful woman like you would be living in a spectacular house on a spectacular piece of land with a spectacular view of the ocean."

"I'm not that successful. Not yet." But she intended to be. One day, she'd have enough money to buy anything her heart desired. "Where I live right now isn't as important as saving as much money as I can."

"You put a whole lot into Crosslyn Rise."

"No more than you." They'd each seen the figures.

"That's a whole lot."

She thought about the sum. "Uh-huh."

"And you want to open your own business."

Her brow went up. "Who told you that?"

"Carter," he answered factually. "When the consortium

was forming. Just like he told you about me. So when do you think you'll do it?"

"I don't know. It depends on how much money we make on Crosslyn Rise and how soon." Her hand went to the first paper on her pile, but before she could address herself to its contents, the waitress placed a large glass of tomato juice in front of her. She smiled her thanks and opened her mouth to speak to John when he stopped her with a hand.

"Not yet. I need food first."

"There's food," she said, pointing to his orange juice. "Drink up, then I'll talk."

Rather than taking a drink of the orange juice, though, he drained the last of his coffee and refilled the cup. "Aren't you happy at Crown?"

After a moment's consideration, she gave a one-shouldered shrug. "As happy as I'd be working for someone else, but I've always wanted to be on my own."

"Independent."

"That's right."

"So you can rake in the most bucks?"

She raised her chin. "It's not as much the money as the freedom. I don't like having to answer to someone else."

"Marty Crown's a nice guy."

"A very nice guy. I could have done a lot worse picking a boss." Not that she'd left that to chance. Before moving up from New York she had researched each and every real estate agency in the North Shore area. She'd picked Crown for its reputation, its connections and Martin.

"Does he know your plans?"

"No, and I'd rather he not," she advised, sending John a look that said she was trusting him to keep her secret. "I've done well for Martin in the six years I've been here. He's made good money from my sales, and I don't begrudge that. It's the way things work. He gets his share in exchange for giving me a forum to work and to learn.

I'm a much better broker now than I was when I came. Whether I have Martin to thank for that, or myself, isn't important. What's important is that if I can take out of Crosslyn Rise double what I put in, I'll be in great shape to make my move." Feeling that to be as smooth a segue as any, she once again fingered the top sheet in her file.

Once again John stalled her. "That's a lot of money," he said with thought-filled preponderance. "I'd have thought you could pretty much set up a real estate brokerage wherever you wanted with little more than a telephone."

"Not the kind of brokerage I want," she said, and let her dreams momentarily surface. "I want something classy. I want to either buy a house and do it over, or rent the best commercial space available. Then I want to decorate with the best furnishings, the best window treatments, the best artwork. I want a secretary, a sophisticated telephone system to make certain parts of my work easier, a computer setup to handle the latest programs and handle them well. I want to design a distinctive logo and stationery, and I want to advertise." She took a breath. "All of that costs money."

"I'll say," John said, and sat quietly back, studying her as though she were something foreign that he couldn't quite understand. "Couldn't you start small? Do you need everything all at once?"

"Yes. That's the whole point. Real estate agencies are a dime a dozen around here. Granted, some are better than others, and those stand out. But for a new one to spring up and attract enough of a clientele to be successful, drastic measures are called for. From the very first, my agency has to be different. It has to attract attention. I think I can do it if, A, my offices are elegant, B, my staff is courteous, hardworking and smart, and, C, I advertise like hell."

"Your staff?"

She sent him a dry look. "I'm not doing all the work on my own. That would be suicide. The whole point is to have people who are answerable to me, to teach them and train them, let them do their work, then take *my* cut in the profits. Isn't that the way successful entrepreneurs do it?"

John didn't answer. He took a slow drink of his juice, set it down, then pushed his utensils out of the way when the waitress delivered plates filled with eggs, meat and toast.

Mindful that once they had food in their stomachs, John would be willing to talk business, Nina began to eat. She cracked her eggs, scooped them from the shell onto the wheat toast, gave them a light sprinkling of salt.

John's fork seemed stuck in the first of his scrambled eggs. "I'm surprised," he said unhurriedly, "that you want to set up business around here. If the goal is to make money and buy your freedom—"

"Not buy. Ensure."

"Ensure. If that's what you want, wouldn't you be better in a large place where, by virtue of sheer numbers of people, the market would be more active?"

"I've been there. I didn't like it."

"Why not?"

"Too impersonal. I may be hard, driven, aggressive, ambitious, even ruthless—people have called me all those things—but I like being able to greet the local grocer by name and have him greet me the same way. Besides," she added with a glance out the window, "I do love the ocean."

John followed her gaze briefly before returning to her. "When do you have time to see it?"

"I see it. Here and there. Coming and going." She nudged her chin toward his plate. "Eat up. Time's passing."

"Ever spend a day at the beach?"

"A day? No. An hour or two, maybe. Any more and I get itchy."

"You never wanted just to lie out on the sand for hours listening to the sound of people and the surf?"

"No. There's too much to do."

He took a bite of his eggs, then swallowed. "That's sad."

"Maybe for you. Not for me. I'd much rather get brief glimpses of the ocean lots of different times in the course of a day, know that it's there, even listen to it at night at the same time that I'm getting something else useful done, than sit doing nothing on the sand."

He looked baffled. "But don't you ever just want to go out and enjoy it for itself, rather than as an accompaniment to something else?"

"Why should I? It's the best accompaniment in the world. It makes anything else I'm doing that much nicer."

"That's sad," he said again, and Nina found herself getting irked.

"I don't see *you* with a tan."

"I haven't had time yet this spring. But I will. You can count on it. As soon as lessons let up a little for my son, we'll be hitting the beach."

Nina was about to ask what lessons he meant, when she caught herself. The child had a handicap. She didn't want to put John on the spot. Besides, his personal life wasn't her affair.

With a tolerant shrug, she said, "Different strokes for different folks. What works for you doesn't necessarily work for me, and vice versa. It's no big thing, John. Really." He didn't believe her, but that wasn't her worry. Crosslyn Rise was. "Listen, I'd really like to get to those papers." She glanced at her watch. "We have to be at the bank in less than half an hour."

"How was your seminar?"

"My seminar was fine." She put her hand on the top paper. "What I have here is my personal recommendation. I've broken the project down by size and expected date of completion—"

"Did you learn a lot? At the seminar."

She paused, stared, nodded. Then she patted the paper.

"The more I thought about it over the weekend, the more I realized that we hit on something good last time we talked. The idea of—"

"Was it worth the four days?"

She took a breath for patience. "I'd say so."

"You're a better broker for it?"

"I'm more knowledgeable." She took another breath. "The idea of pricing the units progressively—"

"Don't you ever get tired?"

She pressed her lips together. "Of work? I told you. I love my work."

"But don't you ever get *tired*?"

"You mean physically fatigued?"

"Mentally fatigued. Don't you ever want to stop, even for a little while?"

"If I do that, it'll take me longer to reach my goal."

"What about burnout?"

"What about it?"

"Doesn't it scare you?"

"Not particularly. If I get where I'm going, I'll have plenty of time to take it easy, without the risks."

"What are the risks?"

"Of taking it easy now?" She didn't have to take time to think. She lived with certain fears day in, day out. "Loss of sales. Loss of reputation. Loss of status in the agency. There are other brokers out there just dying for my listings. If I'm not around, if I'm not working, if I'm not on top of things, if I'm not getting results, I lose."

In a rare instance of expressiveness, his mouth twisted in disgust. "I get tired just listening to you."

"Then don't," she snapped. "Don't ask me questions, and you won't have to listen to my answers. All I want—" she slapped the paper beside her plate "—is to come to some sort of decision here!"

John stared at her. She glared back. Gradually his stare

softened into study, and before she knew it, she felt the same kind of quiet force emanating from him that she'd felt before. As had happened then, her heartbeat picked up, all the more so when his amber eyes began a slow, almost tactile meandering over her face. She felt their touch on her cheeks, her nose, her chin, then her mouth, where they lingered for a while to trace the bow curve of her lips.

The indignation she felt moments earlier was forgotten, pushed from mind by a strange, all-over tingle. "John?" Her voice wobbled. She cleared her throat. "I, uh, really think we should talk."

He wasn't done, though. His gaze dropped to her throat, touching the smooth skin there before slipping down over silk to the gentle swell of her breasts.

Even sitting, she felt weak in the knees, which made so little sense at all that a flare of pique shot through her. *"John."*

His eyes rose. "Hmm?"

"I *need* to show you my *papers*."

"What papers?"

She rapped the folder. *"These."*

He looked at the folder, then looked back at her. Along the way, his mouth hardened. "You won't let it go, will you?"

"Let it go? But this is why we met!"

He said nothing, just stared at her. Not even his glasses diffused the strength of that stare.

She felt penetrated. "Wasn't it?"

Slowly he shook his head.

"Then why?"

"To have breakfast."

"You insisted on this meeting just for *breakfast*?"

Slowly he nodded.

"But *why*? You could have had breakfast for less money and with less hassle if you'd stayed home with your son. Why on *earth* did you drag me out here if you didn't have any intention of discussing Crosslyn Rise?"

"We'll discuss Crosslyn Rise. When we're done eating."

"So what do I do until then?" she asked in exasperation.

"You slow down. You take a deep breath. You look out that window and watch the sea gulls. You have a second cup of coffee and take the time to smell the brew." His voice lowered, growing sharper and more direct. "You're rushing your way through life, Nina. If you're not careful, the whole thing will be over and you won't know what in the hell you've missed."

Incredulity holding her mute, Nina stared. She had to take a deep, deep breath and give a solid swallow before she was able to say, "Last time I looked, this was my life. Seems to me I should be able to do what I want, and if that means rushing, I'll rush."

His voice came out gentler than before, but no less direct. "Not with me, you won't."

She sat back in her chair. "Fine." Two could play the game. She hadn't wanted this breakfast, anyway. All along, she had wanted the committee to take its vote. "Fortunately, I won't *be* with you beyond this meeting." She smiled. "Take your time. Eat. I'll just sit here and enjoy the scenery."

SHE WORKED HARD at doing that. After an eternity, with barely ten minutes until they were due at the bank, John invited her to show him the papers she'd brought. Staying calm, patient and professional, she went through them. With surprising ease, they came to an agreement on the third of her plans. Together they walked to the bank.

Sixty minutes later, when Nina returned to her office, she was like a steam kettle ready to blow. Slapping the folder sharply on her desk, she squeezed her eyes shut, put her head back and let out an eloquent growl. Its sound brought Lee in from next door.

"How'd it go?"

"Don't ask."

"Which plan did he go for?"

"C, damn it."

"And the consortium agreed?"

Nina nodded. Seconds later, she threw a hand in the air. "Don't ask me why I didn't argue more. I should have."

"Plan C is just fine."

"It's not aggressive enough."

"So why *didn't* you argue more?"

"Because—because—" she struggle for the words, finally blurting out, "because John Sawyer wore me down, that's why."

"I thought he was *blah*."

"He is."

"But he wore you down." Lee grinned in a curious kind of way. "That's a change. Usually it's the other way around. You must be losing your touch." When Nina gave her a dirty look, she said in an attempt to appease, "Sometimes the most blah people can be forceful, just because they take you by surprise."

But it wasn't that, Nina knew. It was John's persistence, his molasses-slow approach and a doggedness that was built of reason. His will was stronger than she'd expected, and, as fate would have it, his will coincided with that of the majority of the consortium.

Not for the first time, Nina vowed that she would never again involve herself in a project where decisions were made by committee. Unfortunately, she was stuck with this one to the end. "Crosslyn Rise may be the death of me yet." Snatching up the pink slips that were waiting, she flipped sightlessly through, then flattened them back on the desk. "The *worst* of it is that they want me to keep working with him. Can you believe that? They see him as kind of a lay advisor. So even though consortium meetings won't be held more than once a month through the summer, they're expecting John and I to meet once a week."

"That shouldn't be too hard."

"It's a royal waste of time, a total frustration." She sent a beseeching look skyward. "Someone up there better help me out, or I'll be a raving lunatic by the time summer's done." Eyes dropping back to the desk, she sighed. "At least I can give the printer the go-ahead to print those brochures." Moving the folder aside, she drew up a pad of paper. At the top, she wrote Call Printer. "I want to have an introductory Open House over the Fourth of July weekend, something with lots of hoopla to launch the selling campaign." To the list, she added, Call Christine, then Call Newspaper. Her pen went back to the Christine part. "*If* the model apartment is ready. Chris was aiming for the first of the month. It'll be impressive." Looking at Lee, she asked, "Have you been up there lately?"

Lee shook her head. "I'm waiting for you. Maybe today, after lunch?"

Something about the way Lee mentioned lunch gave Nina pause. She dropped her eyes to her desk calendar. Catching in a breath, she said, "Lunch! That's right!" She had forgotten all about it. With a grin, she looked up. "Happy birthday, Lee."

Lee blushed. "Thanks."

"I'm sorry. Wow, I should have been thinking about that when you first walked in here, but I've been so annoyed all morning. Hey, how does it feel to be twenty-nine?"

"You've been there. How did it feel to you?"

"I don't know. It came and went so fast, I think I missed it." For a split second, she remembered what John Sawyer had said, then pushed her mind on to more meaningful things. "So, we'll go out for lunch to celebrate. Any other plans?"

"I'm meeting my parents in town for dinner."

"Nice," Nina said with enthusiasm, though she couldn't help but wonder about Tom Brody. If there was something real going on between Tom and Lee, he should have been the one to take her to dinner on her birthday.

As though reading her mind, Lee said, "Tom and I celebrated last night." She touched her earlobe. "See?"

Nina was a stickler for her own appearance, dressing for the part she wanted to play. She carefully shopped for clothes and accessories, and wore them unselfconsciously once they were hers. There, though, her interest in fashion ended. She was far more apt to notice the overall effect of a person's clothing than the details of it. That was why she hadn't noticed Lee's earrings before.

Looking back, she didn't know how she'd missed them. They lit up Lee's ears in a way that neither gold, silver nor neon enamel could. "Wow," she breathed, coming out of her chair for a closer look. "Those are *gorgeous*."

"They're three-quarters of a karat each. Tom said to make sure I insured them."

Nina wanted to say that if Tom Brody had style, he'd have given her a year's worth of insurance along with the gift. But Tom had flash, not style. There was a difference.

"Definitely insure them," Nina said. She didn't add that that way Lee would be sure to have something of value when Tom left her behind. Nina wasn't a spoiler. But she felt awful. "It's too bad he can't join you tonight. Has he ever met your parents?"

"No. He has to be in Buffalo. It's just as well," Lee reasoned indulgently. "My parents would be looking Tom over as husband material, and that kind of pressure is the last thing Tom needs. He has enough pressure with work."

Nina felt momentarily chilled. Making excuses for a man was a sure sign that a woman was giving more than she was getting. But before she could say that, Lee made for the door.

"Martin is having a root canal. I told him I'd cover for him. He has some people coming in from the Berkshires.

Their daughter is starting at Salem State in the fall and they want to buy a condo for the four years she's here."

Nina was hearing that same story more and more often. She supposed that if she had kids she'd want to do the same thing, since, given rents versus tax benefits and property appreciation, it made sense. Of course, she didn't have kids, so it was a moot point.

"How about I make reservations for twelve-thirty?" she asked.

"Sounds great," Lee said. "I'll be back here by twelve. See you then."

Nina waved a goodbye, then looked again at her desk calendar. The fact that she'd forgotten about lunch was nothing new. At the end of a given day, when she looked over her program for the next one, business appointments were the things she saw. Fortunately, she didn't have anything that would conflict with Lee's birthday celebration. She liked Lee a lot. She felt good about taking her out.

She was also grateful for the opportunity to eat, since she hadn't had much of the breakfast she had so glibly ordered at Easy Over. John had distracted her. Even when he'd been leisurely eating his own food, she hadn't eaten much. He made her stomach jump.

Annoyance, she told herself. Annoyance and irritation. John was the kind who, in his innocent way, gave people ulcers.

Actually, it was a wonder he was so calm, given the problem he had with his son. It couldn't be easy for him raising a child alone. She wondered about the extent of the boy's problems, wondered what kind of schooling those problems entailed. She wondered whether John ever got frantic, threw his hands into the air and gave up. Some parents did that when confronted with a frightening situation. Her mother had, more than once.

Something nagged in the back of her mind. Lifting the

collection of pink slips that she'd barely seen earlier, she set one after another aside until she came to the one that had caused the nagging. It was a message from Anthony Kimball, the medical director of the Omaha nursing home where her mother lived. The call had come in promptly at nine that morning. The message requested a callback.

Lifting the phone, Nina punched out the number that she knew by heart. "Dr. Kimball, please," she asked. She gave her name, then waited while the call was transferred.

"Nina?"

"Yes, Dr. Kimball. I got your message. Is something wrong?" It wasn't often that Anthony Kimball called her, and when he did, there was usually a problem.

"I'm not quite sure. Your mother had some sort of seizure during the night. Her blood pressure fell dangerously low. We have her stabilized now, and there doesn't seem to be any other side effect from whatever the seizure was, but I thought you ought to know. This may be the start of the weakening that we've been expecting."

Nina swiveled her chair away from the door and bowed her head. "Is she comfortable?" she asked quietly.

"As far as we can tell."

"Is she aware of anything?"

There was a pause, then a quiet, "I don't believe so."

Nina sighed. "I guess we should be grateful for that." She pressed a hand to her eyes. "This weakening. Once it begins, does it go fast?"

"I can't tell you that. Every case varies. It could take one month or ten, but you may want to come out here to see her within the next few weeks."

Nina didn't have to look at her calendar to know that the next few weeks were fully booked. This was her busy season. A trip to Omaha would take precious time, not to mention a toll on her emotions. Seeing her mother was always painful. "Why don't I talk with you next week and see how she is then," she suggested. "If she stays stabilized, I'd rather wait a bit before coming out."

The doctor agreed to that, as Nina knew he would. Though the home was the finest Nina had been able to find, it wasn't unlike others in its overriding concern with money. Nina paid well for the service of having her mother cared for. As long as the checks kept coming, Anthony Kimball and his staff were content.

Hanging up the phone, Nina felt the same hollow ache she felt whenever she thought of her mother. Such potential gone to waste. A beautiful woman now a vegetable. She wished she could credit the damage to a disease like Alzheimer's, but her mother's mind hadn't fallen victim to anything as noble as that. She'd taken drugs. Bad drugs. Too many drugs. Rather than dying of an overdose, she had lived on, simply to languish in whatever position her attendants arranged her.

Nina was the one who felt the pain of it all. She was the one who felt the remorse. She couldn't say that she felt a loss, because her mother had never been hers to enjoy, but there were times, once in a very great while, when she thought of what might have been if things had been different way back at the start.

But they wouldn't be—couldn't be—and thinking about it only caused pain. One of Nina's earliest lessons in life had been that the only sure antidote to pain was activity. It was a lesson she still lived by.

CHAPTER FOUR

SUNDAY WAS MOVING DAY. Nina completed all her weekend showings on Saturday and was up with the sun the next morning to pack the last of her things. Rather than pay a formal moving service, when she had so little of intrinsic value to move, she had hired two young men to help. Between their muscles, the small pickup truck one of them owned and the promise of a generous check for the job, they had successfully transferred her meager furnishings and not so meager personal belongings from the old apartment to the new one by noon.

Shortly after, Nina went to work, first pushing the furniture over or back until the positioning was perfect, then opening carton after carton in an attempt to see what was where. She was standing in the midst of chaos, feeling vaguely bewildered, when she heard a call from downstairs.

"Hello?"

She tried to place it, but she wasn't expecting any guests. "Yes?" she called back without moving.

"It's John Sawyer, Nina. Can I come up?"

"Uh—" she looked around, bewildered, "—sure." John Sawyer? Downstairs? She hadn't seen hide nor hair of him since the Tuesday before, and though she told herself to be grateful, more than once she had wondered where he was. The consortium wanted them to work together, but since she wasn't thrilled with the idea, she'd decided to leave the initiative up to him. She hadn't expected that he'd seek her out in person, much less at her home, much *less* at the home whose exact address he couldn't possibly have known.

Yet John Sawyer it was emerging from the stairwell wearing a T-shirt, jeans and sneakers. His hair was mussed, his nose and cheeks unexpectedly ruddy. He looked fresh and carefree, neither of which she was feeling at that moment, and as if that weren't bad enough, the first thing he did after he came to a halt was to give her an ear-to-ear grin.

John had never grinned at her before. She'd caught a twist of the corner of the mouth once or twice, but never a full-fledged grin. The surprise of it had her insides doing little flip-flops, to which she responded by frowning.

"How did you find me?"

"Your car. You said you were moving to Sycamore Street. There aren't many houses here with bright red BMWs in the driveway."

For reasons unknown to Nina just then, she felt suddenly defensive about the car. "It's not new. I bought it used and had it painted. Some people think it's pretentious to have a car like that when I live pretty modestly, but the fact is that it impresses clients. They like riding around in it."

John studied her, his grin softening into something curious. "Don't you?"

"Don't I what?"

"Like riding around in it."

"I suppose." She frowned again. "What are you doing here?"

"Helping." He stuck his hands into the back pockets of his jeans, a gesture that should have been totally innocent. Given the way his T-shirt tightened over his chest, though, it wasn't. Nina felt a corresponding tightening in the pit of her stomach.

"I told you I didn't need help," she snapped, scowling now.

"Everyone needs help." His eyes skimmed the sea of cartons on the floor. "This place will be a mess until everything's unpacked. Why be burdened doing it after work every day this week, when between the two of us, we can get it all done now?"

He had a point, though she wouldn't concede it. "I'm sure you have better things to do with your time."

"Actually, I don't. J.J. and I were at the beach this morning, but he's gone off for the afternoon with friends, and the store is closed, so I really do have time to waste. I'm in the mood for unpacking." Shifting his hands from his pockets to his hips, he looked around at the cartons. "Where should I begin?"

"Uh—" Nina tried to concentrate, but all she could think about was that she hadn't showered, that she hadn't put makeup on and that between her ultrashort hair and the loose shirt and jeans she wore, she looked more like a boy than a girl. She felt embarrassed. "Uh, really, John, there's no need—"

"Where?" he repeated. Stepping over one carton, he peered down to look at the writing on the side of another. The words *living room* had been crossed out and replaced by *dining room*, but that, too, had been crossed out. *Bedroom* was the word that seemed left, though even from where she was, Nina saw through the open flaps of the box that it contained pots and pans.

"I've used these cartons lots of different times," she explained, wringing one hand in the other. "I kind of gave up on marking things this time, which is why everything's mixed up out here."

"No sweat," John said, lifting the carton. "This looks like it goes in the kitchen." He hitched his chin toward the back of the house. "That way?"

"Uh-huh."

Carrying the carton, he passed her, went through the dining room and into the kitchen. Within minutes, she heard the clattering of pots and pans being stacked. Wondering where he was putting them, she followed the noise to find him on his haunches before one of the kitchen cabinets. "I don't know if this is right, but at least they'll be out of the way. If you find in a week or a month that you want them elsewhere, it'll be easy enough to move them."

"That's fine."

"Why don't you go back into the other room and sort through the rest of the cartons. If I carry stuff into the bedroom, you can organize things there, while I finish up here."

She tried again. "John, this really isn't necessary."

"Of course, it's not. But it helps, doesn't it?"

Given the direct question, she couldn't lie. "Yes, but—"

"Unless there's stuff here you don't want me to see."

"There isn't, but—"

"Or you're expecting someone else and my being here will embarrass you—"

"I'm not and it won't, but—"

"Then there's no problem."

"There *is* a problem," she cried, driven by exasperation to a semblance of her usual force. "I told you this last week. If I wanted help, I'd hire it."

He looked up at her. "And pay for it. With a check. Yes, I did hear that."

"Well, I meant it."

His eyes held hers for a time before he returned them to the task at hand. He had barely set another pot into the nest of them in the cabinet when he looked up again. "This is free, Nina. I'm not asking for payment of any kind, and if you offered, I'd give it back. I'm doing this as a friend. You won't owe me anything."

She felt color warm her cheeks. "I know that."

"I'm not sure you do," he said with a frown. "You've made it clear that you prefer to hire and pay people when you need things done. But when you get someone who's willing to help for free, the only reason I can think of why you'd turn him down is that either you can't stand his company or you're afraid there's a price." His words came slowly but steadily, one sentence flowing gently into the next. "Now, I know we haven't necessarily hit it off on a personal basis, so it may well be that you can't stand my company, and if that's the case, just tell me, and I'll leave. On the other hand, if you're afraid there's a price, I'm telling you there isn't. I'm offering my services free and clear of return obligations." He paused. "Do you believe me?"

After a minute, she said a quiet, "Yes."

"Then why don't you let me help." It was more statement than question. "Come on, Nina. Go with the flow. I'm here and I'm willing. Use me."

Use me. It was usually the other way around, where relationships between men and women were concerned. But he'd said the words himself. He'd offered them. Freely. Just as he was offering his help. "Are you sure you don't have anything else to do?"

"I'm sure."

As he sat there on his haunches looking up at her, it struck Nina that he wasn't bad looking. Not bad looking at all. Actually, rather good-looking, even with those glasses perched on his nose. With his longish hair, his light tan, and his T-shirt and jeans, the glasses made him look oddly in vogue.

Which was a surprising thought, indeed.

"Fine," she said, and headed for the front room before she had a chance to regret the decision. "I'll sort through the cartons. Come back in when you need another one."

With a certain amount of kicking and shoving, she had cartons separated into groups by the time John returned. As promised, he carried everything for the bedroom into the bedroom before continuing with the kitchen.

For one hour, then a second, they worked straight. Nina

was back to being her usual efficient self, in part to keep
her mind occupied and away from the fact of John's
presence in the other room. Come the time when they were
both unpacking cartons in the living room, that became
more difficult. He was never out of sight. She was highly
aware of him. Adding to the problem, most of the cartons
contained books, so John's progress slowed. For every
four that he placed on the shelf, there was one that he
wanted to discuss.

She tried to keep moving. She tried, even when she was
giving her opinion of one book or another, to keep unload-
ing others and lining them up on the shelves. But the
questions he asked were good ones, often ones that
required thought, and she found her own progress slowing
down right along with his. She found herself curious to
know *his* opinions.

Nina had never thought of herself as an intellectual.
She had a college degree more out of practical necessity
than love of learning. John, on the other hand, was an intellectual. It was clear in the way he looked and acted,
not to mention his occupation, and to some extent, she
had assumed that given this difference between them,
they would have trouble communicating. To her surprise,
they didn't. He didn't make obscure references to classical writers or philosophers. He didn't pick apart books
along the lines of arcane theories. He offered honest,
straightforward thoughts in honest, straightforward
English. Pleasantly surprised, she indulged herself the
discussion, letting her defenses down, enjoying the talk
for talk's sake.

Engrossed as she was in it, she was taken off guard
when, in the midst of a discussion of James Joyce and his
wife, Nora, John said, "Have you had lunch?"

Sitting cross-legged on the floor, she straightened,
looked at him, swallowed. Dragging herself back from a

pleasant interlude to the present, she glanced at her watch. "It's after three."

"I know. I'm starved. Did you have anything?"

Silently she shook her head.

"I'll go get something." Coming to his knees, he fished his keys from his pocket. With another smooth motion, he was on his feet. "You'll eat, won't you?"

"I don't need—"

"Are you hungry?"

"I wasn't planning to—"

"Lobster rolls?"

Her mouth watered. "Only if I pay."

He thought about that for a minute. She was prepared to dig in her heels and insist that that was the only way she'd eat anything he brought, when his mouth quirked. "Okay."

He was *quite* good-looking, she realized with a start. Dragging her eyes from his, she looked around for her purse. Unfortunately, it was directly behind him. The only footpath through the cartons took her by him with mere inches to spare. His flesh was warm from work. She felt that warmth, smelled its scent, and where she should have been repelled, she wasn't. John Sawyer smelled healthily male. Attractively male.

Convinced that the tension of the move was jumbling her mind, she quickly found her purse and fumbled inside her enough money to cover sandwiches and drinks. John took the money.

"You do know," he said, and eyed her straight on, "that I'd never allow this if it weren't for the big deal you made about not wanting my help to unpack. The way I see it, your treating me now is payment for my work, so we're even. Got that?"

His gaze was so strong and his voice so firm that all she could do was manage a quiet, "Uh-huh." If he had asked her to say anything else, she'd have been at a loss. Fortunately, he didn't. Tucking the money into his pocket, he went off down the stairs.

During the time he was gone, Nina was a whirling dervish of activity. Bending over and around repeatedly, she emptied two full cartons of books, then moved on to her stereo equipment. She tried not to think about anything but the work she was doing, and to some extent she succeeded. Only intermittently did images flash through her mind—John's long arms flexing under the weight of cartons, John's shaggy hair spiking along his neck, John's very male, very alluring scent—but she pushed them away as quickly as they came.

She had a rack of CDs filled and was halfway through a second when he returned.

"This is a treat, let me tell you," he said with a smile as he began to unload the bag he carried. Shifting a carton from the low coffee table onto the floor, he spread out not only lobster rolls, but cups of potato salad, ears of corn and soda. "Take-out for me is usually McDonald's."

Instinctively Nina knew that the choice had nothing to do with money. "That's what your son likes?"

"He *loves* it. He'd be happy to go there every day of the week if I let him."

"What does he eat?"

"A hamburger, a small bag of fries and a milk shake. He doesn't always make it through the shake, but he devours the rest. For a little guy, he always amazes me."

"He's four?"

John nodded. Sitting down on a nearby carton, stretching his legs comfortably before him, he took a bite of a lobster roll, closed his eyes, chewed softly and neatly. "Mmm," he said with feeling, "is this good."

Nina, too, took a carton as a seat. Using one of the plastic forks that had tumbled from the bag, she sampled the potato salad. "So's this." She took another bite, all the while thinking about her curiosity and the fact that maybe, now that she and John were friends, she could ease it. It seemed she'd been wondering about certain things for a long time.

Shooting for nonchalance, she took a sip of soda, then said, "Tell me about your son."

John's glasses might have hidden the flash of wariness in his eyes had she not been watching him closely. Clearly he guarded his son. She wondered if he'd tell her to mind her own business—one part of her was telling herself that very same thing—and felt deeply warmed when, instead, he said in a low, slow voice, "J.J.'s a sweet little boy who's had a rough go of it in life."

"When did his mom die?"

"When he was one. He doesn't remember her."

"Is that good or bad?"

"Good, I guess. He doesn't know what he's missing."

Nina wanted to ask how the woman had died, but didn't. It was enough that John had agreed to talk about his son. "I'm sure you give him twice the love."

"I try," he said thoughtfully, and took another mouthful of lobster roll. After he'd swallowed, he said, "It's hard sometimes knowing if what I'm doing is right. Normal guidelines don't fit when it comes to J.J. He's a special child."

Eating her own lobster roll, she waited for him to go on. As curious as she was, she didn't want to sound nosy. Surprisingly the silence wasn't awkward. She ate patiently, wondering about all those ways in which J.J. might be special.

Finally John raised his eyes to hers. "What have you heard about him?"

"Just that he has vision and hearing deficiencies."

"That's pretty much it. He wears glasses and hearing aids." With the words, John looked momentarily in pain. "God, it hurts to see him sometimes. My heart aches for the poor little kid. He didn't ask for any of this."

"What caused it?"

He thought about that for a minute, then shrugged. "No one knows. He was born that way."

"Did you know right then?"

He shook his head. "Things seemed fine at the beginning. By the time he was six months old, I could tell that he wasn't responding to sound. It was when I brought him in to be tested that they detected the problem with his eyes. Unfortunately, there wasn't much of a medical nature that they could do about either. They wouldn't even fit him for glasses until he was close to a year. He'd have just dragged them off."

"They must help."

He nodded. "A lot. He reads."

"At four?"

John shot her a quintessentially parent-proud grin. "Nothing's wrong with his mind. He's a bright little kid."

"I'm sure," Nina said.

"I wasn't. Given all the other problems, I'd been told there was a possibility that he'd be retarded. Thank goodness that isn't so. I mean, how much should the child have to take?"

"But you'll be putting him in a special school." That was what she'd been told, the major reason John had invested in Crosslyn Rise. Handled wisely over the years, the profit he stood to make would cover the high cost of that special school.

"I have to. What hearing he has is negligible. He has to learn how to sign, how to read lips and how to talk."

"That'll all start next year?"

"It all started as soon as we diagnosed the problem. He and I work with a therapist every morning, and in the afternoon he's in a play group with children like him. Their parents are trained like I am. The learning for these kids has to be continuous." His eyes widened and he shot a hurried glance at his watch. The abrupt movement, coming from him, took Nina by surprise. Seeing the time, he let out a breath. "I'm okay. He's with one of those other families today, but I still have a few minutes."

"Oh, John, I feel guilty. It can't be often that you get a free afternoon like this, and to blow it away unpacking my things. I'm really sorry."

He regarded her strangely. "Don't be. If I hadn't wanted to do this, I wouldn't have. You didn't exactly invite me." He paused. "You didn't exactly *want* me. I inflicted myself on you, so you don't have anything to feel guilty about." He paused again. "Besides, I got a lobster roll out of it. And some interesting conversation." His voice lowered. "I like you better when you're talking books than when you're talking real estate."

"The feeling's mutual," Nina said, then regretted it the moment the words were out because, behind his glasses, John's eyes darkened. "You're not as bad as I thought you'd be," she added quickly, lest he think she was being suggestive in any way, shape or form.

His eyes remained dark. They dropped to her mouth.

"I think," she babbled on, "that when you only see a person in one context, say for matters involving a business deal like Crosslyn Rise, you get a very narrow view." Her voice seemed to be fading, like the rest of her was doing. Fading, weakening, feeling all warm and trembly inside. "It's nice to know you like lobster rolls."

John's brows drew together in a brief frown before he managed to drag his eyes back to hers. "I do," he said quietly. "But I'd better go, I think." He stood.

Simply so that she wouldn't feel so overwhelmed, Nina stood, too. "Thanks." She waved a hand in the vague direction of the food, then broadened the gesture. "For everything."

He walked slowly to the door, one hand deep in his pocket reaching for his keys, his head slightly bent.

Nina was suddenly nervous. "John? I didn't upset you, asking about your son, did I?"

"No, no." He pulled the keys from his pocket, but he didn't turn.

She moved closer. "I was curious. That's all."

They keys jangled in his hands. "People are."

She moved closer still. "You must be a very good parent. I'm beginning to feel a little humbled."

"That makes two of us."

She frowned. "Two?"

Slowly he turned, and what she saw in his eyes took her breath away. His voice was low, still slow but nowhere near as smooth as it usually was. "I thought I was immune to women like you. I thought that there was no way a woman with a fast-driving career could turn me on, but I was wrong."

A tiny voice inside Nina told her she ought to be angry, to either lash back or turn in the opposite direction and run, but that voice was drowned out by the sound of her pulse beating rapidly, hammering her feet in place on the floor.

His hand shaped her cheek, then slid along her jaw until his fingers were feathered by her hair. "Tell me not to want to kiss you," he said.

But she couldn't. As outlandish as it seemed, given that John Sawyer was the antithesis of the kind of man she usually liked, she wanted his kiss. Maybe, deep down inside, she'd been wanting it since he'd shown up at her door that afternoon wearing a T-shirt that made his chest look heart-stoppingly hard and broad. Maybe she'd been wanting it even longer, since the night she'd shown up at his store and seen him sweating. There was something about sweat that blew the intellectual image. Sweat was earthy and honest. Sweat was intimate. Given the right chemistry between a man and a woman, it was a powerful aphrodisiac.

Whether she wanted it to be so or not, Nina had to accept that the chemistry between John and her was right. There was no way her body was letting her move away from his touch, no way it was letting her evade him when his head slowly lowered and his mouth touched hers.

He gave her one kiss, then a second, then a third. Each one lasted a little longer than the one before, each one touched her a little more deeply. He seemed to be savoring her, reluctantly, if his words were to be considered, but savoring her nonetheless. His lips were firm, knowing, increasingly open and wet. His kisses were smooth as warm butter and ten times more hot.

By the time the last one ended and he raised his head, Nina's breath was coming in short, shallow wisps. Her eyes were closed. She felt miles and miles away from everything she'd always known, transported to a place where kisses touched the heart. She'd never been there before.

"I shouldn't have done that," he said quietly.

She opened her eyes to find his face flushed, his eyes serious. "Probably not," she said softly.

"You're not my type."

"Nor you mine."

"So why did it happen?"

She tried to think up an eloquent answer, but for all the hard selling she'd done in her day, she was without one. The best she could do was to murmur, "Chemistry?"

After a minute's thought, he said, "I guess." As though the admission were a warning, he passed his thumb over her lips—moist now, warm and naturally rouged—before letting his hand fall to his side.

"I didn't come here for this," he said gruffly. "I hope you know that."

She did. Somehow, with John, it wouldn't have occurred to her otherwise. He wasn't a wily sort of man.

"I'm not looking for anything," he went on, still in that

same gruff voice. "I don't have time for this kind of thing. Between the store and my son, I have all I can handle."

"Hey," she said, taking a step back, "I'm not asking for anything." It sounded to her as though he thought she was, or would. "It wasn't *me* who started that kiss."

"You didn't tell me to stop."

"Because I was curious about it. But it's no big thing. It's over and done. Curiosity satisfied. Period."

He thought about that, then nodded. But he didn't turn to leave. Instead, he looked thoughtful again. Then, in a low voice, he said, "Was it good?"

She took a deep breath. "You don't really want to know."

"I want to know."

"It won't help the situation."

"I want to know."

"It'll only make you angry, because the last thing you want is for someone like me to say it was good."

"Was it?"

"John," she pleaded, "why don't you just leave it be?"

"Because I want to know," he said with the stubbornness of a child. Nina had the sudden fear that he would stand there asking until she told him the truth.

Staring him in the eye, she said, "Yes, it was good. It was very good, and I'm sorry it ended. But it had to, because it wasn't right. We're totally different people with totally different wants and needs. You can't understand why I talk so fast, and I can't understand why you talk so slow. I want to make money, you want to meditate on the beach." Her hands went in opposite directions. "Worlds apart, John, we're worlds apart."

"Yeah." His amber eyes moved over her features. "It's too bad. You're awful cute."

She snorted. "Cute is what every woman over thirty wants to be."

"Over thirty?"

"Thirty-one, to be exact."

His mouth quirked at the corner. "I wouldn't have guessed it."

That quirking annoyed her. She didn't like being laughed at. "Well, now you know, and since you do, you can understand that I mean all I say about what I'm doing and where I'm going. I'm not some cute little pixie fresh out of college trying to make it big. I've had years of training in my field, and now that I'm on the verge of getting where I want to be, I'm not letting anyone stand in my way." She stole in a breath and raced on. "So if you think that I'm going to think twice about that kiss, that I'm going to look for a replay or want something *more*, you're mistaken. I'm off and running, and you'll only slow me down. I won't let that happen."

Having said her piece in a way that she felt was forceful and clear, she stood her ground with her jaw set, waiting for John to do his thinking thing then come up with a rejoinder. Not more than thirty seconds had passed, though, when, with a start, he glanced at his watch.

"Damn," he muttered, "I'm late." Raising his arm in a wave, he was fast out the door, taking the stairs at a speedy trot. Nina had never seen him move so fast, but it made sense that if he did it for anyone, he would do it for his son, and she was glad. From what he said, the boy had precious little going for him but a good brain and a loving dad.

Standing there amid the cartons in the living room that didn't feel quite hers yet, Nina's mind traveled back in time to when she'd been four herself. She hadn't had any obvious handicap. Her vision had been fine, along with her hearing, and her mind had been sharp—too sharp, in some respects. Even at that age she had wondered why she didn't have a father. Even then she had known something was wrong when she'd heard gruff voices coming from her mother's room late at night. Even then she had known that the bruises on her mother's face and arms and legs weren't normal.

She sighed. Ignorance would have been bliss back then, but what was done was done. She'd overcome those things that had darkened her early years and was now well on her way to having the security she wanted. Okay, so once in a while she wished things were different. Once in a while she wished *she* had someone rush home to her the way John Sawyer had to his son. But life wasn't perfect, she knew. No one had everything. So if she didn't have that special someone who cared, she had a growing career and a growing name and lots of respect along the way. She could live with that. She had no other choice.

COME EIGHT O'CLOCK that night, she wasn't thinking of choices. Having unpacked the very last carton, the only thing on her mind was soaking in a hot, hot bath. Stripping out of her shirt and jeans, she started the water and returned to the bedroom for a robe, when the phone rang.

Absurdly, her first thought was that the phone would also be ringing at her old apartment, jangling through rooms now empty and forlorn. Remembering the good two years she'd had there, she felt a twinge of sadness.

Her second thought was that Lee was calling in to report on any activity that had taken place at the office that day. Shrugging into the robe, she reached for the phone.

"Hello?"

"Nina?"

It was a man's voice. Though she hadn't ever heard it before on the phone, she knew instantly whose it was. Thoughts of him had been hovering at the back of her mind since he'd left her house in such a rush.

"Hi," she said cautiously.

"It's John."

"I know."

The line was silent for a time before he said, "I, uh, just

wanted to apologize for leaving so abruptly. Time had gotten away from me and J.J. was due home."

"Did you get back in time?"

"Almost."

"No?"

"They were waiting out front in the car."

"For long?"

"Three or four minutes. I'm usually on time. They were starting to worry."

"How about J.J.?"

"He was okay."

"Did he have fun?"

"I think so. Sometimes it's hard to tell whether he had a good time or he's just real happy to be home. One thing's for sure. He ate enough. He was wearing mustard, fruit punch and chocolate all over his shirt."

"Oh, yuck." She thought about single parenthood, and a sudden fear struck. "Are you the one who has to do the wash?"

"You got it."

"Oh, *yuck.*"

"Actually, given all I've had to clean up in the last four years, the dribbles from a picnic lunch are a snap."

Nina found herself picturing those other things. "You changed diapers?"

"All the time."

"What a good father. And husband. Your wife must have appreciated that." Once the words were out, she held her breath.

"Actually," he said after a brief pause, "she took it pretty much for granted. It was part of the bargain we made. I wanted the baby. She agreed to carry it if I was willing to take the responsibility for its care once it was born."

"That's awful," Nina exclaimed without thinking, then she did think and regretted the outburst. If John had adored his now-dead wife, the last thing Nina wanted to do was criticize her. "I mean, I suppose people do what's right for them. Did it work for her?"

"Not particularly. She went right back to work the way she planned, but she felt guilty, and she resented that."

"Oh, dear."

"Yeah." He paused. "Well." Another pause, then a new breath. "Anyway, I'm used to doing everything for J.J. It's kind of fun. Gives me a real sense of self-sufficiency."

Nina thought about that. "Do you cook?"

"Nothing gourmet, but he doesn't mind that. He's big on things like BLTs, and PB and Fs."

"PB and Fs?"

"Peanut butter and fluff sandwiches. Not quite the kind of meal you make, I'm sure."

Remembering the exchange they'd had over cookbooks in his store, Nina felt sheepish. "I don't really do that much."

"Ha," he scoffed. "I'm the one who unpacked your kitchen today. I saw that wok and that clay pot and that fondue dish."

"Those are all for fun. I don't use them often, except maybe for the wok. When I want a quick meal and don't feel like a frozen dinner, I stir-fry something up. I'm pretty good at it, actually. I've found some good recipes. I'll make you something sometime, if you'd like."

For the third time in the conversation, words had slipped from her mouth that she hadn't consciously put there. The idea that John Sawyer, whom she worked with but with whom she didn't have another thing in common except a love for reading, should want to come back to her house—for dinner, no less—was ridiculous. Surely he'd see that.

"Yeah," he said, "well, maybe." He paused. "So. Did you finish with the rest of your things?"

Feeling as though she'd been eased from a precarious place, she said, "Sure did. I'm feeling it now."

"Sore?"

"Mmm. I was just about to get in the—oh, hell! Hold on! I forgot about the water!" All but dropping the phone on the floor, she raced into the bathroom in time to watch the first of a steaming waterfall cascade over the edge of the tub. Frantically twisting the taps, she turned off the water, pulled out the plug, then reached for the towels she'd so recently hung on the nearby bar. "Good show, Nina," she muttered to herself as she mopped up the spillage. When she had the worst of it absorbed, she dropped the sodden towels into the sink, replaced the plug with just enough water left for her bath and returned to the phone.

"I can't believe I did that," she said without prelude. "A fine thing it'd be if the first night I'm here, I send water dripping onto my landlord's head."

"All cleaned up?"

"Enough." Thinking of the still-damp floor, she sighed. "I'd better go finish. Thanks for calling, John. And thanks again for your help. It was nice."

Some time later, lying in the tub with the heat of the water seeping into her tired limbs, Nina realized that it had been nice, both his help and his call. He was a nice man. A *sexy* man. All wrong for her, of course, and there was no point in even *thinking* of a repeat of that kiss. Still, he was nice to be with—which was what she told Lee the next morning when she was asked about the car that had been parked behind her car that Sunday afternoon.

"I was going to stop in and see how you were doing," Lee explained, "but when I saw that, I figured you already had a guest. I never thought it'd be John Sawyer." Her eyes narrowed in play. "Is there something you haven't told me?"

"Nothing at all," Nina said, cool and composed from the top of her shiny black hair to the toes of her shiny purple shoes. "John Sawyer is someone I work with. He knew I was moving, so he stopped by to help."

"I thought he drove you nuts."

"He does when it comes to work. But he's good for lifting cartons. So I used him." More pointedly she said, "That's what you have to learn to do. Turn the tables on Tom. Use him for a change, rather than the other way around."

"I'm not moving."

"Then use him for something else. Ask him to bring the wine and dessert if you're the one who's cooking dinner. Ask him to give you a lift to the service station when you have to pick up your car."

Lee wrinkled her nose. "I don't think he'd appreciate that."

"Probably not." Her voice gentled. "He does things on his terms, and his terms alone. That's not good. It's not fair."

Lee shrugged. "Maybe not, but that's the way it is."

Not for me, Nina thought. *Never for me.* She had her work. It, and the reward it brought, were all she needed.

With that reminder, she swiveled around to face her computer, punched up the current listings and got busy.

CHAPTER FIVE

OUT OF SIGHT WAS NOT out of mind. Nina tried not to think about John. She tried not to think about the way he looked or the way he acted. Mostly she tried not to think about the way he kissed, but it didn't work. Memory was insidious, wending through her mind in brief but potent flashes.

She hadn't had a kiss like that since…she'd *never* had a kiss like that. In her experience, men kissed women either rapaciously, showing their hunger and proud of it, or timidly, showing their fear, hoping to pass it off as sensitivity. John hadn't kissed her either of those ways. His kiss had been forceful in a quiet, thoughtful way, which was pretty much how he was himself. He'd known what he was doing. His mouth had conveyed the attraction he felt. The fact that the attraction was unbidden made it all the more special.

But it was over, and she had put it from her mind, so she immersed herself in her work for all she was worth. It wasn't hard, since she loved what she did. And there was plenty to keep her busy. If she wasn't out showing a piece of property, she was working with the newspaper on fresh copy or doing paperwork for an impending sale or tracking down a competitor with a co-broke offer. When she was in the office, her phone was forever ringing.

None of those calls were from John. As the week wore on, during those brief in-between times when she thought of him, she began to wonder why he hadn't called. He had been so persistent at first that they discuss Crosslyn Rise, and though the decision on pricing had been made, the consortium had very clearly asked them to continue to work together.

She wondered whether he was as bothered, after the fact, by that kiss as she was.

She wondered whether he was embarrassed. Or disappointed. Or disgusted.

She wondered whether he hated her.

By Friday afternoon, she'd just about had it with the wondering. Picking up the phone, she punched out his number.

He answered, his voice deep and pleasantly resonant. "The Leaf Turner."

"John? It's Nina. Am I getting you at a bad time?" Heart pounding, she waited.

His voice came back a little less deep than it had been. "No, not at all. There's actually a comfortable lull here right now. How are you?"

She chose to believe he was pleased that she'd called. "Fine," she answered lightheartedly. "And you?"

"Can't complain."

"How's J.J.?" she asked, knowing it was the one thing that would guarantee a positive response.

"Great. The girls took him out for ice cream. He loves that."

"Girls, plural?"

"Two. Twins. What with J.J.'s problems, I like knowing there are two of them, so that one can keep an eye on him at any given time. You know how baby-sitters can be."

Actually she didn't. An only child herself, she'd never had a baby-sitter, but had been left with a neighbor or, at a frighteningly tender age, alone. Her mother hadn't had the money to pay a sitter. By virtue of that same fact, when Nina had been old enough to work, she had bypassed baby-sitting in favor of a supermarket job with more regular hours and higher pay. It hadn't mattered that the supermar-

ket didn't hire kids under fifteen. She had talked them into
hiring her. Even back then, she'd had a persuasive mouth.

"Do they talk on the phone a lot?" she asked.

"It's not as much that, as getting distracted cooking
pizza or watching television. Actually, these two are pretty
responsible. And they think J.J. is adorable."

"I'll bet he is," Nina said, because if he looked anything
like John, she was sure he was. "Did you get all the mustard
and stuff out?"

"The what? Oh, that. Pretty much."

Again she pictured him doing the wash and felt
admiration. He was a good father. A good man.

Aware of the silence, she cleared her throat and said,
"Uh, I'm actually calling about work, John. I picked up the
finished brochures from the printer today. They're the ones
we'll be handing out at the open house, and then, after that,
in the office to anyone interested in Crosslyn Rise. I
thought you might like to see them."

"That would be nice," he said with what she could have
sworn was a touch of caution.

"I'll be working most of the weekend, so I'll be in and
out, but I have to man the front desk at the office Sunday
morning from ten to twelve." She had thought it all out. Her
calling him was a business move. She didn't want him
thinking it was anything else. Hence, the office. "Do you
want to stop by then?"

After a pause, he said, "I could do that."

"You could bring J.J. if you want." He certainly didn't
have to hire a sitter for something as innocent as a brief
office meeting. "We won't be long. You'll probably want to
take the brochure home to study. I'll be passing out copies
to all of the members of the consortium at our next meeting,
but I thought you might want to see it before then. There
may be some things that you think are stronger or weaker,
that we can compensate for in person at the open house."

"Okay. I'll drop by."

"Sometime between ten and twelve?"

"Uh-huh."

She shrugged. That was that. "See you then."

SHE TOLD HERSELF that it was nothing more than another business meeting and probably wouldn't last longer than two minutes, still she took care in dressing, again passing over some of the more outlandish of her outfits in favor of a relatively sedate slacks set. Granted, the pants were harem-style and the top short and loose, but the color was moss green, the neck barely scooped and the sleeves as voluminous as the legs.

Well, hell, he didn't expect that she'd dress like a school-marm, did he? At least, the outfit wasn't neon pink, like some of hers were, and her nails weren't red now, but beige.

Ten o'clock came and went. She talked with a couple who walked in off the street, people who thought *maybe* they'd look for something new but *only* if they could sell their old place and what were their chances of that. Ten-fifteen became ten-thirty. One of Martin's clients came by to drop some papers he'd signed. A potential buyer called to check on the time of another open house. Ten forty-five passed and eleven arrived.

She was beginning to wonder whether he'd forgotten, when, shortly before eleven-thirty, he came leisurely through the door. He was alone; she felt an unexpected stab of disappointment at that. But the disappointment was brief, because he looked so good. His hair was damp, freshly combed back over his ears and down over his nape. He was wearing a white shirt—open at the neck, with the sleeves rolled—and a pair of jeans that looked relatively new. She wondered if it was his Sunday best.

When he planted himself directly before her desk, she smiled. "You've been at the beach again." His skin had a golden glow, a bit of new color over what she'd seen the week before.

He nodded. "This morning. J.J. is still there."

Her face dropped. "Oh, I'm sorry, John. I didn't mean to drag you away from him. This wasn't so important. We could have done it another time."

"You didn't drag me away. He's with friends. He's happy."

"The same friends who took him out last week?"

He shook his head. "Different ones. They have a daughter with special needs. She's just about J.J.'s age. They're in the same play group."

"Do all the children in the play group have similar handicaps?"

"Roughly."

"How many children?"

"Twelve."

She was stunned. "And they all live around here?" She couldn't imagine so many four-year-olds with similar problems in the immediate area. As populations went, the local tally was low.

"No. Some of them come from pretty far, which means that we go pretty far to see them in return. But it's worth it. Socialization is critical, but it's hard for kids like these to get it through regular channels. I tried J.J. in a local play group when he was two. I figured that he was doing all the same things the other kids were, playing with blocks and all. But he wasn't talking. Since he couldn't hear, he couldn't react to the other kids the way they expected. And he made the mothers nervous."

Nina thought that was awful. "Screw *them*."

He gave a lopsided grin that created a dimple in his cheek—and sent a ripple of awareness through Nina. "I felt the same way. Actually, I felt worse. I was furious. Then I thought about it, and I talked it over with J.J.'s therapists, and the way we reasoned it out, it wasn't so awful. Those women were nervous because they didn't know how to communicate with J.J. They kept expecting him to be just like their own kids, only he wasn't. Isn't. And it didn't matter how angry I got, no way was that experience going to be positive, and that's the name of the game. So now he's with people who understand him. They understand me. We've all been through the same things. We help each other."

"Like watching kids at the beach?"

"Like that."

Nina reached for the brochure that she'd tucked safely to the side. "You'll probably want to take this and leave, then." She held it out, trying to be a good sport. "It's a beautiful day for the beach. You'll be anxious to get back."

He closed his hand around it, but rather than turning away, he arched a questioning brow toward the chair by the desk. She was surprised, and delighted. With an enthusiastic, "Please," she watched him lower himself into the chair, stretch out his legs and open the brochure.

He really *was* handsome, she decided again. He wasn't urbane or sophisticated looking, certainly not slick, still he was handsome. Today there was something western about him. With his fresh jeans and his damp hair and the color the sun had painted on his skin, he looked like a cowboy newly off the range and showered. With high-heeled boots, the picture would have been complete. Then again, she preferred his deck shoes, particularly the way he wore them without socks. She wondered what his ankles were like, whether they were as well formed as his hands and wrists, and half wished he'd cross one of his legs so she could see.

But he didn't. Looking perfectly comfortable as he was, he took his time reading the copy, studying the drawings, closing the brochure to look at the piece as a whole. "This is very professional," he said at last.

She felt inordinately pleased. "Thank you. Do you think it'll impress the people we want to impress?"

"It should." He turned to the last page, where the price guides were listed. "I was wondering whether they'd get these right."

"You mean, you were wondering whether I'd hike those prices back up between the time the consortium voted and the printer printed?" She couldn't quite tell if he was kidding. Rather than overreact if he was, she kept her voice light. "I wouldn't do that, John."

He shrugged. "You never can tell with typos."

"There aren't any typos in that brochure. Not a single one. I've been over it with a fine-tooth comb dozens of times. It's perfect."

Taking several more minutes, he looked through it again. Then, unfolding himself from the chair, he stood. "I like it, Nina."

She hated to see him leave so soon. "I thought maybe you'd have some suggestions."

"This is pretty much a *fait accompli,* isn't it?"

"Yes, it's all printed, but that doesn't mean we can't approach things differently when we're talking with clients, if you think a different approach is called for." She was feeling a little foolish, because he was right. The brochure was done and printed. Everything major was correct. To change something small and reprint hundreds of copies would be an absurd expense.

Still, the consortium wanted them to work together.

Eyes on the brochure, he said, "Why don't I take this home and read it again—" his voice dropped and slowed "—when I'm not so distracted by the piles of soft stuff you're wearing." With each of the last words, his eyes rose a notch until finally they met hers. "I'll call you if anything comes to mind."

She swallowed. "That sounds okay."

He nodded. Raising two fingers in a wave that could have been negligent, bashful or reluctant, he left.

NINA MADE A POINT not to wait for his call. She figured that after the way she'd invited him over when she could as well have put the brochure in the mail, a little aloofness was called for. So she ran around as usual, confident that if he called the office, she'd get his message, and that if he called her at home, he'd keep calling until she was there.

It wasn't until Thursday night that she picked up her phone in response to its ring and heard his voice. "I still think the brochure is fine," he said after the briefest of exchanged hellos. "But I thought maybe we could go up to the Rise and take a look around. I haven't been there in a while. If you're looking for the reaction of an everyday Joe, I'm your man."

Not even at the beginning, when Nina had broken into cold sweats over John's pokey ways, had she thought of him as an everyday Joe, and she certainly didn't now. He was different. He marched to his own drummer. She did concede, though, that of all the consortium members, he was probably the one to give the most off-the-cuff response, so she supposed in a way he was right.

"Okay. When can you go?"

"Tomorrow morning, actually, but I know this is pretty last-minute for you. You probably have appointments all over the place."

She did. She didn't have to dig out her appointment book to know that, and when she did open it, she saw that her schedule was even worse than she'd thought. But John was free, and he was right. They really should get up to see Crosslyn Rise.

"I may be able to shift things around," she said, her mind already at work. "Can you give me half an hour to find out?"

"Sure. I'll call back."

During the next thirty minutes, Nina phoned four clients, one other broker and Lee. By the time John called back, she had cleared a two-hour stretch starting at ten. They agreed to meet then.

No matter how frequent a visitor Nina was to the Rise, she was always amazed at the progress she found with each return. Most impressive this time was the mansion. It had long since been scooped clean of its innards, with little left but structural elements such as the grand staircase and period details like ceiling moldings and chair rails. Renovation was well under way. Woodwork that had been stripped and sanded was now being stained. Walls were being modified, doorways shifted from one spot to another. From the large first-floor room that would serve as an elegant paneled meeting-room-lounge-library, to the large back room that would be a health club, to the totally modernized kitchen, the two private dining rooms, and the charming suites on the second floor that could be rented out to guests, the place was suddenly taking on the feel of something on the verge of being real.

"Does this ever look different," John said as he stood with his head tipped back to take in the height of the huge front hall. "Very nice."

He wasn't bubbly. His voice was as quiet as ever. But Nina, who had studied his face closely in the recent past, could read the subdued excitement there. Taking excitement from that, she waved him on. "Come." She led him from one room to the next, pausing in the middle of each, letting the feel of the place seep in. At spots where there was active construction going on, they had to watch where they stepped and moved, and at those times, John either went first and took her arm to guide her by or cautioned her to take care.

Nina had never been one to cling to a man, but John's touch felt good. Particularly on bare skin. In deference to the June warmth, she had worn a sundress. It was bright yellow, actually little more than a long tank top that, once hiked up at the waist by a wide leather belt, grazed the top of her knees. She had also worn flats for the sake of walking, and the overall effect was to make her feel that much more delicate next to John, who, wearing jeans and an open-necked shirt—a horizontally striped one this time—looked surprisingly rugged.

She stayed close, under the guise of safety, until they reached the outdoors and the danger of flying wood chips was gone. She would have given him more room then, but he didn't move away. He stayed close by her side during the walk down the path toward the duck pond, where the first of the near-completed condos were.

"Such a gorgeous place," he said. "I don't know how Jessica was ever able to give it up."

"She had to. She couldn't keep it as it was, and we couldn't find a single seller who could afford the whole thing. So rather than seeing it broken down by a developer who didn't care a whit about the glory of the Rise, she decided to form the consortium and be the one to call the shots."

"Does she call them, or does Carter?"

Nina looked up to find a mischievous smile touching his mouth. Her gaze lingered on his mouth for a minute before she said, "Jessica does. Carter gives her input, and he runs the meetings, but in the end the decision is hers." She returned her eyes to the path.

"They seem happy."

"They are."

"I think she's pregnant."

Nina's eyes flew back to his. This time John seemed totally serious. "How do you know?"

"She has that look."

"You mean, radiance? For heaven's sake, John, that's a crock."

"It is not."

"When a woman is pregnant, she feels sick. Then fat and clunky. There's nothing radiant about being that way."

"Fine for you to say," John said, kicking aside a fallen twig. "You've never been pregnant. You don't know what the feeling's like."

She laughed. "And you do? I hate to tell you this, John—"

"I remember when my wife was pregnant," he said quietly. Coming to a stop, he looked off in the distance, seeing not the duck pond but another time years before. "She wasn't real happy about it, but I was. I thought it was a miracle, the idea of this little life growing inside her. Long before the baby moved, I could see the changes in her body. First her breasts, then her waist, nature doing its thing in a totally generic way. Maybe she was too close to be able to appreciate it. I was just that little bit removed, so I could see things in a broader scheme. Then, when I felt the baby move in her stomach, everything that had been so broad seemed to focus in on the fact that it was my child growing there." His breath caught on the intake. Seeming surprised by his own words, he looked quickly at Nina. "Sorry. I get carried away. It was an incredible experience."

Standing still beside him, she felt goose bumps running up and down her arms. "You make it sound incredible." And she could almost believe in radiance, because she could have sworn that was the look she had seen on John's face for the few seconds before he'd caught himself.

The look she saw now was more earthy, and there was no way his glasses could mask it. His eyes were on her goose bumps. "Cold?"

"No."

Lightly, starting at her wrists, he ran his hands up her arms. They stopped just shy of her shoulders to gently knead her skin. He watched their progress, first one, then the next. "It's too bad you don't want to have kids. You'd make a pretty mother."

Her skin felt hot where he touched it, and the heat was stealing inside. "People would have trouble telling me from the kids," she managed to say, though her voice was meager.

"Pregnant, I mean. You'd be pretty pregnant."

Her heart was racing. "Maybe more substantial."

"No." His eyes touched her breasts, which rose with each shallow breath she took. "You're substantial now. But it's different when you're pregnant. Not just added weight. Something else." His eyes slipped to her stomach, caressing it through the thin jersey material, causing the same kneading sensation that was so seductive on her arms. She could barely move, barely breathe. Slowly, searing a path along the way, his gaze rose and locked with hers. "I keep thinking about you, Nina. I don't want to, but I do."

At the reluctant admission, she started to shake her head, but he made a shushing motion with his mouth and that stopped her. His voice was low, slow and sandy. "I keep remembering that kiss. It was so good. The only problem was that nothing touched but our mouths."

"I know," she whispered.

While his hands kept up their gentle motion, his thumbs slid sensuously up and down under the thin straps at her shoulders. "I keep wondering what it would be like to touch other places. I lie in bed at night imagining. It's not fun."

She swallowed. "Because you don't want to like me?"

"Because I get hard."

Her breath caught in her throat and stayed there despite the wild skittering of her pulse. She gave a short, sharp shake of her head.

"What?"

"Don't say things like that," she begged.

"Because it embarrasses you?"

"Because it excites me."

The flare in John's eyes told her what her words had done. His thumbs began moving more widely, stroking her skin in small patches that inched downward, under the edge of her dress, over the starting swell of her breast.

"I want to touch you more," he said. With the lightest pressure, he brought her arms just that tiny bit forward to angle her body better for his seeking thumbs. They stroked deeper, even deeper, under her bra now, moving toward the center of her breasts.

Her nipples tightened. "John," she whispered weakly. Heat seemed to be gathering and pooling not only in her breasts, but down low. She clutched his hips for support.

"Let me," he whispered back, as his thumbs reached their twin goals. He circled them once, touched their tips, then moved back and forth in a gentle rubbing.

Catching in a small cry, Nina bit her lip. But the feeling in her breasts was still too intense, so she closed her eyes and dropped her head back.

With a low groan, John caught her to him. His hands left her breasts and circled her, drawing her fully into his body at the same time that his mouth came down on hers. He kissed her long and deep, first with his lips, then his tongue. Wrapping her arms around his neck, she sought his firmness. Opening her mouth wide to his, she tasted his hunger. There was nothing in him that was either rapacious or arrogant. He kissed her like a man who simply needed to be closer.

And closer he brought her. His arms swept over her back, one lower, one higher, pressing her into him at every point. His strength came at her through his thighs, his chest, his arms, made all the more enticing to her by the faint tremor that spoke of his restraint.

When he finally tore his mouth away, his breathing was ragged. Dragging his arms from around her, he took her face in his hands. "What the hell am I going to do with you?"

She didn't know what to say.

"Can you feel how much I want you?"

She hadn't been that long without a man that she didn't know the meaning of the hard presence against her stomach. Unable to take her eyes from his, she nodded.

"So?" he asked in frustration.

"So I don't sleep around."

"Me, neither."

"I don't take making love lightly."

"Me, neither.

"So we can't do it. We're all wrong for each other. We don't even like each other. And we have to work together."

He looked at her for a long time, his amber eyes dark and hungry still. "You're right." His thumbs skimmed her cheeks. "But all that doesn't take the wanting away. I haven't wanted a woman—"

He was cut off by the intrusion of a loud voice on the approach. "Okay, you guys, I think you'd better break it up."

Nina's head shot around as quickly as John's, and she found herself staring into the amused eyes of Carter Malloy, who was coming from the direction of the duck pond. Stopping not far from them, he said, "I think there's something about the air out here. It makes you forget that just anyone could be walking through. Fortunately for you, it's me. I understand these things."

Nina knew her cheeks were red, but she didn't say a word either in defense of herself or protest to John when he slowly released her.

Carter scratched the back of his head. "I nearly lost it with Jessica, just about a year ago, not far from where you stand." He paused, looking from Nina's face to John's. "I think the ducks were less embarrassed then than you two are now."

Nina took a deep, faintly shuddering breath. "You should have called from way back on the path."

"I did."

"Oh."

John had his hands on his hips. "You should have called a second time."

"I did. But, hey, now that you're awake and aware, I'll just be moving along." He gave them a grin and started off. "Catch you later."

He'd gone a good ten yard when Nina called, "Carter, is Jessica pregnant?"

He stopped in his tracks and turned, wearing a guarded look. "Where did you hear that?"

"Is it true?"

Taking a deep breath that straightened his back and expanded his chest beneath the blazer and shirt he was wearing, Carter allowed himself a slow smile. "Yeah, it's true. She miscarried in January, so we've been cautious about saying anything. But she's almost into her fourth month. Things look good this time."

Forgetting her embarrassment, Nina burst into a grin. "Hey, that's great. I knew she wanted a baby."

"We both do."

"How's she feeling?" John asked.

Carter shimmied a hand. "Sometimes nauseous, sometimes not. The doctor says the sickness is a sign that the baby's really settling in, which is good news after the first one. We're keeping our fingers crossed."

"I'll keep mine crossed, too," Nina said.

John put a thumb up and said in a very male way, "Good goin', Carter."

Carter tossed him a macho smile before turning and continuing along the path.

Watching him go, Nina murmured under her breath, "Are you going to say, 'I told you so'?"

"Of course not. The important thing is that it's true."

"Mmm. She did tell me she wanted a baby. I'm excited for her."

"Excited about the baby?"

"Excited because she's getting what she wants. I don't know enough about babies to get excited about them."

"Don't have any friends with kids?"

"A few. But I've never been terribly involved. I'm too busy with work. My friends seem to know that. When they meet me for lunch, it's without the kids." She allowed herself a glance at John. "Which is another reason why you and I are no good. You have a kid. I wouldn't know what in the devil to do with one."

John didn't say anything. He stood there, looking down at her, looking *into* her, seemingly, for something she was sure wasn't there. Looking back at him, all she could see was the random brush of his hair on his brow, the lean contour of his jaw, the straight slash of his nose, the tightness of his lips. It was a face that drew her even when she told herself that it shouldn't.

Finally he raised his head and looked away. "We'd better get going."

Nodding, she started off toward the duck pond, but the glow that had earlier been on the day was gone. In its place was a tension that began in the body and ended in the mind, causing an awkwardness that was underwritten with need.

They walked through the condominium that was to be the model, then through two others. Nina pointed out various features and options, just as she might have if John had been an interested buyer. They avoided looking at each other, avoided standing too close, but that didn't ease the wire that seemed strung taut between them. Whatever the distance, it hummed.

By the time they returned to the mansion, Nina was feeling strung out, herself. She was only too glad to put together a hasty goodbye to John, climb into her car and drive off. She wasn't used to confusion. Hitherto in her life, she had been the sole master of her fate. Now, though, it seemed she was losing control, if not of her fate, then of *something*.

She wished she knew what that something was.

She wished she could stop it from slipping away.

She wished she didn't feel hot, then cold, light, then dark, good, then bad.

Mostly she wished she understood what she was feeling for John. He wasn't like any man she'd ever known. He was maddeningly laid-back, but she respected him. He saw the world differently from her, but she trusted him. She liked him, but she didn't.

And she wanted him. Wanted him. He haunted her for the rest of the day and all that night. She lay in bed wide awake, remembering how he'd kissed her and held her, how safe she'd felt, how valued, how hot and needy. The need returned, making her flop one way then the next, but no position was better for the aching within. *I lie in bed imagining,* he'd said, and she imagined him imagining. She also imagined him hard, and the fever built.

She slept for an hour, then awoke, slept for another, awoke again. When her skin grew damp in the warmth of the night, she sponged herself off, but no sooner did she return to bed than she was sweaty again.

By dawn, she was fit to be tied. No man, *no man*, she vowed, could do this to her. No man was worth it. She had her life, and it was free and independent, just as she wanted. Once she had her own agency, that independence would increase. She was well on her way to where she wanted to be. She didn't need any man, *any man*.

Then, at eight o'clock, her doorbell rang. Sticky, tired and more than a little cranky, she plodded down the stairs. "Who is it?" she yelled through the wood.

"John," he called back.

Moaning softly, she put her forehead to the worn pine. It was cool, with a faint musty scent that took her out of time and place, but the relief was short-lived. John was on the other side. She didn't know what to do.

His voice came more quietly, as though he'd moved closer. "Open the door, Nina. We need to talk."

"I don't think," she said, squeezing her eyes shut, "that this is the best time."

He didn't answer. Had he been another man, she might have wondered if he'd left. But this was John.

After a minute, he spoke again, still quiet, still close. "Nina? Open the door, Nina. Please?"

She might have had a comeback had it not been for his tone of voice. Not even the thickness of the door could muffle the quiet command. But there was something else there, something even more potent. Beneath the quiet command was a hint of pleading.

Fearing she was making a huge mistake but helpless to avoid it, she gave a tiny sound of frustration, took a small step back and opened the door a crack.

CHAPTER SIX

JOHN PUSHED THE DOOR open only enough to slip through. Watching him from the corner by the hinge, Nina felt beset by every one of the wild imaginings she'd tried to stifle through the night. The fact that he wore a T-shirt and shorts didn't help any. The sight of leanly muscled legs spattered with warm brown hair stirred the fire inside her to a greater head.

"I brought donuts," he said quietly, but his eyes hadn't risen above her neck.

She was in the short nightie that she'd put on in the wee hours, and wore nothing beneath it. "I was in bed," she said, feeling the need to explain. She wouldn't normally have answered the door dressed that way. But she felt reckless, at the end of her tether. "It was a bad night."

At that, he did raise his eyes. He'd left his glasses at home, and it struck her that he looked every bit as sweaty as she felt. His hair was damp and disheveled, his skin moist. "I ran." His eyes were intent, the deepest, richest amber she'd ever seen. "I thought we could talk."

"I don't know if I can." Her need was written all over her face, she knew, but she couldn't erase it.

John seemed to see it, consider it, fight it—with about as much success as she had. After an eternity of searing silence, he muttered, "I don't want these." Dropping the bag of donuts onto the stair, he reached for her.

Coming up against his body, winding her arms around

his neck, feeling him lift her nearly off her feet, Nina felt the first relief she'd had in hours. She sighed his name and held tighter, burying her face against his neck.

For the longest time, they stood like that, holding each other tighter, then tighter still, making no sounds but those of quickened breathing and the occasional whimper or moan. Nina might have stayed that way forever if it wasn't for the gradual awakening of her body to the one molding it. She began to move against him in small ways to better feel him, and when that wasn't enough, she started to use her hands.

John's own hands made slow sweeps of discovery over her back. She could tell the instant he knew for sure she was bare under her nightie by the sharp catch of his breath. Fingers splayed, his hands stole up the back of her thighs to her bottom.

"Tell me to stop if you don't want this," he said in a gravelly voice she'd never heard before. It was laced with raw need and was a stimulant in itself.

"I want it," she breathed frantically. Exploring the lean line of his hips, she pushed her fingers over his thighs. The hair there abraded her palms delightfully. "I need it," she confessed just as frantically, then let out a cry when he touched the fire between her legs. "Help me," she begged, and to convince him, she worked her fingers up under his shorts. He wore cotton briefs, but they were stretched taut.

Clearly he didn't need any convincing.

Before she had any inkling of what he was doing, he slid his hands under her thighs and lifted her. When her legs were cinched around his hips, he covered her mouth with his and devoured it whole as he started up the stairs. He didn't stop until he was in her bedroom, where he lowered her to the rumpled sheets and crouched over her.

His voice a rough burr, he drew up her nightie. "I haven't been with anyone since my wife. Do I need a condom?"

Nina helped him pull the thin fabric over her head. As

soon as one hand was freed, she reached for him. "It's been longer than that for me," she whispered hurriedly as she tugged at his shirt. It was over his head in an instant, revealing a chest that was well formed and tapering. A wide wedge of hair narrowed, arrowlike, toward his fly. She reached there and touched him. "No condom."

John lowered his zipper and shifted to thrust both shorts and briefs aside. "Babies?"

"I take pills," she gasped, then, "Hurry, John, hurry." His large hand swept her under him, and no sooner did she open her legs when, like a heat seeker, he was in. Stunned by the force of his impaling, she cried out and arched up.

"Nina—"

"No, no, it doesn't hurt, it feels good, so good."

But that penetration, that first feel of his masculine strength, was only the beginning. What he proceeded to do then nearly blew her mind. He stroked her inside and out, using his hands, his mouth, his sex. He nipped, he laved. He quickened the pace and the force when her breath came more quickly. At times his movements were rhythmic, at times less so. At times he filled her to the utmost, withdrew nearly all the way, then reentered with a sharp pulsing burst that she might have feared was climactic if he hadn't continued right on again.

Hungry for everything he gave her, she touched him wherever she could, but the heat he stoked in her soon drove everything from her mind except the release coming on. She erupted with a vengeance, throbbing against him for what seemed an eternity. Lost on the other side of rapture, she wasn't able to separate her climax from his until she finally returned to consciousness enough to feel the last of the spasms shaking his body.

Slowly, breathing hard, he lowered himself over her. After a long minute, he rolled to his side and drew her along, still inside her.

She looked into his eyes, and for a minute she couldn't speak. Something caught at her throat, something deep and emotional, something she couldn't—didn't want to—understand. Making love with John had been the experience of a lifetime.

As the minutes passed and she regained her poise, she let a smile soften her lip. "Who'd have guessed it?" she finally whispered.

His brow creased in a frown that was here and gone. "Guessed what?"

"That slow, quiet, thoughtful John Sawyer was a crackerjack of unleashed virility in bed."

His cheeks were already flushed, but she could have sworn they grew more so. "I was inspired."

"You certainly were." Her smile faded. She touched his face. "That was special."

He gave a slow, thoughtful nod. "Are you sure I didn't hurt you?"

"Do I look hurt?"

He shook his head. Slowly. "You look well loved." He touched her lips, which were still warm and swollen, then her cheek, then her hair. "How can hair that is shorter than mine be feminine?"

"It's not real hard to have hair shorter than yours," she quipped, and buried her fingers in the thickness at his nape, "but I like it."

"You didn't at first."

"I didn't like much about you at first. You were slowing me down."

"I still am. It's become my cause."

She assumed he was teasing and teased him right back. "It won't work."

"Sure, it will. You're not rushing off to work right now, are you?"

She shook her head. "I don't have to be in until ten."

"If you had to be in at nine, would you be rushing?"

"Maybe." She grinned. "I suppose it would depend on how forceful that *thing* you're anchoring me here with is. Doesn't feel too forceful right now."

He grinned back. "Give it a minute."

"You think so?"

"I know so."

She waited a minute, during which time she touched his chest, tracing the hair there, teasing his nipples. "Hmm," she said, clamping her thigh higher around his when she felt him growing inside her, "I think you may be right."

"Of course I'm right." He caught her mouth and ate at it gently, then less gently as his hunger grew. Fluidly he rolled to his back, bringing her up to straddle him. His eyes were focused on her breasts, which were warm and rose tipped. After guiding her hips for a deeper joining, he left her to her own devices there and touched her breasts.

Nina watched the long fingers she admired curved around her flesh. She watched them trace her shape and weigh her fullness. She watched them knead, then rub her nipples into hard beads, then draw her forward to meet his mouth. The sight of his tongue dabbing the tip of her breast with moisture that his finger then spread, was nearly her undoing. Closing her eyes, she began to move on him, shifting forward, then back and around, feeling him grow and grow inside her until he was rising to meet her thrusts.

He brought her to a first climax by tugging her nipples into elongated points. He brought her to a second one by finding the hard bud between her legs and stroking it to fruition. He brought her to a third one by rolling her over and plunging into her with the kind of savagery she'd never have expected from him, but which drove her wild. By the time he'd emptied himself into her, their bodies were slick and spent.

For a short time, they lay limp and quiet, and at first, Nina enjoyed the closeness. Then her mind clicked on.

Slowly picking up speed, it ran her through what had happened, painting pictures of what it meant, and she grew frightened. She had enjoyed herself too much, far too much. John Sawyer as a lover could be habit-forming. But she didn't have room in her life for a relationship. She didn't have time for a man like John. She had places to go. She couldn't be tied down, *wouldn't* be tied down, not even by her own desires.

"Gotta get up," she murmured from against his chest.

His arm tightened around her. "No, stay."

"Gotta get to work."

"Call in. Get someone to cover."

"I can't."

"I have a sitter till noon."

A sitter. The word represented one of the major differences between Nina and John. Flattening a firm hand on his chest, Nina ignored the lure of damp, warmly furred male flesh and levered herself up. Seconds later, she was out of bed, headed for the bathroom.

"Nina?" John called.

"I have to shower," she called back.

"Put it off."

"I can't."

She turned on the water. As soon as steam rose from it, she stepped under and began to soap herself. She worked methodically, the same way she always did. If certain spots were more sensitive than usual, even tender, she ignored that. She went on to her hair, scrubbing it hard, then rinsed, turned off the water, reached for the towel and began to rub herself dry. By the time she returned to the bedroom, John was propped up against the brass headboard, looking extraordinarily masculine against her bright pink sheets. Everything in the room was bright pink for that matter; still he didn't look foolish. Just masculine.

Ignoring that, too, she took underwear from a drawer and put it on, then a pair of silk walking shorts and a matching silk blouse, both in fuchsia. After hooking a pair of turquoise spangles onto her ears, a matching necklace around her neck and a belt around her waist, she stepped into strappy sandals. Then she shook her head, vigorously, peered into the mirror over the dresser and finger-combed her hair.

"Nina."

She looked over at John in surprise. She hadn't forgotten he was there—no way could she do that—but he'd been so still for so long that his voice, strangely sharp, startled her.

"Is that it?" he asked. His face was expressionless, his eyes level.

"What?"

"We make love, you get up and leave?"

Opening her makeup case, she began to smooth moisturizer onto her face. "I have to work."

"I want to talk."

Eyes on her own reflection, she shook her head. "Can't do that now. Maybe another time."

"When?"

She shrugged. "I don't know. I'll have to see when I'm free."

"You can be free any time you want to."

"I cannot. I have clients to service."

"So what about me?"

Her voice was low, her fingertips busy dabbing eye shadow onto her lids. "Seems to me I just serviced you."

John swore. Kicking back the sheet, he rolled to his feet and came to stand over her. Looking in the mirror, Nina caught sight of his nakedness for an instant before her own body blotted out the image, and not a moment too soon. Naked, he was stunning.

"Don't use that word with regard to what we did."

She forced a shrug, hinting at a nonchalance she didn't feel, and went on with her makeup.

"Damn it, Nina, didn't that *mean* anything to you? I mean, you're the very first woman I've been with—wanted to be with—since the debacle of my marriage, and you say that you haven't been with any other man, yet you can just climb out of bed, get dressed and move on?"

"I have work to do," she said quietly. "I take it seriously."

He rubbed a hand along the back of his neck. She could see that much. Even barefoot, he stood tall over her. Warily, with half an eye, she watched him, waiting for him to move or speak. With the other half, she finished her makeup. He hadn't said anything by the time she snapped her blusher shut and zipped it back into the bag, but he was giving her a baleful stare.

"Okay," she said, turning to him in concession, "so I'm a cold, hard bitch who's in a rush to get back to work. You can think it. You can *say* it. You knew it before this ever happened."

"Didn't this mean anything?"

"Of *course* it did. I told you, I don't play around, and I *haven't* been with a man in years. But just because we made love doesn't change anything. You still have your priorities, and I have mine. Neither of us is going to change. You knew that, John. We both knew it. That's why doing this was so stupid."

"So why did we?"

She tried to find a sensible answer, but the only thing she could come up with was, "Because we couldn't *not* do it. There's something chemical between us. It was building up and building up. This was inevitable." She turned away to reach for the purse that matched her outfit. "Dumb, but inevitable."

He stuck his hands on his lean hips, totally unselfconscious, seemingly unaware of the magnificent picture he made. "And you're sorry we did it?"

She hung her head and fingered the purse. "No. I enjoyed it."

"But you'll just turn and walk away from it?"

Her eyes shot to his. "What would you have me do?"

"Stay here. Talk to me."

"There's no *point*. What's done is done. Now I'm getting back to my life."

"You work too hard."

She made for the door. "What else is new?"

"You looked awful when I walked in here," he said, following her through the apartment.

"That was because of you. I didn't sleep last night. I kept thinking of *you*." As indictments went, it was a revealing one, but her step didn't falter.

"And you think you can stop now?"

"I'm sure as hell going to try."

"How?"

"By *working*." She reached the head of the stairs, and without a pause, started down.

"You won't be able to," he called from the top.

"Yes, I will."

"What we've done just now will haunt you."

"I won't let it."

"You can't even *look* at me!" he shouted.

Nina hadn't ever heard him shout before. The sound shook her from the top of her head to the tips of her toes, but it wasn't enough to make her turn. Lest she be stopped cold like Lot's wife, she hauled open the door and fled without a single glance back.

NINA WAS DETERMINED to do just what she'd said, to get back to work as though nothing as earth-shattering as making love with John had ever happened. Neither John nor his gorgeous body nor his masterful way of loving was going to sidetrack her from her goals of making money, making a name and making a fully independent way of life for herself.

So she poured herself into work more single-mindedly than ever that Saturday. It wasn't until after nine that night that she returned to her apartment, and she was off at seven the next morning to drive to Hartford for a one-day seminar. She was exhausted by the time she returned, feeling hot and sweaty and achy, just as she had on Friday night. Knowing John was the culprit and determined to push him from her mind, she refused to answer the phone—which rang repeatedly through the evening—and instead set herself up with a particularly tricky and, therefore, demanding book of figures relating to home mortgage options, shifting interest rates and tax plans. She worked at it until two in the morning, when a combination of exhaustion and an upset stomach got to her. Fortunately, exhaustion was the stronger of the two. She was asleep soon after her head hit the pillow.

At nine the next morning, Lee popped into her office. "Been here long?" she asked.

Nina looked up from the papers she'd been poring through. "Since eight. I'm off to show 93 Shady Hill in a couple of minutes."

Lee came closer to the desk. "You sound funny."

"Funny?"

"Tired. You look it, too. Pale."

Nina put down her pen. "I think it's a stomach bug or something. Don't come too close." Though she'd tossed the warning off half in jest, Lee backed up to the door.

"Whatever you have, I don't want. I'm making dinner Friday night at Tom's place for us and three other couples."

Nina lowered her head but not her eyes. "You're what?"

"Three other couples, and I know you're going to say

that I'm crazy," she rushed on, "but I want to do it, Nina. Tom didn't ask me to. I offered."

"But he's left you sitting home alone for the past two weekends while he's off playing in New York—"

"Chicago, and it's business."

"Both weekends, *all* weekend?"

"Yes, and he was thinking of me. I showed you the scarf he brought me after last weekend. This weekend he sent flowers. It's not like he's off with another woman or anything." At Nina's dubious expression, she insisted, "He's not. Tom loves me."

Gently Nina said, "He loves what you do for him, and you love belonging."

"So, what's wrong with that?"

"Nothing—" She was about to add an "except" and then go on to say more, but caught herself. Much as she hated to see Lee hurt, she hated even more bad-mouthing Tom all the time. Lee was hooked on the man, so Nina was damned either way. It was a no-win situation. She *hated* no-win situations. Particularly when she was tired. "Listen," she said, forcing a smile, "maybe it'll work out. Maybe I'm all wrong, a cynic to the core." She tried to draw the last, but the draw went flat.

"You *must* be feeling lousy," Lee commented, eyeing her strangely. "We've been arguing about Tom for months, but you've never given up before."

"I'm not giving up. Just taking a breather. You'll hear from me again."

After a minute, softly, a bit worriedly, Lee said, "Are you sure it's just a bug that's getting you down?"

Nina touched the face of a pink slip that lay separate from the rest. "A bug and my mother. She's not doing well."

"Have you talked with her doctor?"

Setting her pink slip aside, she began to gather up her papers. "A few minutes ago. She seems to be having these little seizures. Her condition fluctuates."

"Maybe you should go out to see her."

The doctor had suggested the same thing. Again. "How can I go out there," Nina said, scooping the papers into a folder, "when there's so much to do here? This fluctuating could go on for a while. It's not even like she'd know I was there."

"But she's your mother—"

"And I do all I can. She's in the best possible place, totally at my expense, and I don't mind that. But in order to do it, I have to work. Bills don't get paid by flying all over the country." Setting the folder aside, she reached for her bag and stood.

"It's just Omaha."

"And I'll *get* there. Right now, things are buzzing here. The momentum is on. Business is great. As soon as there's a lull, I'll be on the first plane west." Holding a palm out she said, "I'm coming through the door. Move, or I won't be responsible for my germs."

Lee moved, and Nina was on her way.

THE GERMS LINGERED through the rest of Monday and Tuesday, alternately leaving Nina crampy, then not. By Wednesday, she acknowledged that what was ailing her didn't have much to do with John, other than to kill any thought of sex she might have had. That was why, when John showed up at her door on Wednesday night, she opened it.

Under the light of the porch, he looked furious. "I've been trying to reach you all week. Didn't you get my messages?"

Feeling guilty and sad, then angry at herself for feeling either, not to mention the heartthrobbing that the mere sight of him caused, she said, "I've been busy."

"So busy that you couldn't return a single phone call to the man you took to bed last Saturday?"

"It was the other way around. You took me to bed."

"Want to argue about who was willing?" He barely

paused, something that unsettled her even more than his words. John took his time, always took his time—unless he was upset. "You look like hell."

"Thanks."

"I'm serious." His fury faded some as he studied her face, and his voice, more tentative now, touched her heart. "Are you all right?"

She swallowed. "I'm fine. Just busy."

"What you're doing isn't healthy—"

"Just for a little bit. This is the height of the season. Come next fall—"

"Next fall! You can't keep up this pace till then!"

"I've done it every other year. This one's no different, except that this time the end is in sight. If Crosslyn Rise comes through the way I want, by next summer I'll be out on my own. Then I'll have other people to do the running through the height of the season."

"If you're still alive."

"I'll be alive."

He was quiet then, looking at her, pensive in the way she'd come to find both comforting and provocative. Since she wasn't feeling up to provocative, she took advantage of comforting until he ended it by saying, "What about us?"

"What about us?"

"Can I see you?"

She shook her head. "I need some space."

"How much?"

"I don't know."

"Look, I'm not asking you to give up your work."

"You were last Saturday—"

"Because it was so nice holding you that I didn't want you to leave. But I thought about it after that, and you were right. You had previous appointments, and you hadn't known I was coming. So all I want now is to arrange a time when you *do* know I'm coming."

"John," she whined in frustration, "you don't *like* me."

"I don't *want* to like you. There's a difference."

"If you don't want to like me, what are you doing making a date with me?"

"Trying to find out why I like you, even if I don't want to. That was what I wanted to talk about in the first place on Saturday morning, before we got sidetracked."

Nina saw a complicated discussion on the horizon, but she was in no more of a mood for it than she was for a sixteen-ounce steak. Her stomach was feeling weird, which was how it had been feeling on and off for too long. She would see a doctor if she had the time, but she didn't have the time. Work came first. Everything else would have to wait.

"Can we save this for another time, John?"

"Sure, if you can tell me when."

"I don't know when. If you call tomorrow, I'll check—"

"I call and you're out, and you don't return my calls."

"I'll return your call this time," she said earnestly. She *really* wanted to go upstairs and lie down. "Better still, I'll call you." She was ready to promise almost anything to get him to leave. Feeling worse by the minute, she was using every bit of her strength not to let it show.

Apparently she succeeded, because he looked calmer. "Will you?"

She nodded. "First thing tomorrow, once I get into the office. I'll call and we'll arrange a time. Okay?"

He thought about it for a minute, then nodded. "I'll be waiting."

His eyes fell to her mouth, and for a minute she thought he was going to kiss her before he left. One part of her wanted that more than anything; his kiss was a balm, able to make her feel good. Then again, when his kiss was over and done she always felt worse, and she didn't need that now. She was feeling awful enough without any help from John.

For whatever his reasons, he took a step back, turned

and slowly went down the walk to his car. Taking only distracted pleasure from his tight-hipped walk, Nina closed the door and leaned against it for a minute before making her way upstairs.

Despite the earliness of the hour, she went right to bed. She was hurting too much to do anything else. It occurred to her that maybe people were right and she did need more sleep, and though, given her druthers, she'd rather be working, she figured she'd give it a try.

Sleep came sporadically. She dozed, only to awaken to a knotting in her stomach a few minutes later. After tossing and turning, she dozed again, but less than an hour later she was awake. Her stomach was feeling worse, aching almost steadily. Not one to take pills, she sipped water, then a little ginger ale, but nothing seemed to help. After a while, she slept, only to wake up this time in a sweat with the realization that the ache in her stomach had become a pain.

She began to grow frightened. She didn't have time to be sick. She couldn't *afford* to be sick. Desperately seeking an explanation for what was happening, she thought back on anything she had eaten that might have upset her, but what little she'd had in the past few days had been light and bland. Sipping more ginger ale, she lay down again, but the pain grew worse. Try as she might, no amount of rearranging of her body seemed to ease it.

She began to wish she had seen a doctor. She began to wonder if she should now. But other than her gynecologist, she didn't have one, hadn't ever needed one. Besides, it was after eleven. She couldn't be calling a doctor now. If worse came to worst, first thing in the morning she could make some calls and get a name.

That decided, she managed to sleep for a bit, only to rouse with a sharp cry as an acute pain suddenly tore through her insides. Clutching her stomach, she struggled to sit up, but she couldn't seem to catch her breath.

Fear gave way to terror. Something was very, very wrong. She didn't know what it was, didn't know what to do about it. Worse, she didn't think she would have been able to do anything if she *did* know what to do. She couldn't stand up straight. She could barely move.

Fighting panic, she picked up the phone by her bed, and with shaky fingers, punched out John's number. The phone rang twice before it was answered, but she didn't hear a voice.

"John?" she cried feebly. "Are you there, John?"

After a minute, she heard a groggy, "Nina?"

"Something's wrong," she cried in short, staggered bursts. "Awful pain. I don't know what to do."

His voice came stronger, all grogginess gone. "Where's the pain?"

"My stomach. I wanted to wait. But it's getting worse. I've never had this before."

"Is it cramps?"

"No. Pain. Sharp pain." She was bent in two trying to contain it.

"Which side?"

"I don't know. All over. No, more on the right."

He spoke firmly, exuding a gentle command. "Listen, babe, I'm gonna run next door for a sitter—"

"It's two in the morning. You can't—"

"Can you make it down to the front door?"

"I don't know. I think so."

"I want you to go there, unlock the door and wait for me. I won't be more than ten minutes."

"Oh, God, John, I'm sorry—"

"Go downstairs and wait."

"Okay." Trembling, she hung up the phone. Then, fearful that if the pain got worse she wouldn't make it, she stumbled out of bed and headed for the door. She stopped against the doorjamb, doubled over in pain, caught her breath, then stumbled on. Reaching the stairs, she sat on the top step and, one by one, eased herself down. She barely had time to unlatch the door at the bottom before she crumpled back onto the lowest step, in excruciating pain.

She must have passed out, because the next thing she knew, John was crouching down by her side. "Nina? *Nina*."

His hand was cool against the burning on her forehead, her cheek, her neck, but it was the worry in his voice that reached her. She forced her eyes open. "I'm okay," she said, but even her voice was far away. Her insides were on fire, hurting like hell. With an anguished moan, she closed her eyes against the pain.

"You'll be fine," John said as he lifted her. The words came through a fog, the same way as the feel of his arms did. What was happening inside her body seemed to be putting distance between herself and the world. But trust was an intuitive thing. She trusted John. For that reason, as soon as she was in his arms, as soon as she felt him start to carry her out to his car, she yielded her well-being to him and turned her own focus to fighting the intense pain that was eating her alive.

WAKEFULNESS CAME TO Nina in fits and snatches over the course of the next few days. She seemed able to grasp at consciousness only briefly, enough to find out what had happened and ease the fear in her mind before yielding to the effects of anesthesia, painkillers and illness. At times when she woke up, there were doctors with her, poking and prodding, asking her questions that she had barely the strength to answer. At times there were nurses bathing her, shifting her, checking the fluid that ran from bottles, down thin tubes, into her veins.

At times John was there. Of all the faces she saw in her daze, his was the clearest. Of all the things she remembered hearing, his words were the ones that registered.

"You had a ruptured appendix," he told her during one of those first bouts with wakefulness.

"Ruptured?" she whispered, dry mouthed and groggy.

He was sitting close by the side of the bed and had her free hand in both of his, pressed to his throat. "But it's okay now. You'll be just fine."

Another time, when she awoke to find him perched on the side of the bed by her hip, she asked in a croak, "What did they do?"

He smiled crookedly. "Took out your appendix. Cleaned up the mess in there. Sewed you back up."

Moving her hand to her stomach, she felt what seemed like mountains of bandages. "So much stuff here."

"It'll come off soon. How do you feel?"

"Hot."

"That's the fever. They're giving you antibiotics. It should help pretty soon. Are your hurting?"

"A little. And tired."

Brushing her cheek with the back of his hand, he said, "Then sleep."

Given the quiet command and the warm assurance of his body close by, she did, and those hours of sleep were the best. When she awoke alone, there was an emptiness along with the pain and the heat, and she sought sleep again as an escape. Aloneness was bleak, strangely frightening. Given that she'd spent so much of her life alone, that would have mystified her if she'd been in any condition to analyze it. But she wasn't.

For nearly three days, she was in a limbo of fever and pain. Slowly, on the morning of the fourth, she began to emerge from it. The doctors were the first to visit, in the course of making their rounds. Then the nurses came in to do their thing. And then John.

She was awake this time when he appeared at the door. His face brightened when he saw that her eyes were open.

"Hey," he said, coming inside, "you're up."

"Finally." Her voice was still dry, weak and hoarse, and she was feeling more feeble than that, but the sight of him pleased her.

"You look better."

"I look awful."

"You've been up looking at yourself in the mirror?" he teased.

But she nodded. "They made me get out of bed."

"That's great," he said with enthusiasm, then grew more cautious. "How was it?"

"Terrible. I can't stand up straight."

"That'll come."

"I got dizzy. I nearly passed out, and that was just between the bed and the bathroom. It's discouraging."

"Were you expecting to get out of bed and dance a jig?"

"No, but I thought I'd be able to *walk*, at least. I mean, I've been lying here doing nothing for three full days—"

"Doing nothing?" His brows went up for an instant. When they came down, his expression was dark. "Babe, you were fighting for your life. It was touch and go for a while there. Didn't they tell you that?"

"Doctors exaggerate things."

"Not this time," John said, and his face underscored the words. "You've been really sick, Nina. They wanted to know if there were any close relatives who should be notified."

That sobered her a bit. "What did you tell them?"

"What Lee told me."

"Lee?"

"I called your office Thursday morning to let them know you wouldn't be in, and she was the one who called back. She's been in a couple of times, but you've been asleep." He settled gently on the side of the bed and said in a quiet, compassionate voice, "She told me about your mother. I'm sorry, Nina. I didn't know she was so sick."

Nina closed her eyes. "She's been sick for a long time."

"That's what Lee said."

He grew quiet, giving Nina the opportunity to go on, but she wasn't up for that. During the past few days, on those occasions when she'd woken up alone, she had thought about her mother more than she might have expected. She was feeling very strange about some of the thoughts she'd had, particularly now, knowing how sick she had been herself.

"Want to sleep?" John whispered.

She shook her head and whispered back, "I'm okay," but she didn't open her eyes.

He took her hand. "You can sleep if you want. I'll be here when you wake up."

"You've been here a lot."

"Whenever I could."

"You shouldn't have."

"This is important."

"But you have other things—"

"I have backup. Right now, this is where I want to be."

At the words, she felt a slow knot form in her throat. Turning her head away, she murmured, "I'm sorry."

"What for?"

"Being a pain in the butt. You've got more important things to do than sit here with me. You should be home with J.J."

"J.J.'s with a sitter. He's fine."

She squeezed her eyes shut. "He's with a sitter too much lately, and all because of me. First I drag you out in the middle of the night, then you feel you have to stay here—"

He touched her lips, stilling her words. "Thank God you did drag me out in the middle of the night. If you'd waited for morning, it might have been too late. And as for my staying here, I don't have to. I want to. Think of me as your warden. I'm gonna make sure you don't do too much too fast."

Her warden. She didn't know whether he was that or

something else, but she did know that he was special. Lee might have stopped by to visit, but she'd left. Her other friends had sent cards and flowers, even called. But John had come. Time and again, he'd come. And stayed.

Feeling suddenly weepy, she tried to turn over onto her side, but the attempt brought a wince. John's hands were there, then, helping her, propping pillows behind her to give her support. "Okay, now?" he asked, leaning over her shoulder.

She nodded. Seconds later, she felt him brush at the tears escaping from the corners of her eyes.

"Ah, Nina," he whispered.

"I'm okay," she whispered back. "I'll just rest for a while." Taking his hand from her cheek, she tucked it inside hers, between her breasts. "Rest for just a little while," she murmured, and let herself go to sleep.

John was there when she woke up, then again later that night, then the next morning. He helped her out of bed and into the bathroom, then back into bed. He sat close beside her when she ate Jell-O, then later, custard, then later, a soft-boiled egg. He left for a little while at the end of the day but was back after he'd put J.J. to bed, then sat with her until after eleven.

By the Tuesday morning, her sixth in the hospital, she was finally feeling better. The intravenous solutions had been replaced by oral antibiotics, her stitches by tape. She was still sleeping on and off through the day, but she was beginning to think about work more and more. There was so much she wanted to do. Each day she lazed around in the hospital was another day wasted.

"When can I go home?" she asked the doctor after he checked the incision and her chart and appeared pleased with both.

"Another two or three days."

"*Two* or *three*?" That surprised her. "But I'm fine now.

I'm up and around. The worst of the pain is gone, and without any medication for it." One of the first things she'd done was refuse painkillers. She hated being doped up.

"But there's still the danger of infection," the doctor pointed out. "Your body's suffered a trauma. You need to be monitored for that. And you need rest."

"I can get rest at home."

"But will you?" He was middle-aged, with a pleasant manner, a gentle sense of humor and particularly expressive eyes. Those eyes were now filled with an I-know-your-type look, for which she had only herself to blame. She had told him about her work. In the telling, some of her compulsion must have come through. "You live alone. There'll be no one to keep tabs on how much you do or don't do."

"I'm a big girl. I can keep tabs on myself."

"But will you?"

"I'll rest."

"With a pen in one hand and the phone at your ear?" he chided. "No, I'd rather you stay here a little longer."

"But there's a shortage of beds," she argued, having read that time and again in the paper.

"Not for sick people, there isn't."

"I'm not sick."

"You were. More sick than some. And it didn't help that you were run-down." He looked about to scold her for that. Instead, he simply said, "I'm not sure I can trust that you'll rest at home."

Though she was beginning to tire, Nina wasn't giving up the fight. "I'll rest better there than here. Sleeping was fine here when I was half out of it, but now I wake up with every little noise in the hall, and then you guys come at me at six in the morning—"

"You're still weak, Nina. You need watching."

A low voice came from the door. "What if I were to watch her?"

Nina turned her head to find John there, and felt a little more peaceful than she had moments before. He did that to her, had a way of making her feel safe. It had to do with his confidence, she guessed, and that air of quiet command. He would argue with the doctor. He knew how much better she was feeling.

Responding to his question, the doctor said, "Can you do that?"

"If she's at my house, I can."

His house? But that wasn't what Nina had in mind. Not at *all*. "Uh, wait a minute, John. That would be tough."

"Why so?" he asked, approaching the bed. "I have a perfectly good guest room with a perfectly good bed. You can sleep in it just as well as you can sleep in your own bed, and there wouldn't be the hospital interruptions."

There wouldn't be a telephone, either, Nina knew. Nor would she feel comfortable having people stop by from the office with updates on work. Nor would she be able to call clients. John would never stand for that.

"I could make sure you eat," he went on, "and I'd be able to see if you were worse and get you back here in time." His gaze shifted to the doctor. "Would you let her leave if she stayed with me?"

The doctor didn't have to give it a second thought. "Sure."

His easy agreement infuriated Nina. "That's ridiculous," she said, but more quietly. She was beginning to fade and was appalled by it. Before she totally lost her strength, she said to John, "What about J.J.?"

"What about him?"

"He'd see me."

John considered that. "Yes."

"But you don't want that."

"Uh, listen," the doctor interrupted, "this is sounding like a private discussion." To John, he said, "If you want her, she's yours, but not until this afternoon. I want to do a final blood workup before I discharge her. Why don't you leave word at the desk when you decide what to do. I'll be on the floor for most of the morning."

"Dr. Caine?" Nina called weakly. She wanted to go to *her* home, not John's. She didn't want to owe him a thing. And she wanted to be free to work.

"I'll be back," the doctor said from the door and disappeared.

She took in a big breath and let it slowly out, sinking deeper into the pillows as she did.

"You're feeling tired, aren't you?" John asked.

She wanted to argue, but couldn't. Silently she nodded.

"Caine says it'll be that way for a while."

She wanted to ask—indignantly—when John had spoken to Dr. Caine, but it was a foolish notion. John had brought her to the hospital on that nightmare of a night. He'd been the one to tell the doctor what she was feeling, since she was unconscious. He'd been the one in the waiting room while she was in surgery and the one in her room when she woke up. Of course, he'd spoken with the doctor. Naturally the doctor trusted him.

So did she, but going to his house involved matters beyond trust. It involved an intrusion in his life that was different from the time she'd hitherto taken up. It involved meeting J.J.

As though reading her mind, John carefully lowered himself by her side. "I've thought about this a lot, Nina. The idea of your coming home with me isn't out of the blue. If you're leaving the hospital, you need to be with someone who can take care of you."

"I can take care of myself."

"Maybe in a few days. But not now. At least, not very well. You need to rest. You don't need to be thinking about making a meal when you're hungry or answering the door when the bell rings or doing work. Work will wait," he said with subtle emphasis. "It'll wait till you're well."

In other circumstances, Nina would have argued up a blue streak about that. But either she was simply too weak to argue, or his slow, confident tone was too persuasive. So she let it go for the time being. At the moment, the issue of work didn't seem quite as important as the one of John's son.

"What about J.J.?" she asked again, very softly. "If I were to stay at your place, what would you tell him?"

"Just what I've been telling him all week, that you're a friend who's sick."

"I'll be in the way there."

He shook his head. "You're not demanding. You barely let me do things for you here. I can't imagine you turning into a spoiled witch once we leave."

"But there's *J.J.*"

John's eyes searched her. "You seem hung up on that. He's just a child."

"Just a child? He's *your* child, and he means the world to you. You didn't want me to meet him—"

"Whoa. You said that before. What makes you think it?"

"You always get a sitter when you see me."

His lips grew wry. "Because what I'm thinking of doing when I see you isn't exactly appropriate for a child, any child, to see."

"But that Sunday when you came by my office for the brochure, you could have brought him, still you didn't. You left him with friends at the beach."

"Because he was having fun."

"If he'd started to cry when you left, would you have brought him?"

John was contemplative for a minute. "Maybe." Slowly he added, "But maybe you're right, in a way. I want to protect J.J. from hurt, so I've kept our lives—his and mine—very simple. My job is perfect for that. I haven't brought strangers around often, and in particular, I haven't brought women. I haven't wanted to confuse him."

"If you bring me home now, he will be confused."

He thought about that. "I can explain that you're a friend."

"But I'll be there, in your house, then when I'm better, I'll be gone. Won't *that* confuse him?"

"I'll explain that you're better."

Nina wasn't expressing herself well, and the more she tried, the more frustrated she grew. Closing her eyes, she sighed. "Oh, John."

"What?" he asked with such gentleness that the words, sounding fragile and meek, spilled out.

"I'm awful with kids. I don't know what to do, and J.J.'s not just any kid. He's special. But what if I do something wrong? What if I *say* something wrong?" In the silence that followed, she dared open her eyes. John's were every bit as gentle as his voice.

"You'll be at my place to rest, not to perform," he said, and gave a sad smile. "Besides, you don't have to worry about saying the wrong thing to J.J. He won't hear you, anyway."

Feeling John's sadness, she closed her eyes. From within that cocoon of darkness, she heard his low-spoken words. "I'd like you to meet him, Nina. I'd like him to meet you. It's time."

She wasn't quite sure what that meant, but somehow it didn't seem important. If John wanted her, truly wanted her to recuperate at his home, she'd go. There was a danger in it. She would have to be careful not to compromise her own independence in any long-term way. But she was sick. And he was offering. And there was a small part of her—call it expediency or curiosity or just plain old selfishness—that wanted it, truly wanted it, too.

CHAPTER SEVEN

THE DOCTOR DID HIS workup and was sufficiently satisfied with Nina's condition to release her into John's charge late that afternoon. Wearing the loose sundress and sandals that Lee had brought by earlier in the day, she walked slowly to the elevator, holding lightly to John's arm.

"Just your speed, eh?" she teased.

"I'm not complaining." He studied her face. "Are you okay?"

"Uh-huh." But she wished it was true. Her legs felt weak, and since she refused to walk hunched over, her incision pulled. The doctor had promised that both the weakness and the pulling would get better each day, but she was impatient. She wasn't used to being sick. The thought of being slowed down frustrated her.

Nonetheless, by the time the elevator ride was done and they had crossed the parking lot, she was grateful to sit. Easing herself gingerly into the car, she put her head back against the seat and worked at regaining her breath.

"You're pale as a ghost," John observed the instant he joined her. "Are you sure you don't want to go back in there?"

She shook her head. The *last* thing she wanted was to go back in there. She had places to go and things to do, and though she would rather be heading for her own home, given the doctor's stubbornness, John's home would have to do. At least she'd be able to sleep when *she* wanted to, then use the rest of the time to think. John might not allow her to spend hours on the phone, but she would be able to do some creative planning and write out instructions for Lee regarding Crosslyn Rise.

"I'll be fine," she said in a thin voice. "I'm just not used to being upright for so long."

"Try this." Gently he eased her down so that her head was braced in the fold of his groin. "Better?"

She sighed against his thigh. "Much."

Putting the car in gear, he started off. "You were lying this way when I drove you in last Wednesday night. Do you remember?"

"No. That whole time's a blur."

He stroked her hair. "I was scared."

"Did you guess what was wrong?"

"Uh-huh. That's why I was scared. It used to be that once an appendix ruptured, the person was gone. I figured yours had ruptured, but I didn't know when. It must have been right before you phoned me."

She shivered.

"Cold?"

He was already reaching to lower the air conditioning when she shook her head. "Just remembering. The pain was so awful. I've never felt anything like it."

"Thank goodness you knew to call me."

She thought about that, just as she'd done more than once while lying in her hospital bed. She could have called Lee. She could have called Martin. She could have called 911. But she'd called John. She hadn't seriously considered any other option. And while one part of her—the part that had built a life on the concepts of independence and self-suffi- ciency—resented it, she had to accept the practical fact that of all the people she knew, John had the coolest, calmest head on his shoulders.

Reaching for his hand, she tucked it under her chin. "I

haven't thanked you. You came. You knew what to do and did it. You saved my life."

He cleared his throat. "All we need now are a few violins—"

"I mean it, John. I'm very grateful."

"Good. Then you can show your gratitude by being a good girl over the next few days and staying in bed."

"*Staying* in bed?"

"At least at the start."

She settled in against his thigh.

After a short silence, he said, "What? No argument?"

"I'm too tired," she said in a feeble drone, answering the very question she kept asking herself. Going with John this way was against all she stood for, but the circumstances were mitigating. "I didn't realize it at the hospital. I just wanted to get out." After a minute, she said, "Now I just want to rest."

"Then rest. We'll be there soon."

She let the hum of the car and the strength of John's thigh lull her. "Get me up before we reach your street?"

"Why?"

"So your customers don't see me drag my head from your lap and think awful things."

He chuckled. "I'll get you up. But watch what you say, or you'll get me up, too. Then the customers will really have a show."

Had she been feeling well, Nina would surely have marveled that the bookish John Sawyer was into double entendres. Had she been feeling well, she would have been turned on by it. But she wasn't feeling well. Sex was the last thing on her mind. Or nearly. She couldn't resist a smile at the image of the proper bookseller, improperly aroused, escorting her across the front lawn.

In no time it seemed, John was nudging her awake. "Rise and shine," he whispered, and helped her sit up as he turned onto his street. Seconds later, he turned into his driveway and pulled directly up to the side door. Though Nina guessed that he normally parked by the garage that stood well behind the house, she didn't argue. Walking through the hospital had exhausted her. She was still feeling the drain.

With John's help, she eased herself from the vehicle. As they walked toward the door, her heartbeat quickened. She wanted to attribute it to the weakness of her limbs, and that might in part have been true. But she was also nervous.

"What will he be doing now?" she asked in a whisper. "Does he watch TV?"

John didn't have to ask who she was talking about. "Sometimes. But I think he's out." He pulled the door open.

"Out?"

"With the girls."

"Oh." She was relieved, then again, disappointed. Starting up the stairs with John's arm in light possession of her waist, she said, "I'm beginning to think he's a phantom. He's never around when I expect him to be."

"He'll be back," John said with certainty, and tightened his arm when she seemed to lag. "Maybe these stairs weren't such a good idea," he muttered.

"I'd have had stairs at my place, too," she said, huffing more with each step. "Once I get to the top, I'll be fine."

"Once you lie down you'll be fine."

She agreed with him there. With little more than a vague impression of lots of browns and blues, she let him guide her past the living room and down a hall to the very last room. It too was blue, blue and white, not quite masculine, not quite feminine, not quite decorated, but simple and sweet. The one thing that interested her most though was the bed. It was a double, had two fluffy pillows and was covered with a quilt that had already been turned back. Desperate to lie down, she crossed to it, sat on its edge and, bracing her stomach with an arm, carefully lowered her head to the pillow. John lifted her feet behind her.

She sighed and close closed her eyes. "Ah, that's better."

"You're sweating."

"I'm okay."

"Is there a nightshirt with the clothes Lee picked up?"

"Should be." She heard him take the bag from his shoulder and drop in onto a chair, then unfasten it and rummage through.

"This is pretty," he mused dryly.

She managed to lift her head and open an eye, but what she saw didn't please her. Lee had packed her skimpiest nightie. She couldn't possibly wear it, not with a little boy running around.

With a moan, she returned her head to the pillow. "I'm okay like this for now." She'd worry about nightwear later.

But John had other ideas. Without a word, he left the room, returning moments later with a shirt of his own. "Assuming this reaches your knees, it'll be loose and soft and decent," he said, and began to unbutton it.

Nina was too weak to protest when he helped her off with the sundress and on with the shirt. She managed some of the buttons while he did the others, then, while she lay down again, he rolled up the sleeves. After surveying his work and judging it acceptable, he flipped a switch on the wall. A soft whir of air drew Nina's notice to the ceiling, where a fan had gently started to turn.

"Nice," she said with a small smile, but what was nicer was the clean way she felt in John's shirt, the way the mattress molded to her body as the hospital one had never done, the freshness of the linen by her cheek. "I think I'll just rest awhile now," she murmured and, within minutes, dozed off.

WHEN SHE AWOKE, she was disoriented. At first she thought she was at the hospital, but the smell wasn't right, too pleasant, not antiseptic at all. Then she thought she was at home, but the sound wasn't right, too smooth, almost a hum, like the fan she had always wanted but didn't yet have. Then she remembered where she was and slowly opened her eyes.

Before her, standing nearly at eye level little more than an arm's length away, was J.J. Sawyer. He had thick shiny hair that was a shade lighter in color than his father's dark brown and fell over his forehead in full bangs, skin that was smooth and gently tanned, a small nose and serious mouth. Barefoot, he was wearing a faded T-shirt over denim shorts. His limbs were slender though not skinny. In fact, while she had expected him to look frail, that wasn't the case. Had it not been for the thick glasses he wore and the hearing aids on each ear, he'd have looked like anyone's rough-and-tumble, normal healthy four-year-old son.

Feeling an unexpected tug at her heartstrings, Nina smiled. "Hi," she said. She didn't move other than to lift a hand and flex it in a small wave.

He waved back, but, with the movement of her hand, his attention had been drawn to her wrist. She followed the line of his gaze to the identification band the hospital had put there. She hadn't thought to take it off. Holding her arm out, she let J.J. take a closer look.

He turned the band slowly, first one way, then the next.

Had she been able, Nina would have slipped it off and given it to him, but by design it was too small to slip off. Shooting for second best, she mimed cutting through the band with scissors. She pointed to him, then to the door, then repeated the cutting motion.

J.J.'s eyes, magnified by the glasses, rose to hers. She raised her brows in invitation, smiled, nodded and made the cutting motion again. Without a sound, he turned and scampered from the room.

Only then aware of the quickening of her pulse, Nina

took a deep, steadying breath. Either she'd gotten her point across, or she'd sent J.J. off to his father with reports of a real weirdo in the spare room. But, what the hell, how was she supposed to know what a four-year-old did? All kids used scissors, didn't they? Or was it only ones older than four? She tried to remember what *she'd* been doing at that age, then decided against it. Nothing about her childhood had been normal.

Before she could give it another thought, J.J. ran back into the room, carrying a pair of small, blunt-tipped scissors. Feeling victorious that she had made herself understood, Nina held out her wrist. "Can you do it?" she asked, pointing from him to the bank, to the scissors and back.

Opening the scissors, he slipped them under the band and tried to cut, but the plastic resisted the dull blades.

"Try again," Nina coaxed. Giving him a thumbs-up sign in encouragement, she pushed the band deeper into the jaws of the scissors. He made another single slash with the scissors, but to no avail. His brows came down, his small mouth thinned.

Feeling his frustration, Nina held up a finger to tell him to wait, then pushed the band even deeper into the scissors and made a series of repeated movements with her fingers. He took the hint. Using smaller cuts, he finally managed to pierce the plastic. Once that initial piercing was done, the split grew longer with each cut.

Though he was the one making the effort, Nina was the one who had worked herself into a cold sweat of determination by the time the scissors finally made it all the way through. "Good boy!" she said with a grin.

J.J., too, was grinning when he looked up at her.

"Thank you," she mouthed, and his grin widened, then his eyes followed suit when she offered him the band. "It's yours if you want it. You earned it."

He couldn't have heard her words, wasn't even looking

at her face at the moment she said them, so he couldn't possibly have read her lips, but the excitement she saw in his eyes was an eloquent as could be.

Nudging the band into his hand, she nodded. He took it, turned and ran from the room.

Again Nina felt the race of her heart and concentrated on slowing down. J.J. had done the work, but she was exhausted. Pathetic as it was, it was a fact of life, for this day at least. If she rested today, surely she'd feel stronger tomorrow.

But she had barely closed her eyes when the patter of small running feet returned. J.J was back, one hand holding her band, the other closed into a fist. Squatting down by the side of the bed, he put the band between his feet, opened his fist, rearranged its contents, then stood and offered her the five jelly beans that lay carefully cupped inside.

Nina hadn't eaten much in the past week. Her stomach was just getting back to normal. Sweaty jelly beans weren't the kind of food that the doctor would have necessarily recommended. But she grinned at J.J., put on an honored look and, one by one, telling him how good each was with the roll of her eyes, ate the beans.

"Dee-licious," she said with a final eye roll. Then she settled into a smile and gave him a silent but exaggerated, "Thank you."

With a grin, he retrieved the band from where it had been safely resting and ran from the room again. She half expected him to be back seconds later with something else, but he wasn't, and it was just as well. She was feeling tired again.

Gingerly rolling over, she pulled the sheet up to her chest, closed her eyes and slept. This time when she awoke, the room was bathed in the early-evening sun and the eyes she looked into were John's.

"Hi, there," he said. He was sitting on the side of the bed. She wondered how long he'd been there.

"Hi."

"Sleep well?"

"Mmm-hmm."

"Feeling better?"

"For now." Wryly she added, "In five minutes, I'll be tired again."

"That'll pass."

"I hope so."

"Are you hungry?"

"No. I had a snack last time I was up. Five jelly beans."

"So I was told."

"He's sweet, John. So sweet."

"I think so."

"Does he look like his mom?" Other than the hair, she didn't see the resemblance to John, though that could well have been due to the discrepancy in size and age.

John thought about it for a minute, finally saying, "It's hard for me to tell. When I see J.J., I see J.J. He has a way about him that's all his own, maybe because of the problems, I don't know. But I've never done much comparing of him either to other children or to adults."

"He's bright and quick. He knew just what I was saying."

"About the bracelet?"

"He told you?"

"Showed me. Made me tape it together so he could wear it." His eyes rose and went past her. "Speak of the devil." He gestured with his hand and spoke with the same kind of exaggerated mouth movements that Nina had used. "Come on in."

Too content lying where she was to turn, Nina asked, "How good is he at that?"

"At lipreading? He gets short things, simple things, far more than a normal four-year-old would get but far less than he will in a year or two or three." Scooping the boy onto his lap, he said, "J.J., this is Nina." Then he snickered. "It'd help, of course, if he were looking at my lips, but he's too busy looking at you. Not that I blame him," he added under his breath.

Nina gave the child the same kind of small wave that she'd given him before. With his smaller hand—circled now with the taped plastic band—he returned it. Then she looked at his mouth, which was surrounded by a faint orange ring. "Is that spaghetti sauce I see?" She ran her finger around her lips.

Carefully, J.J. put the tips of his baby fingers together and drew them apart with the faintest of spiraling motions. John made a different motion, bringing one hand down from his mouth, palm up, into the other. Tipping his head back, J.J. gave him a grin.

For Nina's benefit, John explained. "He signed 'spaghetti.'" He repeated the motion J.J. had made, doing it more neatly so that she could see. "I praised him back in sign."

Nina was impressed. "Does he sign a lot?"

"About as much as he reads lips. We work on both with the therapists, and I reinforce it at home. Spaghetti's one of his favorite things. He eats it a lot, so he has the sign down pat." He paused, leaned over, planted a kiss on his son's forehead. "Overall, he does damn well at it, for a four-year-old."

Nina felt a touch of envy for the love passing from father to son. Then she thought of something else and felt a shaft of timidity. "Does he get frustrated with people who don't sign?"

"He gets frustrated when he wants something and can't make himself known, but every kid does that. As far as signing goes, he only gets frustrated when someone who doesn't sign gets frustrated with him."

"Do his sitters sign?"

"A little. The girls do it more than the grown-ups. They think it's a game." Snorting, he nuzzled the top of J.J.'s head. "They wouldn't think it was such fun if it was their only means of communication." Leaning sideways, he signed something to J.J., who promptly nodded. In the next instant, John lowered him to the floor and stood. "He's going to help me bring in your supper."

Nina pushed herself up on an elbow. "John, I can go into the kitchen."

"Not tonight."

"I can do it," she insisted. With her mind clear and her body newly rested, she was uncomfortable in the role of the helpless patient.

"Why should you try, when I can bring it in here?"

"Because you shouldn't be waiting on me."

"Yes, I should. That was the whole point in your coming here. It was the only condition the doctor let you out."

"But I don't want—"

"Tough," he cut in with uncharacteristic sharpness. "It's done." Following J.J.'s lead, he left the room.

Nina didn't resume the fight when he returned with a dinner tray. She only made it through half of the spaghetti and sauce he'd given her, and even less of the salad, before she felt too tired to go on. "I'll have more later," she said, putting her head onto the pillow as soon as he removed the tray. To her chagrin, she fell asleep.

She awoke once not long after that to find J.J. in pajamas, playing on the floor with a brightly colored plastic tow truck and two matching cars. His small head, hair clean and damp, was bent in concentration, and from time to time a low, flat sound came from his throat, clearly an imitation of the truck's roar. She wondered if he ever heard the real thing, or simply felt the vibrations. She wondered if he heard anything at all. He wasn't wearing his hearing aids. She wondered what a totally silent world might be like.

Loath to disturb him, she simply watched for a short time until her eyes felt heavy again. Then, bidding him a silent good-night, she went back to sleep.

WHEN SHE AWOKE at eleven, John was sitting in the nearby chair, reading a book. After seeing her to the bathroom and back, he made her a frothy milk shake that she was sure he'd slipped an egg or two into, but she didn't complain. It was cool and tasty, smooth going down. Feeling comfortably full, she went back to sleep.

When she awoke the next morning, J.J. was on the floor again, this time perched on his heels, reading a book of his own. From what Nina could see, it contained far more pictures than words, but he turned the pages in order and seemed engrossed in what he saw.

She rolled over and stretched, but he couldn't hear the rustle of the sheets. So she ruffled his hair. At that he looked up. Seeing her awake, he jumped up and, leaving the book on the floor, ran for John.

She was sitting on the edge of the bed when he arrived. "Did you have him standing guard?" she teased.

The only answer she got was a shrug. His gaze was fixed on her face. "How did you sleep?"

"Soundly. It's peaceful here."

He continued to study her, finally deciding, "You look better."

"It's about time."

"Want some breakfast?"

For the first time since she'd taken sick, she said. "Just a little." But "just a little," as interpreted by John, turned out to be nearly as large a breakfast as Ronnie's Special at the Easy Over. She came nowhere near finishing. "You're trying to fatten me up," she complained. "Much more of this and my clothes won't fit."

"You're clothes don't fit now. You've lost weight."

She guessed it was true, though her stomach still felt puffy near the incision. "Maybe I could get dressed today and see."

But John shook his head. "Tomorrow."

Figuring that he was taking his orders from the doctor, she didn't argue. But she wasn't beyond bargaining a little. "How about the newspaper, then? I haven't seen one in a week."

He considered that for a minute, then used the tip of his sneaker to gently nudge J.J., who had returned to his book. A brief sign sent the boy scurrying off.

Nina repeated the sign, a double snapping of the heels of her hands with her fingers aimed in opposite directions. "Newspaper?"

"That's right."

She filed the information. "How do you say 'thank you'?"

John mouthed the words.

"In sign," she prompted dryly, and repeated the sign when he showed it to her, then used it when J.J. ran back in, the proud bearer of the morning paper.

Unfortunately, she wasn't as proud of herself when, barely halfway through the paper, she set it aside, slid down on the pillows and fell back to sleep.

The pattern repeated itself through all of Wednesday. She woke up feeling bright eyed, only to wither after a brief time. Fighting it seemed to do no good. Her body had a will of its own.

"Is this normal?" she asked John later that day. Back in bed, feeling as though she'd run a marathon rather than just taken a shower, she was discouraged.

"Perfectly normal," he said, flanking her hips with his hands.

"But I wasn't this tired in the hospital."

"You were, but you didn't think anything of it. Here, you keep thinking you should be up and around."

"I should be."

He shook his head in the slow way that was an answer in itself.

"I should be," she insisted. "When I stop to think about the work I'm missing—"

"Lee is covering for you."

"I know, but I should be doing it."

He pulled back a little, and his look grew dark. "That's exactly the kind of argument that nearly got you killed. If it hadn't been for your compulsion to work, you'd have seen a doctor earlier and gotten by with a simple appendectomy. Instead, you let it go, so you ended up going through ten times more danger and pain. Stick inconvenience in there wherever you want. If you're missing work, it's your own fault."

"But what about Crosslyn Rise?" she asked more meekly. She always felt bad when John raised his voice or spoke more quickly than usual, which was what he was doing then. "We've come so far with it, and it's almost there. If we're launching the marketing program with an open house on the Fourth—"

"That's barely two weeks off, Nina," he interrupted more calmly but with no less force. "You can't hold it then. Put it off a month."

"A *month*!"

He gave a slow nod. "Carter and Jessica have no problem with that."

"You talked with them about my work?" Not wanting to sound annoyed after all he'd done, she spoke with care, but John must have sensed some of what she was thinking, because he came back firmly.

"It's my work, too, and Carter's and Jessica's, and of course I talked to them. They've been worried about you. You're part of the team."

"Part of the team, that's right, and I have no intention of letting down on my end. I can plan the open house, John. Right from this bed I can plan it. Assuming Christine gets the finishing touches done on the model condo, I can handle it. There's nothing much to putting a few ads in the paper, sending around a few invitations, making a few phone calls to get interest humming."

John turned sideways, looking back at her over a shoulder. "And what about standing on your feet for hours on end talking with lookers, not to mention giving tours of the grounds?"

"I can have other people do that."

"Wait a month."

"But the Fourth is a perfect weekend."

"People go away on the Fourth. Wait a month."

"People go away in *August*."

"So wait until Labor Day."

"Impossible."

"Then the last week in July."

"How about the weekend after the Fourth?"

"The last week."

"The next to last week." Wrapping her arms around her middle, she slid lower into the sheets. "And that's as much as I'll give."

Silently he stared straight ahead while she studied his profile, trying to guess at his mood. She knew she irked him at times, particularly when it came to work, but she didn't want him angry.

Anger wasn't what she saw when he turned his head, but rather a trace of amusement. "I'm surprised you gave that much," he mused. "I expected more of a fight."

In another day and age, she might have said something clever, clicked her heels and walked out of the room, but she wasn't up to any of that. "Believe it or not," she said with a sigh, "I don't love fighting even when I *do* feel good."

"Which you don't right now."

"Weak, just weak. Damn it."

Taking a deep breath, John straightened his arms on either side of her again. Looking deeply into her eyes, he said with exquisite gentleness, "Is it so awful to be weak once in a while?"

"I *hate* being weak," she ground out, feeling that hatred in her very marrow.

"But once in a while? Not all the time, just once in a while?"

Nina shut her eyes against the flood of memories that his words brought back. *Once in a while, that's all, I'll just see him once in a while. I can't not see him at all. He's too good to me for that. I need him, Nina. I do.*

"Nina?"

Feeling a great wave of sadness, she opened her eyes to John. At first she didn't think she had the strength to answer. Then she saw the concern—and question—in his eyes and knew that, given all he'd done for her, the least she could do was to tell him the truth.

Quietly, soberly, almost fraillly, she said, "My mother used to ask me that, whether it was wrong to be weak once in a while. Her weakness was men. She loved being held by them and kept by them. She didn't demand anything except that they give her enough to get by, and for years, that's what she did. She got by. She got *us* by. We never had anything extra, and that was okay by me, except that she was never around, and that *wasn't* okay, because I wanted her. When I was old enough to ask her to get a real job with regular hours, she said she couldn't. So-and-so was too good to her. She couldn't give him up. We used to fight about it, more when I got older and the so-and-sos kept changing. I'd tell her she was weak, and she'd say that was okay. Then I started seeing the bruises, and I'd tell her she didn't have to stand for that, but she would. She'd take it over and over again. Then she started in with the pills—"

Nina swallowed hard and, with the motion, felt suddenly more tired than ever before. Wearily she turned her head to the side.

John touched her hair. "Were they painkillers?"

"All drugs are, in the broadest sense."

"She moved from one to the next?"

"Right on up the scale."

Gentle fingers brushed Nina's scalp, soothing her, silently giving her strength. "Was it an overdose that finally did it?"

"Mmm-hmm. Not enough to kill, just to permanently disable." Thoughts she'd had in the hospital came back to her, thoughts about illness and death, friends, relatives. In a shaky whisper, she said, "I should see her. She's lying alone. I hated lying alone when I was sick. But she is, all the time. I should see her."

"Do you often?"

She shook her head. "Too far away. Too much work."

"Too many mixed feelings."

She met his gaze. "How did you know?"

"It follows from things you've said. You wanted her there and she wasn't. You asked her to change, and she wouldn't. You've made your life the antithesis of what hers was." He paused, his thumb tracing small circles on her temple. "Were you around when it got bad with the drugs?"

"Yes. I was in school, and working."

"Where was your father?"

Feeling the same old pain she'd lived with for years, she raised a single shoulder all the way to her ear. Slowly it slid back into place.

"Don't know?"

She shook her head.

"Do you know who he is?"

After a pause, she shook her head again.

Silently John slipped his arms beneath her and brought her up into his embrace. She went limply at first, until the need he felt took her, too. Aloneness was a painful thing. Holding and being held by another person offset that pain. Wrapping her arms around his waist, she clutched at bunches of his shirt.

At first he said nothing, and that was fine. Nina was content to listen to his heartbeat, to let it lull her and offer a comfort of its own. As though she had unburdened herself of a secret that had been weighing her down for years, she grew increasingly relaxed and mellow.

His breath was warm against her hair. "Loving a man doesn't have to be a weakness."

"It's not the loving that's bad," she breathed, "it's the depending. Men meant everything to my mother. When none of them wanted her anymore, she was broken."

"So you never want to depend on a man."

"Mmm. Right."

"You want to be self-sufficient."

"Mmm-hmm." She took in a deep breath, enjoying as much the feel of John as his scent. "I won't let myself get in that bind. Not ever."

Having said that, she felt better. She had warned John. She'd been as blunt as she could be. If he wanted to nurse her, that was fine. If he wanted to wait on her and play guardian, that was fine. She couldn't deny that the coddling was nice, given that her health wasn't yet up to snuff. But once she was well, she would be on her own again.

It was good that he understood that.

CHAPTER EIGHT

THE FOLLOWING MORNING, while John and J.J. were at the therapist's office, Lee came to visit. Wearing the sundress she'd worn home from the hospital—and having polished her nails, which made her feel greatly improved—Nina had progressed to sitting in the den. John didn't know that yet. She planned to surprise him with her strength when he returned at noon.

"Cute place," Lee said with a cursory sweep.

Nina thought so. She had wandered around herself, for the first time, just before Lee had arrived. There were two bedrooms in addition to the one she was in, a large kitchen, a living room, and a dining room that had been converted into the den in which they sat. Nothing was "decorated," yet everything had a lived-in look that gave a feeling of warmth. She liked that far more than she was willing to admit to Lee. So she said simply, "It's clean and functional. Nothing fancy. Definitely a man's place."

Lee nodded. She looked vaguely at the walls, then the floor, then at Nina. "So. How are you feeling?"

Nina couldn't miss the awkwardness in her friend. Unsure as to its cause, she went along with the game. "Better today. I was beginning to wonder when I'd revive. It seems like forever since I've been at work."

"It's only been a week. You still look peaked."

Nina didn't like the sound of that. Lee was usually more complimentary than not, certainly more encouraging.

Something was odd. "My coloring will pick up. I may go out into the backyard later." John would never allow that, but she rather liked the idea. "So," she said, affecting her business tone of voice, "tell me what's happening at the office. Did you have any luck with the Donaldsons?"

Lee opened her briefcase. "Uh-huh. They're interested in buying."

"They are? That's great!"

Lee didn't seem terribly excited. As she busied herself looking through a pile of papers, she said, "Uh-huh. They'll be coming back with a bid later this afternoon. Four o'clock, I think it is."

"Terrific. It's been a long time that they've been looking. I'm thrilled we were finally able to please them."

"Uh-huh."

"Thanks, Lee. I really appreciate all you've done." The fact was that, at Nina's insistence, Lee would get the full commission, so it wasn't work done for free. Still Nina was grateful. By ably taking over for her, Lee was keeping her professional reputation intact. "I know how much work you've put in, not only in this case, but with all of the others this past week. You've been a good friend."

Eyes still inside her briefcase, Lee shrugged. "I have plenty of time. It's nice to be able to fill it."

That sounded odd, not like the Lee Nina knew at all. Lee wasn't one to fill every minute, the way Nina did. Though she always helped Nina out when asked, she didn't actively look for work. She had always preferred a slower pace.

Nina's mind took off in all sorts of different directions until she caught herself and asked outright, "What's wrong, Lee?"

"Nothing."

"Something is. You don't sound like you."

"I'm fine."

"You're *not*."

Retrieving her hands from the briefcase and dropping

them into her lap, Lee hung her head. "You're right." Timidly she looked up, her eyes filled with tears. "Tom's moving. He's getting rid of his place here and moving to Chicago. He says it's an official transfer, but I think he's taking a whole new job. And he's not taking me. It's over, he says. It was nice, but it's over." Pulling a tissue from her sleeve, she pressed it to her nose. "You were right, Nina. You had him pegged."

Heart aching, Nina reached for her arm. "Oh, Lee…"

Sniffling around the tissue, Lee said, "You were right. You knew. And you tried to tell me, but I wouldn't listen. I thought this was it. I really did. I refused to see the truth about those long weekends away. You were that much more realistic than me."

"I just didn't want you hurt."

"You saw it coming."

"I'm jaded, but that's not always so good."

"It sure has worked for you. You're not dangling at the end of Tom Brody's line. He's a rat. All men are rats."

"Not all," Nina said. She was thinking of John, of how giving and undemanding he had been. She was lucky. Strangely so. "You'll find someone else, Lee. Someone better." She squeezed Lee's hand and continued to hold it while Lee cried for a minute longer. "Now that you're free and looking around, you'll see possibilities where there didn't seem to be any before." Unexpected things happen. Nina knew. Not that *she* was looking for a man to marry, the way Lee was. "You'll do fine."

"But I'll miss him."

"I know. But you'll keep busy. I have plenty for you to do, if you want it."

After a bit, Lee stopped sniffling. "I want it," she said with resignation.

"Good," Nina said gently. "Let's talk about Crosslyn Rise."

For the next few minutes, they did just that. Determined to take Lee's mind off Tom, Nina gave her a long list of calls to make regarding a planned launch for the next-to-last week in July. She had calls to make herself, though she didn't rush to make them the minute Lee left. Instead, indulging herself in the tiredness she felt, she turned the stereo on low to a classical station, stretched out on the sofa with her head on the soft leather cushion and took a nap.

The slam of a door woke her. She opened her eyes to see J.J. dash through the room, followed at a more sedate pace by John, who stopped the instant he saw her. "Who let you out?"

"Me." She punched up the cocoa-colored cushion under her head, but made no move to rise. From her vantage point, John was looking tall, dark and handsome. She was in no rush to change the view. "It got a little claustrophobic in the bedroom, and Lee was stopping by, so I figured I'd entertain her in style. How did everything go this morning?"

"Fine." With a slowness that came across as caution, he asked, "How did it go with Lee?"

"Really good. I gave her lots of work to do. There's not a whole lot left for me."

Seeming satisfied with that, he slipped into a chair and stretched out his legs. He was wearing shorts. Nina liked his legs. They were well formed, snugly muscled and just hairy enough.

"Did you tell her about the change in dates for the open house?" he asked.

She dragged her eyes up. "Uh-huh."

"Any problem?"

"No. She'll go along with whatever I say. My worry is more with the consortium. I feel like I'm letting them down."

"You've been sick. They would never hold that against you."

"But I've been telling them that the Rise would be on the market as of the Fourth."

"So you'll tell them differently now."

"I hate to lose those few weeks of potential selling."

"Will it really make a difference in the long run?"

"I suppose not," she conceded, then shifted her gaze to J.J. when he returned to the room. As though he'd plum run out of steam, he was walking slowly, had his thumb in his mouth and was carrying a battered teddy bear. There was something so forlorn looking about him that Nina couldn't resist holding out an arm. Without the slightest hesitation, he went to her.

Drawing him in by the waist, she said, "That's a sad-looking teddy." She fingered the bear's worn nose.

"Not sad," John informed her. "Well loved. His mother gave him that teddy not long before she died."

Nina sucked in a breath. "Does he know?"

"That it was from her? Probably not. But it's special to him. He doesn't love any of his other animals the way he does this one."

Feeling a deep ache for the little boy who would never know his mother, Nina tightened her arm around his waist. He kept up his sucking without complaint.

"What happened, John?" she asked softly. She alternately touched the bear, then the small warm fingers clutching its neck. When silence continued to come from John's direction, she raised her eyes to his. "Tell me about her."

Sitting back in the chair, he crossed an ankle over his knee. Though the pose was relaxed and his voice slow, it lacked the ease that would have normally been there. "We met in Minneapolis. I had a store there, pretty much like the one I have here. Jenna was a market analyst who had just been transferred out from New York."

He rubbed his ankle with the pad of his thumb. After a long minute, he went on. "She wasn't thrilled about the move. Even though she was high up in the office bureaucracy, she felt it was a step down. But the money was good, and she figured that if she was patient, she'd move even higher, and then, if she wanted, she could move out again, preferably back to New York. From the beginning, I knew that was what she wanted, but somehow, when we started seeing each other and then got closer, it didn't seem real."

Breaking away from Nina, J.J. crossed to the television and turned it on. With the sudden blare of sound, John jumped up, tapped the boy on the shoulder and motioned him to turn it down, which he did. John turned it even lower, then turned off the stereo, leaving little to interfere with their talk.

Nina was just noticing that the program was *Sesame Street* and that an interpreter was signing in a corner of the screen, when J.J. returned to her side. Thumb back in his mouth, arm around his teddy, he climbed onto the sofa to sit in the curve of her body.

John was quickly alert. "Is he hurting you?"

"Of course not." She ran a hand down the back of J.J.'s head, over thick, silky hair. "He's so little."

"But your stomach——"

"Is fine. He seems tired."

"He'll take a nap after lunch."

Nina nodded and looked at John expectantly. Apparently satisfied that she was comfortable, he returned to the chair. This time, his legs remained sprawled.

"I'm listening," she prompted.

Though his eyes settled on her, she was sure he was seeing another woman in her place. "I thought maybe she'd change. Even when I convinced her to have the baby, I thought she'd change. I thought for sure she'd take a look at the little kid who was her own flesh and blood, and melt."

Nina didn't know how Jenna hadn't. The little kid who was her flesh and blood was a heart stopper. "Did she have a problem right from the start?"

John nodded. "She resented him. He wasn't any bigger than a peanut and he didn't say a word, but he made her feel guilty about the time she spent working. Unfortunately, her work meant everything to her." He frowned down at his hands. "When we found out about the ears and the eyes, she couldn't take it. Just couldn't take it. It was like he had been declared a troublemaker, so she washed her hands of everything to do with him. She started working longer hours, started taking overnight trips whenever she could. She always brought him things— little cars, balloons, teddy bears—but she figured that the less she had to see him, the better."

"What about *you*? Didn't she want to see *you*?"

The bleakness of his expression said it all. Still he added, "By that time, there wasn't much left between us."

The quiet sounds from the television filled the ensuing silence. Like a puppy snuggling in, J.J. turned sideways to lay his head on Nina's thigh. She ran a hand back and forth on his warm little shoulder, but her eyes were on John. Needing to know, she asked softly, "How did she die?"

He looked off toward the window. "She was driving home very late one night after a three-day symposium, fell asleep at the wheel and hit a tree. Death was instantaneous. No other cars were involved."

Without conscious effort, Nina drew her legs up, tucking J.J. closer to her. "Tragic," she whispered, and felt a private chill. Many a time she had returned late at night from exhausting multiday seminars. More than once, she had stopped for coffee or rolled down the window to stay awake.

John stared broodingly at the floor. "It was a waste. Our marriage wasn't any good, so we'd probably have gotten divorced, but that's the least of it. She had potential. I hated what she did—hated the way she did it with such singlemindedness—but she was good at it. A lousy mother, but good at her work."

The grudging respect was clear in his voice. In turn, Nina respected him for it. Given the way Jenna had left him and his child, he could have easily been filled with scorn.

"You must have loved her once."

He thought about that for a while. "I did, in a dreamlike kind of way. She was like a butterfly, beautiful but elusive."

"Do you miss her?"

He shook his head, and as though the bubble of the dream had burst all over again, his voice leveled. "Like I said, we'd have ended up divorced if she hadn't wrapped herself around that tree. She wasn't an easy person to live with. She was always on, always thinking work. She was always wondering who else in the office was doing what and getting where, and how it would affect her. Her mind was always working on ways she could get ahead. Work was her be-all and end-all, her raison d'être. As time went on, it only got worse."

"*I'm* not that bad," Nina said with feeling, then caught herself, realizing what she'd done. Defensively she said, "You compare us. I know you do."

His eyes held hers steadily. "Do you wonder why?"

In an attempt to be fair, she shrugged. "I can see some similarities. She worked a lot, I work a lot. She was trying to get ahead, so am I. But I'd never have done what she did. I'd never have turned my back on a child. Or a husband. There are responsibilities involved when you marry and have kids. You shouldn't do either, if you want to work."

"It's all or nothing, then?" John shot back with startling speed. "Either you marry and have kids, or you work? No middle ground?"

"Sometimes no, sometimes yes. It depends on where you are in life. I'm at the work stage. I'm not saying that I'll never get married and have kids, just that I wouldn't take on either of those now."

"You couldn't compromise? You couldn't make time for all of it?"

"There are only so many hours in a day, and you're the one who's been telling me I work too much. Where would I find the time to give to a husband or kids?"

He remained quiet.

"Where?" she demanded. If he was putting her on the spot, she could do the same to him.

"You make time for what you want," he stated in a voice that was deafeningly clear. "You give a little here, give a little there. It may mean that one thing or another takes longer to achieve, but it all comes out in the wash."

"'One thing or another,'" Nina echoed. "You mean work. If a woman is willing to sacrifice her career, she can have the husband and kids."

"She doesn't have to sacrifice the career," he insisted, "just defer the ultimate gratification. And that doesn't mean there isn't gratification along the way, simply that the achievements may not be as high until the kids are grown and out of the house."

"She's an old lady by then."

"No way." He sat back and linked his fingers, seeming more relaxed, as though confident he had the argument won. "Take that woman. She had kids in her mid-twenties. They're out on their own by the time she's fifty. Fifty is not old."

"It's too old to start building a career."

"She's not starting. She started years ago. She may have taken a leave when the kids were babies, but after that she worked part-time, maybe full-time as the kids got older. Okay, so she didn't go running off on business trips, or push past a forty-hour week, and maybe that held her back a little. But look what she *has*. She has a solid career. She has a solid marriage. She has kids who probably give her more satisfaction than anything she does at work. And she's only fifty."

With barely a breath, he raised a hand and went on. "Then again, take the woman who put her career before everything else. She got out of school, entered the marketplace and worked her tail off. She started climbing the ladder of success, and the drive became self-perpetuating. The higher she climbed, the higher she wanted to be. The more money she earned, the more she needed. There was always something more, always something more."

"Her being a woman didn't help," Nina put in. "A woman has to work twice as hard."

To her surprise, John agreed. "You're right. And that made her all the *more* determined to make it. So she put off thoughts of getting married, since she didn't have time for that. And she put off having kids, because she didn't have time for *that*. Then she reaches her mid-forties, when theoretically she should be up there on the threshold of the president's office, only there are suddenly four other candidates vying for the job and one of them is the new son-in-law of the chairman of the board. So she misses out. And then what does she have?" He raised a finger. "She doesn't have the corner office." Then another. "She doesn't have a husband." Then a third. "And her childbearing years are gone." He dropped his hand to his lap. "Do you think she's happy?"

His eloquence left Nina momentarily speechless.

"She's alone, Nina," he said more quietly. "She's alone, and she's getting older, and she's beginning to wonder what she'll do with herself if she ever has to retire. Happy? My guess is she's scared to death."

Tearing her eyes from his, Nina looked down at the floor. Aloneness was something that had flashed through her mind more than once when she'd been in the hospital. Different people had dropped by to visit, but John had been a constant in her life. Without him, she would have felt very much alone.

She wondered what, if anything, her mother felt sitting in that nursing home day after day. The doctors had said that she didn't know who or where she was, or who came and went, but Nina had always had a niggling fear in the back of her mind that maybe it wasn't so. Over the years, she had successfully kept the fear hidden in a dark corner of her mind. She was a lousy daughter.

Feeling suddenly very much an imposter in a haven she didn't deserve, she looked at John. "Why am I here?"

He frowned. "What do you mean?"

"From the beginning, I reminded you of Jenna. I'm everything you had once and couldn't stand. I'm a repeat of a mistake. So what am I doing here, interfering with your life?"

"You're here because I want you here."

"But why?"

"Because I like you."

"But I'll only cause you grief."

"Maybe not."

"What does *that* mean?" she cried.

John didn't answer for a while, but sat quietly, eyes downcast, brows drawn together, and Nina didn't prod. She was feeling tired again. Turning her head into the cushion, she closed her eyes.

His voice came gently. "I like you, Nina. Yes, you're right, you did remind me of Jenna, but only at the start and only with regard to work. In other ways, you're different. She was tall, blond and green eyed, you're blue eyed, dark and petite. She dressed to fit in, you dress to stand out. She smiled on cue, you smile whenever you want to. You're your own person far more than she ever was."

Nina had opened those blue eyes and was looking at him, feeling a longing that was only in part physical. "But I love my work."

He nodded. "Yes, you do."

"And you hate that."

Again he nodded.

"So why are you *bothering* with me?"

"Because," he said with a somber look and a surprising

lack of hesitancy, "I like you enough to care. I'm not sure I felt that way about Jenna. I may have loved her once, but I didn't like her. When she was barging headlong toward self-destruction, I did nothing to stop her."

"You were busy with J.J."

"True, but I could have tried more if I'd cared. Then again, Jenna was a hard woman. She wouldn't have listened. Once she set her mind to something, she wouldn't budge." His eyes softened a fraction. "You're not as hard. As determined as you are, you still listen."

She gave a small self-conscious laugh. "I haven't exactly had much choice lately."

"Even before you got sick, you listened. You didn't want to work with me, but you agreed to do it. You made time for it even though you said you couldn't. Besides that, you're more sensitive than Jenna ever was. You feel badly when I have to get a sitter for J.J. in order to see you. You worry that you're going to do something wrong when it comes to him. Look at you," he said with the hitch of his chin, "you've been touching him in some small way, just like a seasoned mother, ever since we got back, and I don't think you even realize it."

Startled, Nina shot a glance at J.J., who was curled up in the curve of her body. Her hand was on his arm, the backs of her fingers brushing ever so lightly over the baby-smooth skin.

When she returned her gaze to John, he was looking satisfied. Pushing out of his chair, he bent over her, putting his mouth by her ear. "Not bad, for someone who doesn't know what to do with kids." On his way to straightening, he scooped J.J. up. "Lunchtime, my man," he said.

J.J., who had neither heard him nor seen his lips, made a loud sound in protest and started to squirm. John immediately set him on his feet and hunkered down before him. "Time for lunch," he mouthed clearly. He tapped his wrist with a finger, then mimed bringing food to his mouth.

J.J. looked questioningly back at Nina.

"She'll come, too," John assured him with a nod, gave him a pat on the bottom and stood. To Nina, he said, "Want to?"

"Sure. What are we having?"

John caught J.J.'s eye. "What do you want to eat?" he asked slowly, signing along with the words.

J.J. made the sign for spaghetti.

John shook his head. "We had that for supper last night."

J.J. made a stirring motion with one hand, then tapped the back of his fist with two fingers.

Again John shook his head. "Mashed potatoes alone aren't enough."

J.J. drew large twin arches in the air.

John chuckled. "Not McDonald's. How about a surprise?" He formed two fingers of both hands into curved Vs, put the fingertips together, then drew them apart with a look of surprise.

J.J. said something that wasn't any kind of word Nina had ever heard but sounded agreeable nonetheless, particularly when he clapped.

"Okay," John finger-spelled, then repeated the gesture for Nina. "I would have spelled out 'bologna,' except that it's too hard a word for him to read. Is bologna okay for you?"

"It's my favorite," she said with a smile, feeling warm and amenable and all kinds of other nice things. The rapport between John and his son was delightful. Being part of their group, undeserved though it was and brief though it would be, was an honor.

AFTER LUNCH SHE napped, then John surprised her by suggesting that, while J.J. was with his sitters and he was at work, she sit out in the backyard. "Great minds think alike," she said. "I told Lee I wanted to sit there, but I didn't think you'd let me."

"You look too pale. You need some color." The corner

of his mouth turned wry. "We wouldn't want people to think you've been sick, now, would we?"

"Certainly not," Nina said, but no sooner was she settled in a chaise lounge, in the dappled sun that danced through the oak boughs, when she thought of what he'd said. He'd been facetious, of course. But, in fact, the rest of the world was waiting. She did have to get back to work.

She'd have to discuss that with John, she knew, but she wasn't looking forward to it. He would tell her she wasn't well yet, and she would feel obligated to say she was getting there fast, and it would go back and forth, as arguments went. In the end, he would wear her down, simply because she wasn't feeling up to par. So, valid or not, he'd have made his point.

Telling herself that she had time to spare, she didn't say a word for the rest of that day. Rather, she lay in and out of the sun for several hours, dozing at some points, watching J.J. play at others. For a time, curious to see what he was doing and how, she sat on the edge of his sandbox and helped him make sand castles. She had as much fun with the sand as she did with J.J. and didn't feel either bothered or frightened to be left alone with him when his sitters went back inside for cold drinks. He was a gentle little boy with the calm temperament of his father. With simple hand motions and facial expressions, she found she could communicate with him just fine.

For dinner, John grilled swordfish steaks, and though J.J. wasn't wild about his, Nina ate every bite. J.J. was wild about dessert, though, a chocolate cake that John had bought at the bakery that morning, and while Nina was watching him eat, John got up to do the dishes. When she offered to help, he refused.

"I didn't insist that you come here, just to put you to work."

"I'm not helpless," she protested.

"But you've been sick."

She wanted to point out that anyone who was well enough to sunbathe and build sand castles could probably handle a few pots and pans, but she didn't. Anyone who could handle a few pots and pans could probably do the cooking as well, which meant that she really should be heading home. But she wasn't ready for that just yet. John kept telling her that she was weak, that she needed more rest, that she had to take it slow if she wanted to regain all her strength. She chose to believe him.

THE BELIEVING WAS all well and good on Saturday. John was in the bookstore all day. J.J. was in and out with sitters. Nina slept a bit, read a bit, boiled up chicken breasts and made chicken salad sandwiches for lunch as a surprise for John.

He was furious. "I don't want you working."

"But I'm feeling stronger, and I'm bored. Honestly, John, what I did was no effort. I'm standing better and walking better. Besides, I have all afternoon to rest."

The look he gave her said that she'd better do just that, but she noticed with satisfaction that he ate every last bite of his sandwich before he returned to the store. Buoyed by that, she did rest awhile. When she woke up, she finished the book he had given to her to read, then went back into the kitchen and cooked up a batch of chocolate chip cookies.

J.J. Sawyer might have had vision and hearing problems, but nothing was wrong with his sense of smell. The cookies were still in the oven when he followed his nose there. He was positively ebullient when she let him peek through the glass.

John's sense of smell was nearly as keen. At the first lull in business, he too materialized in the kitchen, where, hands on his hips, he surveyed the scene. Two fifteen-year-old girls, J.J. and Nina were sitting at the table having an orgy of cookies and milk.

"Better hurry," Nina warned. "They won't last long."

"Should I ask who made them?"

"No."

Eagerly standing up on his chair, J.J. held out a half-eaten cookie to his father. "Are they good?" John asked in sign.

Nodding vigorously, J.J. continued to hold out the cookie until John reached for it, and, with a mischievous grin, he promptly stuffed it in his mouth.

"You devil," his father said, and reached for a cookie of his own. He made a show of taking a bite and thinking about the taste, before downing the rest of the cookie in one large bite.

"You're as bad as he is," Nina said as she rose from the table. Taking J.J.'s eyeglasses from his nose, she washed a chocolate streak from one lens, rinsed and dried both, then carefully slipped them back on. She bent over to study her handiwork. "Better?" Her eyes shot to John's. "How do I sign that?"

He showed her. She repeated the two-part gesture to J.J., who returned it. Eminently pleased with herself and the situation, she took up a napkin, filled it with cookies and handed it to John. "For work," she said.

In a typically John way, he looked at the cookies, looked at her, then slowly took the small bundle. "Thanks," was all he said before he returned to the store.

NINA THOUGHT A lot about that "thanks" during the rest of the day. Even more, she thought about the look that had gone with it, because it hadn't held gratitude so much as puzzlement, even frustration, if she guessed right. But what could she tell him? She liked to bake so she'd baked cookies, which was no more than she might have done if she had been home and snowed in on a winter weekend with no hope of getting to work.

Maybe he was thinking that she wanted to impress him.

Maybe he was thinking that she wanted to impress J.J.

Maybe he was thinking that she was well enough to leave.

She was. She really was. Come Saturday night, when she stayed awake through the entire movie he rented, she knew it. Come Sunday morning, when she put on the bathing suit he'd picked up at her apartment and spent the day—albeit restfully—at the beach with J.J. and him, she knew it. Come Sunday evening, lolling around on the sofa, trying to read but thinking instead about the irresistible lure of John's body, she knew it.

John knew it, too, because shortly after she said goodnight and stole off to her room, he appeared at her door. Little more than a shadow in the night, he crossed to the bed and sat down. No longer a shadow then, he took her in his arms.

Senses that had been gradually reviving over the course of the past few days came fully awake. With a soft moan, Nina slid her arms around his neck. He was so wonderful to hold, so solid, so gentle, virile in everything from his shape to his scent. She felt so alive, restored, whole in mystifying ways.

"I missed this," he murmured. "All the time you've been here, I've wanted to hold you. It was toughest at the beach today. You looked so pretty."

She swallowed against a swell of emotion.

"You want to leave."

"I don't, but I can't stay. I'm getting better. Every day."

For the first time, he didn't refute her argument. Instead, he said, "It's a rat race out there. You don't belong in it."

"I do. It's where I've always been."

"Only because you had no other choice. But you do now. I want you to stay here, Nina. I want you to stay here with me."

Her heart contracted. "Oh, John."

"What does that mean?"

"I *can't*. I can't just give up everything I've spent a lifetime working for."

Pulling back, he took her face in his hands. "I'm not asking you to give everything up, just to add some things. You've been happy here. I know you have. You made up your mind that you couldn't work, and you were happy here."

"But now I *can* work. Maybe not full-time yet, but certainly half-time."

"So go to work from here."

"I can't."

"Why not?"

Unable to resist, she touched his mouth. "Because I'd feel guilty. I've always been independent. I come and go as I please. I can't be doing that from your home. Especially now."

"What does that mean?"

Her fingers moved aside. Inching up, she touched her lips to his, simply because she needed to feel him that way. When she drew back, she knew that what she was about to say was the frightening truth. "Now I'd be tempted, so tempted to play with you. I'd be tempted to lie around reading all night, or spend the afternoon making sand castles, or bake us all into obesity. It's been nice here, so nice, but I have to leave. If I don't, I won't get where I want to be, and if I don't get where I want to be, I might come to resent you, and I'd never want to do that, John."

Amber eyes alive in the dark, he moved his gaze around her face. He followed the eye motion with that of a hand. His voice was low and sandy. "It isn't right that it should be one or the other. You'll be hurt, Nina. I don't want that."

"No hurt," she said, but the accompanying shake of her head was cut short when his hand slipped lower to her neck, then lower still to the budding swell of her breast. She bit down on her lip to stifle a moan.

"You like that?" he whispered. His large hand circled her, moving inward in slow, concentric rings.

"Oh, yes," she whispered back. "You have a way with my body."

"At least I have that."

"You have more—" she began, but the words died when he touched one taut nipple. Another moan came from her throat, this one slipping free into the air.

"Do I hurt you?"

"Only by making me want more."

"Your stomach—"

"No, no." Covering his hand, she pressed it close. "You set me on fire."

The night hid his expression, but the catch of his breath told of what she'd missed. Gently he lowered her to the bed. His mouth followed, capturing hers in a kiss that opened gently, as did her body. Taking advantage of that opening, his hands loved her breasts through the silk of her thin nightie. She felt herself swell to his touch, felt the ache of wanting in her nipples, then lower. Arching upward, she tried to bring him down, but he held himself steadily over her while his hands continued their sweet torture.

The doctor had told her, before leaving the hospital, that her body would tell her when sex was okay. At the time, she'd felt numb and sore. Passion had seemed a distant phenomenon, not the least bit appealing to her bruised and mending self.

Five days of rest and tender care at John's hand had made a world of difference. Though she could feel the intermittent tugging in stomach muscles that contracted with desire, the sensation blended in with her need.

"I want you," she whispered, and slid her hands down his thighs. She was making the upward journey to his groin when he caught her hands and pinned them by her shoulders.

Holding both wrists, he seduced her mouth with a series of deep soul kisses. Then he worked his way down and applied that devastatingly capable mouth to her breasts.

From one hard tip to the other he moved, using his tongue, his teeth, his fingers. The wetter her nightie grew, the hotter she grew inside.

When he slipped his hand under the shirt and touched her between her legs, she cried out.

"Hurting?" he asked in concern.

"With need." She grabbed his wrist to stop him. "Make love to me, John." She arched toward his hips but was only able to make the briefest, glancing contact with his erection when he pinned her down.

"It's too soon."

"No. No. I want you inside."

"Too soon," he repeated, and levered himself up enough to return his hand to her cleft. "This way," he whispered, taking her mouth in an enveloping kiss at the same time that his fingers found their way to her darkest heat.

She was lost then. The best she could do was to flex frantic fingers on his back while he built the fire inside her to an explosive level. He stroked her inside and out, up and down, back and forth, until her shallow breathing caught and she was shot to the pinnacle of orgasmic release.

Her return to reality was a slow one. By the time she could finally open her eyes, she was being cradled against John's supine body. The pervasive weakness she felt told her that, much as she wanted to make love to him back, she wouldn't be doing it that night.

Her "Oh, John" was a soulful sound.

Silently he stroked her hair.

Gradually the trembling of her body eased, leaving a great fatigue in its place. "I want… I want…" The words were slurred, the thoughts behind them muddled.

It wasn't until dawn Monday, when she woke up wanting John and finding herself alone in bed, that those thoughts jelled.

CHAPTER NINE

BY THE TIME SHE HEARD waking sounds in the rest of the house, Nina had dressed, gathered her belongings and packed her small bag. As soon as those other sounds moved into the kitchen, she headed there, too.

John was at the stove frying eggs. At the sight of him, she felt an ache start inside. It had nothing to do with her recent surgery and everything to do with her growing feeling for the man she had to leave.

She hadn't been standing at the door for more than a few seconds when he looked her way, not the least bit startled. She guessed that he'd been expecting her.

Returning his attention to the eggs, he scooped one onto a plate, added a piece of toast and set the breakfast in front of J.J., who was on his knees on a chair at the table.

Looking at the little boy, Nina felt another ache. She had growing feeling for him, too, and that was even more surprising than the other. She had liked John for a while now; in the past ten days, her feelings had only intensified. J.J., on the other hand, had been a stranger up until the Thursday before. Stranger? *Alien being* was more apt. He was a child and he had problems. She had never lived with a child before, let alone one with problems. It hadn't been anywhere near as bad as she'd thought it would be.

Sliding into a chair beside the little one, she stroked his head in wordless "good morning." When he grinned up at her, she grinned back. When he picked up a piece of his toast and offered it, she shook her head and the ache inside grew.

"You're leaving," John said quietly.

She nodded. "I have to."

He could have argued, she knew, but he didn't. They had been through the arguments and exhausted each one. Nothing had changed.

"Will you have breakfast first?"

Though she wasn't terribly hungry, she wasn't denying herself a few last moments of the particular pleasure of being with J.J. and John. "Only if you have enough."

"There are two more eggs here. We'll each have one. Same with the toast."

Clearly he hadn't made extra, hadn't expected that she'd eat. "Oh, no," she said quickly, "you have them. I didn't mean to take—"

He interrupted her with a level stare and a firm, "We'll share. I don't mind. One egg is more than enough for me, and even if it weren't, I don't mind giving a little."

The emphasis on the last few words and the message therein was mirrored in his look. He was saying that life didn't have to be all or nothing, that he was more than willing to compromise if she was.

But she wasn't. Though she nodded yes to the egg and accepted the plate he offered without a word, she felt guilty. She couldn't compromise. She *couldn't*. For too long, she had wanted her independence. With Crosslyn Rise about to go on the market, she was coming close to her goal, too close to give it up.

But what she was giving up on the other end—that was where it was starting to hurt. Her feelings for John were strong and growing more so with each day. To stay would be asking for trouble. Already she wanted things she couldn't have.

I want to make love to you. I want to spend the night with you. I want to stay here forever. Those were the words she might have said if she hadn't been so spent from his loving the night before. Then again, if she'd been in full control of her senses, she wouldn't have said them at all. Leading John on, giving him cause to hope for something that couldn't be, would be cruel.

Did she mean the words? Yes. That was what she'd realized at dawn, why she knew she had to leave. She did want all those things. But she wanted her self-sufficiency more. In her mind—right or wrong—to be dependent on John would be a sign of weakness. She prided herself on being stronger than that.

"Are you going right back to work?" he asked quietly.

She pushed at the deckled edge of her egg. "Tomorrow, I think. I'll get home today, maybe make a few calls. As soon as I get tired, I'll stop." Unspoken was the fact that as long as she felt all right, she'd keep at it. John knew she would. He had experience with her type.

He bit hard into his toast, chewed, swallowed, took another bite.

"We have a consortium meeting next week," she said in an open-ended kind of way. When he didn't respond, she said, "Will I see you before then?"

He shrugged. "Do you want to?"

She was asking herself the same question. On one hand, the thought of not seeing him at all was bleak. One the other hand, perhaps a clean break was for the best.

But they were friends, weren't they? And they'd just come through a harrowing experience together. Surely he'd want to know that she was all right. "I think I'd like to talk. You know, see how things are going here and all."

."Then why don't you call when you have time." With barely a break, he said, "Eat your egg. It's getting cold."

At first she thought he was talking to J.J., but J.J.'s egg

was gone. Seconds later, J.J. was gone, too, off to play in his room.

Nina ate her egg. Not at all hungry for the toast, she held it out as a peace offering to John, but he shook his head, so she put the plate down. He was angry. Maybe hurt. Maybe disdainful again. He wanted her to stay, and she wouldn't. She wouldn't meet him halfway. He had a right to be upset, she supposed, after all he'd done for her.

But that was exactly the kind of thinking that could get a woman into trouble, she knew. So, rather than apologize or try to explain things she'd already tried to explain more than once, she said, "I'd better call a cab, I guess."

John's reaction was fast and furious. "You don't need any damn cab. I'll drive you home." With the scrape of his chair, he rose from the table and carried the plates to the sink.

She met him there. "Let me do that. You can take care of J.J."

"J.J.'s all ready to go," he said, and began loading the dishwasher.

"Then do something else. Let me *help* for a change."

He rounded on her with such suddenness that she took a startled step back. "I don't need your help. I don't need *anyone's* help. You're not the only one who likes to be independent and self-sufficient."

Feeling duly chastised, she said a quiet, "I know. I was just trying to help. You've done so much—"

"And I never asked for a thing in return. I never *expected* a thing in return. So don't feel you owe me, because you don't. I did what I wanted to do, what *I* wanted to do."

When he turned back to the sink with a vengeance, Nina silently withdrew from the room. She got her bag, dropped it by the door, then, without conscious intent, found herself looking in on J.J. He was standing in front of a low bookshelf, on the top of which was a large drawing pad. With crayons from a nearby box, he was making random marks on the pad.

Approaching, she saw that the marks weren't random at all, but his version of letters. There was a wide assortment of them in various shades and sizes, but her eyes were drawn to two deep blue ones, bolder and more distinct than the others, two *J*s.

Grinning, Nina pointed to them. "Look at that. Good boy, J.J." Remembering what John had done, she signed the word "good," then clapped her hands together. Then, while J.J. was beaming with pride, she took a bright pink crayon and wrote her own name. "*N-I-N-A.* Nina." She pointed from the name to herself and back several times, then gently tipped up J.J.'s chin to see if he understood. "Nina," she mouthed, pointing again to herself.

He repeated the mouth exactly.

"Good boy!" she signed, then arched her brows and pointed questioningly at herself.

He mouthed her name a second time, this time pointing to her as he did it.

Grinning widely, she grabbed his hand, brought it to her mouth and gave it a smacking kiss. Then she hauled him in and gave him a full-fledged hug while he giggled and squirmed. She'd miss him, she knew.

But she'd miss his father even more.

HER APARTMENT WAS quiet, the same yet strange. She wandered from room to room, trailing her fingertips over the furniture, trying to reacquaint herself with possessions that were familiar, until she realized that she was the one that was strange. She had been away for a week and a half. A week and a half. Not much. Then again, a long time.

John had insisted on stopping at the market on the way for fresh food so that she wouldn't have to go out, but the emptiness she felt wasn't from hunger. She climbed into bed, thinking that maybe after a nap she'd feel more like herself. When an hour passed and she couldn't sleep, she got up, opened her appointment book and picked up the phone.

Work was what she needed, she knew. It had always been her greatest source of satisfaction. It was what made her tick.

Sure enough, after calling first the office, then several clients to tell them she was back on track, she was feeling fuller. Liking that feeling, she made more calls and would have made even more if she hadn't been legitimately tired by then.

This time she slept, and when she woke up, she made more calls. When she ran out of calls to make, she dialed John's number, only to hang up before the phone had rung. Calling him so soon after she'd seen him was a weak thing to do. She was fine on her own, just fine.

As though to prove that to herself, she grabbed pen and paper and began to organize her thoughts for the rest of the week. With each note she took and each list she made, she felt more convinced that what she was doing was right. Work was *definitely* what she needed. It was the best medicine money could buy.

THE FOLLOWING MORNING, telling herself how great it was to be out and moving around on her own once again, she drove to the office. She didn't stay long, only long enough to let everyone know she was back and ready to work. Armed with a computer printout of the latest listings, she spent the rest of the morning viewing the new entries. By then, to her chagrin, she felt drained. So she went back home, changed out of her dress into shorts and spent the afternoon lounging on the living room sofa, feeling blue.

That was why she didn't call John. She refused to go running to him when she was down. She could pick herself up. She always had before, and she would again.

WEDNESDAY MORNING, things were better. Feeling just that little bit stronger, she took several clients out for showings. By noon, though, she'd had it. She slept most of the afternoon away, picked at the dinner she had halfheartedly cooked, then spent the evening trying to get into one of the books she had brought home from John's. But she was distracted. She kept thinking of him, wondering what he was doing and whether he was thinking of her—then chastising herself for the thoughts. She'd made her choice. She would just have to live with it.

And damn it, if he wanted to talk with her, *he* could call.

THURSDAY MORNING, after showing two clients five separate pieces of real estate with little more than a nibble of interest, she went out to Crosslyn Rise. She needed uplifting. Crosslyn Rise could give her that.

The mansion was moving along nicely. It occurred to her that with the open house pushed back those two extra weeks, something impressive might well be done here. Her mind shifted into gear, turning the possibilities around and around. Pulling a notepad from her bag, she jotted down some ideas.

Then she headed for the duck pond, where the first cluster of eight condominiums was nearing completion, and she was struck, truly struck, by the beauty of the place. The outside hadn't changed drastically since she'd seen it last. She still loved the modified Georgian design, the hints of pillars and balconies, the sloped roofs that hid rear skylights, the cedar shingles painted taupe with cream trim. But something was different. Lowering herself to the ground with her back braced against a tree, she pondered that difference.

After a long time, during which she stretched her legs out in the sun, followed the antics of an occasional duck and breathed deeply of air redolent with the smell of grass, new wood and nature, she realized that it was the trees. With the start of summer, they were fuller and richer than they had been. And the lawn. Sod that had been put down where men and machines had mangled the earth had taken root and was now a deep, healthy green. And the shrubbery. Christine had worked with a landscaper on that, and between them, they had created a masterpiece of color and texture. As the icing on the cake, the greenery worked.

For the first time, Nina wished she could afford one of the units herself. There was something so peaceful about the place. Everything that had been done was of high quality and refined—everything Nina might have let herself dream of owning, but hadn't. She'd always had other dreams. They came first.

Sitting there in the sun, though, lulled by the smells of the outdoors and the sounds of the ducks and the nearby ocean, she didn't want to think about those other dreams. She just wanted to *be*.

Which, to her surprise, was exactly what she proceeded to do for what had to have been nearly half an hour, before two people emerged from the model condominium and approached her.

Tipping her head back against the bark of the old maple, she grinned. "Hey, you guys, what's been goin' on in there?"

Christine shot her husband a mischievous look. "Nothing much—"

"—through no fault of mine," Gideon cut in. "But Chris is all business when it comes to this place. She wants everything done, and done right, in time for your show."

"How are you feeling, Nina?"

Other than squinting against the sun, Nina didn't move. "Fine. Lazy. This place is like a drug. I'm in awe that you both manage to get work done here. Every time I come, I get sidetracked."

This time, the mischievous look Chris sent Gideon was

reflected right back. "We know the feeling," she said, then took a deep breath and tore her eyes from his to look at Nina again. "You're looking good. It's hard to believe you went through what you did only two weeks ago."

"I had good care. I was lucky."

"John was pretty worried about you," Gideon said, more serious now. "When he called to tell us you were sick, he was upset."

Nina chuckled. "He was laying it on thick, so none of you would dare ask me when I'd be getting back to work."

"He was right about the open house, though," Chris put in. "It can just as easily wait until the end of the month."

Gideon draped an arm around his wife's shoulder. To Nina, in a conspiratorial voice, he said, "Especially since the fabric of the living room furniture in the model came through wrong. Chris has been sweating bullets about that. With the few extra weeks, it'll be fixed."

"So. Are you guys buying one of the units?"

They exchanged a meaningful look. It was Gideon who said, "We've been sorely tempted. It'd be a gorgeous place to live in. But Chris's daughter is still in high school. It wouldn't be fair to uproot her and tear her away from her friends—"

"And then there's this little matter of Gideon's dream," Chris put in, looking up at him again. "He's been waking up in the middle of the night with the notion that once Jill graduates we should sell his place in Worcester, buy land somewhere and build a spectacular house of our own."

"It's not a notion," Gideon argued. "It's a full-fledged plan. I can picture the whole house. Hell, I've got the basics already down on paper. It may take us a while to get it built, but when it's done, it'll be super."

He kissed Chris lightly on the lips and looked as though he wanted to do more, when Chris offered a soft, "If we don't get going, we'll be late." To Nina she said, "We're meeting Carter and Jessica for a late lunch. You know that Jessica's pregnant, don't you?"

Nina nodded. "I'm thrilled for her."

"So are we." As they started off, she added, "Listen, I'll give you a call in a day or two. Don't work too hard, Nina. We want you well."

Nina raised a hand in a wave, then let if fall to her lap as Chris and Gideon went farther up the path toward the mansion. She was thrilled for them, too. They were clearly so pleased to be together, so very much in love.

Sitting there, she felt a smidgeon of envy. Christine Lowe had it all—a husband, a daughter, a career. Jessica Malloy was on her way, too. Gideon and Carter were both fine men.

So was John. Fine, and kind, and smart, and sexy.

Feeling, at the very moment, an intense urge to touch him, she moaned aloud. She hadn't seen him since Monday morning. She missed him. Indeed, she'd been missing him all week. It occurred to her that the idea of making a clean break had sounded good but it wasn't much fun.

She deserved a little fun once in a while, didn't she? A little fun wouldn't be compromising her independence, would it?

Determined to call him that night, she pushed up against the tree trunk, returned to her car and drove home. By the time she got there, she knew that a call wouldn't be enough. She wanted to see John. Just a short visit. A drop-in visit. Just to see how he was getting on. And how J.J. was getting on. She could say hello, then leave with her sense of independence and self-sufficiency intact.

SHE WENT SHORTLY after seven. The Leaf Turner was closed then, dinner would be over, and though there was a chance that John might have taken J.J. out for ice cream, she figured that with his bedtime approaching, they'd be back soon.

Her heart did a soft flip-flop when she saw the car parked back by the garage. Driving up to the side door, she rang the bell, then stuck her head inside. "John?" she called. Hearing no response, she went up the stairs.

She found them in the bathroom. John was giving J.J. a bath, though it was questionable who was the wetter of the two. For a minute she just stood at the door and watched. They were an adorable pair, playing under the guise of rinsing. Aside from the sounds that weren't quite like those of other children, J.J. looked like a happy, normal child. But it was to John that her eye kept returning. He looked wonderful, pleasantly wet and mussed, capable, strong. Thanks to the water, his shirt and shorts were clinging to his body more lovingly than they might otherwise have done. To her hungry eyes, he looked extraordinarily masculine.

Suffused with a warm glow inside, she asked, "What's going on here?"

John's head flew around at the sound of her voice. His sudden movement alerted J.J. to her presence. Though the child wasn't wearing his glasses, he must have recognized her overall color and shape, because with the splash of water and a nasal squeal, he began to jump up and down.

"Easy," John said, turning quickly back to him and grabbing an arm. "You'll slip if you're not careful." He said it more to himself, because with one hand on J.J. and another groping for a towel, he couldn't sign. Not that that would have worked, anyway. J.J.'s eyes were riveted to Nina.

Nina was the one who grabbed the towel and shook it open. "Lift him out," she said, "and I'll wrap him up." John did that, and within seconds, J.J. was enveloped in a warm terry-cloth cocoon. Nina gave him a hug, only to pull quickly back when he complained in the most vociferous of ways. "Oops, what'd I do?"

"You wrapped up his arms," John explained quietly. "He can't communicate without them."

J.J. had already set about remedying the situation by

pushing his way out of the towel. Then his little arms reached for her and his little body followed close by. Even if Nina had been wearing her fanciest dress rather than shorts and a T-shirt, she wouldn't have minded the dampness or warmth. Grabbing J.J. around the bare back and bottom, rocking him from side to side, she felt she was holding something more valuable than any property title that had ever passed through her hands. He was precious. He was alive. He was a special, special little boy.

Her eyes rose to John, who was standing near where she knelt. He was regarding her somberly, seeming unsure as to what to make of her arrival.

"I just wanted to stop by and say hi," she explained softly. "To see how you are."

"We're fine," he said as somberly as he was looking. "We weren't the ones who were sick."

"Well, I'm fine, too," she said, but no sooner were the words out than J.J. pulled back and began making sounds. His small hand was at work finger-spelling something, but far too quickly for her to follow, even if she had known the manual alphabet, which she didn't. Something about the sounds, though, the repetition of the syllables, began to ring a bell. Not knowing whether to believe what she was hearing, she looked wide-eyed up at John, who explained.

"He wrote your name for the therapist. She had him practice finger-spelling it, but he wanted to say it, too." Begrudgingly, Nina thought, he added, "It isn't often that he voluntarily speaks. You should feel honored."

"I do," Nina breathed. Looking back at J.J., she grinned and nodded vigorously, then gave him another hard hug, followed by a kiss, followed by, "*Very* honored."

John didn't sound terribly impressed. "It's nice you stopped by so he could try it out on you. He's been asking all week where you were."

She raised stricken eyes to John's, but he turned on his

heel, muttering something about getting pajamas, and left the bathroom. Holding J.J. back, Nina put a finger to the tip of his nose, mouthed, "Thank you," then, tucking him into the curve of her arm, pulled the plug on the water in the tub. When he reached over to take out his rubber duckie, she saw an ugly scrape on his elbow. Forming her mouth into a dismayed "Oh," she took the arm in her hand. "Boo-boo?"

J.J. nodded and signed something that she couldn't understand. She was telling herself that she'd have to learn more signs, when John returned.

"He did that yesterday. Came fast off the slide and scraped it. It hurt."

Gently Nina lifted the scraped elbow and put a feather-light kiss to it. "I'm sorry."

Retrieving the towel, John began to dry J.J.'s back. "It's part of growing up."

"It must hurt you, too, when it happens." She could feel the sting herself.

"Uh-huh."

Little by little, J.J.'s small body disappeared into his pajamas. Sitting back on her heels, Nina watched. She half wished she had someone to take care of like John had J.J. She didn't have the time, of course; still there had been something nice about that warm little body snuggling close.

With a flurry of hands, John and J.J. began to talk to each other. Nina waited patiently, wishing she knew more about signing, making up her mind to learn. Finally John looked at her.

"How long were you planning to stay?" he asked in a neutral tone of voice.

Wanting to stay awhile, but, thanks to that neutral tone, unsure of her welcome, she shrugged. "Did you have plans?"

"J.J. wants you in on a good-night story. He wants you to hold the book and turn the pages, while I sign."

"I'd love to," she said with pleasure. John might not

have been thrilled to see her, but if J.J. was, that was a start. She'd steal time with John any way she could.

The next fifteen minutes were near to heaven. Sitting on J.J.'s bed with the small child nestled close to her side, Nina watched John sign the story of *The Little Engine That Could* as she read it aloud. She knew the story. Her first-grade teacher had loved it, and she had loved her first-grade teacher, so she'd always remembered the book.

She wondered whether John had chosen it for a reason. With its theme of the small engine that, against all odds and by dint of sheer determination, made its way over the mountain to deliver toys and games to the little boys and girls on the other side, it suggested to J.J. that he could do whatever he wanted if he was determined enough.

It suggested the same thing to Nina.

She was still thinking about that when the book was over. A sleepy J.J. gave her a big hug and a kiss, then turned to his father. Not wanting to intrude on their private good-night, Nina quietly left the room. She was leaning against the wall in the hall, with her arms wrapped around her middle, when he joined her.

His look was quelling. "He wanted to know if he could go in and see you in the morning. I had to explain that you wouldn't be here." Without giving her a chance to reply, he took off down the stairs.

Silently she followed. He had a right to be upset on J.J.'s behalf, she knew. But she would have liked it if *he* had been pleased to see her.

He hadn't said a word to that effect. Nor had anything in his look said that he was glad she had come—except maybe for his surprise when he'd first seen her, maybe there had been a little pleasure in that.

He went straight on into the bookstore, to the cartons stacked there, waiting to be unpacked. "It's hard for a kid to understand why someone he likes is there one day and gone the next."

"I know."

His gaze was cutting. "You should, if what you told me about your mother was true."

"It is. But I didn't think J.J. would make such a close tie in such a short time."

"Neither did I, or believe me, I'd never have let you stay here. But it worked between you and him. You're so totally without preconceptions about what a little boy his age should or should not be doing that you accept him completely. He senses that and responds." Swearing under his breath, he pounded the seam of the top box with a fist. Without benefit of a knife, he slipped his fingers into the small slit he'd made and pulled the carton open.

"I'm sorry," she said, and meant it. "But I'm not sorry you had me here. You were right. I couldn't have gone home. I was too weak at the beginning."

She waited for him to pick up on the suggestion and ask how she was feeling now. Instead, he pulled books from the carton and stalked off toward a far shelf. Several minutes later, after he'd taken his time putting those books in the appropriate spots, he was back for more.

"I talked with Christine and Gideon today," she said lightly. "They agreed about postponing the open house. Chris was actually relieved, because some of the furniture for the model didn't come in right, and with the extra time, she can have it done over. She wants everything to be perfect." The last sentence was spoken more loudly to follow John down another aisle with another arm load of books.

Again he was several minutes arranging the books on the shelves. By the time he returned, Nina was growing uneasy.

"Aren't you going to talk to me?"

He was loading his arms a third time. "When you say

something worthwhile. So far, all I've heard is babble."
Off he went.

"It'd help if you'd stop working and look me in the eye,"
she called, growing annoyed. She waited until he returned
before muttering, "And you tell me *I* work too much."

"These books have to be shelved." Tossing one empty
carton aside, he started in on the second.

"Right now?"

"Is there something more worthwhile I should be doing?"

"Talking with me."

"Worthwhile, I said. There's nothing worthwhile in
what we have to say to each other."

"There might be, if you could stop running back and
forth with those books."

His answer to that was to head in a different direction
with a new arm load.

"John! *Please!*" On impulse, she took right off after
him, following him down a short aisle and around a corner.
"I want to talk with you."

He was already putting one book after another in line.
"What about?"

"You. How you've been. What you've been doing."

"Well," he said, raising the last six books and wedging
them in a bunch onto the shelf, "I've been fine and doing
all the same things I always do, so that'd be a pretty worth-
less conversation." He turned to leave.

"John," Nina cried, unable to take any more of his
running. *"Don't!"*

Her cry must have reached him, because he stopped in
his tracks. At first his body was straight. With an expelled
breath, it seemed to sag a little. Cocking a hand on one lean
hip, he hung his head and stood, silent, with his back to her.

She wanted to reach out and touch him, but didn't dare.
Nor, though, could she let him go. More quietly, a little desperately, she said, "Talk with me. Just for a minute. Please?"

At first, she thought he'd refuse. When she was about to repeat her plea, even to intensify it, he straightened his spine and turned slowly. Spreading his arms along the bookshelf at shoulder height, he leaned back against the books and looked her in the eye.

"What did you want to say?"

She saw it then, saw hurt in his eyes, saw confusion and vulnerability and wanting. Long fingers clenched around her heart. She let out a small breath, then swallowed.

"I'm listening," he said evenly.

Swallowing again, she started toward him. Guilelessly, thinking only to tell him what she was feeling, she said, "I've missed you."

"You could have called to tell me that."

"I didn't know it until tonight."

"It just—" arms still outspread, he snapped his fingers "—came to you?"

"Seeing you." Stopping before him, she raised a hand to his face. "I've never missed anyone before." She brushed the wayward hair from his brow, but it fell right back in the way she loved. Entranced by that and by a tug she felt inside, she rasped a palm over the shadow of his beard, touched fingertips to his chin, then his mouth. Unable to help herself, she went up on tiptoe.

"Nina—"

"Don't move," she said in a hoarse whisper, and before he could say another word, she put her mouth to his. It was a simple touch at first, a sweet homecoming that was repeated with additional little touches and tastes. "I've missed you," she whispered again, going up this time for a deeper kiss. His lips resisted. She stroked them gently, traced them with the tip of her tongue, nipped at them until they began to soften. When he opened them enough to allow her entrance, she slipped her tongue inside. He tasted wonderful, so warm and exciting, so like John that when he began to respond to her kiss, she gave a totally helpless moan.

Startled by the sound, she dropped back to her heels. Watching her, John's eyes were alert. They seemed to question and warn, but she was beyond answering and heeding. The only thing she was capable of doing was touching him in response to a clamoring need inside. Raising trembling hands to his shoulders, she tested his strength there before moving inward to the buttons of his shirt.

"Nina, what—"

"Shh. Let me." One by one, she released the buttons, finally spreading the still-damp material to the sides. From the first time she'd seen him bare, she had known he was beautifully made, but memory paled before the real thing. Slightly awed, she caught her breath. Her hands skimmed lightly over his skin, over the cording of muscles higher up, over the wedge of hair that tapered toward his belly, over the dark, flat nipples that grew hard and tight. He was warm and gentle yet masculine through and through. Unable to deny herself the pleasure she leaned forward and put her mouth where her hands had been.

He whispered her name. She shushed him again, this time against the soft hair that swirled over the swells of his chest. She pressed her lips to one spot, put her tongue to another, dragged her teeth over a third. Only once did she stop, with her ear to the rapid thud of his heart and the pad of her thumb on his nipple, but if what she was doing excited him, it excited her as well. While her mouth continued its loving sport, her hands fell to the snap of his shorts.

Again he whispered her name, this time taking his arms from the shelves and framing her head. Still she hushed him. She kissed him lightly, one spot to the next on his chest, while she unzipped him and slipped her hands inside. He was hard and hot, a binding brand against her palm. She traced his length, curved her fingers around him and drew him up, then repeated the stroking until he began to shake.

"Oh, Nina, that feels good."

It was all she needed to hear. Working her way down from his breast, she kissed a trail over his navel to the thick nest of hair that flared at his groin. When she opened her mouth on the velvet tip of his sex, he tried to pull back.

"I'll come, baby, I'll come." His voice was a tortured moan, the sound of a man in the deepest stages of want.

The sound excited her beyond belief. Defying the hands that clenched and unclenched around her head, she loved him in ways she'd never loved a man before, and when his release came she stayed with him, showing him without words how much he meant to her.

Between harsh gasps, he whispered her name. His body seemed held erect by nothing more than the wild trembling that shook it. As the trembling eased, he slid down down until he was kneeling, face-to-face with her. Hands in her hair, he looked at her for the longest time until, brokenly, he said, "No one's ever done that to me before."

"Then it was a first for us both," she whispered back.

His thumbs brushed her cheekbones, his lips caught hers. He drew her against him, only to ease her back in the next breath and tug her shirt from her shorts. "I need to feel you against me," he whispered as he unhooked her bra, and in the next instant he pushed her shorts to her knees and drew her in close again.

Nina couldn't contain the bubble of desire that swelled from her throat into a ragged moan. Large, capable hands covered her back, then her bottom, then worked their way to her breast and her belly.

"Does it hurt?" he asked by her ear, fingering the scar that was still too new to have faded.

Her breath was warm against his neck. "Once in a while, just a pinch."

"Can I make love to you?" he whispered.

"I wish you would," she whispered back.

Very gently then, with a care that brought tears to her eyes and small sighs of pleasure to her lips, he lowered her to the carpet, removed her shorts and his, and filled the place inside that had been wanting him so. Though he held his weight off her stomach, his penetration was deep. He let her set the pace, but he was attuned to her every need. When she grew hotter and her body began straining toward his, he used his fingers to help her to a stunning climax. His own followed soon after, leaving them in a limp tangle of arms and legs.

Snuggling closer into his embrace, Nina whispered a broken, "Oh, John, I was beginning to think you hated me."

He took a long, deep, shuddering breath. "Not hated. Loved. Love, present tense. I love you." Her fingers flew to his mouth, but the words were already out. Taking her wrist, he anchored her hand on his chest. "I do, Nina, and it's hell. I want to be with you all the time, but you have this thing for independence. I've been in agony all week, waiting for you to call."

Shaken by the depth of his feeling, by the intensity in the amber eyes that peered down at her, by the intensity of all *she* was feeling inside in the wake of his declaration, she managed a meek, "You could have called me."

"No. I insisted you come here from the hospital, and while you were here, I insisted you lie around and be coddled. I couldn't insist anymore. You wanted to fly. It was your turn to take the initiative."

She remembered words that had been spoken in anger and frustration on the day she'd left. "You said you were independent and self-sufficient, too."

"I am," he said quickly, then slowly to a more pensive pace, "but it's not how I want to live my life. I don't see anything weak about wanting a woman the way I want you.

I don't see anything weak about wanting to sleep with a woman, or talk with her over breakfast and dinner, or take her to the beach, or eat the chocolate chip cookies she bakes. I don't see that I'd be losing anything by committing myself to you—" he took a deep breath, but when he went on, his voice was harder "—unless you don't make the same kind of commitment in return. I can't live the way I have been this week, Nina. I can't live in a vacuum, thinking of you, wondering, worrying, wanting. I can't sit around waiting for you to call when you chance to get a free minute. And I can't put J.J. through that."

Hearing his words, feeling the beat of his heart and the warm draw of his spent body, Nina was in heaven and hell at the same time. "What are you telling me?"

He was awhile in answering, and during that time, she had the awful feeling that he was savoring the last bits of pleasure before it all fell apart. She was feeling nervous when he finally took a deep breath and spoke.

"I'm saying," he began slowly and with conviction, "that I've been down this road before, only this time there's so much more of my heart involved that I can't, just can't take the risk. I love you, Nina, but if you don't love me back, if you can't marry me and move in here with me and cut back on your work so you can be a wife to me and a mother to J.J., I don't want it." He took another breath, a more labored one this time. "I guess maybe it is all or nothing. I can respect your work. I'd be the first to insist that you keep it up, and if you had an appointment at dinnertime once in a while, I certainly wouldn't complain. But work can't come first in your life. I have to. That's the only way it can be with me. I'm sorry."

Nina wanted to cry. Exerting the utmost control not to, she carefully pushed herself up. "Then—"

"Either we do it my way, or not at all," he said, rising to look her straight in the eye. "Either you love me, or you don't. Either we're together the way we should be, or we break it off. Cold turkey. Over. No phone calls. No visits. No 'maybe, if we find the time.'"

"But…that's not fair."

"Maybe not to you. You'd be just as happy to let things ride for years. But I can't do it. I feel too much."

She was incredulous. "You love me so much you'd give me up in a minute? That doesn't make any sense, John!"

The only response he made was a slow shrug.

"John," she pleaded. When he didn't answer but simply sat there staring at her, she was suddenly lashed by conflicting emotions. She wanted to rant and rave, to hit him, to knock some sense into him; at the same time, she wanted to throw herself into his arms and beg him to hold her, to love her, to keep on loving her while she did what she had to in life.

Overwhelmed and confused, she did the only practical thing she could at that moment. She reached for her shorts and pulled them on to cover her nakedness that had felt so right such a short time before.

"You're leaving then?" he asked.

"I have to. I can't think. I feel confused. I don't know what to do. I need time."

"I don't have time, Nina," he said in a grim voice. "The longer this goes on, the more it hurts."

"Loving shouldn't hurt."

"But it does."

She knew she should argue or plead or throw herself at him and make love to him again and again, until she was so firmly entrenched under his skin that he wouldn't be able to shake her no matter how hard he tried.

But she had too much dignity for that. Pushing her feet into her sneakers, concentrating on willing away the tears that seemed bent on pooling in her lids, fighting the odd sense of near-panic gripping her insides, she stood, straightened her T-shirt and started walking toward the door.

One word from John and she would have stopped. But that word didn't come, so she continued on out into the warm summer night and drove home, shivering all the way.

CHAPTER TEN

NINA WENT TO WORK the next morning, but her heart wasn't in it. She hadn't slept well and was feeling tired and sore and, in general, disinterested in anything to do with real estate. When, after four hours of moving in and out of the office with and without clients, she'd had enough, she prevailed on an accommodating Lee to take over the few appointments she'd made for the afternoon.

Back in her apartment, she was at loose ends. There wasn't anything she wanted to do there, and though she was tired, she couldn't sleep. No sooner did she close her eyes than images appeared behind her lids that kept her awake—John standing on the beach looking out to sea, or kneeling by the tub bathing J.J., or lying naked from the waist down on The Leaf Turner's carpet, between the shelves for Self-Help and Romance. Each image brought back a memory in vivid detail. Each one haunted her.

The one image that kept returning, though, the one that haunted her the most, was the scene in J.J.'s bedroom. She was on the bed with J.J. tucked up against her. A large book was open on their laps, but their eyes were on John, who was telling the story with his hands.

Over and over Nina saw that scene, each time struck by something different. Once there was the warmth—maternal, if she dared use that word to describe what she felt—of holding J.J. in her arms. Another time there was the magnitude of her feeling for John, the sense of trust and respect and attraction that she'd never felt for any other man. Yet another time—and repeatedly—there was the totally unexpected contentment of being a part of an intimate family scene.

John had said that loving her hurt. In those long hours at home, she came to feel the hurt herself. He had given her a glimpse of something she had never expected to experience, and where once ignorance had been bliss, she was ignorant no more. She knew the pain of tasting something exquisitely sweet.

But wasn't independence sweet? Wasn't self-sufficiency? Wasn't freedom?

The more questions she asked herself, the more confused and unhappy she grew. Friday night passed on leaden hands creeping around the clock. By the time Saturday morning arrived, she was feeling no more like going to work than she had the day before, and that unsettled her all the more. She loved her work, at least, she always had. Now, somehow, it seemed inconsequential.

What she wanted to do was to see John, but she couldn't.

Nor could she call a friend. Or take a drive. Or go to the beach. Or the supermarket. Or a movie. She couldn't do anything frivolous, not when she was confronting the most momentous decision she'd ever had to make in her life.

What she did, acting on an instinct that was so nearly subconscious that she couldn't possibly give it much thought, was to pick up the phone and call first the airport, then Lee, then pack a small bag and head for Omaha.

WITHIN MINUTES OF her arrival at the nursing home where her mother lived, Anthony Kimball strode out to greet her. "I'm glad you're here, Nina," he said. After shaking the hand she offered, he guided her down the hall. "I wasn't sure you'd gotten my message. When you didn't return the call—"

"What call?"

"The one I made this morning." He frowned. "You didn't get the message?"

"No." She felt the rise of a cold fear inside. "Is she worse?"

He nodded. With quiet compassion, he said, "It won't be long now. It's good that you've come." At her mother's room, he opened the door. With a sense of dread, Nina stepped inside and moved toward the bed. The tiny figure that lay there seemed little more than a skeleton under a token blanket of skin.

Nina was horrified. "She's so thin."

"The last few months have been hard for her."

"But she doesn't know that," Nina said a bit frantically. "No."

The reassurance was welcome but brief. The very same instinct that had put Nina on the plane that morning was telling her that, as the doctor had said, her mother's death was at hand. And though she had never been close to Maria Stone, though Maria had let her down again and again, though there had been times when Nina had actually hated her, blood was thicker than water. Maria, for all her weaknesses, was still her mother.

Nina didn't realize that the mournful sound she heard came from her own throat until the doctor touched her shoulder. "If you'd rather wait in my office—"

"No," she said and, though determined, her voice was thin, "I want to stay here with her."

She did just that. Sitting in the chair that the doctor brought to the side of the bed, she held her mother's frail hand, studied her expressionless face, stroked her thin gray hair and pretended that things had been different.

Hours passed, still she stayed in that chair. After a time, though, she stopped pretending, because memories started coming from nowhere at all, memories that she hadn't known she had for events she hadn't known she'd lived through. She remembered being very little, falling off a curb and skinning her knees, then being held by a woman with the same delicate profile as this woman on the bed. She remembered fishing funny little noodles out of a soup that she loved, while the woman who had made that soup, a woman with the same bow-shaped mouth as this woman on the bed, looked on and laughed. She remembered the sound of that laugh, and the smell of perfume. She remembered the way that smell had clung to her after she'd been hugged tightly by a woman with slender, fine-shaped hands that, in a healthier time, could well have been those of this woman on the bed.

There had been good times, she realized with a start. There had been some smiles between the frowns, only she'd been so overwhelmed by the need to survive in those frightening times that she'd forgotten them. They had been lost, probably would have been lost forever, had she not, through the force of fate, taken the time out to spend these last hours with her mother.

She wondered at the solace she might have had over the years if she'd taken that time sooner. She wondered whether she would have felt less anger toward Maria and less pity for herself. She wondered whether she might have been more complete a woman. For so long, she had believed that she'd risen way above anything her mother had been. Suddenly she wasn't so sure. Her mother had given her life, then in her own way and working around her own limitations, had loved her. Nina hadn't given anyone life or love. She had been too wrapped up in her own drive to prove that she didn't need either.

But she'd been wrong. Sitting there by her mother's bedside, holding tightly to the hand that had long ago held hers, Nina understood things about herself that she would never have considered before. As the hours wore on, as Maria's skin grew more waxy and her breathing more shallow, Nina was humbled.

Anthony Kimball stopped in before he left for the day. Nurses checked in and out, monitoring Maria's state at the same time that they offered Nina hot coffee and snacks, most of which she refused. She felt a great emptiness inside, an emptiness that wasn't totally foreign to her, but she wasn't hungry. All she wanted to do was to sit by her mother's side, to talk softly on the chance that she could be heard, to warm Maria's cold hands, to let her presence be felt.

She never knew if it was. Shortly after dawn the next morning, when the sun rose with a joy Nina didn't feel, Maria took a last breath and slipped away.

NINA HAD HER buried later that afternoon under a pretty dogwood in a small cemetery on the outskirts of town. After thanking the priest for his kind words and Anthony Kimball for his kind care, she took a cab to the airport. From there, just as her flight was being called, she phoned John.

As though he'd been waiting, he picked up after the very first ring. "Hello?"

With a fast indrawn breath, she said a timid, "John?"

His voice softened. "Nina. Ah, Nina, thank goodness you've called. I've been so worried. Are you in Omaha?"

She nodded, then realized he couldn't see, and said a small, "Uh-huh."

"How is she?"

"Gone. Early this morning—" Her voice cracked. She pressed a hand to her mouth.

"Oh, God, baby, I'm sorry."

"Maybe—" she cleared her throat of the tightness there "—maybe it's for the best."

"Maybe," he said quietly.

"But it's hard—" Again her voice cracked.

"Are you all right?" he asked very softly.

"Uh, I think so." She gulped in a breath. "John?"

"Yes?"

"I'm coming home now. I want—I need—you. Can you—"

"What time? What flight?"

She gave him the information, then hung up the phone and, brushing the tears from her eyes, boarded the plane. She didn't cry during the flight. Nor did she eat or sleep. She felt in a state of suspended emotion, too tired to think or feel, but waiting, holding herself together as best she could.

The plane was fifteen minutes late in landing, which was late indeed, given that it was due in well after eleven Boston time. Putting the strap of her overnight case on her shoulder, Nina followed the rest of the passengers down the aisle of the plane. Passing through the jetway, her throat began to tighten. By the time she made it into the terminal, her eyes were filling up again. Her step slowed as she looked around. She swallowed. She said a silent prayer.

Then she saw John. He was standing off to the side, out of the path of the passengers. Wearing his glasses and a somber expression, he looked tense.

Slowly she started toward him. Her heart was in her mouth, ahead of every other one of the emotions that were clogging her throat, but she kept her feet moving, kept her composure intact. Only when she stood directly before him, when she could feel the warmth, the strength and caring that were hers for the taking, did everything she'd been keeping inside swell up and spill over. Wordlessly she slipped her arms around his waist, buried her face against his throat and began to cry.

At what point his arms closed around her she didn't know, though she felt his support from the start. She cried softly but steadily, unable to stem the tears, barely trying. She cried for her mother, for the years and the love that had been lost, and when she was done crying for those things, she cried for all she'd put John through.

His collar was damp from her tears by the time her sobs

slowed, and by then, the strain of the past thirty-six hours was taking its toll. Bone weary, she mustered scattered bits of strength to raise her eyes to his and utter a whispered plea. "Take me home?"

Something in her tear-damp eyes must have elaborated on the request, because, without a word, John slipped an arm around her waist and helped her out the door to the car. Once inside, he brought her close to his side. Then he drove straight to the small white Victoria that he called home, led her upstairs and, with the most heartrendingly gentle kiss, put her to bed.

THE SKY WAS newly pink in the east when Nina opened her eyes again. Though her memory of the night before was vague, she knew instantly that she was in John's home, in John's bed, wearing another one of John's large shirts. John wasn't as decently dressed. Bare to the hip, at which point he disappeared under the sheet, he was propped on an elbow, watching her. His expression didn't give away anything of what he was thinking.

The lack of knowing, the fear that brought, dashed all remnants of sleep. With a nervous half smile, she said, "Hi."

"How are you feeling?" he returned without any kind of smile.

She was quiet for a minute, looking into his eyes, wanting to melt into him but knowing it was time to talk. So she said, "Sad. Happy. Scared."

"That's a lot. Want to run through them for me one by one?"

Thinking about what she wanted to say was difficult. For a minute, her throat knotted and she thought she might cry again. Determined to be stronger than that, she forced the words out. "Sad, because she's gone and I never really knew her. Happy, because being with her Saturday taught me something that I might not have otherwise known.

Scared, because I know where I want to go now, but I'm not sure I'm worthy of it." Her voice broke, still she went on. "I've been blind about lots of things."

"Like what?" he asked, his eyes level.

"Like her, and the fact that she loved me, even though she was so screwed up she couldn't show it much of the time.

"That happens to lots of parents."

"I know. But I didn't know it when I was growing up, so I got bitter and angry and blamed her for everything that was missing in my life." Her voice dropped. "But I was the one responsible for lots of those things being missing."

"What things?"

"A home and family. Close relationships. I set out to become independently rich, which was something my mother had never been. I was sure that would be a panacea, and I wasn't letting anyone or anything get in my way. Work would fill up my life, I thought. I thought being busy and successful would be enough. But it isn't."

"How do you know?"

"Because," she searched helplessly for the words, "it just isn't."

"Why not?"

"Because—" she wished she could say what she was feeling, but the emotions were so strong, so momentous, so frightening "—it's not the same."

"The same as what?"

"*Being* with people."

"Being?"

"Living with people."

"As in cohabitating?"

"*Loving* people."

John was very still. His amber eyes grew darker, more alert than before. "Are you in love?" he asked softly.

Eyes large and locked with his, she nodded.

"With me?"

Again she nodded.

For the first time, she saw a softening of his expression. "For a lady who can talk up a storm when she wants to make a sale, you're sure having trouble with this."

"That's because it's so important."

"Is it?"

She nodded. "More important than anything I've ever said or done before in my life."

"So. Tell me what you're thinking. Just spit it out."

Taking courage from the gentleness of his face, she said, "I'm thinking that I don't want to be like that lady you once described. I don't want to wake up one day and be alone and empty and too old to have kids." She took a tremulous breath. "I'm thinking that I love you, and want to live here with you and be a mother to J.J. and maybe be a mother to kids we could have. I mean," she hurried to add, "I don't know anything about changing a diaper or making a bottle, but I could learn, if you wanted more kids. But you may not. J.J. is special, and he takes twice as much love."

"I've got more than that," John said softly. Cupping a hand to her face, he rubbed his thumb over her lips. "I've got more than enough for you and him and a bunch of others."

"I want a bunch. That's what I want."

"What about work?"

"I'll work. Just not all the time."

John looked skeptical. "Will that be possible?"

"You were the one who said it was."

"But is it for you? You love your work. It's been your life for so long—"

"Until I met you. It hasn't been the same since. Nothing's been the same since."

He grinned then, the grin she found so sexy, the one that could make her insides go all hot and soft. "I like the sound of that. Now, if I could just hear those other little words again."

She knew which ones he wanted. Swallowing down the last of her fears, she said, "I love you."

"Again."

They came more easily this time. "I love you."

"One more time."

She grinned. It was a snap. "I love you."

Shifting under the sheets, John rolled over so that his long body fit hers. Linking their fingers on either side of her head, he effected a slow undulation of his hips. "Now if we could have the words with a little kiss, then a little touch, then a little—" A loud sound in the hall cut him off. "Damn," he muttered, rolled off Nina and yanked the sheet up to cover her completely. "J.J.'s up."

"He's saying 'daddy'?" she whispered from under the sheet. Her hand was on his hip. She left it there.

"Yup." The door opened and his voice picked up. "Hi, sport, how're you doing?" From under the sheet, Nina could feel the movement as he signed. Seconds later, she felt a small bundle hit the end of the bed, but it slid off nearly as quickly, followed by the patter of small feet leaving the room on the run. "Smart kid," John muttered. "He saw your clothes. He's off to the guest room." Leaning close to the sheet, he warned, "Last chance, Nina. If he finds you in my bed, there's no going back. I can still make up some excuse for your clothes—"

Her hand slid over his hip just far enough to make him jump. "What excuse will you give for this?" He was still fully aroused.

"Uh, he doesn't have to, uh, see that. Damn it, Nina, don't play with me now. Are you staying, or aren't you? I have to know for sure."

"For J.J.?"

"For *me*. He'll have his own life, and I want mine. I want you in it. What do you say?"

"I may be a lousy wife."

"I'll take that chance."

"I may be a lousy mother."

"No way. Come on, Nina. Is it a yes?"

Beneath the sheets, Nina was flying high as a kite. "I need the magic words."

"I love you."

"Again."

"I love you!"

"Louder."

"I love you!"

The shout was barely out when the patter of feet announced J.J.'s return. "Didn't find her?" Nina heard John ask. She felt movement, then all was suspiciously quiet until, with a gleeful guffaw, J.J. pulled back the sheet and jumped on the bed. John caught him seconds before he would have pounced on Nina's stomach, but she was up and laughing, being hugged by them both in no time flat.

Never before had she felt so happy, so whole, so loved.

EPILOGUE

THE SUN WAS WARM on their skin, but it felt good. The winter had been a long, snowy one. Spring had finally come.

Leaning back against John, whose body was a more comfortable chaise than any other she had ever tried, Nina took a deep, deep breath and let it out in an appreciative, "Mmm, does this feel good?"

His mouth tickled her ear. "The sun or me?"

She hooked her arms around his thighs, which rose alongside her hips. "Both. This is an absolutely gorgeous spot."

They were at Crosslyn Rise, sprawled on the lawn that sloped toward the sea. Behind them, on the crest of the hill, stood the mansion, its multichimneyed roof, newly pointed bricks and bright white Georgian columns setting it off against a backdrop of evergreen lushness and azure sky. To the left and right were more trees, many newly budded, and beyond the trees, grouped in clusters, were two dozen condominiums, all finished, all occupied, all spectacular. Before them, at the foot of the hill, was the small marina with its pristine docks and proud-masted yachts, and the row of shops that included an art gallery, a clothing boutique, a sports shop, a video store, two small restaurants, a drugstore and The Leaf Turner.

"Are you sorry we didn't buy a place here?" John asked.

"Not on your life. It's enough that you have the bookstore. Besides, I love the Victorian, especially now." As soon as John had moved the Leaf Turner to Crosslyn Rise, they had repossessed the first floor of the house. What with the professional expertise of Carter Molloy and Gideon and Christine Lowe, they had renovated the place into something neither one of them had dared dream of. Nina might have done even more—finished the attic as a playroom for J.J. or built on an attached garage—had not John been vehement that the bulk of her Crosslyn Rise profit was to go into an account in her own name. He didn't care if it sat there untouched for years, he told her, just so long as she knew it was there, for her, should she want or need it.

He understood where she'd come from. He was special that way.

But then, she mused, lazily shifting her bare feet in the warm, soft grass, he was special in lots of ways. Like his concern for her. There was times when she could swear that his only goal in life was to make her happy.

"Are you sure," his deep voice came now, "that you wouldn't like to rent a small space here for you?"

"Can't do," she said with pride. "We're leased to one-hundred-percent capacity."

"But when something opens up."

"Nope. I'm happy where I am." She was still at Crown Realty, with Chrissie handling her pink slips and Lee, albeit engaged to a wonderful guy now, backing her up.

"You don't ever think about having your own agency, not even for a minute, for old times' sake?"

Tipping her head against his arm, she looked up into his face. How many times she'd seen those strong features in the past two years, seen them in every light and mood, and it seemed that she only loved each one more. "When do I have time to think about having my own agency? My life is so full." Full as opposed to busy. There was a difference.

"But you wanted to be independent."

"I am. I work when I want and come home when I

want." She touched his cheek. "It's a pretty nice deal." She paused. "Why don't you look convinced?"

"I just worry sometimes. I think back to when I met you and remember all the things you wanted—"

"What did I want?" she cut in to ask in a rhetorical way. "I wanted my own business, but that doesn't mean anything to me now, because I have enough else to do that I don't want the responsibility. I wanted lots of money, and I have it, right in the bank."

"You wanted freedom—"

"Which is just what I've got. You've made me free." The words had slipped out on their own, but she thought about them for a minute, finally saying a soft and knowing, "It's true. I used to think that loving meant being a slave to another human being. But loving you isn't that way at all. You make me feel whole and important and secure. You give me strength to do new things." With a mischievous grin, she said, "I've bloomed."

Chuckling, he moved his hand over the flaming orange tunic that covered her belly. "Just a little, but it's in there."

Covering his hand, she held it fast where it was as she looked up into his eyes. "I'm so excited," she whispered, barely able to contain it.

"Not scared?"

"Sure, scared."

"But you've been a super mom to J.J."

"J.J.'s a big boy." Her eyes took on an added glow. "He's doing so well. I'm so proud of him." The special school he was at—the one John had financed with his share of the profit from Crosslyn Rise—was doing wonderful things for him. He had lots of friends. He was reading, writing, signing, lipreading, even talking in his way. He, too, was blooming. "But a little baby, a little baby is different."

"We'll do it together," John said with quiet confidence. Doing things together was pretty much the story of their marriage, which was another reason why Nina hadn't once felt that she'd given something up in teaming with John. He was an able man, an able father and husband. He had been just as self-sufficient, as she before they'd met, and he could easily be self-sufficient, as could she. The fact that they chose to share whatever load it was they were bearing at a given time, was a tribute to their mutual respect and love.

In the months since they had been married, Nina had done something she had sworn never to do. She had grown dependent—dependent on John for his love. But while once that would have terrified her, it didn't now. She trusted him. She knew beyond a shadow of a doubt that she would always have his love.

Feeling happy and hopeful, if hopelessly smitten with the man holding her, Nina gazed out over the picturesque scene ahead and sighed in utter contentment. "There's something about this place. Carter said it once, and I think it's true. There's something in the air here. Crosslyn Rise is a charm. Look at Carter and Jessica and how happy they are with that beautiful little girl of theirs." She grinned. "I'm glad they bought the unit in the meadow. It's perfect for them."

John kissed the top of her head, then murmured into her hair, "It seems right to have a Crosslyn still here."

"Mmm. Even though they spend weeks at a time with Carter's folks in Florida. I understand it's a fantastic place that Carter bought for them." She took a quick breath. "And speaking of fantastic places, the one Gideon is building in Lincoln is going to be *incredible*—" savvy broker that she was, she couldn't resist tacking on a self-righteous "—even if he did overpay for the land."

"He has the money. Crosslyn Rise did well for him."

"In many respects—money, reputation, love. They're so happy, he and Chris. I love seeing them together."

John flashed his wristwatch in front of her nose. "Is it time?"

She shook her head against his chest. "We have another five minutes." Since the Crosslyn Rise consortium had formally disbanded, the three couples—the Malloys, the Lowes and the Sawyers—had taken to getting together once a month or so. Sometimes it was for dinner, sometimes for a show, sometimes for an evening of general playing at one or another of their homes. On this particular day, they were having an impromptu lunch at one of the small restaurants on the pier. Nina was looking forward to it.

Even more, though, she was looking forward to spending the rest of the day with John. Though he was working full-time in the store now that J.J. was in school, he had arranged to have Minna Larken cover for him that afternoon. Likewise, Nina had scheduled all of her appointments for the morning. So they were free. Nina had her monthly checkup with the doctor, which John refused to miss, but after that they were heading into Boston for several hours of walking and shopping and sipping cappucino in sidewalk cafés. They would pick J.J. up at school on the way home.

It was a wonderful life, Nina mused, and all because of John. Shifting impulsively to face him, she slipped one arm around his neck. "Do you know how much I love you, John Sawyer?"

The question alone was enough to bring pleasure to his face, which, in turn, enhanced hers. "I think so," he answered with a soft half smile, "but I wouldn't mind if you told me again."

She didn't have to. Slipping her other arm around his neck, she gave him a long, breath-robbing, arm-throbbing hug that said it all.

MONTANA MAN

CHAPTER ONE

HE WAS A COWBOY. Lily Danziger wasn't blinded enough by the falling snow to miss the faint bow of his long legs or the telltale Stetson on his head. Nor was she troubled enough by the worsening weather to ignore his sheer size. He was a mountain of a man, wrapped in a sheepskin jacket with its heavy collar up against the wind, and he was flagging her down.

She'd never picked up a hitchhiker before. It was lunacy. Just the week before she'd read that a huge percentage of hitchhikers were wanted by the law for one reason or another.

She didn't want to consider whether this one was wanted, or, if so, for what, because her predicament was precarious, to say the least. She was miles and miles from nowhere; hers was the only car on the road; the driving was getting more difficult with the thickening snow; and she was growing more worried by the minute.

What it boiled down to, she decided in the brief time that elapsed from when she first spotted the cowboy's waving hands to when she gingerly applied the brake, was that she was willing to overlook the danger of taking a stranger into her car in exchange for the small comfort it might bring. She'd been alone for the past eight months, but that aloneness was totally different from what she felt now. If her car slid off the road, there would be no one to see, no one to hear, no one to help.

Except perhaps this cowboy.

Her sporty Audi came to such a slow and muted halt that she half wondered if it was final. The thought didn't help her peace of mind much. Nor did the fact that the cowboy had begun to lope toward her even before she'd stopped.

He tugged at the door handle, then bent over to peer into the car, gave an impatient knock and pointed to the door lock.

For the space of a shaky breath, Lily hesitated. Up close and half-covered with snow, the man looked even more formidable than he had before. She thought of the risk. Then she pushed it from mind, because she couldn't *not* open the door, she realized. Not in as remote and hilly a spot in a storm like this. For humanitarian reasons alone, she had to let him in. He hadn't had his thumb in the air. He'd been waving her down as though something were wrong. Something *had* to be wrong for him to be out there at all.

Reaching across the passenger's seat, she released the lock, then returned to her side and watched him open the door, toss a duffel bag onto the floor in back, brush the worst of the snow from his jacket with hands that looked half-frozen, then fold his large frame into the seat beside hers. With the slamming of the door behind him, she felt the chill he'd brought in. Casting a worried glance toward the back seat, she pulled her own thick parka closer against her neck.

"Thought you were going to change your mind," he muttered in a voice that came from deep in his chest. He alternately rubbed his hands together and held them out toward the nearby heating vent.

"I almost did," she said, hoping that it would serve as a warning that she was on her guard. She couldn't see much beyond the collar of his coat, couldn't see whether his features boded well or ill. "What were you doing out there?"

"Trying to beat the storm, same as you." He tossed his head toward a point beyond the hood of her car. "I might've made it if I hadn't gone off the road."

She had guessed he'd been dropped there by someone else, since she didn't see his car. "You were driving?"

"Is there any other way of passing through this godfor-saken place?"

She thought of horseback, then thought again. "Did you skid?"

He snorted. "Fell asleep at the wheel. My car's nose-down against a tree. There's no hope of getting it back up in weather like this."

Peering harder through the swing of her windshield wipers, Lily finally made out the tail end of a car sticking up in the snow. Its presence vouched for the cowboy's story, and while that relieved her, she couldn't help but stare at the car. It was headed down what looked to be a steep ravine.

"You were lucky there was a tree to stop you."

He grunted. Taking the Stetson from his head, he opened the door again, whacked the snow off the hat, stuffed the hat back on his head and slammed the door. Then he tucked his hands in his pockets and slid a little lower in the seat, looking for all intents and purposes as though he planned to resume the sleep his mishap had disturbed.

To Lily's knowledge, he hadn't looked at her once, which was just fine with her. She didn't need charm and conversation as much as a bodyguard. As out of place as a cowboy was in northern Maine, this one would serve the purpose if she got stuck and needed a push.

Aware that the storm was getting no better, she shifted into gear, carefully pulled back into the center of the road and, gripping the steering wheel with both hands, drove on.

"How long were you out there?" she asked.

He shifted his legs, which were too long for the space allotted them. His voice sounded just as pressed. "Better than an hour."

"And no other cars went by?"

He made a sound that was halfway between a grunt and a dry laugh. She thought he was going to leave it at that when he muttered, "Gotta be mad to drive in weather like this."

Or desperate, Lily thought. She wondered which of the two he was. "Where are you headed?"

"North."

That much was obvious, she thought, and hadn't realized she'd said it aloud until he muttered, "So why did you ask?"

She shot him a short, sharp look and decided that he had a chip on his shoulder, which no doubt accounted for his breadth. And while she wasn't one to tackle chips single-handedly, she'd vowed when she left Hartford that she was going to be strong, and being strong meant sticking up for herself. Though she hadn't had much practice at it, now was as good a time as any to start.

"Because," she said, taking a breath, "I was hoping you'd say you were on your way to Quebec to do something innocent, like visit your mother. From my point of view, that would be preferable to your heading for the Canadian border to escape the State Police or the FBI or the DEA or someone like that."

"I'm not running from the law." He passed off the statement with such utter indifference that Lily believed him.

"*Are* you on your way to see your mother?"

"No."

"A friend?"

"No."

"Then you must be here on business." She wanted to believe it. A business trip was respectable.

"You could say that," he answered, sounding more weary. Tugging his hat low over his eyes, he set his head against the headrest in a silent declaration that he was done talking.

For the time being Lily settled for the little she'd learned. She had her bodyguard if she needed him, though what she needed most just then was to concentrate fully on the road.

She drove on. Ten minutes seemed like twenty, twenty like an hour. The snow continued its steady fall, mounting on the car, the road, the surrounding landscape until things began to blur together. She drove at a slow pace, which was as fast as she safely could, and even then her rear wheels spun out every so often before regaining traction. Her fingers grew tighter on the wheel, then tighter still when a gust of wind rocked the car. Her eyes strained to see the road. She held her breath for long stretches, as though that would enhance her control.

Intermittently she glanced at the man beside her. He seemed to sleep for a while, then waken with a small jolt, then stare out the front window for a bit before falling asleep again. Though she couldn't see much more than his eyes in the narrow strip between his hat and his collar, the way his brows hugged them was ominous.

She wasn't surprised when after the car fishtailed wildly enough to shake him from his sleep, he swore. "Damn car's too light for this kind of travel."

"I'm sorry," she said quietly. "If I'd realized it was going to snow, I'd have taken the dogsled."

Ignoring her sarcasm, he grumbled, "Didn't you hear the forecast?"

"Obviously not."

"So you set out into the woods in the middle of January without a thought to the weather."

"I gave a thought to it. I just didn't know what it was going to be." Not that it would have mattered, she knew. She'd had to get away fast. The weather had been the least of her worries.

"Real smart," he remarked.

Lily was thinking it was a case of the pot calling the kettle black, but she didn't bother to say it. There seemed no point, particularly when driving demanded so much of her attention. If anything, the snow was gusting harder. Her windshield wipers were working double-time, yet the glass never seemed to quite clear.

When the road took a sudden turn, she managed to negotiate it with only a small skid—through which, a nervous glance told her, the cowboy slept. Within minutes she handled another turn, and, to her relief, the car began to descend. She figured the lower altitudes would bring an easing of the snow, and, if not that, certainly a return to some form of civilization. She wasn't asking for a thriving metropolis, just a place to take shelter until the storm passed. She wasn't desperate enough to risk life and limb, yet she seemed to be coming closer to that by the minute.

A small motel would be ideal. In the absence of a motel, she'd happily pay for the use of a compassionate Mainer's spare room. Hell, she'd settle for a gas station, if that was all she'd be able to find. She needed gas, anyway.

Almost incidentally her gaze flicked to the gas gauge. Her eyes widened, then returned to the road with greater intensity. Finding a gas station was suddenly her first priority.

To her dismay there was no sign of a gas station, or any other relic of civilization along the road, and where she would have preferred to coast downhill, she had to keep her foot on the gas to propel the car through the drifts. Worse, with each passing minute, the road seemed to narrow. If she didn't know better, she'd have said she was on a logging road in the middle of a forest.

That was impossible, of course, she told herself. Just to prove it, she fished her road map from a pocket on the door. But she couldn't take her eyes from the road long enough to study it. One false move and she'd find her own car hopelessly ground against a tree.

As though goaded by her thoughts, the Audi suddenly slid sideways on the road. She twisted the wheel in an attempt to stop the slide, but the shoulder of the road had angled. After a glide that was brief and utterly silent in contrast to the uproar inside her, the car came to a jarring halt against a cluster of dense, low-growing pines.

The cowboy awoke with a start.

"No problem," Lily said. Determined to ward off panic, she shifted into reverse and stepped on the gas, shifted back into drive and did the same, then repeated the procedure several times.

"We're not moving," he stated.

"Give me a minute. One of the tires is bound to catch on something."

"Or get buried deeper." He swore, then growled, "Leave it to a woman," and opened his door. "Put it in reverse," he ordered as he climbed out. "I'll push."

Lily was grateful she hadn't had to ask, grateful that he seemed willing to take charge. She readily obeyed him, all the while fighting off the terrifying thoughts that seemed to be rushing headlong her way.

Bracing his hands on the front of her car, the cowboy pushed when she gunned the gas. The car moved a bit, but slid right back to where it had been the instant he let up the pressure. He gestured for her to try again. She did. The car moved a bit more, then a bit more. It was only a matter of time before they were back on the road, she told herself, grasping at fragile threads of hope.

The next time she stepped on the gas, though, the engine sputtered, sputtered some more, then went dead, and those fragile threads snapped. Nervous perspiration beaded on her nose as she repeatedly pumped the gas pedal. She shifted from one gear to the next, praying that anything else was wrong with the car but what she feared.

The passenger's door flew open. "What in the hell's wrong?"

"Nothing's happening!"

He slid into the seat, bringing the snow and cold right

along with him, and promptly leaned sideways to study
the dashboard.

Lily shrank into the far corner of her seat and waited for
his explosion. It didn't take long.

"God*damn*it!" Straightening, he pushed back his hat,
turned to glare at her and said in a voice that was low and
threatening, "You're out of gas."

His voice wasn't all that was threatening. For the first
time, she saw his face, and a darker one she'd never met.
Tension radiated from his features—from the lean line of
his mouth, his straight nose, the low shelf of his brow. His
skin was bronzed, and there were crow's-feet at the corners
of his eyes much as she'd have expected of a man who
spent a good deal of his life squinting against the sun. But
where she'd always assumed cowboys to be mild-
mannered sorts, this one wasn't. His eyes were coal black,
even darker than the hair that had escaped from his hat to
fall in scattered spikes onto his brow. Those coal-black
eyes bore into hers.

"I've been looking for a gas station," she argued in her
own defense, "but there wasn't one."

"Surprise, surprise."

"I've been looking for a long time."

"Not long enough. Don't you know to gas up before you
hit the back roads?"

"I did. I started with a full tank."

"When?"

"This morning."

"Where? New York?"

"Hartford. And I didn't think I was *on* the back roads.
The line on the map was thick and black."

His mouth tightened. "Thick and black. So what did
you think you were seeing out here? Superhighway?
Didn't you begin to wonder when there weren't any other
cars on the road?"

"I assumed that's just how Maine roads are."

He nodded. "You assumed that's how Maine roads are." His voice hardened. "Baby, no main road is like this." He shot a scowl through the windshield. "Where the hell are we, anyway?"

Grateful to have something to do, Lily quickly lifted the map from her lap and studied it. "Here, I think," she said, pointing to a thick black line that undulated through northwest Maine.

"You think wrong," the cowboy informed her, "unless you've managed to cover a hundred miles since you picked me up." They both knew she'd come nowhere near that. "I went off the road right about here." He fixed a lean, blunt-tipped finger on a spot some distance from her thick black line.

"But I wasn't supposed to be there at all," Lily protested. Her voice shrank. "I must have missed a turn."

"You must have missed more than one. That's quite a feat."

"I followed the road. Where it turned, I turned."

"You were supposed to stay on the main drag."

"I thought the turns *were* the main drag. In case you haven't noticed, the visibility's awful!"

"That's because we're surrounded by trees."

He seemed to have an answer for everything. She tried a few of her own. "It's because the storm's worsening. And what were you doing when I made those wrong turns? Maybe if you hadn't been sleeping—"

"Goddamned thing doesn't look like much of a road at all," he decided, ignoring her accusation. He studied what he could of the landscape.

Lily was beginning to tremble. "It has to be. I was following *something*."

"Damned if I know what it was," he growled and speared her with a condemning look. "Damned if I know where we are. Damned if I know how we're gonna be found. You didn't listen to the weather, you didn't get gas, and you didn't bother to stay on the main road. Baby, when you blow it, you really blow it." He sat back in his seat, returning his glare to the window. "Just my luck to be picked up by a spoiled little rich girl."

Lily had never been that in her life. The irony of his thinking it would have made her laugh, if he hadn't followed up with "Fancy car, fancy clothes, fancy face—" he turned his head slowly her way "—and...no...brains."

The tension inside her burst into anger. "I had enough brains to pick you up."

"No brains there. It was a stupid thing to do. You don't know a thing about me. For all you know, I'm a killer."

"If that were true, I'd have been dead by now, and I'm not. So where would you be if I hadn't stopped?"

"In someone else's car, safe and warm and on my way north."

"Or frozen to death by the side of the road."

"It's not that cold."

"Good," she said, raising her head a notch. "Then you can get out of my car and walk. If you're in such a rush to get to wherever it is you're going, be my guest. *Hoof* it. You're not much use to me anyway. You couldn't even push my car out of a rut."

His dark face came closer. "Rut? You call what we're in a rut?"

She refused to back off. "Go on. Get out and walk."

His dark eyes flashed. "You're the one without the brains, lady. Me, I'm a survivor. I don't go out walking lost in the woods in the middle of a blizzard with night closing in."

Her bravado faltered. "Night's not closing in."

"It's dusk."

"No. It's only dark because of the trees."

"It's dusk. Look at the time."

Lily did. "It's not even four-thirty in the afternoon!"

"Dusk *falls* at four-thirty in the afternoon this time of year."

She swallowed. "It can't!"

"You gonna stop it?"

Her mind raced on. "After dusk comes darkness, and once it's dark, we'll be stuck."

"We *are* stuck. When's that gonna sink in?"

She fought it, though her insides were shaking harder. "Stuck in the snow, but—"

"Stuck out here. Lost. Marooned. Isolated. Cut off from the rest of—"

"Maybe you could try pushing again?" she interrupted, begging and not caring that she did.

"But you've got no gas!" he shouted as though he'd decided she was deaf as well as stupid. In frustration, he slammed a fist against the roof. "I don't believe this. I should've stayed with my own car. Better marooned on the road with myself than on some cow path with a woman—" A sound from the back seat cut him off, and he went utterly still. When the sound came again, he glanced sharply around, and when it continued, he managed a low "What in the hell's that?"

Snapped from oncoming panic, Lily was already dropping the back of her seat. When it was as flat as it would go, she climbed over it to the carrier that was safely strapped behind the cowboy. "It's my baby," she said softly and not at all apologetically. If there was one thing she'd done right in her life, it was giving birth to the small bundle that she now lifted into her arms. "It's okay, Nicki," she murmured softly, gently, more calm than she'd been moments before. Settling in directly behind the driver's seat, she eased the baby's snowsuit back from its face and put a slender fingertip to first one side of the infant's tiny mouth, then the other. "Shhh. Mommy's here." The baby quieted like a charm.

Twisted in his seat, the cowboy stared back at her in disbelief. "A baby?"

"Yes."

"You've got a *baby* in this car?"

She shot him a dry look.

His voice rose a notch, horrified, now, as well as disbelieving. "We're stuck in the middle of nowhere, for the night—maybe longer—and you've got a *baby* in this car?"

Ignoring his prediction, she smiled at Nicki. "I do believe that's what I'm holding."

"How can you say it so *calmly*?"

"How can I not?"

"Aren't you worried?"

Her smile was gone when she looked up at him. "I'm terrified. But it won't do any good to let the baby know it—unless you'd like to listen to her scream for a while."

The cowboy dropped a frown to the bundle in pink. "She'll probably do that anyway."

"Not for long. She's a good baby."

"All babies scream."

"She's a good baby," Lily repeated, but no sooner had she said it when the baby began to whimper. "Oh, honey, what's wrong?" she cooed softly. She clicked her tongue several times and began a gentle rocking motion, but the baby's whimpers were soon full-fledged cries.

"She's hungry," he informed her.

Lily turned her back on him. "I know that."

The baby's cries were small, but so was the car. Lily was used to it. Clearly the cowboy wasn't.

"Well, aren't you going to do something about it?" he demanded. His dark eyes looked a little wild. "Don't you have a bottle or something? Christ, you don't even have any way of warming milk! Didn't you think *any* of this out before you left New York?"

"Hartford. I left Hartford."

"Same difference. So what are you going to do about that baby?"

"Feed her," Lily said. Sitting sideways on the seat facing away from him, she pushed aside the layers she'd been unbuttoning, unhooked her bra and put the baby to her breast.

The silence inside the car was sudden and sweet, as was the gentle tugging created by the baby's suckling. Settling the infant more comfortably in her arms, Lily rested her cheek against the velour upholstery. Outside, the snow whipped the world into a wild frenzy, but she closed herself in a small cocoon with her child.

For the longest time the cowboy said nothing. Lily refused to look up, refused to let him intrude on her private time with Nicki. Nor did she want to be made to feel self-conscious. She wasn't in the habit of nursing the baby in front of people, much less strange men. She kept herself safely angled for privacy, and what the position didn't do, the layers of clothes surrounding her did.

Though she wasn't watching, she clearly felt it when the cowboy finally faced forward. He remained silent for a time. She was beginning to wonder what scathing comment he'd come out with next, when he asked, "How old is she?"

His voice was lower, more civil. Responding to that, Lily said, "Five weeks."

After a short pause came a scathing, "How can you subject a five-week-old child to this?"

She knew he was facing front, looking out at the storm. She didn't have to look to feel the wind. "I think," she said quietly, "that we've been through this before. I had no idea the weather was going to get so bad."

"Why didn't you stop somewhere when the snow began to pile up?"

"There was nowhere to stop. I kept thinking that it might be worse if I turned back. For all I knew, the center of the storm was where I'd come from. Besides, I hadn't passed anything alive for miles, so there was nothing to go back to. I figured there had to be something ahead."

"Might've been if you'd stayed on the main road."

Lily didn't respond. She worked her way through the fold-over mitten of the baby's snowsuit and watched the infant's tiny fingers curl around hers. They were so perfect, those fingers, so small, but perfect. So was the little chin, and the button nose, and the soft gray eyes that held hers.

Lily wondered what those eyes saw. The books she'd read said that during the second month of life those eyes would be unfocused when the baby sucked, that the child couldn't actively look and suck at the same time. Lily wasn't sure she believed it. Her baby's eyes were clear, and she could swear they were focused. Of course, it was possible she was simply seeing her own very focused reflection in them.

Her head shot up when the cowboy suddenly opened the door and started to get out. "Where are you going?" she asked quickly.

"I'm taking a look around while there's still some light left." He slammed the door loudly behind him.

"Go ahead," she said lightly, then whispered to the baby, "That's fine. We don't need him in here. Now, if he scouts around and happens upon a bustling logging camp, we'll be forever indebted to him." She gently waved the tiny hand that held hers. "What do you think of that idea, Nicki? Hmm? Sound like an adventure?"

Nicki continued to suck at a steady pace. After a bit Lily looked up and around, searching for sign of the cowboy. But the snow was covering increasingly larger portions of the windows, and, to her horror, the light beyond was indeed growing dim.

For a split second, she imagined the cowboy not returning. She imagined being left alone, totally alone in the woods in the storm with Nicki, and she felt chilled to the bone. A disgruntled bear of a man was better than nothing, she realized.

Swallowing away her fear, she said to Nicki, "Whaddaya think? Think he'll find a logging camp out there?"

Nicki broke the suction of her tiny mouth.

"*Are* there logging camps nowadays?" Lily asked in a deliberate singsong as she raised the baby to her shoulder and gently rubbed her back. "It's the middle of January. Would loggers be working through the dead of the winter? I can't imagine it, but you never can tell." She gave several pats. "He'd better find *something* out there, or we could be in big trouble—"

The baby burped.

"That's my girl," Lily said with a grin and transferred the infant to the cradle of her other arm. Normally she'd have taken a minute or two to play at that point, but she wanted to finish nursing before the cowboy returned.

Nicki began to take her time, though. As her stomach filled, she grew increasingly content—which wasn't to say that she was done. Lily knew from experience that if she forced an end to the feeding, there'd be fussing. That—and a weakening sense of relief—was why she didn't so much as move a muscle when the door opened and the cowboy slid back into the car.

It was a minute before he brushed himself off, another before he fit himself satisfactorily into the seat. Still he didn't speak.

Unable to bear the suspense, Lily finally blurted out, "Did you find anything?"

"Woods," he said without turning.

"No camp?"

Apparently he hadn't shared her fantasy. "Camp?" he asked blankly.

"Settlement. Houses. House, singular."

"No."

Her hopes sank. She looked down at the baby and, for her own comfort as much as the child's began a slow rocking back and forth. "I guess we stay here, then?"

"You guess right." Though his trek through the storm had taken the edge off his anger, his voice remained hard. "Some shelter is better than none. Come morning, when we're guaranteed light, I can go farther looking for help."

"Maybe the snow will have let up by then."

"Maybe."

"Do you think—is there a chance that someone will pass by here?"

His snort was eloquent.

But Lily wasn't quitting. "What if you tried hiking back the way we came? You'd hit the main road and—"

"I'd be lost in the storm long before that."

"Maybe in the morning?" she asked more timidly. She needed something to cling to.

He turned to her quickly, about to speak, then faced front again just as quickly and growled, "How long does that take?"

She knew what he was talking about. She'd felt the same jolt he had when he'd looked back. As irrelevant as it seemed, there was still something about his being a man and her being a woman. "Usually about forty minutes. She's almost done."

"How often does it happen?"

"Every four hours. She goes for a longer period during the night."

Pulling his hat off, he drove a handful of fingers through his hair. "Knowing my luck, she won't this time."

"She will. She has to. And if she doesn't, I'll just feed her more often."

"Great," he muttered under his breath.

Lily studied him. Though the light in the car was growing

dimmer by the minute, she could see that his hair was dark and thick and that though it needed a cutting, the last one had been good. He didn't look unkempt. His jacket and jeans, which was all of his clothing that she could see, looked comfortably worn but clean, and he didn't smell of horse.

Okay, so he was embarrassed when she nursed the baby. There were worse things he could be.

Then again, there weren't many worse situations she could imagine herself in. His earlier words came back to taunt her. In a small, discouraged voice, she repeated them. "I really did blow it, didn't I."

He pushed out a breath. "Yup. Too bad you can't fill up this tank the way you do that kid."

Ignoring his crudeness, she turned her attention to Nicki, who was by now clinging to her nipple for the sake of comfort alone, rather than the nourishment. "All done?" she asked softly. Disengaging the baby's mouth, she put the child to her shoulder, alternately rubbing and patting her back until she'd bubbled. Then, righting her own clothes, Lily tucked her close to her warmth.

"Would you turn the car on for a minute, please?" she asked.

The cowboy looked back and, seeing that she'd finished nursing, held her gaze this time. "What for?"

"Heat. I know it'll drain the battery but—"

He looked like he wanted to laugh but wasn't sure how. "You won't get any heat out of this car. Not without gas."

"Sure, I will. Try it. Turn the key."

"If I turn the key," he said in a slow and tempered voice, "The fan will go on. Just the fan. By now the engine will have cooled off. You won't get a thing but cold air, probably colder than what's in here now."

Refusing to believe that, Lily held his dark-eyed gaze. "Try."

"It'll be counterproductive."

"Try anyway."

He did. Within seconds, cold air was blowing from the vents. She had enough time to extend the fingers of her free hand to discover just how cold that air was before he turned off the fan.

"You were right," she said in a small voice.

"Naturally." He faced front.

"Are you always right?"

"Usually."

"No modesty there," she softly told Nicki. "Too bad he fell asleep while I was driving. If he'd been paying attention to where I was going, we wouldn't be in this mess."

"I thought you admitted you were the one who blew it," came the grim voice from the front.

"I think I'd rather share the blame." She felt the weight of responsibility on her shoulders, and if he was going to be arrogant about it, he could just take a little of that weight.

The only problem was that aside from getting nervous about the baby, he struck her as a competent man. There was a firmness to his voice and a directness to his eyes. While she started to shake each time she thought about what lay ahead, he was calmer. Annoyed, yes, and disdainful of her, but calmer. She guessed he was a practical man, and, just then, with the snow blowing and night falling, a little practicality was in order.

"What do we do now?" she asked.

"Nothing."

"We just sit here?"

"And try to keep warm." He turned to scan the back seat. When he had trouble seeing what he wanted, he went front toward the glove compartment. "Have you got a flashlight in here?"

"I…no."

He slammed the cover and sat still in his seat. She didn't doubt for a minute what he was thinking. But she'd never in her life had use for a flashlight in her car, and there'd been no way she could have known she'd need one now.

Feeling more inadequate than ever, she asked, "Do you want to turn on the overhead light?"

"Not until we're desperate. The battery will only last so long." He turned to her. "Our major worry is warmth. Since we won't get any from the engine, we'd better start thinking about substitutes. I don't know what you've got stashed back there, or in the trunk, but if you've got anything we can use, we'd better get it now. It's gonna be pitch-black before long."

The thought of things being pitch-black sent a shiver through Lily. She tried to concentrate on all she'd packed into the trunk of the car. "The diaper bag is back here. There are lots of clothes in the trunk—mine, and the baby's."

"Baby clothes won't keep us warm."

"There's an afghan." It was the last thing her mother had made her. She hadn't been about to leave it behind. "And two heavy coats. One of them is a fur." On principle alone, she hadn't been about to leave that behind.

"Ah, the advantages of wealth," the cowboy murmured as he reached for the keys, but Lily stopped him.

"You can only do it from in here." Holding Nicki tightly to her, she came forward, barely managing to wedge open the door on the driver's side enough to flip the trunk release on the side panel. She slammed the door as fast as she could, but not before snow fell into the car. "Hell," she whispered, brushing snowflakes from the baby's face.

The cowboy was already out, wading through the snow toward the trunk. Covering Nicki as snugly as she dared, Lily returned the infant to her carrier and scrambled over the seats after him.

Cold nuggets of snow hit her the instant she got outside, and she sank knee-deep. Without a thought to the fine leather of her boots, she pulled up her hood and, head-down, worked her way to the back.

The cowboy was standing by the open trunk trying to figure out what was where. Within seconds Lily had her hands on the two coats and the afghan, all of which had been tucked around her suitcases. He took them from her and quickly deposited them in the car. Under the faint illumination of the trunk light, they soon had their arms filled with the heaviest and warmest of the clothes Lily had brought.

"Any food back here?" he yelled above the wind.

She shook her head and headed around the car. By the time she'd tossed in what she carried and climbed in herself, Nicki was whimpering again, and Lily knew why. Wet diapers had a way of upsetting even the most peaceful of babies. Pushing aside the clothes she'd been carrying, she set about remedying the problem.

It broke her heart to have to expose the baby's skin to the chill, to see the tiny legs shake and touch the baby's new, paper-thin skin with her cold hands. The darkness didn't help. Nor did the setup in the car, which was a far cry from the convenience of the white wicker dressing table she'd had for the baby in Hartford. Fumbling around when necessary, she worked as quickly as possible, all the while crooning sweet nothings to Nicki and trying not to think that this could be the best it would be for a while.

The cowboy, meanwhile, made several more trips to the trunk. By the time he climbed into the front and closed the door behind him, there was a mountain of clothing on the driver's seat. Lily didn't realize how much he'd carted in until she had Nicki put back together and snugly zipped into her snowsuit.

"What have you *got* there?" she cried.

"Insulation," was his succinct response. He lowered the back of his seat and reached for the baby carrier. "How does this thing come undone?"

"Why?"

He paused in his groping to look at her. Though his face

was shadowed, his tone left little to the imagination where his opinion of her intelligence was concerned. "If I can move it, I can get back there and stuff clothes under the window. In case you haven't realized it yet, the longer we sit here, the colder it's going to get. This car may be state-of-the-art chic, but it ain't gonna keep us warm for long without heat. So we need insulation. Understand?"

Lily did and was annoyed at herself for not anticipating what he had in mind. To compensate, she reached down and released the seat belt that held the carrier in place. Once the bulky piece was wedged between the two front seats, she set Nicki in it and began helping line the back window, then the seams of the doors and the front windows with shirts, skirts, slacks and sweaters. She was grateful for the activity. Not only did it warm her up, but it kept her mind off the reality of what was to come.

Too soon, the cowboy muttered, "That'll have to do." Curving his spine to the back seat, he extended his long legs over the lowered front.

Nightfall had further darkened the interior of the car, but Lily's eyesight adjusted to some extent. Sitting back on her heels, she looked around. The afghan, the coats, several sweaters and the baby things were dark blurs on the driver's seat and in the hollows before the two front seats. She dragged the afghan back to where she was, then reached for Nicki. With the child in her arms, she pulled the afghan up chest-high and made herself as comfortable as possible in her own corner of the back seat.

Outside, the snow swirled relentlessly. Lily listened for a bit, rocked Nicki for a bit, tried to imagine the future when she might look back on this experience and laugh. Laughter of any sort was hard to imagine now. Her sense of optimism seemed to be hovering, not sure which way to go.

She glanced at the cowboy. "What do you think?"

He didn't answer at first, and when he did, his voice was

low and tight. "About what?" He had his head back and his eyes closed.

"Can we make it?"

"We have to."

"I know that, but can we?"

"If we're lucky."

"Lucky how?"

"If the snow stops before too long. If it doesn't get too cold after that. If someone sees my car and starts wondering—"

"Were you expected somewhere?" Lily asked hopefully. "Will someone be looking for you when you don't show?"

He killed her hope with a short, deep "Nope," turned his head against the seat back and opened his eyes. "How about you?"

She shook her head.

"No one?" he asked.

Again she shook her head.

"What about the kid's father?"

"He's not in the picture."

The cowboy's gaze pierced her through the darkness. "You just got knocked up for kicks?"

"No, I—"

"—had the hots for a married man and didn't stop to think of birth control."

"No, I—"

"—wanted a baby. Didn't want a husband."

"*No*. I *was* married. I'm just not anymore."

"But you have a five-week-old child. Surely the father knows about it and is going to worry when you don't show up somewhere."

"He knows about the baby. But he won't worry. He doesn't know where we are, where we're going or what we're doing. He doesn't want us any more than we want him."

The cowboy stared at her. Lily refused to look away, but she felt as though she were being skewered. Clearly he was wondering what was wrong with her that her husband would divorce her when she was pregnant. It was a typically male way of thinking. Lord, she was tired of it.

"We wanted different things," she finally said when she could take no more of his silent scrutiny.

"So you took the car, the fur and the kid."

"And my clothes. And the afghan my mother made me. And what little was left of my pride." There were other things she'd taken, but she saw no need to enlighten the cowboy further.

"Then this is the big escape?" he asked with dawning awareness. "You're not just off to see someone or take a vacation?"

"It'll be a long time before I take a vacation, and there's no one I want to see," she said and for an instant regretted her forthrightness. But she pushed her regrets aside. Nothing about the cowboy had suggested that he'd hurt her. She had no reason to believe him to be evil.

Of course, he was a man, and she wasn't thinking too highly of men as a group just then. Then again, she didn't have to like him. All she had to do was weather his company until they found a way out of the mess they were in.

The cowboy straightened his head and closed his eyes.

"Are you going to sleep?"

"Might as well."

"Whenever you go to sleep, something happens. First your car went off the road and then—"

"I'm tired."

"You must be, to have fallen asleep at the wheel in the middle of the day."

"I've been up for nearly thirty-six hours straight getting this far."

"Where did you start?"

"Montana."

"Where are you headed?"

He was quiet. Lily wondered if he'd fallen asleep when his voice came to her, deep and slow. "New York, I thought, but when I got to New York, they said Boston, and when I got to Boston, they said Quebec." He yawned. "If I don't find what I'm looking for in Quebec, I'm goin' home."

She was surprised that he'd said as much. He'd been more laconic until then, keeping personal things personal. Perhaps, she decided, he realized the impossibility of privacy in their situation. Or perhaps her opening up had inspired a little in him. Or perhaps it was simply fatigue, doing in his defenses.

Whichever the case, she wanted to take advantage of it. "What are you looking for?" she asked.

But he didn't answer.

"Are you asleep?" she whispered loudly.

"Almost."

"You won't tell me what you're looking for?"

"Not now," he murmured sleepily.

"What if you fall asleep and freeze to death?"

"You'll wake me before that."

"What if *I* fall asleep and freeze to death?"

"The kid will wake you before that."

"What if she freezes first?"

"Wrap her inside your coat and she won't. You've got body heat. Use it."

His suggestion was a good one, particularly since Lily had a canvas carrier tucked into the diaper bag. By strapping Nicole to her chest, zippering her own coat around them both and covering them with the afghan and a coat, she stood a fair chance of keeping the baby warm.

Not that she was moving just yet. The baby was happily clutching her finger, and the air inside the car was far from frigid. But it was a good thought for the future.

On its heels came another thought. "Is there any chance of our asphyxiating closed in here like this?"

The cowboy didn't answer.

"Uh...excuse me...are you still awake?"

"Barely," came the deep, distant voice.

"Did you hear what I asked?"

"Mmm." He paused, then mumbled, "No gas, no fumes."

She breathed a sigh of relief. "That's good."

"I'm goin' to sleep now. Can you keep still?"

Lily wasn't sure she wanted to keep still. Talking, hearing the sound of her voice, hearing the sound of his was a comfort in the dark. But he was exhausted. Thirty-six hours was a long time to go without sleep. She had to respect his needs if she wanted him to respect hers.

"I'll be quiet," she agreed softly. After no more than a minute, though, she said, "What's your name?"

"I thought you were going to be still?"

"I will. Tell me your name first. That way I can wake you before you freeze."

He was quiet for a very long time. Watching him, Lily could have sworn that his eyes were open for part of that time. At the end, though, they were closed and his breathing was low and even. She was about to give up on him when he said, "Quist."

"Excuse me?"

"The name's Quist."

"Quist?"

"Mmm."

She'd never heard anything like it, didn't even know whether it was a first name or a last name, but when she would have asked, he suddenly shifted, turning away from her.

She let him be. It was only fair, she reasoned. Besides, if luck was on their side, morning would come and with it rescue, and she would never need to know anything more than that the man she'd been stranded with for a night in the snow was Quist from Montana.

CHAPTER TWO

QUIST CAME AWAKE to a strange sound. At least, it was strange until he got his bearings. There had never been a baby in his life, not of the human variety. He'd had his share of experience with newborn calves, colts and fillies, dogs, cats and the occasional bear, but he'd been spared the joy of human squalling until now.

Opening his eyes to the darkness, he looked around, remembered where he was and why, and slowly turned his head. Though the woman had her back to him, the car wasn't large enough to separate them by much, particularly since they were both stretched out from the back seat forward. If he moved his arm, it would brush her shoulder.

He didn't move his arm.

She was shushing the baby, but the baby had a mind of its own and kept crying while she started fiddling under the afghan. Then came the silence, as abrupt as it had been earlier, and Quist knew she was nursing the child.

He wasn't sure why that made him uncomfortable, and he wasn't about to brood on it, but it did.

He hadn't thought she'd be the type to nurse. Nursing babies was for women who were willing to be tied to home and hearth for months, and he wouldn't have pegged her that way. She looked rich. He guessed that her sporty red car was no more than a year old, that her hip-length turquoise-and-white parka had a designer label inside, that her boots were imported, that her pencil-slim jeans cost three times as much as one pair of his functional Levi's.

Besides that, she didn't look hardy enough to nurse a child, let alone give birth to one. Thanks to the bulky parka, he hadn't been able to see much, but what he'd seen looked small. Her face was slender, her features delicate. Her legs were slim. And standing, as she'd done for a brief time by his side when they were digging things from her trunk, the top of her head hadn't reached his shoulders.

There was a fragility to her. He kept thinking about how she'd gone through childbirth only five weeks before. Her body had to still be recovering. And beyond the physical was the emotional. She might be calm with the baby, but she meant it when she said she was terrified. He'd seen it in her eyes, even when she tried to keep her voice calm.

She had every right to be frightened. They were lost in the woods in an area that very possibly hadn't seen traffic in years. If the situation were different, just him and her, they could stay with the car until the snow ended, then bundle themselves up and hike back toward the main road, even if it meant several days' exposure to the cold.

But he wasn't sure how far she'd make it in the snow, and then there was a baby involved. A five-week-old infant couldn't survive exposure like that. So the options were limited and the responsibility greater, none of which pleased him.

He wanted to be in Montana, not Maine. He wanted to be back home on the ranch, which he knew and loved. He worked hard there, but the work made sense. There was an order to it. Emergencies cropped up all the time, but he could deal with them. He could deal with most anything on his own turf.

This was something else entirely. But then, women had always been the bane of his existence. He doubted that was ever going to change.

"Quist?" came a whisper from the edge of the afghan. He grunted.

"We woke you, didn't we?" She paused. "I'm sorry. I settled her as soon as I could, but everything's so dark that I had to fumble around." She paused again. "It's still snowing."

That figured. He didn't expect things to get easy all of a sudden. They were bound to get worse before they got better, and worse, at that moment, meant colder. His feet were feeling the drop in temperature in the car.

Sitting forward, he thought of the advantages of being car-bound with someone rich as he reached for the fur coat and wrapped it around his lower half.

"My boots got wet when I went outside," Lily said quietly. "They're still damp. I wasn't sure whether I'd have been warmer if I'd taken them off. You left yours on, so I figured I'd do the same."

"Are you cold?"

"I'm okay."

"What does that mean?"

"It means that I'd be a lot more comfortable if we could build a fire in here, but that I don't think I'm on the verge of frostbite yet."

"How's the baby?"

"She's all bundled up. It's a miracle I can find her under the hat and hood and snowsuit. I've kept her inside my coat, like you told me to. She's still pretty warm."

Quist looked at his wristwatch, then burrowed more deeply into his coat.

"What time is it?" Lily asked.

"Almost ten."

She moaned. "I feel like I've been sitting here forever. I was sure it had to be at least one or two in the morning."

"Time flies when you're having fun."

His sarcasm went right by her. "I want morning to come. I don't like the dark."

"Did you sleep?"

"Uh-uh. I'm too nervous." She'd spent the time since he'd fallen asleep imagining any number of possible scenarios for the next twenty-four hours. Most of them were depressing.

"Are you hungry?"

"Starved. I was waiting for you to wake up to eat."

That brought Quist slowly around. "You have food?"

"Leftovers from lunch. There's a bag on the floor on my side. Can you reach it?" She would have done it herself if Nicki hadn't been so comfortable, attached to her breast.

When he leaned over to feel around on the floor, the side of his head touched her thigh. Though she was covered not only by jeans, but by the afghan and her coat, she still felt a moment's awkwardness, which was probably why she began to talk more quickly.

"There was a Burger King on the highway. I stopped there to use the rest room and change Nicki, and I figured that I had to get something, even though I wasn't very hungry." When he straightened with the bag in his hand, she felt a little less crowded. "I don't think there's more than half a hamburger, a few fries and some cookies, and they're probably rock hard by now, but they're better than the rest of the food this airline's serving."

Quist snickered.

"If you don't mind my germs" she added.

Germs were the least of his worries. Removing the contents of the bag, he laid them out on the empty baby carrier.

Lily eyed the dim shapes. "I suppose it's lucky we can't see. We might think twice about eating."

"Not much chance of that," he said, but he made no move to take any of the food.

"I'm sorry there isn't more. I should have ordered a whole lot, but I never dreamed dinner would be a problem."

Neither had Quist, and as he stared at the meager spread,

he couldn't help but wonder how many dinners in the
future would be a problem. Reaching to the floor on his
own side this time, he tugged out his duffel, opened it and
rummaged around inside. He set down several foil cubes
beside the Burger King remains, rummaged again and
came up with several more.

Lily couldn't make out details in the dark. "What are
they?"

"Chunky bars."

"Chunky bars?" Her voice rose. "I haven't had a
Chunky in years!"

"Don't get excited. We'll have to ration them, too. It
may be a while before we get our hands on anything more."

"Ration. Right."

"It's a sensible thing to do, isn't it?"

"Sure. Ooops—okay, Nicki," she said softly as she lifted
the infant to her shoulder. She put her mouth to the baby's
cheek and began to pat her back, breathing, "That's my girl.
What an angel you are. Got a bubble in there for me?"
Stopping her patting for a minute, she groped in the diaper
bag, which was jammed between her leg and the side of
the car. Coming up with a cloth diaper, she slid it between
the baby and her shoulder. "Just in case," she murmured
under her breath and started patting again.

"In case what?" Quist asked.

"In case she cheeses on my shoulder. It smells vile."

"Oh. Great. By all means, then, take the precaution. The
last thing we need in here is something that smells vile."

Lily bit her lower lip, wondering what he was going to
do when she changed certain diapers. In that respect she
was grateful Nicki was so young. Even the worst smells
weren't all that bad. Of course, that was easy for Lily to
say. Nicki was flesh of her flesh.

Nuzzling the infant's cheek, she found pleasure in the
sweet baby scent that lingered even now from her morning

bath. How long ago that seemed, a world away. That sweet scent would disappear, she knew, if they didn't somehow get help. Thought of Nicki going without a warm bath, without lotion and powder and clean clothes disturbed her. Oh, she had the lotion and powder and clean clothes with her, but there was no way she was going to undress the infant for other than the quickest diaper change. It was too cold.

Quist interrupted her grim musings. "The only thing here with protein is the hamburg. I think you should have half now and save the rest for tomorrow."

"Me? What about you? Don't you want some?"

"I can do with the other stuff."

"But you said it yourself—this is the only thing with protein. There's none in the other stuff."

"You need it more. You're the one who's eating for two."

"That was when I was pregnant. Nicki eats for herself now."

"What—hamburg? French fries?"

"Uh, not quite."

"Exactly," he said, annoyed that she was making him spell it out. "She drinks milk. Does she eat anything solid yet?"

"No."

"So milk is it, and you're the only milkman around here, which means you need that protein more than I do."

"But you're the one who's going out in the snow tomorrow looking for help."

"I'll be fine."

"You may be walking for miles."

"I'm in shape."

"To go through a blizzard?"

"I'm not going through a blizzard. I'm not budging unless the snow stops."

"What if it doesn't" Lily asked. She tried to keep her voice steady, though it was higher than before. "What if it keeps on for two or three days—or more? What if four or five feet pile up out there? I've read of that happening in the North, and we're pretty far north. What if—"

Nicki burped. Lily held the breath she'd been about to expel, then released it slowly.

"It won't do either of us any good to worry about *what if*s," Quist said, using an assured voice in the hope of calming her. "The fact is that for now, we're okay. We have shelter and a little food. We'll make that last as long as possible and then worry. One thing at a time. Okay?"

Lily wished she could see his face, but it was too dark, so she had to put her faith in the low command of his voice. "Okay," she whispered, then added, "I'm sorry. I try to be strong, but it doesn't work sometimes."

Her whisper, and the words she said, did strange things to Quist. Something stirred inside him, something like compassion. It was totally uncharacteristic and entirely unwanted, but he felt a definite softening. He guessed it was her honesty. At least he thought it was honesty. It had been so long since he'd connected honesty with a woman that he wasn't quite sure whether to buy it or not.

"Take the hamburg," he insisted crossly and thrust it in her direction.

"Let me finish with Nicki first."

"I thought you were starved."

"I am, but another fifteen minutes won't hurt."

"Can't you eat and nurse at the same time?"

"Yes, but then I'd be diluting each of the pleasures."

He put the hamburg down again and drawled, "And you're a lady who likes her pleasures."

Vaguely stung by his sarcasm, Lily said, "Certain ones more than others. Nursing Nicki is the best. It's the most rewarding experience I've ever had in my life, and the most innocent pleasure in the world. It's a time when there's just the two of us, and we're both doing what we were made to do. While I'm nursing, I like to give her my undivided attention. So why should I eat? It's not like I have a whole list of things to do when she's done."

That said, she transferred Nicki to her other arm, tucked her inside her coat and began the second half of the feeding.

Quist took several of the fries, slouched back into his side of the car and began to eat them slowly, one by one.

"And anyway," Lily's voice came through the darkness after several minutes, "there haven't been as many pleasures in my life as you think. I've earned everything I have."

"You work?"

"Every woman works."

He grunted. "In some form or another." He was thinking of Belinda McClean and the horizontality of her occupation. Not that he was a hypocrite. He'd enjoyed Belinda plenty and had paid her well. Then she'd gotten greedy and had blown the arrangement to bits. But that had been years ago. Ancient history.

Lily coupled his muttered comment with something else he'd said. "You don't like women, do you?"

"I don't trust women. They're only out for themselves."

"I could say the same about men."

"Then you've just met the wrong ones."

"Maybe. And maybe the same is true with you and women."

"I doubt it. In forty years, I've seen lots of women come and go, and not one of them's been able to change my mind."

Given the iron beneath his words, Lily had no doubt that he fully believed what he said. "That's very sad."

"No, it's very smart. I know what to expect and what not to. I go through life with my eyes wide open. Wide open." Having issued what he felt to be an adequate warning, he fell silent. But something was nagging at him. After several minutes, he gave in to that nagging. "So what *do* you do to get paid so well?"

"I never said I was paid well. I said I've earned everything I have."

"Did you earn the car? The clothes?" He'd seen quite a few of those clothes when they'd been taking things from the trunk, and everything he'd touched had been top-notch.

"Every last piece," she said with conviction.

"How?"

"By making a warm, welcoming home for a man who took every possible opportunity to put me down. By cooking for him, only to be told that the meat was tough—and cleaning for him, only to be told that the professional service did it better—and dressing up for him, only to be told that the particular color I'd worn made me look sick. By being there when he needed me, then having to stand by and watch when he decided he needed someone else." She caught a quick breath. "He was never particularly generous. Maybe he was just distrustful, like you. Maybe he felt that I was out to take him for whatever I could get, so that made him cautious. But what he gave me, I earned. So help me, I did."

Her voice hung in the silence of the car for a minute, then dropped, leaving nothing but the sounds of the storm to fill the void. Listening to the elements' anger, she was drained of her own. After several minutes she breathed out a small, rueful laugh.

"So much for giving Nicki my undivided attention." She pressed a gentle kiss on the infant's forehead, and said in a soft breath, "Forgive me, Nicki? I think it's the darkness that brings out the demons. Either that, or I just need to hear the sound of someone's voice, even if it's my own. I'll be better from now on. I promise I will."

True to her word, she spent the rest of the feeding doing all the little things, some vocal, some not, that told Nicki how much she was loved. And through it all, Quist sat and listened. There was more he wanted to ask, but he couldn't get himself to interrupt. Strangely, though he'd felt uncomfortable earlier, he suddenly wanted to turn on the overhead light for a minute. He wanted to see the lady beside him. She was taking on a personality, shaped by voice and words, but there was an unreality to it in the darkness.

He waited until she'd put the baby to her shoulder again. Then he asked, "How old are you?"

The question surprised her. She hadn't thought he'd care one way or another how old she was. But she had no big secrets on that score. "Twenty-nine."

In turn, that surprised him. He'd have guessed she was younger. "How long were you married?"

"Four years."

"And he just walked off with someone else and left you with a newborn child?"

"Oh, no. He left me the day I told him I was pregnant. He said I'd plotted it just to keep him." She pressed her cheek to the baby's and whispered, "As though I hadn't wanted you all along. I'd been trying all that time to get pregnant and he knew it." She spoke up again for Quist. "He thought I knew he'd been fooling around, the jackass. I wouldn't have put up with that." Her voice fell, though this time not for the baby's sake. She'd thought long and hard about what might have been, and each time she had doubts. "Then again, maybe I would have. If he'd said that his thing with Hillary was a mistake and that it was over, I might have stayed. I'm not sure I would have been able to believe him, but I did want the marriage to work."

"Why?"

That was harder to answer, because it went beyond self-doubt. Lily knew what her weaknesses were, and she wasn't proud of them. Not even cover of darkness—or the fact that Quist was a stranger—made it easy to confess. "Oh, lots of reasons," she murmured, but said no more.

He let it go, mainly because he didn't feel he had a right

to pry further. The reasons why she'd wanted her marriage to work had no bearing on their present predicament. As to that predicament, all he needed from her was a little cooperation, and he felt sure he'd get that. What they *both* needed was a little luck.

Finishing off the last of the few fries he'd allotted himself, he listened to the wind and wondered about his luck. Actually he'd had his share. He had the ranch, which he'd won in a card game twenty-one years before. He'd been nineteen and brash as all get-out then, and though he hadn't known what in the hell to do with two hundred acres of land, three ramshackle buildings, a small herd of cattle and two aging cowhands, he'd known enough to take advantage of the windfall. Working his tail off and learning as he worked, he turned the ranch around, eventually adding to the acreage, the buildings, the herd and the crew. Sure, hard work had been most of it, but he'd had certain breaks, too. He'd lucked out more than once when it came to contacts and timing and deals, health and weather.

He sure as hell hadn't lucked out with women, though.

"I take it you're not married," Lily said. Much as she tried, she couldn't put the discussion to rest.

"You take right."

"Have you ever thought about being married?"

"Nope. Never even came close."

"I mean, have you ever imagined yourself being married and thought about what it would be like?"

"No."

"Never thought about how you'd handle it, how you'd react to some things as a husband?"

"Never."

Since she wasn't getting the answers she wanted, she turned her attention to Nicki. "Where's that bubble?" she whispered gently. She brushed her lips across the infant's forehead, then ran a thumb over her cheek and would have repeated the gesture if her hands hadn't been so cold. Tugging the sleeves of her jacket over them, she began rubbing firm, flat-handed circles over the baby's back. Several rounds of that brought a soft burp from the small bundle. Lavishing whispered praise, she righted her clothes and returned the baby to the crook of her elbow.

Quist propped a foot on the gear shift. "Why do you ask?"

"Ask what?"

"About marriage." There had been three questions, one right after the next, all about the same thing. He wanted to know why.

"Oh, I was just wondering about something, but if you've never imagined what married life would be like, there's no point in my asking."

"Ask."

"No. I think not."

"Why?"

"Because you don't like women, so I know just what you'll say."

"That's one of the things I like *least* about women. They think they know it all." He raised his voice. "You don't know me. How can you know what I'll say?"

Annoyed that he was making something out of nothing, she burst back, "All I wanted to know was whether you thought Jarrod was right. If you got married, if you took vows and promised to be faithful, would you turn around and cheat on your wife? Do all men do it? Is there some justification for it that I'm missing? I mean, I took those vows seriously. Am I the one marching to a different drummer? Is that my problem? Am I misinterpreting the rules of the game?"

Quist didn't know what to say. She was clearly hurt, but he was no healer.

"And it wasn't only Jarrod," she went on, as though once started she couldn't hold it in. "It was loads of guys we knew. I always heard women talk about this one or that one who was fooling around. No one ever named Jarrod in front of me, and I was never sure whether to believe them about the others until Jarrod told me, and even *then* I might have thought he was exaggerating, trying to okay what he'd done by claiming all the guys were doing it, until Michael came on to me. *Michael*. Jarrod's own *broth- er*—"

Only after she'd said it did she realize what she'd done. Breathing hard, she buried her face by Nicki's until she'd regained a bit of control. Then she raised her head enough to be able to speak clearly—softly, but clearly.

"I'm sorry. I got carried away. It's history—water over the dam. There isn't a lot I can do about what happened. But it still hurts. I guess I'm still pretty angry."

Quist could believe that. But he wasn't about to pass judgment, to say whether or not she had a right to that anger, because he'd only heard one side of the story. For all he knew, the innocent-sounding little mother huddled close by had been a shrew of a wife. For all he knew, she was a lousy lover, or, conversely, a pathological liar who hadn't taken her marriage vows half as seriously as she'd like him to believe. For all he knew, she'd been feeding him a line of bull.

He didn't think so, but what the hell, he didn't even know her name. It was, he realized, time to change that.

"Who are you?"

"Excuse me?"

"Your name—you never told me what it was."

She was silent for a minute. He was starting to think that she did indeed have something to hide, when she laughed. It was a soft, self-conscious sound. "I don't believe it. I just dumped all the sordid little details of my marriage in your lap, and you don't even know my name."

"Well?"

"Lily. Lily Danziger."

"Is Danziger your—"

"Maiden name. Nicki's birth certificate reads Danziger, too." Her voice hardened. "Jarrod didn't want any part of us, and the feeling's mutual."

"What about child support?"

"What about it?"

"Don't you want any money?"

"No."

"Don't you *need* any money? I hear raising a kid is expensive these days."

"It's always been expensive, but people manage."

"How will you? Do you have money of your own?"

"I'm not independently wealthy, no."

"Then you must've got a great divorce settlement."

"Why do you say that?"

"Because it makes sense," he said, and because he was naturally cynical when it came to women. "The guy you married has money—he leaves you for another woman the day you tell him you're pregnant—you go through the pregnancy all by yourself and give birth to the child alone. I mean, it's a tear-jerker."

"I don't hear you crying."

He snorted. "I'm not."

"You're just a hard-as-nails kind of guy."

His voice took on the hard-as-nails sound she'd heard so much of at the start. "I'm a survivor. I do what I have to do, say what I have to say, feel what I have to feel."

"And you're out for number one, just like Jarrod."

"Lady, if I was out for number one, I wouldn't have offered to share my Chunky bars with you."

"It's Lily, not lady," she huffed, "and you can keep your damned Chunky bars. I wouldn't eat them, anyway."

"Why not?" he asked, vaguely affronted.

"Because if I eat chocolate while I'm nursing, the baby is apt to get diarrhea."

"Oh."

"Yes, oh." With that, she turned her back on him, making herself as comfortable as possible with Nicki safely tucked inside her coat. She didn't want to talk to Quist anymore. He annoyed her. So she half sat, half lay on her side of the car with her hooded head pressed to the wool slacks she'd used to line the window.

The wind blew. She tried not to hear it, tried not to hear the hard nuggets of snow that swirled with it, hitting small bared patches of the car. She tried not to think about the cold that had settled in her hands and feet and threatened to spread, and she tried not to think about the future. Mostly she tried not to cry, which was what she really wanted to do. She'd been wanting to do it a lot lately, and it had nothing to do with a snowstorm. It had to do with facing a future that was unknown and daunting. It had to do with feeling very alone and very frightened.

Quist, too, listened to the storm, but his eyes were on her huddled form, trying to make sense of it in the darkness. He didn't know why he bothered, didn't know why he didn't just turn over and go back to sleep. He was still exhausted, but he wasn't as cold as he figured she was, and that made him feel bad.

She seemed so damned fragile. He wanted to think her irresponsible when it came to driving, lousy when it came to keeping a husband and greedy when it came to getting rid of one—still, she seemed fragile. And if there was one thing he had to hand her, she seemed like a devoted mother.

Which was a hell of a lot more than his own had been, he mused, then broke into his musings when he heard a strange sound. It wasn't the baby, at least he didn't think it was.

He held his breath for a minute and listened, then cautiously said, "Lily?"

There was a pause, then a muted, "Mmm?"

He waited, trying to hear the sound again, but it didn't come. "Are you all right?"

After another pause, she said, "I'm fine."

Sitting up, he reached forward and switched on the overhead light.

Lily's head came around fast. She didn't have to squint; the light was too small for that. But it wasn't small enough to hide the tears that pooled on her lower lids—or the defiance behind those tears.

"Don't you dare say a word," she warned, eyes glittering. "Don't you dare tell me that I'm weak or that there's something wrong with me—because I'm tired of hearing it."

He hadn't been about to say either of those things. He'd been about to swear, because tears usually meant that a woman wanted something, and he didn't have a damn thing to give just then. But he decided that swearing wasn't such a good idea, either. It would only upset her, and he didn't want her upset. It wouldn't help the situation.

"I just wanted to make sure you eat," he said. He picked up the half hamburger and held it out. "Like I said, you're the only one who can feed the kid."

The sight of the cold sandwich reminded Lily of how hungry she was. "Can you tear it in half?" she asked. When he'd done it, she took one of the two pieces. "Are you sure you won't have the other?"

"I'm sure."

"If you want it later, you can have it."

But he shook his head. He felt guilty enough about eating the few fries he had, since she wouldn't share his candy. So what was hers was hers. He'd still give her a Chunky if she changed her mind—and it might come to that if the choice were between some milk and no milk—but he wasn't taking any more of her food. She needed it.

Setting the uneaten quarter hamburger on the carrier with the rest of the food, he turned off the light again and sat back. He could feel Lily beside him, eating slowly. He couldn't hear whether her breathing was even—the wind made that hard—but at least he didn't hear another gasp or swallow or whatever the hell it had been. He didn't want her crying. He didn't like women at all, but women who cried were the worst.

On that thought he closed his eyes, slid lower on the seat and went to sleep.

When he awoke, it was six-thirty in the morning, dawn was just beginning to break and Lily was feeding the baby. He wasn't at all where he wanted to be, which put him instantly on his guard and made him cross. He would have complained that the infant's cries had woken him if it were true. But he couldn't remember hearing the baby. He'd been exhausted. Though he'd gone with little sleep many a time back home, the sheer frustration of this trip had taken the toll that physical strain rarely did.

Now there was physical strain, too. Gingerly he stretched muscles that were stiff from the unnatural position he'd slept in and from the cold.

Feeling his movement, Lily peered around the hood of her parka. She was relieved that he'd awakened to face the day with her, but Jarrod's dark early-morning moods had conditioned her to caution.

Quist had never awoken to a woman's stare before. "Something wrong?" he demanded in an edgy voice.

"No."

"Why are you looking at me that way?"

Quickly she looked away, toward where Nicki was nursing under the afghan. "No reason." She took a fast breath. "The wind is down, but I can't tell if the snow has stopped. Everything's quiet. That has to be a good sign, doesn't it?"

Quist flexed his shoulder. "Snow doesn't make much noise when it falls on itself." He studied her downcast face.

Even in profile, even in the dim light of dawn, he saw signs of strain. "Did you sleep?"

"I dozed. I kept thinking...lousy things."

He didn't want to hear what those lousy things were.

But she couldn't help herself. The night had been so long, hour after hour with only the briefest of catnaps, and during those waking times her imagination had been in full swing. Now that there was someone to talk to, she needed reassurance. "I kept thinking that maybe there'd be so much snow piled up around the car that we wouldn't be able to open the door."

"We'll be able to open the door."

"I kept thinking that maybe it would freeze shut, and that we wouldn't have any way of melting the ice, so we'd be stuck in here, *really* stuck in here." She swallowed and whispered, "That won't happen, will it?"

"No." The question, he knew, was whether there was anything outside that could offer them better shelter than the car. Sitting forward to stretch the cramped muscles of his back, he glanced around toward the general vicinity where the baby would be under the afghan. "Is she all right?"

Lily nodded. "She slept, thank goodness, and she's drinking well. I don't look forward to changing her. She's so small, and it's so cold. Her legs tremble pathetically. But if I don't change her, she'll be uncomfortable that way, and if she gets diaper rash, it'll be worse." She fell silent for a minute, then raised her eyes to Quist and said in a small voice, "When I'm not thinking about being frozen solid in this car, I'm thinking of being rescued. Do you think it will happen?"

"Nope," was Quist's blunt reply. "No one's going to find us here. It's up to us to find someone or something out there." He reached for one of the Chunky bars, peeled back the foil covering, snapped the bar in half and popped one of the halves into his mouth. Rewrapping the other half, he put it back with the rest of their meager store of food.

Then he crawled into the front seat, jammed the Stetson onto his head and forced the door open. He was out, with the door slammed shut behind him, before Lily could tell whether the swirling snow was simply snow dislodged from the car or a continuation of the storm.

The minutes crept by, and with each, Lily grew more apprehensive. She had no idea whether Quist was gone for the day, gone for good, or simply looking around outside. As had happened the evening before when he'd left the car, she felt an overwhelming aloneness. At least it was getting lighter out, but that was small solace if, in fact, he'd set off on his own.

When the door opened, she felt an inordinate sense of relief. Her gaze clung to his snowy figure as he slid back into the car. Nervously she awaited his verdict.

Hauling his duffel from under the seat, he began rummaging inside. "It's stopped snowing for now, but there's more to come. The sky's still filled with it. I'm going to see how far I can get before that happens." Shrugging out of his heavy sheepskin jacket, he pulled a sweater on over the one he was already wearing.

Lily's eyes clung to his shoulders. Their breadth represented the strength she'd soon be losing. "Which direction are you going in?"

"Ahead." He pulled on the jacket. "Behind is a waste. You didn't see anything there yesterday. There won't be anything there today." Reaching into the bag, he pulled out several pairs of socks. "Besides, it's all uphill, and I don't have snowshoes. Better to hike down. I'll go for three or four hours or until the road comes to an end. With luck I'll hit something before then." He stuffed a pair of socks in each of his pockets, took a third pair in his hand and looked her in the eye. "It may be a while before I get back."

"How much of a while?" she asked, unable to hide her fear.

"That depends on what I find. But I don't want you to

leave the car. Do you understand that? If you start wandering around, you'll get lost."

"What about you? What if you get lost?"

"I won't. I'm a tracker." His eyes sharpened. "But it won't do me any good to go out searching for help and come back and find you gone. Stay right here with the baby. I don't care how impatient you get, do not wander away from this car. If you start stumbling around in the snow, you'll be in trouble. Do you understand what I'm saying?"

He was speaking in such a slow, clear, elementary kind of way that she couldn't help but understand. "I'm not dumb."

"But you're scared, and scared women do crazy things. So I'm telling you—stay here, stay as warm as you can and remember to eat. Sooner or later, I'll be back."

"Sooner or later?" she echoed in a small voice.

"I can't tell when it will be."

"Will it be today?"

"With luck."

"And if it's not?"

"If it's not, you'll spend another night like the one you've just spent, and I'll be back tomorrow."

"Will you?"

"Yes."

"Do you promise?"

Quist wasn't used to having his word questioned. He wouldn't have put up with it, if Lily hadn't looked so damned frightened. And vulnerable. Damn, he didn't need vulnerable. "I just said it, didn't I?"

She nodded. "But can I believe you?"

He studied her closely. "You're not a very trusting sort."

"I've trusted and been hurt."

That much was clear from the factual way she said it and the sober look in her eye. It also jibed with things she'd told him about herself. Feeling an empathy he didn't want, Quist drew himself up as straight as he could within the confines of the car. "Then you've trusted the wrong men. Me, I'm a man of my word. If I say I'll be back, I'll be back."

Looking into the coal-black eyes that told her nothing in the dim light of dawn, Lily wavered for a minute. Then she thought back on the past fourteen hours and realized that though Quist had his moods, he'd behaved responsibly. She also realized that she had no choice; if she was to make it through his absence with her peace of mind intact, she had to believe that he'd be back.

"Okay?" he asked in a low, cautious tone.

She nodded, then watched him tuck the half of the Chunky bar he hadn't eaten into his pocket.

"In case I get hungry," he explained, then snorted and added, "as if I couldn't eat ten of them now." His dark eyes met hers. "So you've got the rest of the food. I'll have to come back to get it, won't I?"

Before she had time to respond, he let himself out and slammed the door.

CHAPTER THREE

FOR QUIST, THE TRUDGE through the snow was cold and frustrating. He followed the narrow break in the trees on the assumption that it was a road, though eighteen inches of snow had obliterated any sure signs. Save for that lean swath, the landscape was reduced to an endless expanse of snow-laden woods. A winter wonderland? More like the twilight zone, he knew. Oh, he was hardy enough. He could survive cold and lack of food; he'd done it before and he'd do it again.

The problem was Lily. He figured she'd be able to make it through another couple of nights in the car, but after that there'd be trouble. She was cold, and unless he got something to eat, her milk would dry up, and if that happened, the baby would starve, and if *that* happened—he didn't want to even think about it. God only knew why he cared; Lily Danziger and her baby were nothing to him but a pain in the butt. Still, he couldn't just let them freeze.

The more he thought about it—and he had little else to think about as he trudged on through the snow—it was incredible. From the cradle on, he'd had no need for a woman, yet he'd been involved with his share, and each one had been trouble. Hell, he would never have been in the goddamned Maine woods in the first place if it hadn't been for a woman, and now another's plight had him stomping his way for help.

Sure, he'd be stomping his way for help even if he'd

been the only one stuck. He wasn't about to freeze to death, either. But the fact was that if he'd been alone, he'd never have left the main road in the first place. And if he were alone, he wouldn't feel the responsibility he did now.

He knew what he wanted. He wanted to hit a bona fide thoroughfare, flag down a car, find a can of gas and some chains to get Lily's fancy red Audi out of the snow. He wasn't even sure if chains would do the trick, especially if it started to snow again. Playing it safe, he'd probably snag a tow truck to go in after her. If all went well, he'd be in his own motel room for the night, then back on his way to Quebec in the morning.

If all went well.

Somehow he didn't think it would. After plodding through the snow for nearly two hours, he saw no sign of civilization. There wasn't the faintest smell of a wood fire. There wasn't the slightest sound of a snow plow. Maine was nowhere near as big as Montana, and the terrain wasn't nearly as rugged, still he felt well and truly isolated from humanity. In Montana that was good. In Maine, he wasn't so sure.

FOR LILY, THE wait was interminable. With the full dawning of day, she stepped out of the car into knee-deep snow, which did nothing to reassure her. Even if she had gas, she doubted the Audi would be able to make it back to the main road. True, it had stopped snowing, but the sky was still that pregnant, pale gray shade it had been the day before. Quist was right. The snow wasn't done.

Back in the car, she piled every imaginable layer over her for warmth, then played with Nicki, who was right with her under all the covers. She sang; she cooed and babbled and hummed. She took advantage of daylight to do all the things she wouldn't be able to do once night fell again, though she prayed something would happen before then. She wasn't a camper. A city person born and bred, she'd never spent time in the country. As hard as it was to believe that she'd already spent one cold night in the car, it was that much harder to believe that there might be more nights like it.

She wondered how long she'd be able to survive that way, then decided not to think about it. But minutes later she was wondering what would happen if Quist was lost or hurt in the snow and never made it to civilization. Her car, she realized, could be sitting just where it was, unseen by human eyes until spring came, if then.

She wouldn't let that happen. If Quist didn't return in a day or two, she knew that despite what he'd told her, she'd set out on her own. She wasn't about to let Nicki die. She wasn't about to die, herself. She had something to prove, something to do with basic human worth, and she was damned if she'd let a snowstorm and a few wrong turns stand in her way.

Still, her empty stomach knotted. She listened for the sound of a rescuing tow truck, but none came. She waited for Quist to return with the news that he'd found a settlement several hills over, in which case they could laugh at the night they'd spent thinking themselves marooned. But he didn't come.

One hour passed, then two, then three. Nicki slept for a bit and awoke hungry. After Lily fed her, she finished off the last of the cold hamburger. An hour later she had a cookie, but by then she realized the importance of saving whatever she had. Quist had been gone for four hours. Clearly he hadn't found something nearby. Things didn't look good.

Noontime came and went. She rocked Nicki, sang playful songs to her, though playfulness was the last thing she felt. At one point tears came to her eyes and, holding Nicki tight, she cried quietly. She felt she had that right. With the exception of Nicki's arrival, the past year had been a nightmare, and the nightmare went on, more vivid, if anything, in the week now past. From Michael's attack, to her precipitous departure from Hartford, to the long drive, the snowstorm and now this—she feared to think of where it would end.

If her parents were alive, she'd have had a haven, humble as it was. But her mother had been dead for ten years, her father for four, and she had no siblings to ask for help. All she wanted, she realized, was to feel a little less alone.

Sitting in her car, snowbound and lost in the middle of God's country, did nothing to ease that feeling of aloneness. Nor did Quist's continuing absence. By the time one o'clock came, he'd been gone for nearly six hours. She told herself that he'd reached help, but that it would take time for that help to get back to her. Still she felt abandoned—and colder and more frightened by the minute.

At one-forty, just when she was beginning to despair, there was a sudden wrench on the door. It opened with a yawn and a snow-covered figure fell inside.

Had it not been for the Stetson, Lily wasn't sure she'd have recognized him, but the Stetson came quickly off, as did the socks that had been tied end-to-end to cover his ears and the large sheepskin jacket, and before she knew what was happening, he was in the back seat with her, crawling into the nest that her body heat had managed to keep warmer than the air.

"Damn, it's cold out there," he said hoarsely. He pulled her close, baby and all.

"You're freezing!" she cried. She was shocked not only by the chill of his body but by the sudden intimacy he'd forced on her. Much as she told herself that the circumstances were extenuating, it had been a long time since she'd been so close to a man.

"I know. Warm me a little before we go back out?"

Her shock yielded to a glimmer of hope. "You found something?"

"A cabin. It's a one-room job, but it's been lived in as recently as last summer." He took a shivering breath against her forehead. "There's a woodstove, plenty of wood and some food—canned goods and staples. I would've lit the stove if I hadn't been afraid to leave it untended. Didn't want to get you and the kid there and find the place burned down." He paused. "It's a three-hour walk. Can you make it?"

"I can make it."

"You just had a baby. Are you sure?"

"It's been five weeks."

"Still, you must be—your body can't be right yet."

"It's okay. I can make it."

He figured he had to take her word for it. "Fine, then. Strap the kid close to your body and wear as many layers of clothes as possible. We'll carry whatever else we can. God knows how long we'll be there."

Lily started to get up, but he snagged her back with an arm around her waist.

"In a minute," he murmured, his voice a deep rumble against her temple while his legs tangled with hers. "Just a minute. You're the only thing warm worth a damn for miles, and I'm cold. Give me another minute. You owe me that much."

He was right, she knew. He'd found a place that would keep them alive, and he could easily have stayed there to warm up, eat and relax for a while, but he'd turned right around and come back to her. That had to say something for his character.

Not that his body was all that bad, either. With the passing of her initial shock, she realized that the closeness felt good. She guessed it had something to do with the hours she'd just spent alone and fearing the worst. She half suspected she'd have welcomed the closeness of a baboon. But Quist was no baboon. He smelled of the cold outdoors, of snow and of man in a pleasant sort of way. Though he burrowed close, she didn't feel stifled, and beneath the surface chill of his body was a certain strength.

She could have done worse, far worse than this cowboy, she knew, and yes, she owed him.

Maintaining a safe grip on Nicki, she slipped her free arm around his head to cover his ears, which, in spite of the thick hair that brushed them and the makeshift earmuffs he'd worn, were red from the cold.

Quist wasn't about to reject the gesture. He welcomed anything of a warming nature after the trek he'd made, and the trek wasn't over. They had to make it back to the cabin by nightfall, which wouldn't be a problem if he was alone, but he doubted Lily could match his pace. The snow on the ground was deep, and new snow had begun falling a short time before. The additional inches wouldn't make things any easier.

He supposed that the sooner they set out, the better. But he didn't move. It felt too good to lie there absorbing the warmth of a woman, even if she was a scrawny thing—with a bawling kid.

"What's wrong with her?"

"I think she's being squished," Lily said and loosened the arm she'd wrapped around Quist's head. It was a minute before she extricated herself enough to push up against the seat, another minute before she'd worked through the layers to reach the baby's face. "What is it, pumpkin?" she whispered. "Shh. It's all right. Shh."

Nicki kept crying, her tiny features pinched and pink.

"Is she hungry?" Quist asked, sitting up beside them.

"She shouldn't be. Not for another hour."

"Can you put her down while we get ready to go?"

"She'll cry, but that's okay." She paused. "If you can take it." Expectantly she looked up into his face. It was closer than she'd thought, and though he wore a day's worth of stubble and a frown, she wasn't frightened.

Intrigued was more like it. Tanned from the sun and ruddy from the cold, he was the image of health. With his shadowed jaw, the squint marks by his eyes and the general set of his features, he was also the image of ruggedness. Not bad looking, she had to admit. Something like the Marlboro man.

She'd never met a Marlboro man before. Ruggedness wasn't something a man developed at Harvard Law, or Columbia Law, or Yale Law, and since she'd worked in posh law offices for years, most of the men she'd known had gone to one of the three. That meant they'd graduated with credentials to match their egos—largely overrated, in her modest opinion.

Ruggedness, on the other hand, was hard earned. In that sense, Quist was refreshing. He was also looking into her eyes in a way that was every bit as cock-sure as any one of the high-powered lawyers she'd known.

"I can take it," he said. "We'll stuff my duffel and one of your bags. And that diaper thing over there. And anything else that can be strung over a shoulder. Right before we leave, feed her, change her, do whatever else you have to to keep her happy while we hike. You won't be feeding her again until we reach the cabin."

Lily agreed that the plan made sense. "Is the cabin on the main road?"

"Main road?" he asked in a mocking tone that brought back yesterday's folly.

Lily figured she owed him that, too. "This road," she conceded without a fight. "Will we have any trouble finding it?"

"I'm a tracker. I told you that. I don't get lost." He didn't tell her that he'd had to try several different forks in the road before he'd found one that led to a cabin, because it didn't matter. He had found the cabin. And he could find it again. Enough said.

Lily studied his face for a minute longer, then took a deep, resigned, if faintly unsteady breath. "You came back for me when you didn't have to. I suppose I can trust you not to lead me out into the snow for nothing."

The element of resignation struck Quist the wrong way. He bristled. "It's my life, too, lady. Just remember that."

"Lily. It's Lily, not lady."

He put his face even closer. "Warm me up, and it's Lily. Talk snotty, and it's lady."

"I didn't talk—"

"You sounded all stuck-up and put out."

"I didn't—"

"You're the one who got us into this mess, remember?"

"I thought—"

"You thought wrong. Fancy city girl screws up again, only this time the stakes are higher than usual. Face it, sweetheart, you need me."

"I am not your sweetheart."

His eyes flashed hotly. "And ain't it a shame. You'll never know that particular pleasure, will you?" Leaving Lily tongue-tied, he bolted forward, tugged on his coat, hat and makeshift earmuffs, then stomped out of the car to get a bag from the trunk.

Lily spent a minute getting over her astonishment, then another trying to figure out what had happened. Snotty…stuck-up…put out…she hadn't felt any of those things. She thought she'd been telling him she trusted him. It should have been a compliment. Obviously he hadn't taken it that way. He certainly did expect the worst where women were concerned.

But he expected other things, too. That last look in his eyes told her so. It had been different. Hot and flashing. Challenging in a sexual kind of way. No doubt he'd been thinking of one of the women he loved to hate.

A dull thud from the trunk brought her around. Reluctant to give Quist cause for further complaint, she gave the still-crying Nicki a quick hug. "Hush, Nicki. I have to put you down for a couple of minutes. Please don't cry. Please." When the crying momentarily lessened, she set the infant in the car seat and quickly went out after Quist.

It didn't take them long to select the most malleable of Lily's canvas bags and empty it of all but practical items. Returning to the car, they repacked it with the heavier clothing that they'd brought in the evening before. When that was done, they stuffed Quist's duffel and the baby's bag with more of the same, sliding diapers into every imaginable crevice.

They worked in silence. As though to compensate, Nicki kept up a stream of sound that varied from faint whimpering to all-out rage. Finally Lily picked her up and changed her, then put her to her breast. Only then was she still. And only then, with that brief idle time to pass until they left, did Quist pull a can from his pocket. Using one of the arms of his pocket knife, he opened the can, and using a flat blade, scooped out a helping of its contents.

"Here." He held out the knife with its offering. His tone brooked no argument, and Lily gave him none. She was desperately hungry, feeling weak from it. "Carefully," he warned as she closed her mouth around the food. Gingerly she drew it into her mouth without cutting herself on the blade.

"Hash?" she asked with a curious smile. It was hard to tell with everything so cold and Quist's large hand obliterating the label on the can.

He helped himself to a mouthful, talking around the food. "Sure ain't caviar."

"It could be. It tastes heavenly. Thank you for bringing it."

"I figured it'd help before the walk."

"You figured right. My legs are a little wobbly."

He gave her another helping of the hash. "Are you sure you can make it? Better think about it before we set out."

She swallowed. "What's my alternative?"

"Staying here. Waiting for me to bring help back in."

"That's no alternative. I'm going."

"It's a long walk. If you get tired, I can't carry you."

"You won't have to," she informed him with her chin set firm. "I may have just had a baby, but I've probably had more exercise since she's been born than in the year before. I can hold my own. And Nicki. All you have to do is lead the way."

Between the look in her eye and the determination in her voice, Quist saw that she meant it. "Done," he said and knifed more hash into his mouth. He continued alternately feeding Lily, then himself, while she fed the baby beneath cover of her clothes. When she'd finished, she strapped Nicki onto her chest, pulled on several additional sweaters, her long woolen coat, then her parka, secured the fastenings as best she could, grabbed hold of the diaper bag and followed Quist out of the car.

As promised, he led the way. Carrying both his duffel and her large bag, with her fur draped over his head, he looked even more mountainous than he had when Lily had first picked him up. She had a better idea of what was inside now, though, and he wasn't the enemy.

Nature was. Snow was falling in large, moist clumps that accumulated with frightening speed on top of all that already lay on the ground. With each footstep, she sank up to her knees in the stuff, and though she walked in Quist's tracks, her boots were quickly coated.

Mercifully there was little wind, which meant that the cold wasn't exaggerated. But it was bad enough. Stealthily it crept through seams, folds and the tiniest openings that she'd thought secured. She feared to think what would have been if she were less voluminously covered. Though the layers of bulky clothing she wore made walking more difficult, they were a protection. Keeping Nicki from the chill was critical. She felt she was doing that.

The first hour passed. Quist, who had been regularly turning to check on Lily, waited for her to catch up. "Are you okay?"

She managed a stiff-jawed, "I think so."

"Need to rest?"

"No!" she insisted. "Keep going!"

With a single nod he turned and headed off again. He'd have stopped if she'd had to, but he, too, wanted to keep on. The large, moist flakes of snow had given way to smaller, colder chips that were coming down in even greater intensity. If he were to guess, he'd say that those chips were the start of an entirely new storm, which meant that the sooner he and Lily reached the cabin, the better.

By the end of the second hour, Lily was tiring badly, but again, when Quist asked if she wanted to stop for a rest, she refused. She set her sights on resting at the cabin, with a roof for shelter and a woodstove for warmth. She didn't protest, though, when he pressed one of the leftover cookies into her mouth. She needed quick energy. She needed energy, period.

On and on they plodded. Lily kept her head tucked low against the sharp nuggets that were being driven now by a rising wind. There were times when she closed her eyes and concentrated on nothing more complex than the heavy rhythm of the trek. Once when she was doing that, she plowed right into Quist, who had stopped for a minute. She nearly fell. He steadied her with a hand on either arm.

His eyes sought hers. "What's wrong?"

She wanted to tell him that she felt lousy, that her back hurt, her shoulder pinched, her insides ached, her feet were half-frozen and *where was his goddamned cabin already*. Instead, she said, "Nothing."

"How's the kid?" he asked. Thinking to lighten the mood, he quipped, "Is she still alive and kicking in there?"

It was the wrong thing to say. Lily's eyes filled up. "Of

course, she's alive! I can feel her squirming. But you don't hear her screaming, do you? She's being good. So good."

Quist wasn't sure he'd be able to hear a thing through the layers Lily wore, and what small peeps might have escaped would be swallowed up by the wind. But he wasn't about to make the same mistake twice. "You're right. She's being very good. We're lucky." He paused. "Think you can make it a little longer?"

She nodded.

Some of her discouragement must have shown in her eyes because he said, "You're doin' real well, Lily. Keep it up, we're almost there," before he turned and went on.

The third hour was the tough one, as Quist knew it would be. For one thing, dusk was approaching, and though there was still enough light to see the way, night became a deadline, fast closing in. For another the terrain grew trickier closer to the cabin, and Lily's fatigue didn't help. She had trouble on the inclines, even more on the declines. He could feel the strain of those downhill stretches in his own thighs and had to believe that it would be even worse for her. At one point he turned to find that she'd stumbled and fallen in the snow, and the look on her face was so pathetic when he helped her up that he stayed by her side, rearranging the bags on his shoulders so that he could link an arm through hers to help her along.

Once she recovered from the fall, she protested his help. "I'm okay."

"You're not."

"I can manage."

"Another fall like that and you might really hurt yourself."

She'd already hurt herself, if the new discomfort in her wrist was any indication. "But I'm slowing you down."

"You'd slow me down whether I was holding your arm or not. Now keep still and walk. We're almost there."

He'd been saying that for hours, Lily thought, but she

didn't have the energy to point it out. And the fact was that she did appreciate his help. Her legs seemed a great distance away, barely belonging to her, they were so cold and numb. Her gloved hands were nearly as bad, and the rest of her felt a rising chill.

Aside from the occasional stirring she'd mentioned, Nicki slept on, for which Lily was overwhelmingly grateful. She wasn't sure whether it was the steady movement that kept the infant sated or the crying she'd done that had exhausted her, but Lily couldn't begin to think of what she'd do if the baby woke and began to fuss. She couldn't very well change a diaper in the snow. Or nurse. If her milk wasn't frozen solid. Lord, what would she do if something happened to her milk?

The storm intensified as dusk deepened, and every one of Lily's fears paraded in turn through her panicked mind. While not panicked, Quist grew increasingly concerned. The cabin was ahead; he knew he hadn't taken a wrong turn, but he feared he might if they didn't reach it soon. Between the wind-whipped snow and the dark, visibility was decreasing by the minute.

"Where is it?" Lily wailed at the moment her knees buckled.

Quist caught her up. "Whoa," he said, hugging her to him for a minute, "take it easy. We're almost there. Almost there."

"I don't feel well," she cried softly.

"Just a little longer. Hang in there just a little longer."

"How much?"

"Ten, fifteen minutes, maybe."

"I don't…know if I can."

"Sure you can. You've come this far. A little longer's a piece of cake."

"No, it's hell."

"Then it's hell," he agreed in a harder voice, "but you've got to do it. If you can't do it for yourself, do it for Nicki.

Or do it for me. I've been puttin' out for you all day. It's right time you put out for me, babe."

She was silent for a minute, and he was beginning to fear he had a *real* problem on his hands when she muttered stiffly, "It's Lily. Not babe. Lily."

"Fink out on me, and it's babe. Give me that extra go and it's anything your sweet little heart desires. So. Are we on?"

In answer, she straightened, pulled herself away and set off—unfortunately in the wrong direction, but Quist was quick to correct that, and they were soon once again huddled together, plowing through the storm.

Ten or fifteen minutes, he'd said, but Lily's concept of time was as distorted as the landscape, an endless expanse of snow and trees of a deepening indigo hue. She was sure they'd been walking for another hour before they stumbled over a rise and he tightened his grip on her arm.

"There. There it is. See it?"

She wanted to so badly, but things were blurring. "No," she cried feebly. Her lungs hurt. "It's too dark."

"Come on. When we're closer you'll see."

And she did, though at first she thought she was hallucinating. Quist tugged her up to the door and pushed it open, then pulled her inside and shouldered the door shut against the havoc of the snow. Leaving her balanced against the rough-hewn wood, he dropped the fur coat and made his way in the dark across the small room to the table where he'd deliberately left a hurricane lamp and a box of matches. It took a bit of fumbling—his fingers weren't much warmer than Lily's and he was trying to hurry—but he soon lit the wick. The lamp cast a low glow to the room.

Lily didn't think to look around. Sliding down the door to the floor when her legs refused to support her any longer, she kept her eyes on Quist, who went on to light the wood-stove. Dry and ready, the kindling caught, then the logs, and the glow cast by the lamp was heightened by a warmer one. He knelt for a minute with his hands held out to that warmth before tossing aside his hat and earmuffs. Sitting back on the floor directly in front of the flames, he tugged off his boots, then stood and went at his coat. When it was off, he looked back at Lily. She hadn't moved.

Swearing softly, he crossed to the door and knelt before her. Small baby sounds were coming from under the layers of her clothes. Lily heard them, but for the first time since the baby's birth, she simply lacked the strength to move.

"I'll just…rest for a minute," she whispered.

"Nuh-uh. Not yet." He tugged her feet out from under her, ignoring the muffled moans the movement caused. When he'd pulled off her boots, he unfastened both her parka and the wool coat she'd worn beneath it.

"Nooo," she cried softly when he slid a hand inside and pushed the two coats away. "I'm too cold."

"The fire will warm you now." As quickly as he could, he stripped off the two oversized sweaters she'd worn. With the baby still strapped to her chest, he scooped her up, carried her the short distance to the woodstove and sat her down on the floor. "Don't move."

Why she'd have wanted to, she didn't know. He was right; the fire was warming. She couldn't quite feel it in her hands and feet, and those parts of her face that had been exposed still felt as though they belonged to someone else, but elsewhere she was beginning to feel the blessed relief of the newborn fire. If anything, though, that small thawing made her more aware of her exhaustion, which raised another point. She couldn't have moved if she'd *tried*, other than to keel over, and she didn't want to do that. The baby was crying. She had to take care of the baby.

Quist returned, dragging a mattress across the floor. With an ease that belied his own fatigue, he lifted her onto it, repositioning her directly before the flames. In the next minute he was draping an old blanket around her shoulders, and in the next, he was beside her, trying to figure out how to lift the whimpering baby from her chest.

He'd never held a baby before, and even if he knew what to grab, this one was bundled up in a snowsuit that made it difficult to see what was where. He pushed a hand between the back of the snowsuit and the canvas carrier, but there was no hold there. He reached for either arm of the snowsuit, but the baby's own arms felt so fragile through the bulky material that he was sure he'd break something if he pulled. Carefully he closed his fists on the snowsuit material alone, hoping to haul the child up that way, but the entire carrier rose with his tugs. Frustrated, he began to fiddle with the carrier itself, but the only thing contact with the side straps taught him was that though Lily's body was slender, her breasts were firm and full.

Snatching his hands away, he growled. "How in the hell does this come off?"

Lily's numbness was beginning to fade, but she'd started to shiver. It was the cold's way of exiting her body, she supposed, and in that it was good, but it did nothing to help the cause of her hands. Futilely she picked at the fastening that held the carrier close, but it was Quist who completed the job, while she cupped an arm around Nicki.

Bending forward, she deposited the baby onto the mattress, and, by a miracle of will, managed to unzip the snowsuit on the first try. She got as far as freeing the baby's tiny arms and legs from their covering when she stopped, eyes filling with tears.

She wasn't sure if it was the sight of Nicki, so relieved to be out of her snowsuit for the first time in a day and a half that she'd stopped crying and was propelling her little arms and legs in wild circles. Or if it was the simple realization that they'd made it alive through the storm. Or an accumulation of everything that had happened. But the tears trickled down her cheeks while more welled up, and she could do nothing but yield to the quiet sobs that shook her.

Staring at her, Quist felt more helpless than he ever had in his life. Oh, yeah, she was a crier, and he hated women who cried, but this one was different. Her tears were spontaneous. She wasn't turning them on for his sake, because he doubted she was aware of his existence just then. She was crying because she'd gone through a hell of a lot in the last day and she needed the outlet.

He wasn't sure he could complain. She'd been strong when strength was called for. She'd made her way through the snow—albeit with a little goading now and then—and when it came right down it it, she hadn't slowed him down much more than the storm would have done, anyway. He supposed she deserved a bit of respect for that.

So he granted her the respect, but he was feeling something else. He was feeling compassion again, and the strangest need to take her into his arms. She really was a small thing. Sitting there in a sweater and jeans, with her hair—light brown, he saw now, and matted from spending so long under her hood, but still pretty—brushing her shoulders, her head bowed and her arms drawn into herself, she was the embodiment of loneliness. At least, it seemed that way to him. Looking at her, he relived every lonely moment he'd had in his own life, and though he hadn't needed the solace then, he did now.

Gently he pulled up the blanket, which had slipped to the floor. Then he wrapped an arm around her shoulder and drew her against his chest. She didn't melt; her body remained stiff, and her sobs continued to come, but she didn't push him away, and he was glad for that. Holding her made him feel better. And that was all he did, just held her. He didn't stroke her or whisper soft words that he didn't mean. He just held her, just let her feel the solidity of his body and hear the beat of his heart.

After several minutes her sobs subsided, and he could have sworn he felt the slightest relaxation of her body against his. Before he was quite sure, though, she took a deep, shaky breath and made a small movement in search of her freedom. He dropped his arms and sat back on his heels to watch while she gingerly eased herself down on the mattress and drew the baby close.

Her movements were unsteady, not quite coordinated. She was physically hurting, and he could understand that, since he was feeling the same way. Everything that had been close to frozen not long before was beginning to ache—that, in spite of the fact that the warmth from the woodstove felt wonderful.

Lying on her side with an arm draped lightly over the baby, Lily closed her eyes. Quist guessed that she was asleep in less than two minutes, and though he had plenty to do—not the least important of which was to fix something to eat—he sat for a while watching her.

She'd pushed herself to the limit that day, he knew, and though neither of them had had a choice in the matter, he wondered once again whether she'd been up to it. Lying there curled up, with the blanket half-on and half-off, with her hair fallen into her face and smudges visible beneath her eyes, she seemed a far cry from the woman he'd first seen the day before. The sporty car was left behind, her makeup worn off, her fancy clothes, pared down to the basics. She could almost have passed for a ranch girl.

Almost. But not quite.

The baby made a sudden squeak. Quist's eyes flew to her. She was batting the air with all four limbs. He moved closer, wondering what was wrong with her. He fully expected her to start crying any minute, and while he thought that would be a shame, when Lily was finally getting a rest, he wasn't about to save the day by picking her up.

Strangely she didn't start crying, but made another sound, this one the tiniest coo that he almost suspected came out by accident, if the look of surprise on her face was for real. As he watched her, Quist found other things even more surprising.

For one thing, she was even smaller than he'd thought. No longer hidden by the snowsuit, she was wearing a one-piece terry-cloth thing that moved with her. The only point of padding was her diaper, which crinkled softly as she kicked. Though her feet were covered, her hands were free, and smaller, more delicate fingers he'd never seen in his life.

For another, though she didn't have much hair to speak of, she looked like a girl. No doubt, he decided, it was because she was wearing pink and because he *knew* she was a girl. Still, she had the same delicacy to her features, albeit small-scale, as her mother. He couldn't imagine a baby boy looking like that, or if one did, he pitied it.

For a third, she was looking at him as though she possessed some sort of advanced intelligence. She didn't blink. She just stared right at him with eyes that were large and gray. He moved a little to the left; she followed him there. He moved back to the right; so did she. He felt as though he ought to be carrying on some sort of intent conversation with her, but for the life of him, he didn't know what to say—and he could have sworn she knew it, the minx!

Then she sneezed. Her tiny body recoiled along with the small, sweet sound, face puckering, arms and legs flinching. Quist was entranced—until her face stayed puckered and she started to cry.

Lily moved at the sound. She opened her eyes, groggily lifted her head and reached out for the baby's hand, which instinctively curled around her thumb. "Shh," she whispered and closed her eyes again. "Let Mommy rest a little more. Just a little more."

But Nicki wasn't about to do that. She was hungry, and she had no better way to communicate it than to intensify the force of her cries. She proceeded to do just that.

Lily gave a soft moan. She ached all over, and what didn't ache, tingled. Beyond that, she felt totally drained, not at all up to shouldering responsibility. She wanted to *have* a mother right then, not *be* a mother. But the clock couldn't be turned back. And this particular responsibility couldn't be handled by anyone else.

Without rising, she drew Nicki close, unbuttoned her sweater and bared a breast for the child's taking. At the first hint of the nipple's presence, Nicki turned her little head and latched on. In turn, Lily closed her eyes and focused on this small pleasure to counter her larger aches.

Quist hadn't moved. He sat on his heels not far from Lily, his hands splayed on his thighs, his eyes glued to the tableau before him. It was the first time he'd watched her nurse, and though a small amount of the discomfort he'd felt on other occasions remained, something stronger held him in its thrall. He wasn't quite sure what it was—whether it had to do with the bend of Lily's slim legs under the blanket, the graceful line of her back and the curve of the arm that held the baby close, or the peaceful look that had crept over her face. He wondered whether it had to do with the exposure of her breast, which looked full and creamy, or the disappearance of her nipple into the baby's mouth, or the small, sucking motion of that mouth, or the tiny hand that looked so pink on Lily's ivory flesh.

He guessed that it wasn't any one of those things, but several or all of them that contributed to his fascination. The picture before him was very beautiful. It stirred him.

Realization of that stirring was enough to break the spell. Closing his eyes tightly, he hung his head, and, without conscious intent, swayed on his heels against the pain he felt deep inside. It was the pain of sadness, the pain of wanting something and knowing that it was never to be.

The pain lasted for just a minute. In its wake came the

refortifying of Quist's defenses—and an anger that those defenses had been breached at all—and the determination that it wouldn't happen again.

CHAPTER FOUR

WHAT THE CABIN lacked by way of running water and a bathroom, it made up for in food. The kitchen, which consisted of a full wall of shelves and a large sink, contained canned goods ranging from soups and stew to fish, vegetables and fruit. Airtight containers held staples such as sugar, flour and salt. There was a large jar of peanut butter, several smaller jars of wax-sealed jelly that looked to have been home done, and a tin of thick crackers. And there were envelopes of powdered milk and cocoa.

Not bad, Quist decided. If need be, they could stay holed up there, well-fed for a month. Not that he had any intention of doing that. He wanted out, and the sooner the better. He still had Quebec to hit—though whether Lily's little folly would screw that up, too, he didn't know. If he was so late getting to Quebec that Jennifer had run somewhere else, he'd be pissed off. He wasn't sure he'd follow her. Enough was enough. He wanted to be back home, where things were normal.

Taking a handful of crackers from the tin, he sampled one. It was bland and stale, still he chased it down with a second. Intense hunger had a way of humbling even the most discriminating of men, and he'd never been that. Maybe in some things, but not food.

He shot a glance at Lily, thinking to start her eating, too, but her eyes were closed. She was in another world. He had no wish to intrude.

Setting the rest of the crackers within munching distance, he took a large can of stew from the shelf, opened it with the can opener that lay nearby and dumped the contents into a saucepan. When he was satisfied with the way the stew was starting to heat on top of the woodstove, he put on his boots, took a large pot and headed outside to fill it with snow.

He hadn't even reached the door when the cold hit him. It hadn't been as noticeable before, since he'd been so cold himself, but now that he'd warmed up, the contrast was marked. The cabin might have been lovingly used in spring, summer and fall, but he doubted that its owners used it much in winter. If so, they'd have insulated the walls better against storms like this one. Frigid air, even bursts of fine snowflakes were driven by the wind through cracks that the human eye could barely see. That made the temperature by the front walls, where the two cots flanked the door, a good twenty degrees cooler than the air by the woodstove, which stood deeper into the cabin. It was a sure bet that he and Lily would be centering their existence by the latter, and a small space it was, indeed.

On that discouraging note, he slammed out the door.

Lily roused at the noise and looked around just as Nicki was taking a break. Struggling to a sitting position, she laid the baby across her lap and gently burped her, then put her to the other breast.

Moments later Quist returned. He brought with him a fierce gust of wind and a large pot of snow. After brushing himself off, he set the pot on the floor by the woodstove. Once melted, its contents would provide water for drinking, washing and whatever else they wanted. What *he* wanted was a double shot of whiskey. Naturally, it was the only thing the kitchen didn't have.

Ignoring Lily as best he could, he stirred the stew, then put several scoops of snow into a smaller saucepan and set it on to heat for cocoa.

"We lucked out, huh?" Lily said softly.

He shot her a glance, then looked away when he found she was still nursing. Her breast was very much covered to the point where the baby's mouth was attached. Still, the image was there, etched deeply in his mind along with memory of the stirring he'd felt. That stirring meant trouble.

"Lucked out?" He wasn't so sure. There was nothing lucky about being a sap, and if he allowed Lily to get to him, that was just what he'd be. She was a woman, with an agenda of her own. It was totally different from his.

"Warmth. Food. It could have been worse."

"Wait till you see the plumbing."

She looked around, searching the shadows at the perimeter of the room.

"Don't bother," he said. "It's nonexistent. There's an outhouse. The door's half-off, but it serves the purpose." He paused, waiting for her reaction to that bit of news.

If there was dismay on her face, it was lost amid the fatigue. "That's okay," she said quietly—so quietly that he didn't feel any of the satisfaction he'd hoped for. Against his will, he was vaguely concerned.

"How do you feel?"

"Okay."

"Tired?"

"Very."

"Sore."

"A little." It was more than that, but she didn't want to complain. A good night's rest and the soreness would pass, even that in her wrist, which was throbbing. Fortunately it was her left wrist. She could work around it.

"Are you warm enough now?"

"I think so." She glanced at the lower half of her jeans. "These are wet. I'll change when I'm done with Nicki." She kept her head low. "Quist?"

He was wondering what he was supposed to do while she

changed. The cabin was a single, open room with neither a divider nor facility for one. His first thought was to watch her, and that angered him. So he snapped, "What?"

At his tone she hesitated, but only for a minute. "I'm sorry—about before. I don't usually fall apart that way, but it's been hard—" Her voice cracked. She took a deep breath. "I've always been one to cry. I cry at everything— books, movies, graduations, weddings, funerals, you name it—but lately it's been worse. It must be post-partum depression, or something."

"Yeah, well…"

"Crying is a sign of weakness."

"Who told you that?"

"Jarrod. Over and over and over again."

"He sounds like an asshole."

She raised tentative eyes to his. "I'd have thought you'd agree with him."

"I do in one sense. I hate crying."

She waited for him to go on, brows lifting slightly. He'd have been happy to leave the subject there and then, and might have if it hadn't been for that silent invitation. In its innocence, it was powerful, a challenge to his own sense of truth.

"Crying can be manipulative," he said. "It can be melodramatic and phony as hell. And messy."

Still she waited with that same air of expectancy, and it occurred to him that he was being manipulated without a tear in sight. The thought wasn't terribly reassuring. Still, he was driven to finish his thought.

"But it can also have a positive purpose. Certain of life's circumstances are pretty hefty. At those times, crying can be the expression of honest, gut-wrenching emotion, and in that sense, it's a strength." He paused, his frown deepening at the slight change in her expression. "What's the matter now?"

She shook her head. "Nothing."

"Why are you staring at me like that?" He felt as though she were judging him, and he didn't like it one bit.

She looked away, then back. "I'm surprised, that's all. I didn't expect an answer like that. I mean, it's almost like you've spent time thinking the whole thing through—"

"You didn't expect me to think?"

"It's not that. I didn't expect that you'd—"

"Feel? What do you take me for, an ignorant clod?"

"Of course, not."

"Ah, but I'm a cowboy. I'm not supposed to be a hell of a lot brighter'n my horse."

"You're a *man*," she cried in frustration. "Men aren't usually insightful, or sensitive when it comes to feelings. They don't say things like you just did. They have an image to uphold, and crying doesn't fit the image."

"I didn't say that I cried," he warned.

"See? You say it can be a strength, but still you want to make it clear that you don't do it. That is very male of you."

He shook his head. "Practical. It's practical. I don't cry, because as an outlet it doesn't work for me. I'm not saying it never did, just that I don't do it now."

"You used to cry?"

He shrugged.

"When?"

"I don't know."

"When you were little?"

"Every kid cries. You did. I did." He tossed a hand toward Nicki. "She does."

"But when you were five. Or six or seven. I can't picture you crying then. You're too tough."

"I cried," he argued. He wasn't ashamed of feeling what he had at that point in his life. It showed that he was human, and that he had depth. Suddenly telling her became a matter of pride. "My mother walked out on my dad and me soon after I was born. I didn't miss her at all except for certain times, like birthdays and Christmas and special days at school when all the other kids had mothers visiting. I hated those times. I felt angry and hurt and alone, and I didn't understand any of it. So I used to race home, run down to the basement of the triple-decker we rented, hide behind the furnace where no one would hear me and cry."

Lily's eyes had widened as he spoke. They envisioned a little boy, a confused little boy who wanted something without quite knowing what it was. "That's so sad," she whispered.

But he didn't want her pity. "That's not the point. The point is that I cried because at that time it was the only way I could express what I was feeling. When I got older, I found other ways."

"Like?"

"Like pounding fence posts into the ground, or hacking old cedar stumps to bits, or riding hell-bent for leather to the outer pastures to check on my stock." He took a fast breath. "So don't think I don't think or feel just because I don't cry like you do. I handle my feelings differently, that's all." He stirred the stew with more force than was necessary, and announced sharply, "This is almost ready. When are you going to be done?"

"Soon," Lily said distractedly. She was still thinking of Quist as a little boy, and looking down at Nicki, she felt an awful fear that without a father the child might experience similar pain. "Not if I can help it," she whispered fiercely as she bent low over her. By the time she'd relaxed her grip, Nicki had had enough milk. Lifting her to her shoulder, Lily looked around.

The cabin was a utilitarian affair. A small trestle table flanked by broad benches stood not far from the wood-stove. Closer to the front of the cabin were a pair of Adirondack chairs with cushions of a nondescript brown plaid. The front wall held the cots, which doubled as sofas, she guessed, and just around the corner from those were two crudely-fashioned dressers.

With an effort and a small, involuntary groan, she managed to get to her feet. Her legs still felt foreign—stiff and shaky at the same time, and weak—but they did respond to commands of her brain, enough to get her to one of the dressers. The drawers held towels and more blankets, but she wasn't interested in their contents. Finding an empty one, she used her right hand to haul it completely out and lug it toward the woodstove, while she kept her left arm curved protectively around Nicki.

Dropping the drawer on the mattress, she lined it with the blanket Quist had put around her, then double-lined it with the softer receiving blanket that she took from the baby's bag. Nicki had burped by then, and Lily gently lowered her to the makeshift crib. The fit was fine. Eyes on her mother, the baby gently waved her arms and made such sweet gurgling sounds that Lily couldn't help but lean forward and laugh. Nor could she help but congratulate herself on her inventiveness. To date, Quist had been the one in charge. It was time she took over some, at least where she and her child were concerned.

Bearing that in mind, she forced herself back to her feet and once again left the circle of the woodstove's warmth. The floor by the door was littered with all they'd discarded when they'd first come in. Most of it was wet, now that the snow had melted, and she knew that anything that wasn't spread out or hung to dry would stay wet. So she picked up first her boots, then Quist's and stood them against the side of the chair facing the fire. Then she went back for more.

"What's wrong with your hand?" Quist asked. He was leaning against the trestle table, watching her.

"Nothing."

"You're favoring it like it hurts."

She shrugged off the problem. "I landed on it when I fell, but it's just a sprain. It'll be fine."

"Let me see." He started toward her, but she held up a fast hand to stop him.

"It's *fine. Really.*"

At the insistence in her tone, he backed off, but he continued to watch. His mouth twisted when he saw her pick up the fur coat. He should have known she'd worry about it, and he supposed he couldn't blame her. It was worth a mint. Still, she had quite a time spreading it out on the bare metal springs of the cot whose mattress he'd moved. She made a show of using her left hand, but her right was the one that did all the work. Likewise when it came to draping her parka over the back of a chair. When she bent to pick up her wool coat, he'd seen enough. "Leave it," he barked, turning away.

Lily, who had been concentrating on the mechanics of the chore, whirled around. "What?"

"I said, leave it. You can pick up later. Supper's ready."

Supper. The word alone made her mouth water, but she'd been in the outer parts of the cabin long enough to be acutely aware of her legs. "Give me a minute. I have to change."

Dragging her bag onto the cot, she fished inside until she found the warmest wool slacks she'd brought. Then she paused, wondering where she was supposed to change. She was in the darker part of the cabin, still Quist could see plenty.

"Do it there," he told her, as though he'd read her mind. But his voice was more impatient than smug. "I won't look."

When she glanced over her shoulder, he was turning away. Determined to seize the moment, she quickly reached for the top button of her jeans. But what was simply done with two hands wasn't quite as simple with one. She pushed, pulled and tugged, but the metal button wouldn't slide through its hole. When she tried to use the fingers of her left hand to anchor the denim, the only thing to come from the effort was a low moan of pain.

Clamping down on her lower lip, she worked fever-ishly at the fabric until, at last, the button was freed. But there were still four more. With a whispered cry of frus-tration, she went to work on the second.

"Let me see your hand," Quist demanded.

Lily jumped. He was right behind her, then beside her. "You weren't supposed to be looking," she protested.

"You were taking forever. The stew's done, and I'm hungry. Let me see your hand." He reached for it before she could pull away, and then the only thing she could do to minimize the pain was to move right along with the hand. That brought her flush against Quist. Leaning over her, he began to examine her wrist.

Despite his gentleness, she sucked in her breath.

"Hurt?" he asked.

"Yes," she whispered.

He moved his fingers, prodding as lightly as he could while still assessing the damage. "Here?"

She gasped.

"A lot?" he asked.

"Enough."

He probed one more spot, using his thumbs to explore. This time, she would have jumped sky-high at the pain if he hadn't had her anchored to him with his elbows. "I think you've broken the wrist," he announced.

She shook her head against his chest and said in a shaky voice, "Oh, no. It's not broken."

"How do you know?"

"I know. It's not broken."

"I felt it, Lily. That last time, I felt the bone moving. And see how swollen it is." Putting his palms under hers, he held her hands side by side. The difference between them was marked.

"It's sprained. That's all. If I pamper it a little, it'll heal just fine."

"It'll take more than pampering. It should be immobilized and elevated. I'll have to splint it."

"But it's not broken," she insisted, tipping her head back this time to look into his face.

He'd never seen such pleading or such fear, and he was touched so quickly that he didn't have time to tell himself that he didn't want to be touched. "I'm not going to cut it off. Just splint it."

"But if it's broken, I can't use it," she said in a small, high voice. "And I have to use it. I have to be able to take care of Nicki. She has no one else, just me."

"She's a little thing. You'll be able to handle her fine."

"Not if you do something to my hand."

"You're the one who did something. I'm only going to try to fix it."

She looked down at the hand and repeated firmly, "It's just a sprain. No big deal. Leave it alone, and it'll be better in the morning. You'll see."

"Leave it alone, and it'll be worse," he argued, then deliberately gentled his voice. She felt so small and vulnerable, leaning against him like she was. "I'm telling you, Lily, I know about these things. Bones break lots in my line of work. Ignore them, and you're in big trouble. If the bone you've broken knits wrong, you'll have a choice between surgery to rebreak and reset it, in which case you'll be in a cast even longer, or a permanently bum wrist." He paused and tipped his head, coaxing, "All I'm suggesting is that you let me immobilize it until we reach civilization. You can have it X-rayed then, and you'll find out for sure whether or not it's broken. If it's not, good. You'll have taken a precaution, that's all."

Lily was torn. His deep voice was so reassuring, his body so large and warm and supportive, that she wanted to say, "Yes, yes, do whatever you want, take the responsibility, I'm so tired." Still, she didn't want to believe that anything was seriously wrong with her wrist. When and if they were rescued, she had so much to do. She had to finish the drive north, find a place to stay, a job, a bank, a supermarket, a pediatrician, day-care—the list went on. A broken wrist would complicate things horribly.

"It isn't broken," she stated in a last-ditch attempt to believe it.

Removing his hands from hers, Quist held them up and took a step back. "Okay. It's not broken. I guess you know best." She was a big girl, he decided. He couldn't force her to do something she didn't want to do. It was her wrist, her future. If she wanted to mess it up, so be it.

Without another word on the subject, he returned to the stove and began to dish out the stew. After a minute, Lily followed him. He sent her a scowl.

"I thought you were changing your pants."

"I'll do it later," she mumbled.

He stared at her averted face for a minute, then swore and dropped the spoon back into the pan of stew. "You'll do it later, hah. You won't do it later, any more than you'll do it now, because you can't manage those stupid buttons with only one hand." Taking her firmly by her good arm, he ushered her back to her bag. "What in the hell possessed you to buy button-fly jeans, anyway? They went out when zippers came in, for one good reason. When a man wants his pants open, he wants them open fast."

Lily would have gasped at what he said if he hadn't said it so factually. "Button-fly jeans are in fashion," she offered meekly. He made a sound that told her what he thought of fashion. When he began pulling things from her bag, she cried, "What are you doing?"

"I thought I saw you pack a pair of sweatpants in here. Where are they?"

She had her hand on them quickly. They were pink,

rather than gray, which was probably why he hadn't spotted them. "What do you want with my sweatpants?"

"I don't want them," he growled, squatting before her. "*You* do." Before the words were out, he was working on her pants.

She tried to stop him. "What are you *doing*?"

He pushed her hand away. "Undoing these. You can't manage it yourself, and there's no other way to get the damned pants off." With half of the buttons undone, he paused and looked up at her. "You're going to have to take them off sooner or later, whether it's here or in that outhouse. Better here—take my word for it." He returned to his work. "And better now. You need dry and warm, not wet and cold." He tugged at one stubborn button. "Besides, these jeans are skin-tight, and you haven't eaten all day. Once you've had a little of that stew, there'll be even less room to maneuver the buttons."

Lily turned beet red. "I know. My stomach isn't as flat as it used to be." All the buttons were undone. He began to work the denim down her legs. She clutched his shoulder for balance, speaking quickly to cover her nervousness. "I've been doing sit-ups. That helps. It's much better than it was at first. I only gained twenty-three pounds during the pregnancy," she balanced on one foot, while he freed the other, "and all but the last five are gone, but those five pounds don't want to move." She shifted her balance. "Some women are lucky and have no problem. I guess I'm not one of them."

Quist tossed the jeans aside. He wanted to say something about Lily's propensity for problems, but the words didn't come. His attention was focused on the five pounds she'd been talking about. Only he couldn't seem to see them. He saw a slim waist and hips, and a stomach that was ever-so-gently rounded as to be utterly feminine. She wore a pair of white bikini panties, nylon with lace that dipped in a V beneath her navel and was a perfect foil for that soft, gentle rounding.

She was lovely. Soft, gentle, feminine. Unable to help himself, he let his eyes run down her legs. They were slender but shapely and sheathed in the same ivory hue as her stomach and her breasts. He curved a hand around her heel and skimmed it lightly up over her calf, past the back of her knee and her thigh to come to a whisper-soft halt just under her bottom.

That was when he realized what he was doing. It was when he noticed the fine tremor in his hand, and when he saw the movement at Lily's middle that reflected her own quickened breathing.

His eyes met hers, which were wide with something that wasn't quite fear, wasn't quite surprise, wasn't quite desire but had elements of all three. Awareness. That was what he saw. In the instant when he'd touched her, she'd become aware of him as a man.

Her hand, which had never left his shoulder, was gripping it more tightly. At the same time, he caught an almost imperceptible shake of her head.

So she didn't want it, either, he realized and felt a glimmer of relief. If there had to be an attraction between them, at least it was mutually unwanted. It wasn't that he didn't trust himself—though he supposed he didn't. When he was attracted to a woman, he usually followed the attraction to its limits. Sometimes he did so against his better judgment, but if the woman was willing, his brain didn't have much of a chance against the demands of his body. He was glad Lily wasn't willing.

Tearing his eyes from hers, he reached for the pink sweatpants. He knew he should get up and walk away, but he was determined to finish what he'd started. In the process of doing that, the first thing he touched was her damp socks. Reaching again, this time into his own duffel, he replaced those damp socks with a pair of his own clean, dry, wool socks. He figured it was some compensation for thinking lascivious thoughts. Besides, there was nothing at all sexy about a lady wearing wool socks that were way too big, or about a lady wearing pink sweatpants over those socks.

"There," he said when he'd finished, but he had to clear his throat before he spoke again. "The elastic waist is easier."

Rising to his full height, he had to stifle a moan. He was stiff in more ways than one. Peeved at that, he crossed the room and finished spooning stew into the bowls.

It was a minute before Lily followed. She spent that minute trying to understand the warm curling she'd felt inside when Quist had seen her undressed. And when he'd touched her. That had been incredible. The feeling had been so unexpected, but good. She couldn't deny that. Of course, good was all there was to it—a moment's pleasure from physical contact with another person, flesh on flesh, a deeper warmth. It wouldn't go any further than that. It was the circumstances, that was all.

Feeling a slight chill, she took a pair of sneakers from her bag and, perching on the edge of one of the Adirondack chairs, tried to put them on. The bulk of Quist's wool socks would have made the task next to impossible even if she'd had both hands to work with, but without both hands, she couldn't even come close. About all she could do with her left hand was to pick at the laces, and ineffectually, at that. Rather than make an issue of her wrist again, she gave up the struggle.

Shoving the sneakers out of sight, she took several small, bright, rubber toys from the baby's bag, put them on the trestle table and went to get Nicki. She managed it by sliding her right hand under the baby and using her left elbow to help. Grateful that she could do that much, she put Nicki on her stomach on a receiving blanket on the table.

Quist set down the bowls of stew, deposited the tin of

crackers nearby and sat opposite Lily. If there was a lin-
gering awkwardness from what had happened before, it
quickly passed. Hunger and its assuagement was foremost
in their minds. They ate in a silence broken only by Lily's
occasional soft chatter to the baby. Quist refilled each of
their bowls, and they efficiently went through seconds.

Lily was still savoring the very last of the stew, thinking
that nothing canned had ever tasted so good, particularly
when she'd been growing up and canned food was frequent
fare, when Quist set a mug before her.

"Milk," he said. "Powdered. Probably tastes lousy, but
I think you need it."

She did. Since midway through her pregnancy, she'd
been drinking several glasses a day. Now, nursing Nicki,
it was more important than ever, yet she hadn't had a drop
in a day and a half. She didn't care how the powdered
version tasted. For Nicki's sake, she'd drink it.

It wasn't half-bad, she found. She was thirsty anyway,
and it quenched that thirst. Quist was drinking cocoa. She'd
have loved to have had some of that, but she didn't dare.

Stacking the bowls, she gave a vague look toward the
sink. "I'm not sure how to do this."

"Never roughed it?"

"Why are there spigots if there isn't any running water?"

"There is in the summer. Whoever owns this place
drained the pipes before winter so they wouldn't freeze and
burst. Makes sense."

She supposed it did, but that didn't solve the immediate
problem. Of course, the immediate problem was exacer-
bated by the pain she felt each time she moved her left hand,
but she was going to have to learn to work around that, too.

Quist watched her face. He could practically read the
thoughts going through her mind, particularly since she
was gingerly holding that left hand at her waist. It needed
to be splinted, and badly. But she was going to have to

reach that conclusion herself. He wondered how long it would take her.

Though his first instinct was to do the cleanup himself and let her concentrate on the baby, he sat back leisurely drinking his cocoa. "There's a basin by the sink," he said. "Fill it with the water that's left on the stove. Add enough cold water from what's on the floor so you don't burn yourself. Soap and stuff is by the basin."

It sounded nearly as simple as it was. Lily managed to clean everything they'd used for dinner, and conveniently there was a draining rack by the sink, so she didn't have to worry about drying, which she guessed would be more difficult.

When she was done, she felt buoyed. Returning to the table, she sat down, put her face on eye level with the baby and said, "How's it going, Nicki?"

Nicki, who'd been nudging a soft plastic ring in the general vicinity of her mouth, lifted her head and looked at Lily with round eyes that expressed excitement at having her mother's attention again.

"What a bright little girl," Lily whispered in praise. Smiling, she ran her hand over the baby's soft brown hair.

"What does she do?" Quist asked.

Lily looked up. "What do you mean?"

"Is this it? She sleeps, eats and cries, lies around kicking her arms and legs and making faces?"

Lily wasn't offended. Quist just didn't know. Two months before, she'd probably have asked the same question. So it was easy to be patient. "She looks around. She absorbs what she sees and tries to make sense out of it. She responds to the people she's with." Lowering her head again, Lily said in a soft, mommy voice, "Isn't that so, Nicki? There's so much to see in the world, even in this dark, old cabin. There's the sound of the wind and snow outside, and the buzz of the fire and the light from the lamp.

There's my face and his face and the table and your toys—" She broke off, because Nicki grinned, and it was such a delightful thing to see that Lily laughed. When she reached for the baby to hug her, though, the laugh ended with a sharp cry. Without thinking, she'd tried to use her left hand. It was a mistake.

Coming to her feet, she did manage to get Nicki into her arms, but the hug she gave her was selfish, more to comfort herself than anything else.

"Your face went white just then," Quist informed her.

"Thanks."

"It's going to get worse."

"No. I just forgot for a minute. When Nicki smiles, I forget about everything else."

Quist hadn't seen the smile, because he'd been studying Lily's face at the time. He'd been trying to understand how a woman who looked tired and bedraggled could suddenly start to beam. He supposed it was what she said, that Nicki made her forget about other things, but having never had an experience like it, he couldn't quite understand. He'd never been so caught up with another human being that he'd forgotten who he was, what he was doing and why.

"Does she smile often?" he asked.

Cradling Nicki between her body and her left arm, with the injured hand angled away, she used her right to tease the baby's chin. "More and more now. Her first smiles came and went so fast that I wasn't really sure what I'd seen, or whether it was a real smile or a gas pain. Lately the smiles come at appropriate times." Lily grinned and her voice went up. "Like now."

He saw it that time, toothless and wide, and there was something about it that made him smile inside. She looked so happy, Nicki did, so happy in such a wholehearted, innocent way that it would have been impossible for him to do anything else. When her smile disappeared, he was sorry and found himself watching closely to see if it would come again.

It did. So did several others, all in response to Lily's coaxing and cajoling. In time, though, as was inevitable, Nicki tired. Her little face remained serious. Then she began to squirm and grimace. Lily did her best to restore her good mood, hoping, among other things, to prolong her wakeful period as much as possible so that she'd sleep longer through the night. But the whimpers came next, and when they persisted, Lily knew she had to do something.

Changing a diaper, particularly those of the disposable, painless variety, was a relatively easy chore. Lily had changed dozens in the past five weeks. She felt she'd become an expert.

Always before, though, she'd had two hands, and never before had she had an audience. If she'd thought ahead, she'd probably have changed the baby in her drawer on the floor, where her one-handed awkwardness would have been hidden. But she didn't think beyond the ease of changing the baby on the table, and once she'd managed to scoop up the diaper bag from the shadows, juggle both the bag and Nicki, then deposit Nicki on the receiving blanket, she wasn't about to lift her again so fast.

So with Quist watching, she went about the task. Unsnapping the lower part of the terry jumpsuit was easy enough to do with one hand, as was freeing the baby's tiny feet. Lifting the jumpsuit out of the way without lifting the baby was a little tougher. Lily pushed and tugged. She tried to act natural doing it, though she was sure that she looked incompetent, which was very much how she felt. But the diaper had to be changed, and there was no one to do it but her.

She kept at it. Talking soft gibberish to Nicki, which was what she always did when she changed her, she ever so carefully held one part of the diaper down with the very tops of the fingers of her left hand, while she tore first one tape, then the other. Thanking her lucky stars that the baby was only wet, she lifted the two little feet in her right hand and pushed the diaper out of the way with the side of her left.

That brought a closed-mouth moan.

"Lily," Quist warned.

"It's okay," she said quickly.

"Each time you do something like that, it makes it worse."

"It's sore. That's all."

"You're risking greater damage."

"Oh, hush. You're just trying to make your point."

"Damn right, I am. That wrist is broken—"

"Sprained. It'll be fine," she said with determination. Drawing the new diaper close, she lifted Nicki's feet again and nudged the diaper under her. Though she didn't moan that time, tiny dots of perspiration broke out on her nose. Weak-kneed, she lowered herself to the bench.

"What's wrong?" Quist asked, concerned by her pallor.

Lily took a premoistened towelette from its pack. "I wish I could bathe her. It's been so long."

He was relieved that was all. "She looks pretty clean to me."

"She is, I suppose." Using her one good hand, she managed to wipe the baby's bottom.

Quist watched everything she did. He wasn't feeling as smug as he had before. She wasn't giving in to the pain like he thought she would, and he was beginning to really worry about her wrist. But aside from that worry, he watched out of pure curiosity. Without her sleeper, Nicki was smaller than ever. He couldn't say that she was scrawny, because she looked healthy and well fed, still she was small. He doubted her foot was as big as his thumb. Looking at her, he found it hard to believe she would grow up one day to have the kind of gentle, womanly curves her mother did.

Annoyed that he'd even thought that, he scowled. Seconds later, when Lily liberally coated the baby's bottom with Vaseline, he said on a note of distaste, "That looks like the most uncomfortable thing in the world. Who wants to go around with a greasy butt?"

"A baby who doesn't want a rash. The Vaseline protects her." Lily arched a brow his way. "She's not riding a horse, Quist."

That shut him up, but it was a short-lived victory for Lily. Securing the new diaper on Nicki was a trial, as was getting her dressed again. By the time she was done, Lily was frazzled and her wrist was worse.

"What now?" Quist asked. He hadn't moved an inch, still sat at the table with his forearms flat and his mouth set.

"I'm going to bed," Lily answered. She didn't know what else to do. She was feeling lots of things—annoyed that he'd watched her struggle without offering to help, afraid that he was right about her wrist, fearful that the storm had worsened and that they'd be stuck in the cabin for days. Mostly, though, she was feeling exhausted. She hadn't done more than doze the night before, and now, with a full stomach after a day that had been endless and tense, she wanted the blissful escape of sleep.

First, though, she had to put Nicki into her blanket sleeper. She did it with the baby in the drawer this time, still it was an ordeal. Between the frustration and the pain, Lily was near tears by the time she finished. Sheer force of will kept her from breaking down again—that, and Nicki's precious face looking up at her from amid the blankets.

"You're such a love," she whispered, leaned low and kissed the baby's soft cheek. The contact felt so good that she stayed there for a minute. For another minute she actually debated having Nicki sleep with her on the mattress. She wanted to hold—or be held—anything to ward off the fear she felt.

Given the tender state of her wrist, it was a bad idea, she

decided. So she took a deep breath and stood. With her back to Quist and her head down, she said, "I have to use the outhouse. Where is it?"

Quist closed his eyes briefly, only then admitting to the suffering he'd felt watching Lily try to manage Nicki with one hand. Now she had to use the bathroom, which meant putting on boots and a coat, then taking them off again. He'd wanted to make a point before, but he just wasn't enough of a bastard to carry it to the extreme.

"Come on," he said and went for his boots.

Lily grew alarmed. "Uh, you don't have to go out. Just tell me where—is it to the right or the left—how far away—"

"It's wild out there."

She could hear it. The wind had been howling around the corners of the cabin since they'd arrived and showed no sign of letting up. Still, she didn't want Quist taking her to the bathroom. It was embarrassing.

"I'm taking you."

"That's not necessary."

"I think it is," he said firmly. He knelt and held her boot.

Lily stared at the boot for a minute, but that was all it took for her to realize that, as had been the case with changing her pants, embarrassment was impractical. Gripping his shoulder, she pushed her foot in. After he'd held the second boot in the same manner, he held her coat for her. He was duly patient when it came to the left hand, which she took more time easing in.

When he tossed on his own coat, she made a final plea. "I'd feel better knowing you were here with Nicki."

He shot a fast glance at the baby, but she was little more than a silent bundle of blankets in her drawer. "You think she might get up and run off?"

"Of course not, but—"

"Someone may come and abduct her while we're gone? A kidnapper? In this blizzard?"

"What if something happens, like a spark coming out of the woodstove—"

"I've been watching that woodstove since I lit it, and it doesn't send out sparks. It's perfectly safe."

"Still—"

"Look at it this way," he said with a tired sigh. "The chances of something happening to Nicki alone in here are far less than something happening to you alone out there. So I'll come—unless you're planning to spend two hours in the outhouse, in which case, thanks, but I will stay here."

"I'll only be a minute."

"That's what I thought. Let's go." Pushing the Stetson onto his head, he took the hurricane lamp and her arm and drew her out the door.

The storm was as wild as he'd said. Snow was heavy underfoot and overhead, a fury of bright white dots whipping around in the light of the lamp at the mercy of the wind. She ducked her head against the cold, stinging flakes and let Quist forge the way. She heard him swear, or thought she heard him, though with her hood over her ears and the thunder of the wind she couldn't be sure. But she was glad he'd come. Even if she'd known where she was going, she wouldn't have liked being out there alone. It was dark and cold and wet and scary.

The outhouse stood a dozen yards behind the cabin in what seemed a never-never land of snow. By the time they reached it, Lily wouldn't have cared if Quist had come inside. But he shoved her in with the lantern, yelled, "Hurry," and pulled the door closed.

She was as quick as she could be, given her hand, the cold, and the utter foreignness of the place. She didn't stop to look around; she was afraid of what she'd see. So she simply relieved herself, thanked God that Quist had had the foresight to put her in sweatpants, straightened her clothing and left.

Not about to waste the trip, Quist took his turn while

Lily stood outside, huddling against the snow-encrusted wood with her arms wrapped around herself and her face buried in her coat. As soon as he came out, they trudged back to the cabin. The return should have been easier, since they'd already made tracks, but the sheer volume of snow worked against them.

Once inside, Lily went straight to Nicki, who was sound asleep, none the worse for the few minutes she'd spent alone. Quist made no comment, but helped her take her things off, then took off his own and dropped into one of the Adirondack chairs.

Taking a pillow and blanket from another of the dresser drawers, Lily lay down on the mattress in front of the stove, shivered under the blanket until the cold from outside had left her, then closed her eyes. She felt bone tired, more so than she could ever remember feeling. But sleep didn't come. Her wrist hurt. She shifted from one side to the other, from her back to her stomach, but there wasn't any escape from the pain. It was relentless, stretching each minute to an agonizing extreme. She tried to will it away, but Quist's words kept echoing in her mind.

"It's broken...I felt it...I felt the bone moving...see how swollen it is...it should be immobilized and elevated."

Shifting her head to one side of the pillow, she propped her wrist on the other. He'd said to elevate it, and that was the one thing she could do without much effort. It was also, she realized after what seemed another eternity of trying to sleep, not doing as much as she'd hoped. The throbbing went on.

"That wrist is broken...you're only risking greater damage...if the bone knits wrong."

Sitting up, she eyed the wrist as though it were an old friend that had turned traitor. It looked guilty—fat and ugly. And broken. There. She admitted it. But admitting it didn't make the pain go away.

She looked over her shoulder at Quist. He was slouched in the low chair with his legs outstretched, his fingers loosely laced over his middle and his head back against the slats. At first she thought he was asleep. Then she caught the tiny flicker of light reflected in his eyes, and she knew he was looking at her.

"Can you do something?" she asked defeatedly.

"About what?"

"My wrist."

"Not much to do for a sprain," he said, but she heard the challenge in his voice.

She lowered her head. "I can't sleep. It really hurts. I think you're right. It may be broken. I don't want it to be, but what I want isn't always what I get." She raised her eyes to his. "Please."

Quist was out of his chair in a minute, silently cursing himself for making her spell out what she wanted. He didn't like hearing her beg. Somehow it didn't seem right. From what she'd told him, well apart from her wrist, things hadn't gone her way much. If she'd been stubborn before, it had been out of fear. From what he'd seen of her, she wasn't naturally mulish.

"Go sit at the table," he said. He went to the far corner of the room where the dry logs were stored.

Lily wondered what he was doing, but she did her wondering from the table. She watched him take several somethings from the corner, then go back to their bags and get a pair of socks from hers and a shirt from his. She was looking nervous by the time he joined her, which prompted him to explain exactly what he was going to do.

"These are pieces of shingle. I saw them when I took wood for the stove. Someone must have done some repair work on the roof last summer and left the remnants there." He took one of her socks, which were long and cotton, stretched the neck enough to get the piece of shingle going, then shimmied it inside. "They're fiberglass, so they'll be rigid enough to work as a splint without being heavy." He repeated the process with the second piece, then began to tear strips from his shirt.

Lily couldn't believe he was ruining a perfectly good shirt. "Wait, there must be something of mine—"

But he ignored her. "These will hold the whole thing together. You won't be able to move your wrist, which is how we want it." Swinging a leg over the bench, he came down behind Lily. With an arm on either side of her, he was positioned to work on her hand as though it were his own. "I'll have to touch it again to make sure it's okay," he warned. His voice was low but gentle, his breath fanning her temple.

Lily steeled herself for the pain. When it came, she bit her lip and leaned back into him. It was as though one part of her had to escape his prodding, though she didn't move her hand. It was also a move toward a haven that promised warmth and strength.

As gently as he could, Quist continued to probe his way through the swelling to feel the bone that was broken and make sure it was straight. He knew the discomfort he was causing, and again wished for that double shot of whiskey, though not for himself this time. Lily did her best not to make a sound, and except for sharp little gasps when the pain was at its worst, she succeeded. But he could feel the way she pressed back against him, leaning away from the pain, and the way she clutched the table with her good hand and the way she was beginning to tremble. At one point, when she seemed particularly tense, she pressed her face to his arm. He wet his lips and probed on.

"I think that's it," he murmured when he was satisfied that he had the bone aligned. Carefully he slid one of the sock-covered shingles under her hand. He put the second shingle on top, then bound and secured the cotton strips.

"I've left your fingers hanging out. You'll be able to use them a little once the swelling goes down."

"When will that be?" she asked. Her face was no longer buried against his sleeve, but her voice was thin. It would have told him she hurt even if he didn't already know.

He rested his hands beside hers, making no move to get up. "As soon as tomorrow, if you keep it raised. The point is to elevate it above your heart so the blood runs away."

"When will it feel better?"

"Tomorrow or the next day, if I've done it right. As long as the bone is aligned and you can't move it, there should be steady improvement. I may have to tighten these strips once the swelling goes down, but that's no big deal."

"Fine for you to say. You're not the one in agony."

He almost wished he were, he felt so badly for her just then. "Got any aspirin?"

"No."

"There's a first-aid kit on one of the shelves." It was a small pack that didn't look capable of containing much more than Band-Aids and disinfectant. But it was worth a try. "Maybe it has aspirin, or something stronger."

"No," she said quickly. "I don't want anything."

"It would help with the pain."

"I can bear the pain as long as I know it's not permanent."

"It's not permanent," he assured her and continued to hold her gently. The tension he'd felt in her body while he'd been working was beginning to drain away, leaving her limp and pliant. She conformed nicely to his frame. While he wasn't sure it was wise of him to appreciate something like that, he knew he'd stay exactly where he was until she showed signs of wanting to move.

After sitting for another minute with her head lolled back against his chest, she slowly drew herself forward. "I should let you sleep."

"I'll sleep later."

"Then I should let me sleep."

It was what she needed most, he knew. He also knew that he wouldn't sleep until she did. Leaving the bench, he went back to the dressers and took out another pillow and three more blankets. He returned to the woodstove just as Lily was checking on Nicki.

"Sleeping?"

She nodded. "I don't know for how long. It could be another hour, or five."

"Then you'd better try to get whatever rest you can now."

She nodded again, but she stayed where she was, sitting on the edge of the mattress with her splinted hand carefully placed on her thigh. Her eyes were soft with fatigue when she looked up at him. "Where will you be?"

He shrugged. "I'll sit here a little, then bring over the other mattress."

She studied her hand for a minute, then looked up again. "Thank you for doing this."

"How does it feel?"

"It still hurts."

He imagined that would go on for a while yet, and since she wouldn't take aspirin, the only other thing he could do was to elevate her hand and try to give her a little relief that way. Without thinking of the absurdity of it, he dragged one of the Adirondack chairs forward, propped a pillow against it and sat down on the floor. Then he took Lily's pillow, put it against his stomach and gestured for her to lie down.

Lily wasn't thinking of the absurdity of it, either. She was remembering how nice it was to be close to Quist's body. She wanted more of that comfort. It would be better than aspirin, she knew.

Crossing to where he sat, she put her head on the pillow and her splint on the blanket he folded on his knee. She felt him cover her with the third blanket, but she'd already closed her eyes, and she had no intention of spoiling the moment by uttering so much as another thank-you. Just before she fell asleep, she imagined she felt a hand smooth her hair back from her cheek. She held the gesture to her until exhaustion took it and all else.

CHAPTER FIVE

BY THE TIME Nicki stirred, Lily and Quist had shifted to the mattress. They were tucked against each other with Lily in front, nearest the woodstove. Her wrist was still elevated. Quist had woken periodically to make sure of that, and though the wrist still ached, the throbbing had eased. She'd actually been sleeping quite soundly when she'd heard the first of Nicki's tiny cries.

Maternal instinct had awoken her then, a second sense that registered certain sounds while overlooking others. Not being a mother, Quist was without benefit of that instinct. The first he knew of anything amiss was when the softness that had been pressed against him stirred, then inched away. He was slow to realize what was happening, but once he did, he came quickly awake.

"Don't lift her," he said suddenly and loudly.

About to do just that, Lily jumped. She was sure she'd left him asleep. "I have to take her out to feed her," she explained. She returned her attention to Nicki, who wasn't pleased with the delay, but she'd no sooner freed the fussing infant from her blanket than Quist materialized on the opposite side of the drawer.

He was hunkered down, hands poised, voice all business, if a bit groggy. "Tell me what to do."

He was so earnest about it that Lily couldn't help but stare. "You can't feed her, Quist."

"I know that, Lily," he mocked, "but I can get her up and

put her in your arms. There's a reason why I made the effort of splinting your wrist, and I didn't have fun doing it, no matter what you think. So let's give the damn thing a chance to heal, huh?" He looked at Nicki again. "Now what do I do? What do I grab?"

Lily felt suddenly light-headed. She figured it had something to do with sleeping so soundly and waking abruptly. She wondered if it had to do with sleeping with Quist. As a compromise she decided it had to do with simple relief that he'd offered to help. Between that light-headedness and the absolutely precious look of intensity on his face, she wanted to laugh. She knew better.

"Slide one hand behind her head and neck, and the other under her bottom. Head and neck. That's right. There, she's fine."

"Why's she screaming?"

"Because she's hungry." She held out her arms.

But Quist kept staring at the bundle in his hands. "She doesn't like the way I'm holding her."

"She likes it just fine." Just as she'd known not to laugh, Lily knew what to say. She was no fool. Quist's offer of help was a godsend. She wasn't about to offend him by telling him he was holding the baby like she was a sacrifice to a pagan god, though the image was apt. He did look half-heathen, dark and mussed and badly in need of a shave, and his arms were tense. "You can relax your hands a little. They're big and she's small—they'll support her without much effort. That's right."

"She's still crying."

Again Lily reached for her. "She wants milk." When he still made no move to hand Nicki over, she lowered her arm and said, "Try bringing her in a little closer to your body. She likes to feel sheltered. There's a comfort in that." As Lily knew from personal experience. "Ah, see? She's quieting down."

"Not all the way. I'm still doing something wrong."

"No, you're not."

"She's uncomfortable with me."

Lily wanted to say that Nicki was wet and hungry and would be uncomfortable with *anyone* who held her just then, but in fact she was crying less loudly than she'd been a minute before. "Hold her like she's a football."

He was horrified by that idea. "Are you kidding?"

"No. You know how they do it when they've got the ball and they're running down the field? Well, shift her around a little so her head's kind of tucked into your elbow."

"How do I do that without dropping her?"

"Slide the hand that's under her head down her back so that your arm keeps supporting her head."

"It'll wobble if I don't, won't it?" he said, but he was following her direction and there wasn't a bit of a wobble.

"That's it. Now ease her up into the crook of your elbow. There." Inordinately pleased, she sat back on her heels. "Perfect. You can even take away the other hand. She's very comfortable there."

Indeed, she was. She'd stopped crying altogether, and although her little mouth was set in a way that threatened she might start in again at any time, she simply looked up at Quist.

He made a small, weighing motion with his arm. "She's very light."

"She's very little."

"Littler than most babies?"

"Littler than some, but none are real big at this age."

He made the small, lifting motion again. "This isn't so bad."

"What did you expect?"

"I don't know. I thought maybe she'd squirm right out of my hands. Know what I'd feel like if that happened and she fell on the floor?"

Lily had asked herself the same question dozens of times in the past five weeks. "She won't."

Nicki continued to study Quist with eyes that looked large and round in her face. Only her hands moved. They were linked in a random way that kept shifting, one tiny index finger on a knuckle, then a pinky around a wrist, then a thumb in a palm. Intrigued, Quist followed the changes.

"Does she know she's doing that?"

"She knows she's touching something that's reassuring and warm. Does she know it's her own hand? Probably not."

"She looks like she does. She looks like she knows a whole lot more than we think she does."

Lily felt a swell of pride, but said nothing. She thought Nicki was brilliant. That didn't mean she was going to boast about it to strangers.

Then again, Quist wasn't really a stranger. Not anymore. She didn't know the details of his life, didn't know what kind of ranch he had or how many men he employed or why he'd been heading for Quebec, but she had a feeling that she knew things about him that other people didn't. She knew that there was a gentle side beneath the gruffness, a caring side beneath the indifference. She knew that though he claimed to dislike women, he didn't like seeing one hurt, and that his aversion to babies wasn't so much aversion as fear, and that though one part of him didn't want to, he liked physical closeness a lot. What else could explain the way he'd chosen to sit when he'd tended her wrist, or the way he'd held her while she'd fallen asleep, or the way he'd kept her curled against him after that, or even the way he was holding the baby now. He still wasn't entirely comfortable with it, but he didn't rush to hand her back.

He was, Lily decided, an interesting man. She'd taken one look at him in the snowstorm and labeled him a cowboy, but there was much more to him than a Stetson.

He had a depth that few of the men she'd known possessed. Thirty-six hours—not even that—she'd spent with him, and together they'd run through a gamut of emotions. Still she had a feeling that she'd only seen a few of his layers.

Strange, she mused as she continued to study him, but that top layer had changed since they'd met. She hadn't thought him particularly attractive at first. He'd been too large, too dark, too forbidding. She saw him differently now. Beneath the bulk of his outer clothing, he was well built. Though his shoulders were broad, they tapered to a lean waist and hips and long, strong legs. And while his face was shadowed by a two-day stubble, he didn't look darker, so much as rugged. He had high cheekbones and eyes that weren't coal black, as she'd originally thought, but softer, rich like sable, warm when the defensive walls inside him began to melt. They were doing that now, and he wasn't looking at the baby. He was looking at her, in a way that said they shared something special.

She'd never seen that kind of look in a man's eyes before. God knew Jarrod had never looked at her that way. It made her heart beat faster and her blood heat and her breath trip over itself before rushing on.

In that rush, with her eyes still on Quist's, she whispered, "Maybe I'd better feed her. It's still the middle of the night. I've been trying to teach her that I won't play with her when it's dark. That's the only way she'll learn to sleep through." She took a fast breath. "Besides, I'm feeling full. It's time."

Quist's gaze fell to her breasts. He didn't say a word, just looked, but Lily felt an intense tingling warring with that sense of fullness. This tingling went deeper, curling down through her body until it settled in her womb. The sensation was nothing like the contractions she used to feel when the baby nursed. This sensation was sexual and unexpected. It had been a long time since Lily had thought of herself as a sexual being.

He raised his eyes to hers for a final, hot second before turning his attention to Nicki. Very slowly and more than a little awkwardly, reversing the motions that had brought her in to his elbow, he handed her over. Lily was able to take her in her left arm without hurting the splinted wrist, while she used her right hand to unbutton her Henley-style sweater. She was about to push the wool aside, when she paused. Her bra was already undone, since she hadn't been able to do it up with one hand after the last feeding, and pushing aside the wool meant baring her breast. Quist had seen it before, but that had been when she'd been cold and exhausted and hurting. She hadn't been thinking about him then.

She was now. She was thinking about the heat in his eyes and the heat inside her. She was thinking that it was both inappropriate and frightening, and that the smartest thing would be to turn away while she nursed. But when she started to do that, he said, "Don't. Let me watch."

His voice was low and smoky, a caress and a plea, and she couldn't say no. After all he'd done, she couldn't deny him this. Or so she told herself as she gently eased back the wool, tucked it outside her breast and brought Nicki to her nipple. But there was more. Though she kept her eyes on the baby, she could feel Quist's eyes on her. She could feel the heat. Yes, it was inappropriate and frightening. But it felt good.

Quist wasn't so sure. He was aroused—the pressure behind the placket of his fly was fierce—and he didn't know where it had come from. One minute he'd been holding the baby, thinking totally innocent thoughts, and the next he'd looked up to find Lily looking at him in a way that had turned him on.

He didn't know what was so arousing about her. He liked his women tall and shapely, with long, thick, wavy hair that could toy with a breast before he'd even put his fingers there. Lily wasn't like that at all. She was small and slender. Her hair just grazed her shoulders. Granted, her breasts were large, but that was because they were filled with milk, and because of that, he reasoned, they shouldn't turn him on.

So what was it? He supposed it was lots of things, and he supposed it had been building for a while. Nursing or not, a breast was a breast, and he was definitely a breast man. He guessed he had felt something the first time he'd seen Lily's. He knew he'd felt something when he'd helped her out of her jeans, when he'd seen the shapeliness of her legs, the softness of her skin, the curvature of her stomach. She'd been embarrassed by that, but he'd thought it sexy as hell.

And then she'd looked at him as if she found him attractive, when he'd counted on her not wanting him. He'd counted on her nixing anything before it started. He'd counted on her being the ice water to cool his fire.

Maybe it was an aberration. Maybe she was thinking of someone else, like her ex-husband or that brother-in-law she'd mentioned. No, not one of those two, he decided, but maybe someone else. He knew she was headed for Quebec to start a new life, and he knew she was alone. Still, maybe there was an old love in Quebec, someone she was planning to see, someone she'd been thinking about when she'd looked at him that way.

The thought angered him, but then, he was easy to anger when he was aroused without hope of relief. He was still aroused. *Why didn't the damn thing go down?*

It didn't go down, he told himself, because he'd asked her to let him watch her nurse, and a strangely erotic sight it was. His gaze drifted from her bare breast to her bent head to the slender fingers that, over and over, smoothed the baby's fine hair. Yes, it kept him aroused, but there was also a peace to the scene that held him there. Lily was nurturing her child as women had nurtured children since the start of time. She was loving that child in unspoken ways, and the feeling that emerged was one of serene beauty.

Quist watched with growing envy. The one thing he'd missed in life had been the kind of relationship that was so close as to be beautiful. Lily had it. Nicki would grow, and perhaps mother and daughter would have their differences, but at the moment they had something precious.

Aware that his body had finally begun to relax, he got up and added wood to the stove, then sank into the chair to watch it burn while he thought about relationships and what made them the way they were. When he saw Lily take Nicki from her breast, he found himself sitting forward and quietly asking, "Need help?"

But she easily shifted the baby to her shoulder. "I'm okay."

"Does the wrist hurt?"

"It aches, but it's better than it was. The splint helps."

Quist sat back again, this time propping his jaw on a fist. He thought back to the start of the time they'd spent together, when he'd been able to chalk Lily off as just another troublesome female and ignore her. That time had passed. He didn't think he'd ever be indifferent to her again. Even now, when his body was finally under control, he'd leaned forward and asked for more. Either he was a masochist, or Lily sparked something in him that no other woman ever had. He wasn't sure he wanted to know which it was, but in either case, he knew he couldn't sit by and watch her struggle. Time enough for struggling once they were back in civilization and went their separate ways.

Prompted by the thought, he went to the window, pulled back a shutter and peered outside. It was too dark to see much, but the low light leaking from inside the cabin revealed snow sweeping past the pane. He couldn't detect the slightest letup of the howling wind. It made him nervous to think about how much more snow had accumulated since he'd been out last.

"What time is it?" Lily called softly.

"Four-fifteen."

"No improvement?"

"Nope." He returned to his chair and sat there until Nicki was done. When Lily laid her on the mattress, he came forward. "What can I do?"

She reached for the zipper of the sleeper and began working it down, jerk by jerk, with one hand. "Uh, I don't think you want to do this."

Pushing her hand aside, he had the zipper down in a minute. Then he sat back on his heels. "What next?"

"Her legs. You have to take them out of the sleeper."

He managed that a little more slowly, gingerly holding her legs with his thumb and forefinger. Remembering what Lily had done the last time, he unsnapped the bottom of the jumpsuit, then pulled the terry cloth until first one, then the other of Nicki's feet popped free. Lily lifted both feet in one hand.

"Push the stretchsuit out of the way."

He did that. Again remembering, he carefully tore each of the diaper tapes. Then he sat on his heels and tucked his hands into the back of his jeans. He couldn't have said, "This part's yours," any louder.

Lily didn't complain. She was impressed that he'd done so much. As quickly as possible, given the handicap of her wrist, she did her part. When she reached for a clean diaper, he came forward again to help, and though he did things more slowly than she might have if she'd had two hands, he worked faster than she could with one.

When Nicki was back in her drawer with the blankets pulled up around her, he went for the second mattress and put it foot-to-foot with the first.

Lily was vaguely disappointed. She'd enjoyed the warmth of Quist's body. But separate beds were the wisest thing, she knew. Vividly she remembered the heat that had simmered between them, and though it had cooled to a comfortable level, she knew it could rise again. Separate beds were definitely the wisest thing.

Quist turned down the hurricane lamp this time, leaving the cabin lit only by the golden glow from the stove. With the pain in her wrist nowhere near as sharp as it had been, Lily fell quickly to sleep.

As though sensing her mother's need to rest, Nicki slept for a full five hours. It was after nine-thirty in the morning when her small cries woke Lily from a deep sleep.

She yawned, then stretched, and the first thing she thought of was not her daughter, but a delightful warmth by her feet. It was a minute before she realized that those feet were entwined with Quist's. For a minute they remained that way. She could hear the storm raging outside, and the warmth inside felt so good that she didn't want to lose it.

But Nicki wanted attention. Reluctantly Lily sat up, only to have Quist wave her back down. "I'll get her," he murmured in a groggy way that was offset by the speed with which he was on his feet. He lifted the baby a little less awkwardly this time, and when she immediately stopped crying, he scowled at her. "I thought you were hungry."

"She just wanted to get up," Lily explained, rubbing sleep from her eyes. "She's probably hungry, too, but the first priority is recognition."

Quist went on scowling at Nicki. "They learn fast."

Lily considered that as she came fully awake. "We teach them. First children, especially. From the start, we come to them when they cry, so they start crying when they want us to come. Some mothers have the demands of other children or a husband or a job, so they don't do it as much. Me, I only have Lily. I've spoiled her, I guess."

"She doesn't have any grandparents?"

"My parents are dead, and if Jarrod's know she exists,

they don't care. It's just as well, I suppose. If they wanted to see her, I'd have to take her back to Hartford to visit, and I don't want to do that."

The hardening of her voice was subtle, but Quist caught it. He knew that her marriage had ended badly. As odd as the time seemed now, he wanted to know more. "Was it bad all the way through?"

Disentangling herself from the blanket, Lily pushed it back and got up. "Not really." She went to her bag, took out a brush and worked it through her hair.

"What does that mean?"

She sighed. The last thing she wanted to discuss, especially two minutes after she'd woken up, was her marriage. But she couldn't be angry with Quist. He was being so helpful, and he was only curious. "It means that while I was living through it, I thought it was okay. It's only afterward that I look back and know differently." Returning the hairbrush to her bag, she looked longingly at the clothes she'd brought. She wanted to bathe in a bad way and, even more, to put on fresh things. But that would have to wait.

Coming back to Quist, she saw that Nicki was perfectly happy. Lily wasn't quite sure why, since he was holding her as if she was a sack of potatoes, albeit a valuable one, but she guessed that the novelty of his features intrigued her. Funny, his darkness hadn't made her cry. But then, she was too young to put a symbolic meaning to dark and light. Or maybe she was too smart.

"You have a way with her, Quist."

He grunted. "She'd be staring at me even if I was a side of beef."

"No. She doesn't like sides of beef. I tried that in the supermarket once. She screamed. Actually, it wasn't a side of beef. It was a steak that I put into the carrier with her. Something about it frightened her. You're much bigger, but she's not frightened." She paused to look up at him. "Will you hold her a minute longer? Since she's quiet, I can try to get some breakfast going. She may not be starved, but I am."

So was Quist. "There aren't any eggs."

"I didn't expect there would be."

"Or bacon or sausage."

So he was an egg and bacon man, she mused, crossing to study the kitchen shelves. Actually, she was an egg and bacon woman, but she hadn't expected to find either of those, and she wasn't complaining. Yesterday's fear of starvation was too fresh in her mind.

She lifted a few lids and peered inside, then bent down to scan the contents of a lower shelf. "Quist?"

"Yes?"

He was directly behind her. She shot up straight, then went red. "Sorry."

He noticed the color on her cheeks and realized that she looked better. The shadows under her eyes had faded. She didn't look as frightened or as helpless, though there was still a question in her eye. For a split second, he entertained the notion that the question had to do with sex. Then he forced himself to think sanely. "You started to ask something."

It was a split second before she remembered what it was. "The weather. We're not going anywhere today, are we?"

"Not unless the wind suddenly dies and the snow stops within the next half hour."

"Why in the next half hour?"

"Because when I go out, it's got to be first thing in the morning. It may take me a while to reach help, then a while to get it back here, and I want to be back by nightfall."

She wanted to ask why, but that seemed like pushing a good thing too far. Still she was touched. He was an incredibly kind man. For that, she decided, he deserved the best breakfast she could invent.

Actually, she didn't have to invent a thing, since pancakes had been breakfast fare for generations. She supposed lacing them with peanut butter was a novelty, and she doubted she'd want to enter the recipe in the bake-off, but the end result was edible and nourishing.

Quist loved it. He was great at opening cans and cooking up frozen dinners and reheating leftovers, and he could fry a mean egg and grill a rasher of bacon just right, but he wasn't one to put together a meal from scratch. He was surprised that Lily had done it. He hadn't expected she'd be much of a cook, but she'd managed well, even with a bum hand. Nicki had started to cry just as the first batch of pancakes were done, so he'd taken over with the spatula, but that was okay. It wasn't like Lily had left the kitchen in the middle of things to polish her toenails. He could wield a spatula. And the pancakes were great.

With Nicki fed and changed, Lily laid her on the table and sat down for her own breakfast. Nursing a second cup of cocoa, Quist watched her eat. Though she talked softly to Nicki from time to time, she seemed otherwise content with the silence. He wondered whether she'd become as used to solitude as he had, or whether she'd always been that way. He didn't ask, though. The silence was too comfortable just then.

When she'd finished, Lily looked at him and smiled. Seconds later, she shifted her gaze to the window and the smile faded. "This is unreal," she murmured.

He'd liked her smile. It had done things to him, and he was sorry it was gone. But he knew what she meant. Unreal was one word for their situation; bizarre was another. "Uh-huh." He saw her looking down at her splinted wrist. "How does it feel?"

She hesitated before answering, "Okay."

"Does that mean better?"

She nodded. It still ached, but the ache was more dull than acute. One part of her wanted to think that it wasn't broken, after all. The other part recalled the pain she'd felt when Quist had manipulated it the night before. No sprain felt like that.

"I should have known it was broken."

"You didn't want it to be."

"No, but I should have known. I always manage to do things like that."

"You didn't do it on purpose."

She sighed, still looking down. "I didn't purposely come down with chicken pox the night before I was to play Dorothy in my seventh grade class's production of 'The Wizard of Oz,' either. Or break out with poison ivy the day before my high school prom. Or have my rental car stolen with all my things inside when I was driving to college to start my sophomore year." She frowned, feeling the pain inside her head rather than at her wrist. "This couldn't have happened at a worse time." Her voice dropped to a whisper. "I have so many things to do."

"So you'll just do them slower."

She shrugged and got up from the table with the dishes. She didn't want to think about it. It was too discouraging. So many things to do, simple but important things that were going to be twice as difficult for her now. It wasn't fair.

Quist carried a pot of hot water to the sink. "I'll do them this time."

"*I'll* do them," she insisted. Swishing the dishes around in soapy water was one of the few things she could do single-handedly, and while she regretted her snappish tone, she had to be assertive. Quist was doing far too much.

Preoccupied wondering how she was going to do all those other things, she finished the dishes without another thought to Quist. When she was done and turned, though, she went very still.

He was shaving. Sitting at the table with his back to her, he was stripped to the waist. A small mirror was propped against the worn leather shaving kit. A small pan of hot water stood before that. He was stroking the blade up his neck, making neat, consecutive furrows in the shaving cream.

But it wasn't his neck to which her eyes were drawn, so much as his back. It was a broad expanse of skin stretched over tight muscles that moved with each stroke. She'd already guessed him to be fit. She'd already guessed at his tapering shape. She hadn't guessed at the raw power of his body, or at the powerful effect seeing it bare would have on her.

Her heart began to pound as she stood there, unable to take her eyes away. She noted the way spikes of dark hair fell over his nape when he tipped up his chin, the way the muscles of his shoulder bunched when he reached the apex of each stroke, the way tufts of dark hair shadowed his armpits. She saw a pale scar, jagged but old, lying somewhere in the vicinity of his waist, but it was hard to tell just where that waist was, since his jeans rode low on his hips. She traced his spine up to his shoulders, then dropped her gaze again until it hit his jeans. But her mind didn't stop at denim. It went on to the small of his back, then stole around to his front to see what was there.

Covering her eyes with her arm, she tried to get hold of herself. The baby would help, she decided, so she went to the table, leaned over Nicki, cooed to her for a minute and lifted her. Then, with the baby held tightly in her arms, her eyes went to Quist.

His chest was breathtaking, his muscles well-defined without being overdeveloped. He wasn't heavily haired, but what there was created a soft pelt that was broad and tapering, a visual echo of the shape of his body. His nipples were small and dark brown. He had a beauty mark just below the right one and a scar several inches below that.

"Lily."

She raised her eyes to find that he'd stopped shaving.

"What are you doing?" he asked in a low voice.

She tried to moisten her lips, but the inside of her mouth was dry. Her throat must have been, too, because her voice came out sounding parched. "Holding Nicki."

"That's not what I mean."

She swallowed. "I'm thinking that maybe I could bathe her when you're done."

His eyes glittered, daring her to tell him the truth.

"Well, you were just sitting there," she burst out. "I mean, I was doing the dishes and suddenly turned around and there you were with your shirt off. What did you expect me to do?"

"I didn't expect you'd stare that way," he said very quietly. "You've seen a man with his shirt off before."

"I know."

"You've seen a man shave before."

"Yes, but—"

"Is it just that it's been a long time, that you're hungry?"

"I'm not!" she cried. "I just had a baby. The *last* thing on my mind is sex."

He paused before saying, still in that same very quiet voice that was more pointed than a shout and every bit as dangerous, "It was there just now."

"And it's your fault!" She dropped her voice to mutter, "Sitting there like that, with a chest like yours," then raised her voice again, "What do you expect?" Turning on her heel, she stomped off to the front of the cabin and glared at her open bag.

"I expect," Quist said from directly behind her, "that you'll use a little self-control. I'm a man. You can't count on me for it."

"You don't need it. I'm not the one who's sexy."

"Who told you that?"

"I know it. I'm not gorgeous to begin with, and now that I've got a baby, I'm about as attractive to a man as a piece of mush."

His voice was closer. "I wouldn't say that."

"You would if you weren't shut up in this tiny place with me."

"But I am shut up in here with you, and it doesn't help things when you look at me the way you just did."

She knew that he was directly behind her. The heat of his body reached out to her, joining with the images of his bareness in her mind to play havoc with her insides. To blot out those images, she buried her face against Nicki's head, but the name she whispered was Quist's.

The heat came even closer then, a line of fire touching her from her shoulders to the backs of her knees. "I want you, Lily."

She shook her head, but couldn't utter a word.

Lowering his head over hers, he put his lips to her temple. The rest of his body did a similar kind of nuzzling. "You're not my type, still I want you. Can you feel it?"

A little frantic, she nodded.

"Then I would suggest," he said slowly and with deliberation, "that you make a point not to encourage me. If you let on that the feeling is mutual, I can't promise I won't take you." The last was said against her neck and was punctuated by a slow, suckling kiss that made Lily feel faint. But just when she needed him most, he stepped back. Furious in her frustration, she put a hand to the spot he'd kissed and whirled on him. "You gave me a hickey."

"Not this time," he said. More softly, he promised, "Next time," and before she could think of an appropriate comeback, he was sauntering back to the table.

Senses in an uproar, she collapsed onto the bare springs of the cot, held Nicki close and rocked back and forth. The squeaking of the springs joined with the sounds of the storm to emphasize the absurdity of the situation, as did a certain scent that was coming to her. It wasn't exactly the musky, male scent that had already etched itself on her brain, but a more immediate scent.

Touching her temple, she brought her hand down with traces of shaving cream. She found them on her neck, too, and would have screamed if it would have done any good. But self-control was what she needed, certainly not another confrontation with Quist. She was attracted to him. Okay, she was. But she'd get past it. It was nothing more than another hurdle to be cleared.

Taking several deep breaths, she sat up straight and turned her attention to Nicki.

Quist finished shaving and bathed himself as best he could with the water that remained and one of the towels he'd taken from the drawer. When he was done, he went for a clean shirt. That meant passing close by Lily, but she seemed determined not to look. He looked at her, though, as he buttoned the clean shirt, and when he was done, he said, "Do you want to bathe the kid?"

"Yes."

Pulling his boots on, he went outside to refill the largest pot with snow. He set the whole thing on top of the stove to melt. The process gave Lily plenty of time to undress Nicki, which she did on a blanket directly in front of the woodstove, where it was comfortably warm. By the time the water was hot, she was ready to go.

Quist watched. He told himself that he wanted to make sure Lily didn't injure her hand, but there was a definite curiosity factor involved. He wanted to see what she was going to do and how. He also wanted to see her doing it, because he liked watching her care for Nicki. It brought out the serenity factor, and though it reminded him of everything he missed, and in that sense was painful, he was helplessly drawn to it.

That serenity factor wasn't as strong, now, though, as it had been at other times, and Quist could see why. Splinted and awkward, Lily's wrist kept interfering with what she was trying to do. She shifted, lifting Nicki different ways, doing the best with what she had, but it clearly wasn't enough to satisfy her. Though she continued to talk softly and gently to the baby, her features grew tense, reflecting her frustration.

By the time she'd wrapped a wet and naked Nicki in a towel, she was near tears. That was when he came forward. "Damn it, won't you ever ask for help?"

She sat back on her heels, put her hands on her hips and, looking at the baby, said stonily, "I don't want help."

"Maybe not, but it'd be a hell of a lot easier on both of us if you admitted you could use it."

"I have to do this myself."

"Why?"

"Nicki's my responsibility."

"Yeah, but I'm sitting here doing nothing. Why not make use of me?"

She looked him in the eye. "Because that puts us close. Better we shouldn't be close."

He ran a hand through his hair, which had already dried from the dunking he'd given it and fell right back over his brow. "Better you should get this done. It's worse watching you."

Lily wasn't sure exactly what that meant, but she didn't have time to ask before he was leaning over to pat the baby dry. While Lily took care of the delicate parts, he helped with the others, and Nicki was happy enough with the dual attention to kick and coo and smile. By the time he handed her over, she was dressed in a pretty pink stretchsuit, her hair was brushed and her cheeks had the polish of early apples. Closing her eyes, Lily breathed deeply of that sweet baby smell she adored, and smiled. When Nicki yawned, she kissed her tiny, button nose and held her for several more minutes, then neatened the drawer and put her in for a nap.

Quist's voice came from the world behind her. "Are

you next?" He had a clean towel in his hand. Rising, she took it. He lowered his voice. "Want me to help?"

"Of course not," she whispered, eyes wide and glued to his.

"Can you manage by yourself?" The intimacy of his tone was matched by his look.

"Yes," she said in the wisp of breath he left her. She was able to breathe more deeply only when he turned away.

Disposing of the water she'd used for the baby, he refilled the smaller pot with hot water and set it on the table. When he looked at her again, his eyes were dark and sensual. "If I were a martyr, I'd offer to go out and wander around in the storm for fifteen minutes, but I'm no martyr." He turned one of the Adirondack chairs so that it faced the front of the cabin, dropped into it and said, "I won't watch."

Lily swallowed and stood stock-still. The air was pregnant with a silence that not even the storm could fill.

"Well?" he prompted without turning. "You'd better get to it. Like I said, I'm no martyr. I won't sit here forever."

That brought her to life. Taking clean clothes and a small bottle of lotion from her bag, she went to the table. For another minute she looked at Quist; only his dark hair and navy sweater were visible through the slats of the chair. Realizing that she had no choice but to trust him, she turned around, eased the sweater over her head, then over the wrist with the splint, and began to wash.

Quist didn't look once. He wanted to, and several times he came close—mainly because he hoped that the real thing would be less impressive than his imagination—but he stayed true to his word. His mind was so preoccupied thinking about what she'd be like naked, though, that he was unprepared when she materialized by his side fully clothed, looking fresh and combed and even more sweet-smelling than the baby. She wasn't on a pleasure mission, though.

"I think this needs tightening," she said quietly, cradling the splinted wrist in the good one. She looked a little pale.

"It hurts?"

She nodded.

Urging her down in front of him, he took the wrist onto his thigh and, one by one, released and retied the strips of cloth that held it tight. When he'd finished, he took the fingers extending from the splint and very gently moved them.

"Hurt?"

"A little."

"But not as much as yesterday?"

"No."

"That's good." With the splint braced on his thigh, he held her fingers in his palm, traced their slenderness with his thumb. "You don't wear a ring."

She looked at her hand, saw what his thumb was doing, found it soothing. "I'm divorced."

"Did you get the divorce, or did he?"

"He did. He wanted it fast."

"What was the rush?"

"His girlfriend was pregnant."

"So were you."

She raised her eyes. "So?"

"So his loyalties were misplaced. You were his wife. He should have stayed with you until you'd had the baby."

"I didn't want that any more than he did," she said, and he saw the pride that lifted her chin.

"But it must have been hard, being alone through all that."

"It would have been worse if we'd been together. Everything would have been right there—the anger, the resentment, the distrust. I'd have been a nervous wreck, and Nicki would have suffered." She shook her head. "Better being alone than living with that."

He could understand the rationale. It was one he'd adhered to most of his life. "Did you ever see him after that?"

"Not if I could help it."

"What about your brother-in-law?"

Her features tightened. "What about him?"

"Did he offer to help?"

She looked back at her hand in time to see her fingers curving around his. "Did he offer to help? I guess you could call it that." She took a shaky breath. "He offered to take credit for Nicki in exchange for my...servicing him."

At thought of the service, Quist swore softly. At thought of Nicki, he said, "Take credit for her? But she already had a father."

"That's right. Michael threatened to say that he'd had an affair with me, that Jarrod wasn't her father at all. The only way I could keep him from doing that, he said, was to sleep with him."

"Did he want you that much?"

"Me?" She gave a brittle laugh. "He didn't want me. He wanted to sock one to Jarrod. They'd been rivals all their lives. He thought he could take advantage of the way I was feeling to get back at his brother. It would have given him great pleasure to let Jarrod think he'd been making it with his wife."

Quist made a face. "What kind of sickness is that?"

"Sickness?" She raised sad eyes to his. "You don't know the half. When I refused him, he got ugly."

"Ugly? Like how?"

"Yelling. Name-calling. Violent, I guess."

"You guess?"

"He started throwing things. If it hadn't been for my next door neighbor knocking on the door, I'm not sure what I'd have done."

Quist was quiet, staring into her eyes for a long time. At last, very quietly, he asked, "When was all this?"

Taking her hand back into her lap, she stood. "Three days ago." She went to the window, wrapped her arms around herself and stared out at the gusting snow.

It was easy enough to figure out. "So you ran."

Hurt in her eyes, she whirled around. "I had to. I couldn't stay there, not living under that kind of threat, *especially* not with Nicki's welfare to consider." Her eyes followed him, barely aware that he'd come out of his seat. "You don't know these people, Quist. They have power and money, and they have no qualms about using either or both when it suits their purposes." Her eyes rose as he approached. "Michael would have kept after me, maybe threatened something else, and Jarrod might have lashed back, but I'd be the one hurt. Me, and Nicki. So why should I stay in Hartford? I stayed there during my pregnancy because my doctor was there and a few friends, but all along I knew that I'd be leaving. There was no future for me there. Thanks to Michael, I made the move sooner, that's all."

Feeling the need to comfort, Quist lightly stroked her arms. "What's in Quebec?"

"I'll find out soon."

"Do you know anyone there?"

She shook her head. "It's supposed to be a nice place, and if I don't like it, I'll move on. I'm a legal secretary, and a good one. I can work anywhere there are lawyers."

"What about Nicki?"

She swallowed hard. "I'll find someone to look after her while I work."

"Is that what you want?"

"It's not what I want at all," she cried, "but what choice do I have? I'm not like Jarrod or his family. I don't have contacts in scads of cities. My parents were quiet, private people who struggled to pay the bills until the day they died." She caught in a breath and added, "I thought I'd escaped that."

"Is that why you married him?" Quist asked, but even before the words were out she was shaking her head.

"I thought I loved him. I thought he loved me. I thought we were a solid couple, because I was a foil for his flamboyance. I calmed him down, so he said. I thought it was true. I thought that I was sensitive enough to understand his mood swings and smart enough to anticipate his needs. I thought that the differences in our backgrounds didn't matter and that his parents would come around in time. I thought we'd have a house and a car and kids and a dog. I thought—I thought we could have it all." She sucked in a breath and held it for a shaky second before releasing it in a ragged whoosh. "I thought wrong."

Tears shimmered on her lower lids, underlining the anguish in her eyes. Quist felt the pain of that anguish, but before he could act on it, she said in a soulful whisper, "All I wanted...all I wanted was to be a good wife. I didn't want personal recognition. I didn't want a career. I didn't even want to be named to the board of one of the corporate subsidiaries. All I wanted was to keep house, to be a good wife and a good mother. Was that so awful?"

He drew her close and wrapped her in his arms. She didn't cry. But her body trembled as it sank into his, and her arm stole around his waist and clung.

She drank in his strength without thought as to why she shouldn't. She needed him just then, needed him to hold her, to tell her she was worth holding. She'd been alone for too long with her fears and her worries. She needed to feel that she had a friend.

She'd never had one quite like this, though—one whose body could protect and comfort and at the same time excite. She'd never had one who made her feel delicate, while he held her so tight, or one who felt so vibrant or smelled so good in such an unadorned way.

So many sensations, so many emotions. She felt dazed when he drew back and looked down into her face. His own was as dark as always, but his eyes were alive, relaying the

message of his body. Her lips softened. Her pulse raced.
She wasn't so dazed that she didn't know what was happening when he lowered his head—nor was she so dazed
that she didn't know that, right then, she wanted his kiss
more than anything else in the world.

CHAPTER SIX

HIS MOUTH TOUCHED hers. It was a tentative touch, a brief sampling that quickly called for another. The second, then the third were the same, gentle enough to be nonthreatening, firm enough to offer the comfort for which they had been originally intended.

At least Quist told himself he was offering comfort, but the question was to whom, and the issue was drawing the line between comfort and desire. He knew he was doing something to Lily, because her lips softened beneath his and her body went pliant, losing the tension he'd felt when she'd been telling her story and he'd first touched her. And he knew that he felt better with her in his arms, tasting her mouth, breathing in her sweet woman's scent. But his body wasn't pliant; it was growing harder by the minute. So, was desire a comfort? That depended on where it led, he supposed.

But supposition had its place, and it wasn't there, at that moment in time. Sensation was taking over, driving him to deepen the kiss. His tongue outlined her lips, first outside, then inside. When it met resistance at her teeth, he returned to a more innocent caress, and soon, with a tiny sigh of surrender, she asked him in.

He didn't wait to be asked twice. With gentle force, his tongue swept the hidden depths of her mouth. He breathed her breath and gave his own in return, and in so doing, possessed her in ways that went far beyond a kiss.

She was lost, unaware of anything but Quist. The storm

might well not have been, nor the cabin, nor Nicki. Quist filled her senses to overflowing—the strength of his body as he held her, the gentleness of his touch, the fire he sparked. He made her forget everything else, and she needed that. He made her feel feminine, and she needed that, too. But he gave her a sense of hope, and that was what she needed most of all.

It was also, in the end, what made her draw back. Her body was heated and trembling, arching into his with a primal ache, yet she made a small sound and tore her mouth away. She didn't release her hold of his waist; she couldn't quite let go of everything at once, and besides, she didn't trust her legs to support her. But she laid her head on his chest and closed her eyes in an attempt to corral her senses into some kind of order.

Quist kept one arm around her back. He cupped her head with his free hand and held it close while he raised his own high and dragged in labored breaths in an attempt to regain firm footing on the ground. Only when he felt he'd done that did he lower his head.

"Lily?"

Her voice was muffled against his sweater. "I'm okay."

"I won't apologize for that."

"I don't want you to." She paused, then asked very cautiously, "Was it me?"

He didn't know what she meant. "You?"

"Me. As opposed to someone else."

"There's no one else here."

"In your life."

"What are you talking about?"

She let out a small, muffled sigh. "Has it been a long time since you've been with a woman?"

"It's been a while."

"Oh."

She sounded disappointed, which surprised him. He'd

have thought she'd be pleased. Bemused, he cupped her head with both hands and turned her face up. Her cheeks were flushed, her eyes large and gray. He would have kissed them closed if he hadn't been distracted by her reaction. "What in the devil's going through your mind?"

"You're horny."

That much was obvious, since his erection was pressing against his jeans, which were in turn pressing against hers. "A man can't hide things like a woman can."

"But you're horny because you haven't had a woman in a long time. So it wasn't me. It was my being a woman. That's all."

He was beginning to get her drift. She was feeling insecure, and based on what she'd said about her marriage, he could understand why. She was also distrustful of men, but she'd told him that at the start. He hadn't imagined then that it would bother him so much.

Tightening his hold of her head, he said with some force, "I see women. I see them all the time. I may be a goddamned cowboy, but it's not like I'm out on the range for six months at a time. I'm in town two or three times a week, and I travel farther at least once a month. So there are women. If I haven't had one for a long time, it's by choice, which means that it's also by choice if I want one now."

His eyes fell to her lips and lingered there. "You taste so damned good," he muttered under his breath. As though chagrined by the admission, he looked her in the eye and went on more sternly. "So don't ever suggest that I'd take just any woman. I'm picky. I don't make love to one while I'm thinking of another, and I don't make love *at all* unless it's to the woman I want." He stared hard at her for another minute before softening. "I've already said you turn me on. You'd better believe it."

Lily wanted to. Then again, she didn't. In fact, the more she thought about it, the more she realized that she didn't want to believe it at all. She didn't want it to be so. She didn't want to be involved that way with Quist, not when her life was in such a state of confusion.

"I need a friend," she whispered, "not a lover."

Arching a dark brow, he drawled, "That wasn't no friendly kiss you just gave me, baby."

"I didn't give you anything. I just...*let* you—" she gritted her teeth "—and it's Lily, not baby. I hate being called something I'm not." Pulling free of him, she moved a step back. That was all it took to put her up against the wall. To compensate, she tipped up her chin.

Quist took in the staunchness of her expression and re-membered other times she'd taken similar exception to what he'd said. Suddenly he realized why. "He did that, didn't he? Your husband did that."

"Ex-husband, and yes. When I worked in the office, I was his girl. When I dated him, I was his honey. When I married him, I was his sugar. But the worst, the *worst*, was baby. That started sometime during the second year of our marriage, when the glow had worn off and the monotony set in. I told myself it was nothing more than another little term of endearment, but it always bothered me. It was short and crude and condescending. More than that, it's a cop-out. A man can call any number of women baby, or sugar or honey. It's easy. He doesn't have to remember a name, and he doesn't risk using the wrong name on the wrong woman." She took in a fast breath and her tone grew pleading. "So, please, call me Lily. Not lady, or sweetheart, or baby. Lily. Or nothing at all."

As abruptly as she finished talking, she dropped her chin and looked at the floor. Quist allowed that for just a second before he took her chin in his fingers and lifted it.

"Let's get a few things straight," he said.

"A few *more* things," she corrected.

"Okay. A few *more* things. First off," he began, dark

eyes flashing, "I am not like your ex-husband. I don't use women—or if I do, they know it right from the start and agree to the terms. Second, when I use words like lady or sweetheart, I do it to express something I'm feeling at that moment, whether it's anger or affection. I don't do it to avoid calling one woman by another's name. I don't have to. Because—point number three—I believe in monogamy. I have never been involved with more than one woman at a time. One woman is about all I can handle, and if she isn't, then she's all wrong for me. And fourth," his fingers tightened on her chin, "I want *you*, not just any woman, and not just because we're marooned out here in the middle of a goddamned blizzard. There's nothing sexy about being stuck here when I'm supposed to be somewhere else, and there's nothing sexy about that bare-bones mattress on the floor over there. I'm forty years old. I've roughed it plenty. I've earned the right to creature comforts, and making love on a skinny, lumpy bed isn't one. Nor is doing it on a hardwood floor or against a drafty wall."

He paused, mesmerized by the wide-eyed look on her face. She was so innocent. It was hard to believe. "Besides," he said more quietly, even distractedly as his attention drifted to her mouth, "There's no way I could confuse you with any other woman I've known. You're different from the rest in every possible way."

Lily wanted to think that was a compliment, but she wasn't sure. "What are the others like?" she heard herself whisper.

With a sniff, he shot a glance toward the eaves. "Tall. Buxom. Curvy. Blond." He brushed the pad of his thumb on her chin. "And none of them have kids."

"Why didn't you marry one of them?"

"I'm not interested in marriage. You should have guessed that."

"Because you don't like women?" He'd been blunt about that from the first. "For a man who doesn't like women, it sounds like you've been involved with an awful lot. I'm surprised one of them didn't con you into it."

He straightened. "No one cons me into anything. And that's a vow." As though to second it, the muscle in his jaw jumped.

Lily knew what he was thinking. "It's not a vow, it's a warning, but it's unnecessary. I couldn't con you if I wanted to. I don't know how. Besides, I don't *want* to con you into anything. The only thing I want is to get my car out of that snowdrift and get back on my way to Quebec."

Curling his fingers around her neck, he said, "It'll be at least two or three days before that happens, and in the meantime…"

"In the meantime, what?" she asked, but she could tell from the look in his eyes what he was thinking.

"In the meantime, anything can happen."

"It won't."

"It almost did, right here, a minute ago."

"That was just a kiss, for God's sake."

"It was more than that, and you know it. It was a preview." He leaned closed. "You felt it deep inside, just like I did."

She shook her head.

"Yes, you did, Lily." His voice lowered. "You feel it even now." His hand came from the back of her neck. He rubbed the backs of his fingers over her throat. "And don't say you've just had a baby so you're not interested in sex, because I'm not convinced one follows the other. You may not have kissed me back, but you enjoyed what I did."

"I didn't ask for it."

"But you enjoyed it." His voice grew more intimate. "And you'd enjoy it if I touched you more." He ran the backs of his fingers down between her breasts to her middle, ignoring her gasp of surprise. "Come to think of it, having a baby is a pretty sexy thing. There's only one way to get pregnant."

Lily's heart was beating faster. "Not today. There are lots of ways today."

He was drawing light circles just above her navel. "But sperm has to meet egg and do its thing. There's something inherently sexual about that, regardless of where it takes place."

"You're playing with words," she said a bit breathlessly.

"And you're picking at straws." His hand came slowly up, fingers dragging along her sweater, creating friction and an incredible heat. "Admit it. You're feeling sexy."

"I'm not."

He caressed the side of her breast. "How about now?" She shook her head.

He brushed her nipple. "And now?"

A tiny sound came from the back of her throat, still she shook her head.

"You're a liar," Quist whispered, but with an odd affection, as he settled his hips against hers. "Why deny it? It's no crime." Back and forth went the backs of his fingers over that tightly budded crest. His cheek was against her forehead, his voice not much more than a breath against her eyes. "I can feel it. It's hard and aching."

Lily could feel it, too, but from the inside. His touch was pulling all kinds of strings linking her breast to the center of her being. "I don't feel sexy," she managed in a husky voice. "I feel aroused. There's a difference."

He was willing to settle for aroused. God only knew he was that, himself. Breathing more roughly than he had moments before, he opened his palm and cupped her breast fully.

"Don't."

"Shh. It's okay. I won't hurt you."

Hurting her wasn't the problem, at least, not in the traditional sense. She was beginning to ache inside, wanting something she couldn't have. And his hand wasn't helping with its sweet stroking, the kneading that gave definition to her flesh. Each time he buzzed her nipple she felt a surge of heat.

"Please," she gasped.

"Please, what?"

"Stop. Please, stop."

But he didn't. He kept touching her, and she didn't so much as grab his hand, because what he was doing felt so good. She felt as though she was awakening after a long sleep, as though she was stretching and purring and coming alive in ways she'd never been before. Her breathing was shallow and fast, her forehead pressed to his cheek. She felt female all over.

Quist thought so, too. While one of his hands stroked her breast, the other was exploring things like her waist and her hips, even her thighs, and nothing he found was a disappointment. But he was, after all, a breast man. Wrapping that other arm fully around her waist to anchor her close, he slipped a hand under her sweater and, before she could protest, cupped her swollen flesh.

She gasped, then followed it with a tiny moan of helpless pleasure and mindless need. She hadn't expected the sensual onslaught. She wasn't prepared for it at all.

"Quist," she whispered, and there was a frantic edge to the sound.

He heard it. Not for a minute did he think it anything but what it was. She wasn't asking for more, though one part of her wanted it. She was asking him, one last time, to stop. She was saying that she wouldn't be able to ask him again, but that she didn't want to make love. She was frightened.

So was he, in his way. He'd had his fire stoked many a time, but never to quite the combustible level he was at now. His muscles were tight, his blood heated. He was on the verge of losing control. He had to think, had to decide whether that was what he wanted to do.

Breathing hard, memorizing the feel of her for a final greedy moment, he dragged his hand over her flesh and out from under her sweater. "This is absurd," he grumbled. "This whole thing is absurd. There shouldn't be any attraction between us."

"I know," she cried in a wobbly voice.

"We're as different as night from day."

"Yes."

"We want different things. Once we leave this cabin, we'll go our separate ways and never see each other again."

She nodded against his chest.

"So what are we doing?"

"I'm not doing anything. You're the one who's doing— and don't say that I didn't fight you, because I know I didn't, so I'm as bad as you are."

"Worse," he said. Unfulfilled desire always made him cranky. "I told you not to count on me for control, but you did it. So where does that leave us now? I'm hard and you're scared."

"Maybe you'd better let me go."

"But I like the feel of you against me."

"It's useless. It can't go anywhere."

He moved then, not far, but enough to allow for breathing space. "Can't?" It was a possibility he hadn't considered, but he eyed her in concern and considered it now. "Was there some problem when you had Nicki? Are you not completely healed or something?" She'd done pretty well going through the snow, right up until the end. It was hard to remember she'd been through childbirth such a short time before.

"I meant can't, as in won't."

But he wasn't convinced about the other. "Are you okay, Lily? If things were different, if we knew each other in normal circumstances, if you wanted to do it, could you make love?"

She was a long time answering, and then it was in a defeated voice directed at the far wall. "I should say no. That would be best for both of us. You'd know that you couldn't do it, and I'd know that I lied, so I wouldn't deserve to do it." She looked meekly up. "I haven't been to the doctor yet. I was supposed to see him next week." She hesitated for another minute, finally admitting very quietly. "But I'm fine. I know my body. It's healed."

Quist was glad for her, not so glad for him. Temptation was staring him in the face, and he didn't like it.

Crossing her arms over her waist, Lily balanced her splinted wrist in the crook of her elbow. Her face was averted. "I was only with one man before my husband, and that was long before my marriage. I'm not good at things like this."

"Neither am I," Quist said. "The other women I've been with have known the score."

Her head went lower. "I'm sorry. I wish I was more sophisticated—"

"Oh, please," he snarled, turning away with a hand at the back of his neck. "If you were more sophisticated, I probably wouldn't want you so much. Besides, wishes are pointless. They don't do us any good."

She pulled in her arms. "What will?"

"Determination." He faced her again, and his expression was as firm as his voice. "We're not making love. That's that. The attraction is skin-deep. You don't want a cowboy any more than I want a new mother. We'll be here together for another one, two, maybe three days, but after that it's over. So we're just gonna have to use a little self-control."

"You said I couldn't count on you for it."

"I'm not sure you can. I'll try. You just be sure to try double hard."

Lily put her head back against the wood and closed her eyes for a minute. She could try double hard. She was good at doing that. It seemed she'd been doing it all her life. Ah, but she was tired of the struggle.

Her eyes flew open when Quist suddenly grasped her arms and hauled her away from the wall. She was thinking that his resolve hadn't lasted long at all, when he said, "You'll freeze standing there." He dropped one hand, kept the other at her arm as he led her to the chair nearest the woodstove. When she'd settled into it, he turned the other around to face the same way and sank down. He stretched out his legs, propped his elbows on the broad wooden arms, pressing his fists together against his mouth. Seconds later he mumbled something.

Lily looked up. "Hmm?"

He dropped his fists to his lap. "You didn't feel the cold, did you?" It was more a statement than a question. No, she hadn't felt the cold, and they both knew why. "And your wrist wasn't hurting." He didn't even attempt to make that one a question. She'd been aroused. Everything in the periphery had fallen away. "It was powerful," he said a bit wistfully, keeping his eyes on the slow-burning logs.

There wasn't much Lily could add. He'd captured the feeling in two short statements and three words. Dwelling on it, though, wasn't going to help with self-control. They needed a diversion.

"Why are you headed for Quebec?" she asked. It seemed as good a diversion as any, and besides, she wanted to know.

He shot her a fast glance before looking back at the woodstove, and he was silent for a while. Finally he rubbed a finger across the bridge of his nose. "I'm looking for someone. Last I heard, she was there."

"She?" Lily felt stung.

"My half sister."

The sting eased. "Your mother's daughter?"

His nod was slow and tight. "She's in some kind of

trouble. Called me two weeks ago from New York and asked if I'd come, but when I got there she'd gone to Boston, and when I got there, she'd gone to Quebec. I'm giving it this one last shot, and if she isn't in Quebec, I'm on my way." He half sang the last, the message being that he'd be on his way without regret.

"What kind of trouble is she in?"

"Man trouble. She got involved with someone who wasn't very nice. The question is whether he takes the fall alone, or whether he drags her down with him."

"What can you do?"

"Get her a good lawyer."

"She can't do that herself?"

"She's only nineteen."

"Nineteen! That's…surprising."

His mouth grew hard. "My mother was seventeen when she had me. She was thirty-eight when she had her. For all I know, there were others in between, but I only heard of Jennifer. I got a call from a lawyer one day saying that my mother had died and there was a daughter I was supposed to be told about. So I was told."

There was more that he wasn't saying. "You've never seen her, have you?"

"Nope."

"Were you in touch with her at all before this?"

He pursed his lips and shook his head.

She offered him a tentative smile of admiration. "Still you've come all the way across the country to help her. I think that's nice."

"Not really. I'm just satisfying my curiosity."

"It has to be more than that," she chided, still wearing that tentative smile. "If it was only curiosity, you'd have come to take a look at her long ago."

"I didn't know about her long ago. It's only been five years since my mother died."

Lily's smile faded. "Did you ever see your mother again, I mean, after she left?"

"No."

She rubbed her arm against the chill in his voice. "You never tried to find her?"

"Why would I have done that? She was the one who left. She didn't give a damn about me. Was I supposed to care what happened to her?"

"Weren't you ever curious?"

"I had enough to keep me busy so I didn't have to think of it."

"But she was your mother."

"An accident of birth."

Lily glanced toward the drawer in which Nicki was napping, and it occurred to her that one day her daughter would say the same thing about Jarrod. And Lily would do nothing to discourage it. Lord knew, *she* didn't want contact with Jarrod. "But Nicki may be curious," she told herself. Realizing that she'd spoken aloud, she sent Quist a self-conscious look. "I was thinking about Nicki and her father."

"Obviously."

"I'm not sure how I'll handle it."

"When she asks about her father?"

Lily nodded. "It's not an immediate problem. While she's little, she'll accept the answers I give her. But if she decides she wants to see him when she's older, I don't know."

"You can't forbid it."

"I don't want her hurt. What if she pops up on his doorstep and he slams the door in her face? Can you imagine what she'd feel?"

"I can imagine," he said, and Lily realized that he, more than most, could imagine, indeed.

"God, I hope that never happens," she whispered, nervously fiddling with the ragged ends of the cloth strips binding her splint.

"What if he comes looking for her one day?"

Her eyes flew up. "He has no right."

"He has every right. He's her father."

But Lily was shaking her head. "As far as I'm concerned, he surrendered his rights where Nicki's concerned the day he walked out on us."

"A court would say differently."

"Whose side are you on?" she cried.

"I'm not taking sides. I'm just being realistic."

Calming herself a little, she realized that he was right. Only he didn't know the facts. "I have papers. Jarrod signed them. He agreed to leave us alone."

Quist considered that. "In exchange for what?"

She had to hand it to him; he was quick. And it seemed silly, since she'd already told him so much, not to tell the rest. "A lump-sum settlement that was below what I might have gotten if I'd wanted to fight him. Jarrod's family is powerful. They never accepted me as one of them, and I could imagine all kinds of nasty things happening if they decided they wanted part of Nicki. I won't have her used that way. I was willing to give up the money for a certain peace of mind."

"So now you have to work."

"I don't have to. The settlement was still a good one. But I want to put it away for Nicki—for education, maybe travel or a home when she's grown." She rubbed her arm. "I don't want that money for myself. I'd rather work."

Quist had to admire her for that, but his thoughts were straying. He was remembering what it was like growing up with one parent and no siblings. "She'll be lonely."

"Maybe not. I'll be there most of the time. And if I meet the right man, I'll remarry and have more kids."

He eyed her warily. "Is that what you want?"

She had no qualms about saying, "Yes," and looking him in the eye. "I meant it when I said I didn't want a

career. I can work, and I'll happily do it as long as I have
to, but I'm not ambitious that way. I want a home and a
family. I want to bake bread and drive car pools and
barbecue hotdogs on Sunday afternoons. That's all I've
ever really wanted."

When she'd said it before, it had been in the context of
her marriage to Jarrod. He hadn't given it much thought
then. Now he did. "You're a throwback. Women aren't
wanting to do things like that nowadays. They want to be
out having fun, making money, putting men in their places,
or trying to."

"Not me," she said simply. Resting her head against the
back of the chair, she closed her eyes.

Quist stared at her, waiting for her to look at him and
tell him how cynical he was, or that he knew the wrong
women. The fact that she didn't move, didn't speak, didn't
even open her eyes somehow gave greater credence to her
claim. If she was a throwback to women of an earlier age,
she was making no apologies for it.

He almost envied the man she married, and she would
marry, he knew. She wasn't meant to be a loner. She'd
make some man a good wife. She was nice to be with,
eager to please, willing to do her share of the work. She
was bright and attractive. And sexy. He looked at the way
her sweater fell loosely over her breasts and remembered
how that flesh had felt in his hands. Too quickly he felt a
stirring in his loins.

Fortunately Nicki woke up just then, and he was almost
relieved. He needed something to take his mind off Lily's
body. Picking the baby up, carrying her to Lily, helping
change her diapers were the kinds of things that—novice
that he was—demanded his full attention. He had to
confess that he liked it when Nicki looked at him and
smiled, which he found he could make her do by tickling
her under her chin, which he could do without a lot of fuss

while Lily's back was turned. He liked doing it then. He didn't feel foolish. And with Lily off across the room, he knew Nicki's smile was for him. That gave him an odd kind of satisfaction.

Odd or not, he needed *some* satisfaction, because with Lily so often close, the breaks were few and far between. He spent the time she was nursing Nicki at the window, looking out at the storm, wishing it would end, wondering when it would, planning the action he'd take when it happened, but no sooner did he return to the center of the room than he felt that same unbidden excitement deep inside. Increasingly that excitement led to a sense of deprivation, which made him testy.

Lily's version of testy was edgy. No matter what other things she thought of, when Quist came near, she was acutely and physically aware of him, and when that happened, she got nervous. She fumbled around his large hands for the diaper tapes, bobbled the can of soup he opened for her to heat, twice lost the stirring spoon in the pot. Though she could blame the clumsiness on her splinted wrist, she knew its true cause.

Quist was exceedingly virile. Everything about him smacked of man, from his height, to his physique, to the gentle bob of his Adam's apple when he drank, the fine hairs on the backs of his hands and the veins on his forearms. His walk, especially, intrigued her. It was tight-hipped and spare of movement, but it got him where he was going just when he wanted to be there. Of course, he wasn't going far within the cabin, but that meant that wherever he did go, she could watch.

It was a trying pastime. Too often, when their eyes met, that special heat flared, and their eyes met often. Sheer boredom led to that. There wasn't much to keep either occupied in a way that was separate from the other. The cabin was too small, their activities too enmeshed.

Lily was taking her turn at the window, looking help-lessly out at the storm, when, from out of the blue, she said, "Are you really a cowboy?"

Quist was feeding the stove, whose heat was slightly depleted after having provided them with a lunch of hot soup. Her question made him pause. Twisting on his heels to look back at her, he said, "I thought that was a given."

She came away from the draft. "Are you one?"

He shrugged and turned back to the woodstove, pushing the log where he wanted it. "Depends how you define the term. If you mean, do I live on a ranch with cattle and horses and branding irons and dust, the answer is yes. If you mean, do I swing into the saddle every morning wearing chaps and spurs to do all kinds of fancy tricks with my rope, the answer is no." He closed the grate and stood, brushing his hands against each other. "My ranch is a business. When I'm not in my office, I'm in town contracting for supplies, and when I ride the range, it's usually in a Jeep."

Nothing he said diminished the slightly romantic notion she had of a cowboy and his life. She could see him doing those things. Dark head, bronzed skin, tight hips and long, denim-covered legs—he made a handsome cowboy. "Do you like the work?" she asked and watched him sink into the chair she'd come to think of as his.

"Yes."

"Do you miss it now?"

He stretched out his long legs and nodded.

"Is it nice, Montana?"

He shot her a glance. She was standing by the chair he'd come to think of as hers. "Never been there?"

She shook her head.

"It's real pretty. Green and blue. Lots of wide-open spaces. I like wide-open spaces."

She could imagine he would, given his size. She could picture him standing on his front porch, taking a long, deep breath of the fresh air, then striding easily off toward the corral. He was the commanding type, with the more to command, the better, she guessed.

That raised another issue. "Who's taking care of things while you're gone?"

"I have a foreman."

"Is he good?"

"He's been with me for fourteen years. I trust him." He looked at her again. "Why all the questions?"

She shrugged. "I don't know. I was just wondering. That kind of life is totally foreign to anything I've ever known."

"A city girl born and bred?" he asked with a dry twist to his lips.

"Something wrong with that?" she asked right back. Picking a fight with him was better than panting after him.

"Wrong? That depends on what you want in life. City living's great if you want headaches, stomach aches, traffic jams, lines everywhere you turn and either cockroach-infested apartments or ticky-tacky houses on quarter-acre lots. Me," he took a breath, "I'd die living like that."

She brushed her fingertips on the arm of the chair. "But you did it once."

"Did I tell you that?"

"You said you lived in a triple-decker. I've never heard of a ranch with a triple-decker. You know the pitfalls of city living very well. And then there's the way you talk. You don't talk like a cowboy."

He was amused. "How is a cowboy supposed to talk?"

"With a drawl. With *ain't*s and *dunno*s and *mama*s. And *darlin'*s. You've never called me darlin'." She slipped into the chair and settled back. "If you were a native cowboy, you'd have done that."

He snorted. "You've been watching the wrong programs."

"Cowboys don't use words like that?"

"Some do, some don't. But you're right," he hurried on,

because she'd already picked up on too much, "I was born in the city." And once started, it seemed a shame not to tell it all. "We lived in Seattle, my father and me. Then we moved to Denver, then Detroit."

"Why so many moves? Did it have to do with his work?"

"Maybe. He was a restless kind of guy."

"Do you think he was looking for your mother?"

The muscle in his jaw jumped. "If he was, he never told me, and he sure as hell never found her."

Lily was amazed at the anger that the mere mention of his mother stirred in Quist. Not wanting to make things worse, she redirected her questions. "What happened after Detroit?"

"*In* Detroit. He died."

She turned her head against the wood slats to find him staring at the woodstove, not quite angry, but sober. "And?"

"I raised hell for the next four years. Then I won the ranch."

"Won?"

"In a game of five-card stud."

"You're kidding."

Slowly he shook his head.

"You *won* it?"

He nodded.

"Men actually do that—put something as valuable as a ranch up as a stake?"

"Damn right they do," he said, but he remembered how stunned he'd been, himself—no, what had stunned him was the lousy hand the guy had. Poker players were usually more careful when something as vital was at stake. "Not that the ranch was worth a hell of a lot back then, but it was more than I'd ever had." He looked at her. "So I took it."

"That's incredible," she said with a smile of amazement. "And you made it work."

He basked in her smile, letting its warmth seep through him. She was so pretty when she smiled, he thought. No, she was pretty all the time, but when she smiled, she lit up, and that lit him up inside.

Her smile, he realized, was totally innocent, seductive in the broadest sense of the word, and dangerous.

That thought was sobering. In a darker voice, he said, "I made it work, all right. I fought and sweated and bled to get it in shape, and once I'd done that, I fought and sweated and bled some more to get it growing. That place is me."

"Mmm. Big and dark and rough," she teased, but he didn't smile.

"Not dark, but big and rough. It's a man's place."

"Without a woman's touch?"

"Don't need a woman's touch."

"Do the women who see it agree?"

"Women don't see it."

Lily frowned. "Where do you see *them*?"

"Anywhere but the ranch. The ranch is mine. Besides, a ranch is no place for a woman."

Lily stared at him, then made a face. "That's the dumbest thing I've ever heard. Women have lived on ranches since the beginning of time. Who do you think did all the cooking and cleaning and sewing while the cowboys were out getting dirty?"

"Correction," he said, looking back at the fire. "A ranch is no place for the women *I* know. I love it—they'd hate it. I don't need that kind of grief."

Whether it was something in his voice or the grim set of his face that did it, Lily wasn't sure. But she suddenly wondered whether he was afraid of rejection. After all, he'd been rejected early on by his mother.

"Why would they hate it?" she asked more gently.

"It's not fancy. It's not society. It doesn't have four-star restaurants or exciting nightlife. It doesn't have nightlife, period, because the days begin at dawn. It relies heavily on routine. It's quiet and isolated. And peaceful," he tacked on, because that was the way the ranch made him feel.

Lily thought it sounded nice. "What about creature comforts?" she asked, teasing again.

This time, his mouth relaxed into a sheepish half smile. He remembered what he'd told her. "It has those."

"Then maybe it isn't so bad. Maybe you underestimate your women."

His smile went the way of the warmth in his eyes. "No. Never that." He was out of his chair in a minute, stalking to a corner of the kitchen. There, he turned to glare at Lily, who was sitting demurely in her chair. "Don't look at me that way." She didn't blink. "What are you staring at?"

"You. You really do know the wrong women. You're typically male."

"What do you mean by that?"

"Men want women who are fast and free and glitzy. What was it you said—your women are tall, buxom, curvy and blond? It's an ego thing. You think you're hot stuff if you attract hot-shot women." She pictured Jarrod, pictured his new wife, whom she'd known quite well and who was the embodiment of glitz. Then she deliberately blinked them away. "Well, of *course* those women won't fit on a ranch. That's not to say that other women wouldn't do just fine."

"They would not."

"They would, too."

"Ranch life is hard."

"Uh-huh, with your office and your Jeep and your creature comforts."

"Ranch life is *hard*."

"And a woman's too soft?" She heard just about enough. Coming out of her chair, she advanced on him. "You want to believe that. You want to believe it so bad that you keep your eyes closed to the alternative." Her own eyes were angry. "For your information, women can be every bit as hard as men, if not harder. We have to be, if only to survive the mess you guys make of things!"

She whirled away, but he caught her arm and whirled her back. "I've never made a mess of anyone's life—"

"—but your own. You're missing out on a whole lot, Quist, and some day you'll die a lonely old man!" As soon as the words were out, she regretted them, and it had to do only in part with the rigidity of his features. She'd confused the issues, let her own anger jade her judgment. "I'm sorry," she whispered. "I shouldn't have said that. It's not my place to tell you what's right or wrong. I haven't done such a super job with my own life."

Quist wanted to say, "Damned right, you haven't," but the words wouldn't come. He stood there staring at her, wondering how she could be hard and soft at the same time, knowing she was. She was so different. Whether she was being quiet and vulnerable or vocal and insistent, he wanted her.

He could see that she wanted him, too. It was there in her eyes as she stood before him. It was there in the faint tremor that gave her body a gossamer feel, and in the quickening of her breath.

Taking a deep one of his own, with his hand still on her arm, he led her across the room. "We're going out," he muttered.

"Out?" she said shakily. "We were out before, and it's still snowing."

"I need fresh air."

"Then you can go out."

"You need it, too," he said and looked at her in such a way that she didn't say another word. She submitted to being helped on with her boots and her coat. She waited while he put on his own things. Then, holding the back of his coat, she let him lead her out into the storm.

Heads bowed against the wind, they waded through the

thigh-high snow to circle the cabin twice before making a stop at the outhouse. Quist, who had that much more strength than Lily and commensurate sexual energy to expel, made two more circles before joining her inside. She'd managed to shrug out of her coat and work her boots off with her feet, but when she turned to him, he caught his breath.

Her hair was still matted by the hood of her coat, and the moss-green sweater she wore didn't exactly go with her pink sweatpants. But her eyes were clear, her cheeks red, her lips moist. She looked good enough to eat.

In the space of a breath he was before her, taking her face in his hands, covering her mouth with his. He kissed her with the hunger he thought he'd just walked off. Then he murmured against her mouth, "This isn't going to work. I want you too much."

Lily moved her hand over his jaw, trying to warm it with a hand that was none too warm, itself. Then, trying to warm her hand, she buried her fingers under the crew neck of his sweater. The skin there was warm and firm, and just that little bit fuzzy.

"Lily," he warned.

"I know," she said quickly and withdrew her hand. "It's okay." She turned from him. "Nicki's due up any minute." Sitting on the mattress beside the drawer, she held her hands in her lap and watched the baby until she awoke.

But Quist was right. It wasn't going to work. No matter how hard she tried to concentrate on the baby, she was aware of him. If it hadn't been for her wrist, she decided, she'd have been able to do everything on her own. But her wrist was broken. So she needed help. And he was more than willing—no, he insisted on giving it.

Afternoon wore into evening. The snow let up a little, which was the only hopeful thing that happened. They continued to struggle with thoughts and looks and accidental touches. Tension ran high between them, and though it was sexually-induced, it took different outlets. Quist snapped at Lily for using up the hot water without telling him; she snapped back at him when he diapered Nicki too loosely; he told her that the bread she'd made to eat with the stew wasn't real bread at all, and she said that it couldn't be since she didn't have yeast, so it was quick bread—and between them they ate every crumb.

By the time Nicki went to sleep at eight o'clock, Lily felt the night had already been endless. She sat by the stove for a bit, then lay down on the mattress and pulled the blanket to her chin. But though she was tired, she couldn't sleep. Her insides were astir with feelings and thoughts that she shouldn't have been feeling or thinking. So she tossed and turned on her mattress.

In time, Quist lowered the lamp and turned in, too, but his rest wasn't any more peaceful than hers. At one point, without considering for a minute that she might be asleep, he growled, "Is it your wrist?"

"Is what my wrist?"

"Whatever it is that's making you squirm."

"No, it's not my wrist."

"Do you have to go to the bathroom?"

"No! I'm restless. That's all."

"You're keeping me up," he alleged.

"You're keeping yourself up," she told him and flopped over again.

Quist was in fact up in the most sexual of senses and had no way to relieve it. He ached to take Lily, but he wouldn't. His body was punishing him for his chivalry.

After long periods of thinking about the ranch, plotting strategies for diversifying his herd and counting the heads of cattle in the pen he drew in his mind, he fell asleep. When he awoke, it was four in the morning, Nicki was whimpering, and he was hard as a rock.

Ignoring the last, though it caused him a moan when he pushed himself up, he went to the drawer, lifted the baby and deposited her into Lily's waiting arms. On impulse, he sat down at the base of the chair and pulled Lily back against him. "Do it here," he said with a huskiness that could have been due to a number of things. "Indulge me."

"Quist…"

He fitted her more snugly into the notch of his thighs. "Nothing can happen. You've got Nicki."

On the one hand, he was right. Lily drew up her sweater and put Nicki to her breast, and all was fine. She switched breasts midway through, and all was still fine.

The trouble came when she was done.

CHAPTER SEVEN

QUIST CAREFULLY PUT Nicki back in her drawer and watched Lily tuck her in. But when she turned toward her own mattress, he caught her hand and in a single fluid movement had her in his arms.

She barely had time to cry his name when his mouth came down over hers, and what she'd so diligently tried to suppress for so long sprang to life. There was nothing tentative or exploratory about this kiss, nor was it gentle. It was hard and hungry, like Quist's body, and it wasn't about to be denied.

His mouth plundered hers. It slanted and sucked, drawing her deeper into his desire. She was stunned by the force of that desire, stunned even more by the understanding that the desire was her own. She'd never thought of herself as a woman who craved. In times past when she'd been with a man, his needs had directed and dominated the dance. Jarrod had barely cared whether she achieved satisfaction, and, in truth, she hadn't cared much, either. The pleasure was in the giving.

Something was different now. She opened her mouth to Quist, took his tongue and gave her own in return, but the giving was greedy. She'd never felt such hot and intense a need, and though a small voice in her brain warned her to caution, the rest of her didn't listen. She was caught up in sensation and in an irrational but irrevocable feeling that what she was doing was right.

Quist wasn't thinking any more clearly than she was. Holding her head still, he devoured her mouth. He tasted her, drank her, breathed her until even that wasn't enough. Sliding his arms around her body, he crushed her to him with a force that made Lily cry out.

Immediately he loosened his hold. "Are you okay?"

"I think so," she said with a breathless little laugh. When he backed into the chair he'd just left and brought her down on his lap, she whispered a hurried, "Maybe we shouldn't, Quist." Her arms, even the one with the splinted wrist, were draped over his shoulders, and though she was having trouble catching her breath, her eyes held his.

"We have to," he answered. Voice, gaze, touch—all smoldered with barely banked heat. "We have to. I can't explain the need," it was as much emotional as physical, as much a need to stake a claim as to slake a desire, "but it's too strong." He took her head in his hands. "I need you, Lily. I'm making you mine."

Like the fierceness of his kiss, the boldness of his words excited her. He didn't ask. He didn't beg. He told her what was going to happen and why, and since Lily was feeling everything he was, she couldn't argue with his conclusion. Instead, her body began to tremble in anticipation.

He kissed her again until she was gasping for breath. Then he brought the hem of her sweater up and took it over her head and off, leaving her naked above the waist. He held her back to look at her, first her eyes, then for a long time her breasts.

Her breath came more shallowly. She was acutely aware of her nakedness, of the rapid rise and fall of her breasts, of their heaviness, of the paleness ribboned by veins that had come with motherhood, and she might have tried to cover herself if it hadn't been for the look in his eyes. That look was incredible. It made her feel warm and beautiful. And sexy. No man had ever made her feel sexy like that. Not a word, just that look, and she soared.

But the soaring had just begun. When he put his hands on her breasts, she sucked in a breath. She let it out in a soft sigh of pleasure when he began to knead her flesh, and when he lowered his head and took a distended nipple into his mouth, she cried out.

He paused, fearful again that he'd hurt her, but she pushed her fingers in his hair and urged him back to her breast. He lingered there just long enough to drive her wild before relinquishing the wet nub to his fingers and moving on to the next. Small sounds of pleasure came from deep in her throat. She urged him closer, then closer still as the crux of the heat moved downward. Pressing her legs together didn't help. Neither did shifting her hips.

Clutching fistfuls of his hair, she whispered his name and tugged. He lifted his head and looked at her, still with the desire and appreciation that made her feel so wanted. The wanting made her desperate.

"I'm on fire," she cried brokenly. "Help me."

He didn't need further urging. His hands went to her sweatpants and pushed them down. He shifted her until the heavy material was free of her hips, then her legs, leaving her in the V-shaped scrap of silk and lace that he found so sexy. With the flat of his hand he touched her stomach, her hips, the small of her back, her bottom, and by the time he returned to her front, he'd breached the barrier of her panties to find the dampness that gave proof to her arousal.

Lily hadn't been so indifferent to satisfaction in the past that she'd never had an orgasm. She knew the feeling, knew when it was imminent, and at that moment she was on the edge. If Quist touched her more deeply, if he slid a finger inside she'd come, and she didn't want to. Not without feeling the iron of him, not without knowing that they were fully coupled.

"Your sweater," she cried against his mouth as she

grabbed a handful of it and pulled. More than ever before, she wished for two good hands. Fortunately, Quist had them.

Setting her on her feet, he rose and tore off his sweater. She barely had time to reacquaint herself with the marvel of his chest when he had his zipper down, then his jeans. When he came back to her, he was buck naked and magnificent. Kneeling, he slid her panties down, leaned forward and put his mouth to the hair that was still too short to curl.

Her knees buckled. She slid down until her breasts grazed his chest, and he lowered her to the mattress. His breathing was rough; his arms shook with the force of his desire as he held himself above her, poised between her widely parted thighs.

"Hurry," she whispered and lifted toward him. She was frantic to have him where it seemed he belonged. That sense of rightness had survived the fire of foreplay and was as strong, if not stronger than ever.

But he held back. He looked into her eyes, looked deeper, into her soul and felt touched to the core of his being. She was his. She was bare before him, inside and out. He felt responsible for her, and while he'd always before shunned responsibility where women were concerned, this time he welcomed it. It made him feel possessive, protective and strong. It was also humbling, so much so that instead of thrusting hard into her as his body was telling him to do, he moved forward more gently.

Lily would never know how he'd known to do that, but it was another thing to marvel at. She was tight. She hadn't realized how much so. Involuntarily her body tensed at his initial incursion and she gasped.

"I'm hurting you," he whispered against her temple.

"No. It's...from the baby...I'm very..."

Sealing her mouth with his lips, he began to caress her, first her breasts, then her belly, then the small bud that had hardened between her legs. Little by little, he pressed inside as he built her arousal to an ever higher pitch. He moved his hips in slow, gentle circles, stretching her, allowing her to get used to his size. Only when he was fully buried inside her, when he felt her tightness hugging him to the hilt, did he allow himself a moment's selfishness. Closing his eyes, he arched his long torso, threw his head back and shuddered with pleasure, then, unable to help himself, gave a low cry of triumph.

The triumph was Lily's, too. She'd never felt so much a part of a man, and it wasn't just that Quist was more man than she'd ever met. There was something else. They shared a special feeling. She couldn't comprehend the extent of it just then, because all that was happening inside was near to overwhelming, but she was more satisfied by what they were doing than she'd ever been by any orgasm.

Sensing and sharing that satisfaction, Quist held himself still. After a time, he breathed in a long, shaky breath, opened his eyes and looked down at her. What he saw made his heart pound harder against his ribs.

Lily's gray eyes were warm and velvet and there was a soft smile on her lips. Her cheeks were pink, her skin dewy. Her breasts rose and fell with the short breaths she took, while her knees hugged his sides. She looked as though she'd be perfectly content to stay right where she was for an eternity, and he wasn't sure he'd have minded. She was without a doubt the most beautiful, the most serene, the most honest woman he'd ever made love to.

He gave a small smile. "Ahh, Lily." When her brows rose in question, he whispered, "I could almost be tempted to look at you like this all day." Bowing his head, he opened his mouth on her neck and gave her the hickey he'd promised.

"You rat," she whispered back, but her smile grew wider. "Haven't you got better things to do with your mouth?" Coming up off the mattress, she used her own on his nipple. When he let out a guttural cry, she wound her arms around his neck and gave him the kind of kiss that made him think of all those better things he could do.

He did a good many of them in the next few minutes, and if there were some that he missed, neither of them noticed. Laying her down, he made love to her fully—withdrawing and gently reentering, withdrawing and coming back harder, withdrawing and thrusting home with the force of his ardor.

Lily egged him on. Once past her initial tenderness, she was a creature she'd never known. She writhed in response to the fire he lit and demanded he tend it. It never occurred to her to lie still, as a vessel for his pleasure; that simply wasn't part of their relationship. With Quist, she was a free agent, a woman letting herself blossom without set rules or preconceptions. He was a rough-edged man prone to wild passion, and wild passion was what he inspired. She gave and she took with rapturous fury.

Their bodies grew sweaty as they worked toward a near-violent crest. At its height, she felt a moment's fear, the sensation was so intense. His name was a frantic cry on her lips, but he was fast to soothe her.

"That's it, Lily," he panted, pumping more quickly. "Let it come. Let go for me. That's it."

Catching in a breath, she arched up off the mattress, closed her eyes and went very still for an instant before erupting into a series of shuddering spasms. She was still in their grip when Quist thrust deeper than ever. With a low, agonized sound, he gained his release—but not before he'd found the wherewithal to pull out of her.

Lily missed him instantly. Though their damp bodies remained entwined, she felt a sudden and stark emptiness inside. It brought tears to her eyes. "Quist?" she whispered, still breathless from the power of what she'd experienced.

It was a minute before the harshness of his breathing eased, another before he raised his head from her shoulder.

One look at the tears in her eyes and he said, "Oh, no, don't do that." He brushed the moisture from her lids with his mouth. "Don't cry. Not now."

"Why did you do that? It was so perfect until that."

He'd been afraid she regretted having made love and was deeply relieved it wasn't so. Shifting to cradle her gently against him, he lifted her splinted wrist to his chest. Then he ran his thumb under her eyes to catch the tears that remained. "You've just had a baby," he said and felt protective. "You don't want another so soon."

Lily was surprised; thought of birth control hadn't entered her mind. In self-defense, she said, "I wouldn't have gotten pregnant. It was just one time."

His smile was indulgent, the rolling of his eyes more eloquent than that. So she tried again.

"A woman can't get pregnant while she's nursing."

"Is that a fact? Has it never happened? Not once?"

"Well, maybe once or twice," she conceded, "but those are the exceptions."

He studied her face, stroked her damp cheek. "Look at you," he said, feeling concern this time. "You have a new baby and no home. Can you even begin to imagine what it would be like to be pregnant on top of that?"

It would be terrifying, she knew, still she felt the same emptiness she'd felt when he'd first withdrawn. "I liked being pregnant," she said almost as an afterthought and lowered her face to his chest. He had a nice chest. It was firm and well shaped and had just enough hair to lightly cushion her cheek. Besides, his chest held his heart, and its steady beat was a comfort by her ear.

Looking over the crown of her head to the ivory skin that extended below it, Quist felt a swell of affection. She was so incredibly sweet, sweet to taste, to smell, to hold. And she said sweet things. No other woman had ever complained when he'd put on a rubber. He hadn't had a rubber here, but he'd deliberately waited until she'd climaxed to reach his own peak and withdraw. Still, she was sorry he'd left. That made him feel special.

In fact, he was feeling special in lots of ways. And relaxed. And content. Which was really odd, given the cabin and the storm and the fact that he still had to find his way out of it. Still, at that particular moment, he felt special.

"Quist?"

When she used that tentative tone, he knew something was up. "Mmm?"

"Do you really think I'm sexy?" she asked, keeping her eyes on the lean plane of his middle.

"How can you ask that, after what we just did?"

"For all I know, you go wild with every woman you bed."

He rolled on top of her, partly to feel her again that way and partly to set her straight. "I like sex, and I like it hard and fast. But I've never done what we just did."

All eyes, she looked up at him. "What do you mean?"

He couldn't answer at first, because he wasn't sure *what* he'd meant. Then again, he was. What he'd done with Lily had been more than sex. It had been lovemaking. He couldn't tell her that, though, because she might get the wrong idea. She might think he loved her, and it wasn't that at all. He liked her, liked her in some ways that weren't at all physical, so that when he'd taken her physically, he'd felt more than usual. But like wasn't love. And she was waiting for an answer.

Wrapping himself in the velvet of her gaze, he said in a voice vibrant with attraction, "I've never entered a woman slowly, the way I entered you. I've never really cared if she was uncomfortable at first." He stopped for an instant. "I've never taken a virgin before."

"I'm no virgin," she whispered, cheeks going pink.

"But I imagine it was like that. You were new. You haven't been touched since the baby." He thought about that and slid halfway to her side so that she wouldn't bear the brunt of his weight. Then he asked in a quiet voice, "You were cut there, weren't you?"

She nodded. They'd just made love, which was as intimate as two people could get, still his question seemed even more so. His interest made her warm all over.

"Did it hurt?"

"There was local anesthesia. I didn't feel it."

"Afterward?"

"I felt it then, but it didn't bother me. It was part of having Nicki. I'd do it again in a minute."

"In a minute?"

She smiled. "Well, maybe not so fast, but I wouldn't hesitate to have more children."

"You really enjoyed being pregnant?"

She nodded, and Quist believed her. It was in keeping with everything else she'd said. Besides, she didn't lie. He'd already learned that, though at times like this he wished it weren't so. She was looking up at him with such guileless warmth that he felt his blood stir. Slowly, inevitably, his gaze fell from her face. He moved to see her body better, and when the visual wasn't enough, he touched her.

His hands were large, his fingers callused but gentle. The heady combination sparked a renewed tingling deep in Lily's belly. Grabbing his hand, she dragged it to her throat and held it there.

"What's wrong?" he asked.

She took in a shaky breath. "You touch me and I start to burn. I don't know what it is about you, Quist. I was never like this before."

He seized her mouth to still her words, which were as much a turn-on as anything else. But a taste of her mouth led to a taste of her neck, then one breast, then her stomach. She'd released his hand by then and was touching him wherever she could, and by the time he straightened beside her, he was feeling hot and bothered. Taking her hand, he lowered it on his body. "Touch me," he whispered hoarsely. "I've dreamed of having your hands on me here—" He groaned the last as he curled her fingers around his arousal. Oh, yes, he'd dreamed of that; it was why he'd been so hard when Nicki's cries had woken him. But the dream paled in comparison to reality. He hadn't dared to dream that Lily's fingers would take him higher, and with such untutored skill.

The skill was a product of instinct, in turn a product of curiosity and desire. Lily was intrigued by the length and strength of him. She explored his thickness, the velvety tip and the heaviness beneath, and felt pride when he grew even harder.

His low moan brought her gaze to his face. In the dim light filtering from the woodstove, she saw that it was covered by a sheen of sweat. His eyes were closed, his mouth drawn into a thin line as he struggled to retain a measure of control.

She wanted him to lose it. To that end, she grew even bolder with her hand and her mouth. Tasting his body, brushing her nose through the hair on his chest, dragging her lips along the line that tapered to his navel while she continued to caress his hardness—he was soon breathing roughly, and she wasn't doing much better. Everything about him turned her on. She felt a flame inside that was every bit as hot as it had been not so many minutes before.

Wanting to see how far she'd go, Quist drew her on top of him. Knowing she couldn't put weight on her left wrist, he supported her under each arm. Her legs straddled his hips, and for a prolonged minute of torture, she held herself just inches above him while, taking short, shimmering breaths, she looked down into his eyes. Then, closing her own, she let her hips settle, taking him fully in one smooth glide.

Quist felt possessed. It was a turnaround, but he wasn't displeased. He filled Lily, yet he was the one who felt filled, and the filling was with an almost unbelievable pleasure. It smacked of oneness, which was something he didn't know much about. But like Lily, he acted on instinct, and that instinct was to help her, to make her movements his own, make her rapture high.

At first, he did nothing more than lightly run his hands over her body. When she began to undulate with him inside, he drew her forward so that he could love her breasts with his mouth, and when she dropped her weight to her elbows, he grasped her hips. Guidance or caress— the line blurred, and it didn't matter, because neither of them was analyzing what happened. Instinct and sensation dominated the thrusting sweep of their bodies, and if instinct and sensation were in turn dominated by a deeper underlying emotion, neither of them was analyzing that, either.

They burned, then exploded. In the end, Quist rolled over Lily and afforded her the same protection he'd given the first time. Though she knew what he was doing this time, she still felt the loss, but the heat of her climax carried her through until he held her tightly to his side again.

There were no words when it was over, nothing to describe what had happened. Their bodies continued to communicate for a time, lying limply, then more peacefully entwined. When Quist drew up the blanket, they fell asleep. Neither one of them moved again until Nicki's small cries broke through the morning silence.

Lily stirred first, trying to burrow more snugly against the warmth of Quist's large body. When she realized what the sound was that had awoken her, she started to turn, but he held her still.

"I'll get her." His voice was groggy, and, contrary to his words, he drew her in closer and buried his face in her hair.

Nicki cried again.

"I'd better go," Lily whispered.

But with a kiss to the top of her head, he disengaged himself from her body. "Stay here. I'll bring her over."

Settling her head on the pillow, Lily watched him climb out from under the blanket. His body was beautiful, not only in the throes of passion but now in the morning's light. What she'd only felt earlier she could finally see, most notably the masculine make of his legs and the way his sex lay amid a dark nest of hair. He was impressive in any state of arousal, a pleasure to look at.

But he was reaching for his pants, threatening to deny her that pleasure.

"What are you doing?" she asked, vying with Nicki to make herself heard.

He balanced precariously on one foot as he tried to get the other into his jeans. "I can't very well go to her like this." He glanced down at himself.

Lily was torn between admiration of his body and amusement. "Why not?"

"She's a girl. She could be traumatized."

"She's just a baby. She won't see a thing."

"She sees," he said earnestly, as though he had great insight into the matter. "She understands more than you think."

Pressing her lips together to stifle a grin, Lily gave a slow but confident shake of her head.

He paused. "No?"

She repeated the slow headshake.

"But I'm a strange man. She doesn't know me. I'm not even her father."

"She knows you better than she does her father," Lily said, "but that's neither here nor there. The fact is that she won't know whether you're naked or not, and I don't want you dressed."

That brought a softer look to Quist's face. Nicki kept

on crying, but he stayed still where he was with his jeans on one leg and no more. "You don't?"

She shook her head.

"Are you sure?"

She nodded.

Nicki's cries grew more strident. Shucking the jeans, Quist strode to where she lay and picked her up. She quieted right away, which made him grin. "Like that, do ya?" he asked the child in a voice that was light, a little playful, very masculine. "Are you a sexy little thing like your mama?" He placed her carefully in Lily's arms.

"I'm not sexy," Lily chided in a half whisper. Turning onto her side, she put Nicki to her breast.

After fueling the stove, Quist pulled the blanket up to cover Lily's back and stretched out, propping himself on an elbow, to watch her nurse. "What do you mean, you're not sexy?"

"I'm not."

"Sure could've fooled me. Sure could've fooled my body."

Lily felt a heat rise in her cheeks, but she kept her eyes on Nicki. Quist watched them both. He thought of the first time he'd seen her nursing and remembered how uncomfortable he'd felt. He was jealous then. He saw a closeness that he'd never had, and irrationally, he was jealous. That jealousy had eased, mostly because he'd become involved with Lily. Now when she nursed Nicki, it was a specific, rather than a generic activity. But there were still times when he felt pangs of something else, when he looked at the two of them and the warmth they shared and ached to be part of it.

This was one of those times. To get his mind off the aching, he asked, "What does that feel like?"

"It's peaceful," Lily said, smiling into Nicki's eyes. "And very satisfying."

"I mean physically. When she sucks. Is it like when I do it?"

The color in her cheeks deepened. After a minute, she raised her eyes to his. Her voice was feminine without being seductive. "It's the same, but it's different."

"Explain that." When she sent him a pleading look, he said in a voice that was masculine without being seductive, "I want to know."

"But it's hard to explain, and it's embarrassing. Here I am, at the same time nursing my baby and thinking about a man doing…putting…"

"Sucking." His mouth twitched. "Spit it out, Lily. No need to play prim. After all, you're the woman who insisted I stay naked."

"You keep me warm when you're naked." She looked at his chest. "Besides, I liked what we were doing."

"We were sleeping."

"Before that," she said and took a breath. He was right. There was no reason to be prim, after what they'd done with and to each other. Meeting his eyes again, she said, "The difference between what you do and what Nicki does is in intent and outcome. When Nicki nurses, the sucking sensation brings out maternal things like love and pride and protectiveness. The satisfaction is in the doing. When you, uh, do the same thing, it makes me want more."

He grinned. "Does it now?"

She nodded, and for several minutes, they simply looked at each other, neither one of them saying a word. Finally, with a bit of the devil in it, his grin broadened. "There. You did a real good job with that explanation."

Lily was entranced by his grin. It made him look younger, less stern, almost happy, and the bit of the devil in it was highly endearing. Without thinking, she raised her splinted wrist and touched the tips of her fingers to his chin. He took her hand and gently held it to his neck.

"How does it feel?" he asked.

"Rough. A little stubbly. Very manly."

"Not my chin. Your wrist."

"Oh. Okay."

He sighed. "What does 'okay' mean?"

"Better than yesterday."

"Still ache?"

"A little. It's more an annoyance than anything."

He lightly rubbed her arm just above the splint. "First priority when we hit civilization is a hospital. A cast will be neater and easier to manage than this."

When we hit civilization. The words echoed in Lily's mind, but they didn't have the element of relief they'd had twenty-four hours before. She was feeling safe just where she was, she realized. Safe and happy. Holding Nicki, looking at Quist, it suddenly occurred to her that she wouldn't mind it a bit if they were snowbound for months.

But that made her stop and listen, and what she heard was silence. Eyes widening, she glanced toward the window, then looked back at Quist. "It's over?"

"Sounds it," he said calmly. Rather than getting up to check, he waited to see what she was going to say next.

She didn't say anything at first. She looked down at Nicki, lowered her head and rubbed her cheek against the baby's hair in an attempt to recapture the sense of solidarity she shared with Nicki. They were a twosome, mother and daughter. They'd gone through nine months and five weeks together. They'd left Hartford to make a new life for themselves, and that was just what they'd do.

Now, though, there was Quist. She wasn't sure where he fit into the life they were making, but it had to be somewhere. He was too special; what she'd done with him was too intimate. Even if their relationship proved to be nothing more than an aberration, a product of being caught together in an isolated cabin in the midst of a blizzard, she'd remember him. She wasn't sure she was ready to say good-bye.

When she raised her eyes to his, they were filled with tears. "We were just starting to have fun," she whispered.

Quist didn't know whether to laugh or cry. He'd been thinking the same thing, but hadn't wanted to say it. "Don't you dare go weepy on me now."

"If the snow's stopped, you'll be leaving."

"I don't know for sure that it's stopped."

"Aren't you going to look?"

"Me? And freeze my butt off? I'm not dressed." He took a lazy breath. "Maybe later."

"But you said you'd have to set off first thing in the morning," she argued. Even as she did it, though, something in his expression registered. He was looking a little too content, almost to the point of smugness. Slowly the meaning of the look set in. He was giving them an extra day. "Thank you," she whispered, and this time the tears that welled were ones of happiness.

Quist wanted to scold her, but couldn't. Her tears, he was learning, were as expressive of what she was feeling as a laugh or a sigh or a moan. They came and went quickly, and were eminently honest. He couldn't fault her for that, particularly since in this case she was crying because she was pleased to be spending another day with him.

He wondered what was going to happen when the time came for them to part. It wouldn't be the lightest of moments, he knew, and determined to push it out of his mind.

Actually that was easily done. Once Nicki was fed, they did dress to make a trip to the outhouse. The snow had stopped, and the forest was beautiful, which added to the idyllic feeling they brought back into the cabin with them. While Lily played with Nicki, Quist put together a breakfast that, while it wasn't quite as imaginative as Lily's had been, filled their stomachs. When they were done, he helped her bathe the baby, and when they were done with that and Nicki had been rocked and sung to and put in for a nap, they bathed themselves. All three baths were a joint effort. The last two led to something far hotter than the water.

"I've never been like this in my life," Lily murmured when, once again, they lay sweaty and spent in each other's arms. "You've corrupted me."

Quist gave a weak laugh, which was all he could muster after the physical exertion he'd just made. "I think you got that backward. You're the corrupter. I'm just an innocent cowboy."

"For an innocent cowboy, you sure know how to do some naughty things."

He opened an eye and looked down at her. "And you loved them. Admit it. You loved them."

"I admit it," she said simply. Pressing a kiss on his chest, she put her head down. "This is all so unreal," she breathed.

"Mmm."

"Hard to believe how we met."

"Hard to believe what we've done since we met."

She laughed softly, almost to herself, but the laugh quickly died. She was thinking that it would be a story for the books, one to tell the grandchildren, only she didn't know whose grandchildren she'd tell. She and Quist wouldn't have any together.

"Quist?"

"Mmm?"

"When do you think you'll leave?"

He was quiet for a time. Finally he said, "Tomorrow. You ought to have your wrist casted right, Nicki's running out of diapers and I'm getting sick of hash."

He was right on all counts, she knew. She also knew that she'd give just about anything to stay another day, then another day after that. But it couldn't be. He had to leave. Thought of that brought new worries.

"The snow's deeper now than when we hiked in here. The going will be tough."

"I've got long legs."

"But you may get lost."

"I'll follow the break in the trees, same way I did to get us here, and I won't have the wind and the snow."

"What about animals? They'll be out foraging for food. I think I read somewhere that there are bears in northern Maine."

"They're in hibernation." Taking her chin, he tipped her face to his. "I'll be okay, Lily."

"I'll worry."

"But I'll be okay. And you will be, too."

Lily wasn't so sure. The thought of Quist leaving, of his being gone for a long time gave her a desolate feeling. She was going to have to learn to live with it, she supposed, but that didn't mean it wasn't real.

"Kiss me," she whispered, wanting a little forgetfulness.

He gave her that and more, then repeated the good deed while Nicki was napping that afternoon. He might have been sick of hash, but his appetite for Lily was endless, so much so that he was almost willing to consider staying put for another day when the decision was taken out of his hands. The sound of an engine broke through the silence of the forest, waking him from a doze. Slipping out of Lily's arms, he went to the window in time to see the arrival of a pair of snowmobiles.

In an instant he was back shaking Lily's shoulder. "Up you go, sweetheart. We've got company." He was into his pants in a flash, then helped Lily into hers. She had just managed to pull on a sweater when the door burst open.

Their guests, it seemed, weren't guests at all, but the son of the owner of the cabin and his girlfriend. It was a toss-up as to who was the most uncomfortable—Lily and Quist for having been caught in the love nest they had created, or the two younger lovers who had come to create their own.

Civilization, it seemed, was an hour away by snowmo-

bile. With a little arm twisting, Quist managed to convince
his male counterpart to return with him for help. Leaving
the young girl with Lily, and feeling better that she wasn't
alone, he set off.

Shortly before dark he returned with a snowplow and its
driver, the boy and his snowmobiles, plus two gallons of gas.

CHAPTER EIGHT

THE NEXT FEW HOURS passed in something of a blur for Lily. With Quist's help—and that of the young girl, who was anxious to see them gone and be alone with her boyfriend—she neatened the cabin and repacked the things they'd carried through the snow. Strapping Nicki to her chest, she climbed into the cab of the truck to sit between the driver and Quist.

The distance to the car was no more than four miles. What had taken Lily and Quist more than three hours to trek through on foot in the storm took the snowplow thirty minutes. Between the two men, the Audi was shoveled off, towed onto the newly plowed path, gassed up and warmed in another thirty minutes. By the time darkness was complete, Lily and Quist were following the truck back to town.

Quist drove. With his Stetson on his head and the collar of his sheepskin jacket up, he looked so much like the distant cowboy she'd picked up in the storm that Lily felt lonely again. Occasionally he glanced at her, but the night masked his expression. Only once, when he reached out to touch her, did she feel a breath of the warmth they'd shared.

He stopped in town to settle up with the driver of the snowplow and make arrangements to have his abandoned rental car retrieved and returned to an agency outlet. Then, as promised, he set off for the nearest hospital. It turned out to be an hour north of where they'd emerged from the woods. Nicki, who had awoken hungry halfway through

the drive, was already fed by the time they arrived, and
again, Quist took charge. Holding the baby like a pro, he
ushered Lily inside, had an X ray taken and an orthopedist
examining her arm before she'd had time to do more than
fill out a cursory form, and while Nicki slept in his arms,
he watched the doctor put a lightweight, waterproof cast
on Lily's wrist.

Back in the Audi, parked under the bright lights of the
emergency entrance, Quist turned to her. His voice was
deep, quiet. "Quebec is four hours north of here. It's ten
now. We could be there by two. Or we can find a place to
spend the night and make the drive in the morning." He
watched her closely, trying to look through the frail mask
of her defenses. Cautiously he said, "I say we find a place.
I want a hot shower and a big bed. How about it?"

He'd read her well, she mused with a smile and a nod.
She was feeling tired, though she didn't know why she
should, since she and Quist had dozed on and off for a good
part of the day. Perhaps more than tired, she was drained.
Leaving the security of the cabin had thrown her once
more into the limbo of her life. Finding a room somewhere, with four walls and Quist, sounded just right.

What they found, actually, was a ski lodge that had plenty
of midweek vacancies. They took one room; there was never
any question of taking a second. Quist registered in his name,
and if the clerk chose to assume that they were a family, that
was fine. All they asked of him was the room key and a
portable crib, both of which he produced without pause.

The room wasn't fancy, but it was warm, carpeted and
blessed with a king-size bed. Nicki was quickly changed
and put into the portable crib, and while Lily rubbed her
back to help her fall asleep, Quist took the shower he'd been
dying to have. When he'd finished, he came back for her.

Reluctant to wet her cast until it had fully hardened, Lily
opted for a bath, and nothing, she swore, nothing had ever

felt so good—at least, that was what she told Quist, who was helping her at every turn. The fact that he made her feel better than the bath was something she kept to herself. She wasn't sure whether he'd take it as calculated flattery, and she didn't want that.

What she wanted was to go to Montana with him. She wasn't sure when she'd gotten the idea, but it had come to her and stuck like glue. But she knew what he thought of women, in general, and women on a ranch, in particular. Granted, he had to know by now that she wasn't a piece of fluff, still she had to be careful. She couldn't do anything to suggest she was trying to manipulate him. If she was to go to Montana, the idea had to come from him.

So she simply smiled her pleasure as she floated in the hot bath water. He helped her soap up, even washed her hair, and by the time he'd finished drying her off, the towel he'd wrapped around his hips was too small.

They made love on the clean sheets of the king-size bed, and even apart from the cleanliness of the bed and their bodies, the experience was new and different, special in ways that Lily couldn't begin to name. Hunger, greed, joy, desperation—so many things entered into their mating that it was hard to sort one from the other. The past was a dream, the future an enigma, yet they were affected by both. And in the aftermath, when Lily lay with her head and an arm on his chest and a slender leg between his longer, more ropey ones, she knew that she loved him.

Morning came all too soon. Though they lingered in the waking, taking time with Nicki and each other, and then lingered over breakfast in a nearby coffee shop, inevitably they had to drive on.

It was midafternoon when they reached Quebec. Again Quist took a room, this time at the Hilton, which, he told Lily, had a shopping arcade so that she'd have something to do while he was out taking care of business. Lily wanted to tell him that she didn't like shopping, and that she'd be glad to go with him to confront the half sister he'd never seen, and that if anything she ought to be looking for an apartment for Nicki and herself.

She didn't tell him any of those things, not because they weren't true, but because he was gone before she'd had a chance.

So she stayed in the room to feed and change Nicki, and by the time she was done, it was too late to start apartment hunting. Besides, she wanted to be there when Quist returned, if only she knew when that would be. He had an address, she knew, but whether he'd find his half sister there, or whether he'd have to go elsewhere, and if he did find her how long they'd spend talking, Lily didn't know.

The complicating factor, of course, was that Lily didn't know quite where she stood with Quist, and that was the one thing that made her most uneasy as the minutes piled up. Playing with Nicki was a distraction and a comfort, but when Nicki began to doze off, the distraction was gone. So she bathed. With the comfort and compactness of the cast on her wrist, she had greater use of her fingers than she'd had before. She brushed her hair until it shone, put on the smallest bit of makeup, dressed in a sweater and skirt. Frustrated with the waiting, she put a sleeping Nicki into the carrier, slid the straps over her shoulders, anchoring the baby to her front, and went down to sit in the lobby and wait for Quist there.

He returned ninety minutes after he'd left. Lily saw him instantly as he strode from the revolving door. Even without the Stetson, which he held in his hand, he stood head and shoulders above the rest, but he didn't look pleased.

Hurrying to join him, she weathered a tense glance as they stepped into the elevator. He didn't say a word, simply punched their floor then stood with his jaw set and his eyes on the digital readout. With other people in the car she knew he wouldn't talk, but once they reached the privacy of their own room, she waited apprehensively.

He stalked to the window, pulled back the sheer and stared at the night lights of the city.

"Quist?" she prodded.

Slowly he turned and in an equally slow but very angry voice said, "She wasn't there. At the first place they sent me to a second, and at the second they sent me to a third. At the third place they told me she'd left town." His nostrils flared with the carefully controlled breath he took. "She left town. I came all this goddamned way, lost three days in a damned blizzard, not to mention the two days I spent checking out New York and Boston, and she left town."

Lily gave a small moan of disappointment. "When?"

"Day before yesterday."

"In the storm?"

"They said it wasn't so bad here. She probably figured she'd use it to her benefit by getting a jump on anyone who might be on her tail." He thrust a hand through his hair, then hooked both hands on his hips and scowled. "If I'd have gotten here when I was supposed to, I'd have caught her, and if I'd have done that, I'd be back home right now."

"And if I hadn't taken the wrong turns," Lily put in, because she knew he was thinking it, "you'd have gotten here when you were supposed to." She paused. "I'm sorry, Quist. I messed you up."

"Women always mess me up," he grumbled without acknowledging her apology. "I'm the man, but they're the ones doing the screwing. I haven't met a woman yet who was good for her word. Jennifer calls me and asks if I'll come—I come and she's gone. She's just like her mother. Runs away and keeps running. I don't know why I thought it would be any different."

Lily didn't like being lumped with his women, particularly since she'd been honest from the first. But the argument was better saved for later. When it came to anything to do with his mother, and Jennifer had to do with his mother, he was raw. "Did they say where she'd gone?"

"Chicago."

"Chicago!"

"That's what I said."

"What's she going to do in Chicago?"

"Same thing she was going to do here, I guess—hide out until things quiet down."

"But if you were able to find out where she's headed, so will whoever it is who's following her."

He shook his head. "She had protective friends. I had to show an ID to get the information. At least she had enough brains to give them my name and say I'd be coming. But what in the hell does she expect me to do, follow her all over the goddamned northern hemisphere?" Swearing again, he turned back to the window.

Lily took in the rigid set of his shoulders and his tight stance, and although the circumstances were completely different, she couldn't help but remember when they'd first met. He'd been angry then, too—at himself for falling asleep at the wheel, at her for being a woman picking him up in a sporty red car, at the world for stranding him on a mountain road, at whatever it was that had made it snow.

She'd been able to shrug off his anger then, because she hadn't known him at all. She knew him now, though, and it bothered her to see him upset. Slipping her arms out of the carrier, and laying Nicki in the center of the bed, she went to him.

"What will you do?" she asked in a softer voice. When he didn't answer, she put a tentative hand on his back, and when he didn't move away, she slid it up and began to lightly massage his shoulder. "She's young. Probably frightened and confused."

"She should have stayed put," he growled. "I told her I'd come."

"But she doesn't know you. Maybe she's as wary of men as you are of women."

"Then she shouldn't have called me in the first place."

"But you're her half brother. You may be the only living relative she has."

"Does that give her the right to use me?"

"It gives her the right to ask for your help. You could have refused her at the start."

"I should have."

"Why didn't you?"

"Because she's my half sister," he snapped. "She may be the only living relative *I* have."

Which said a lot, Lily mused. It said that though Quist didn't have family, he wanted it, and that made her love him all the more. Unable to help herself, she slid an arm around his waist and fitted herself to his side. "You're a softy, do you know that?"

"I've never been a softy," he muttered.

"Maybe not on the outside, but inside—" she flattened a hand on his chest "—you've got heart."

"I won't be taken advantage of."

"Who's trying to?"

He hesitated for a minute before shooting her a look. "You. I know what you're thinking. You're thinking that if I've come this far, I owe it to myself to go to Chicago. It's on the way home, if I was driving. But I'm not, and you know it."

"I wasn't thinking that at all, but since you mention it, it's not such a bad idea."

"She could be gone when I get there. This has been a wild-goose chase so far. Who's to say Chicago isn't just the next bogus stop?"

"Can you call her first? I assume you have an address. Do you have a phone number?"

"No, and I can't get one. She's staying with a friend. I have the address but no name, and the lady I spoke with didn't know it."

"Chicago is on the way."

"Not as the crow flies."

"But as American or Delta or TWA flies. You could easily stop there on the way home."

He grimaced. "Damn it, I shouldn't have to do that."

"What's your alternative? After you've gone through all this, can you really go home and forget about her? Won't you always wonder what happened? Won't you wonder whether she got into trouble? Won't you feel guilty that maybe you weren't there when she needed you?"

"I *was* there, but she *moved*," he argued, feeling more frustrated than anything else.

Quietly, Lily said, "You'll always wonder, Quist."

He stared at her hard. "You're laying a guilt trip on me."

"No. I'm trying to put into words what you won't. You make yourself out to be a callous kind of guy, but you're not that at all. And I think that if you don't follow this thing through, you'll always wonder if you should've."

He continued to stare at her, but the hardness was easing. "You're being manipulative."

"Me? Manipulative?" She'd tried so hard not to be. "How am I being manipulative?"

"Your words. Your tone. They're so damned reasonable. And the way you've got yourself plastered to my side—how can I think straight when you do that?"

She started to move away, but he tugged her right back, and then it was his long arm that sandwiched her in. "If you're such a tough guy," she said, tipping up a defensive chin, "you should be able to withstand anything I do. And while we're on the subject," she grabbed at a breath, "I want to make a couple of things clear. I am not a manipulative woman, nor have I ever tried to take advantage of you—" her voice dropped "—well, maybe I did when we first met, because I thought you could help me if I got stuck in the snow, but after that plan fell through, I wasn't thinking at all in terms of what I could get out of you." She paused to recoup, and her voice rose again. "And the fact that I'm telling you this should make my next point. I've never lied to you. I've never gone back on my word. So don't group me with women you've known in the past. It's not my fault you're a lousy picker of women."

Finished, she closed her mouth, but in the next blink it was open again. "If it hadn't been for the storm, we'd never have met. If you'd seen me on the street, you wouldn't have looked twice. You've said it yourself, I'm not your type. Well, I say 'hallelujah' because it doesn't sound to me like your type is so hot."

Held captive by the vibrancy of her features, Quist felt a swelling in the area of his heart. Lily was unreal, that was all there was to it. She was a vision he'd conjured up to fill the void in his life—which was truly remarkable, since before this trip he hadn't given great thought to that void. She was sweet and agreeable, industrious, domesticated, feisty when she felt he was being unjust, and dynamite in bed.

She gave him a dark look. "What are you grinning at?"

"You're dynamite in bed. Do you know that?"

She made a face. "Is that relevant to this discussion?"

"I think so." His gaze fell to her lips and stayed there.

"How?"

"It has to do with our relationship," he said, but his voice was lower, almost distracted as his eyes traced the shape of her mouth. "You turn me on even when you're telling me off. How can that happen?"

A slow warmth was starting to seep through her. "Maybe because what I say is the truth, and because an honest woman turns you on."

"I doubt it. I think it's because you're such a little thing,

and when you get up on your soapbox your cheeks turn pink
and your eyes flash, your lips caress the words and your
breasts go up and down with each breath. I'm a breast man."

"Do tell."

"I'd rather show." But it was her chin that he took in his
fingers, and her mouth that he seized. His kiss was long
and thorough. When he let her up for air, he said against
her mouth, "So you really think I should go to Chicago?"

Her voice was a wisp of air. "Think? How can I think
anything when you kiss me that way?"

"You said I should go to Chicago. I want you to come."

Her head cleared a little. "To Chicago?"

"To Chicago." He gave her another long, drugging kiss.
"Or else I might change my mind halfway there. You're my
conscience."

"I thought," she whispered, "I was dynamite in bed."
Her eyes were heavy-lidded, her head back, her lips moist
and parted.

Unable to resist their lure, he kissed her again, and this
time he couldn't stop. His hands got into the act; his whole
body got into the act. In no time, it seemed, clothes were
strewn around the room, and they were making love on the
plush dove-grey carpet. At one point Lily thought she heard
him murmur, "I need you with me," but, if so, the words were
overshadowed by deeds, and she lost all but the moment.

There was, of course, no question but that she'd go to
Chicago with him. She loved him. As improbable as it
seemed, when a week before she hadn't known he existed,
she'd fallen hard. While her feelings for Jarrod had been
conscious and rational, what she felt for Quist was more
passionate on every count. It wasn't necessarily wise; she
had no idea where it would lead, but it was strong enough
to keep her from turning away. She was happy. Traveling
with Quist, spending days and nights with him gave her
pleasure. She had a right to that, she reasoned.

Quist was strong, perhaps headstrong at times, but gentle and caring as well. As angry as he might be at the fates, he couldn't sustain anger against her. Looking back on it, she realized he'd never been able to do it. Even at the beginning, he'd been more bark than bite. He made her feel protected; more than that, he made her feel worthy of his protection.

And he was good with Nicki. Lily loved the way he held the baby, careful but now steady and competently. Despite all his grumbling at the start, he seemed genuinely attached to Nicki. He didn't shy from carrying her, bathing her, even changing her diapers, and Lily suspected that if there was food to be spooned in, he'd do that, too. She wanted to believe that having Nicki and her in his life meant something special to him, and though he hadn't said as much in words, nothing of his actions suggested differently. After all, he could have been free of them in Quebec, but he was insisting they continue on with him to Chicago.

So she was going. Quebec held nothing special for her. She'd chosen it because it was new, because she'd heard good things about it, and because it was a safe distance from Hartford and the long arm of Jarrod's family. The irony that she'd met Quist because his half sister had chosen to run there, too, didn't escape her. But she didn't dwell on it. Nor did she dwell on—or Quist raise the issue of—if, when and how she'd return to Quebec. She was taking one day at a time.

That seemed to be what Quist was doing, too. Though he kept a steady pace, he didn't break any speed records on the way to Chicago. He was keeping in daily touch with the ranch, though, enough to know that snow had fallen there, too. If there was more, he told Lily, and if the temperatures fell much, he was going to have to airlift hay to large numbers of his herd. He had to get back soon, he knew. Still, he wasn't racing.

Chicago was their crossroads. Though neither of them said as much, both knew that there were decisions to be made there. It was one thing to leave Quebec and head for another way station, but once they left Chicago—and Quist swore he wouldn't, couldn't go any farther in search of Jennifer—the next stop would be Montana. Lily's going there was a step that would take some discussion.

The discussion, though, once they reached Chicago, revolved around Jennifer. Reaching the city in the middle of the afternoon, they drove directly to the address Quist had been given. It was a small house on the outskirts of the city, modest verging on shabby. Lily was surprised. With the jumping from large city to large city that Jennifer had done, she'd expected something more cosmopolitan.

"They've all been places like this," Quist told her as he studied the house. "Very plain." He looked at Lily. "I'll go see if she's here. If she is, I'll be back for you." To the objective observer, he looked perfectly calm, but Lily had spent long enough studying his face to recognize the subtle tightness around his nose and mouth.

"Won't you want to see her yourself?" she asked. "Nicki and I can wait here."

"In the cold, no way. If I go in, you go in." He paused. "Aren't you a little bit curious?"

She gave him a crooked smile. "I suppose." She offered her mouth when he leaned over in search of it, then she watched him unfold his tall frame from the car and approach the house.

Two minutes later he came back for her. The tension remained around his nose and mouth, and Lily could have sworn she saw something approaching fear in his eyes. But it was gone before she could be sure, and after he helped her out, he took Nicki in his arms.

It occurred to Lily then that she and Nicki were Quist's security. They were his family as he confronted someone who was also his family but in whom he had no faith at all. Lily knew that she was a calming force for him; she'd seen it different times when he'd been tense or angry, when looking at her or touching her had relaxed him. The situation with Jennifer clearly put him on edge. It also opened up feelings of vulnerability. If Lily gave him confidence, that was good. She found deep satisfaction in being there for him.

Jennifer Simmons had no one to give her confidence. Her vulnerability was right there on the surface, along with features that were young and lovely and eyes that were years too old. She was dressed simply, in jeans and a shirt, and she looked up at Quist as though she didn't know whether to hug him or run away.

Awkwardly she introduced them to the older woman with whom she was staying, and showed them into the house. When they were seated in the living room, she swallowed hard. She looked down at her hands, which were pale and tightly clenched. She looked up at Quist.

"Thank you for coming," she said in an unsteady voice. "I wasn't sure you'd follow me here."

Quist wanted to be angry with her. She was his mother's daughter, and he'd been angry at his mother all his life. But at first glance Jennifer looked more unwitting than evil. So rather than be angry, he was cautious. "You gave my name to your friends. I assumed you expected me."

She shook her head. Her hair was dark like Quist's but shorter and fine. It hugged her head and would have made her look waiflike if she hadn't been so tall. Lily guessed her to be five nine. She also guessed that she could have been a model if she'd wanted to.

"I didn't know what to expect," Jennifer said, still unsteadily, "but I had nowhere else to turn."

Where else but to blood kin, Lily thought as dozens of questions flooded into her mind. If she'd been Quist, she'd have been wondering whether Jennifer looked like her

mother, whether they'd been close, what her mother had
been like, whether Jennifer had any other siblings, whether
her mother had remarried and finally settled down, whether
she'd ever mentioned Quist.

Quist wasn't unaware of those questions. But he was
guarded, not yet ready to open up that part of the relationship. "You told me there was a man, that he was involved
in embezzlement and that he planned to implicate you in it."

Jennifer held herself straight, but there was a fine trembling in her arms that made her shirt shimmer as though
there was a wind whispering through the weave. She hesitated for just a minute, seeming as reluctant to trust Quist
as he was to trust her. Then a tiny flicker of resignation
crossed her features, suggesting that she had no choice.

"His name is Walker Keane. I've known him most of
my life, but it's just been the last two years that we've
been together."

"You're having an affair with him?" Quist asked bluntly.

She looked down. "Yes. We—I thought he was a good
person. He had a nice place to live, and he was always
buying me things. All he asked was that I look good for
him. He liked to show me off. I made him feel younger."

That sounded ominous. "How old is he?"

"Forty-three."

Quist was silent, trying to reconcile the twenty-four-year
difference in ages. He thought of Lily's being eleven years
younger than him, but eleven years wasn't twenty-four.

Jennifer made no attempt to rationalize the difference.
If anything, she seemed eager to get away from it. "We
were living in Albany. He was a free-lance business
manager. He would hire himself out to different companies
for a limited period of time. That meant he could work as
much or as little as he wanted to, and it meant that we could
go away a lot. He liked doing that, going off on trips."

"Did you?"

She hesitated, then nodded. "Walker's the only man I've ever really known. I trusted him. From the first I can remember, he was always around, and even though he used to get into some awful battles with Mom—"

"He's been around that long?"

"Since I was seven or eight."

The guy sounded perverse to Quist. "He was attracted to you back then?"

"Not to me," Jennifer said. "To Mom."

Nicki started crying. Only after Quist handed her over to Lily did he realize how tightly he'd been holding her. With a determined effort, he relaxed his muscles.

But Jennifer was leaning forward, smiling at Nicki in a way that made the girl look fifteen. "She's adorable. How old is she?"

"Almost six weeks now," Lily said.

Jennifer's gaze skipped back and forth from Nicki's face to Lily's, then Quist's. "She looks like you," she told Lily, and Lily didn't say a word as to why that should be so.

Neither did Quist, but only in part because he didn't mind being mistaken for Nicki's father. The other part was still trying to comprehend what Jennifer had said about her mother and Walker Keane. It disgusted him to think that mother and daughter had been involved with the same man, even if it had been at different times.

"How did Keane get into trouble?" he asked a bit sharply.

Jennifer looked up from Nicki, and her smile quickly faded. "I'm not sure how or when it started. All I know is that he's been accused of stealing hundreds of thousands of dollars from different ones of the companies he worked for."

"Where do you come in?"

"He doesn't have much of a defense, I guess, so he's going to say that I put him up to it."

"A nineteen-year-old girl?" Quist asked skeptically.

"And before me, my mother. He'll say that the original scheme was hers, and that I just carried on after she died."

"Does he have proof?"

"How can he have proof if it's not true?" she cried. It was the first time she'd betrayed any of the frustration she was feeling, but she quickly regained control of herself. "He has proof that we helped him spend the money, and we did that, only we thought he'd come by it honestly."

"Your mother cared about things like honesty?" Quist blurted out. He couldn't control the asking any more than he could the bitterness behind it.

Jennifer remained quiet, thinking, choosing her words. "I know you have no reason to feel anything for her. She wasn't much of a mother to you."

"Much?" he echoed tartly.

"Okay, she wasn't a mother at all," Jennifer said, and both her tone and her look said that her guard was down. "But she was to me. She never got divorced from your father, so she never married mine, and he didn't stick around long enough for it to matter. So I grew up with one parent, too, except that after a little bit we had Walker. But the whole time, Mom tried. She worked as a bookkeeper until Walker said she didn't have to work anymore, and I was glad he said it. She worked too hard. She worked too hard trying to be good with Walker, too. Sometimes she was his mother and sometimes his lover, and sometimes she was something in between. That was when there was trouble. But all she wanted was to have us be together, Walker and me and her. Maybe she felt she'd blown it once—I don't know, because she never mentioned you to me, but I do know that she liked the idea of family."

She stopped and was studying Quist. "You're older than I thought you'd be."

"She was seventeen when I was born."

"Maybe she was too young to handle having a baby. Did she love your father?"

"I doubt it."

"Do you remember her at all?"

"No. I was an infant when she left."

Jennifer frowned and looked away. "I wonder what she did all those years in between." She looked back up at Quist. "What do you think? She never talked about the past. It was like her life began when I was born. When I used to ask her questions about where she was born or what it was like when she was little, she'd give me general answers that said nothing at all."

Quist wanted to offer some kind of dark speculation as to what the woman had done after she'd abandoned his father and him, and though he had plenty of words at the ready, he couldn't get himself to utter a one. He was coming to wonder whether Jennifer Simmons wasn't, in her way, a victim of her mother, too. Jennifer had loved the woman. He couldn't see deliberately hurting her for the sake of his own vengeance. Far safer to stick to Jennifer's present predicament.

So he cleared his throat. "Where is Keane now?"

"In Albany."

"Has he been indicted?"

She nodded. "He's out on bail."

"And he actually told you what he planned?"

"He was drunk, but he didn't deny it when I pinned him down the next day."

"So you ran?"

"As fast as I could. I went to stay with someone in Albany, but he came for me there. I thought I could lose him in Manhattan, but I got a call saying he was on his way."

"Who are the people you've been staying with?"

"Friends of my mother. We used to visit them a lot when I was little but not so much after we moved in with Walker. I was counting on their loyalty lying with me."

Quist was grateful she'd had that much sense. She'd been pretty dumb carrying on with a hand-me-down from her mother, but then, she was young, seventeen at the time she'd started in with Keane. Seventeen was the same age his mother had been when she had him and left. And at seventeen, he'd been no cherub, himself. Maybe bad judgment at that age ran in the family.

But that was as far as he wanted to go with family analyses. "What do you want from me?" he asked. It didn't matter that he felt an unbidden affinity for the girl; he wasn't about to be used without knowing the score.

"Advice." She looked at him straight on and would have conveyed utter confidence if it hadn't been for that same fine trembling in her arms. "I think I need a lawyer, but I don't know the first thing about how to go about getting one who would be good for something like this. I tried to reach Henry Melnick—he was the lawyer who called me after my mother died and told me about you—but he's dead, and I don't know where else to turn. My mother's friends—the people I've stayed with—don't know. Walker was in control of just about my whole life." Looking off to the side, she said more quietly, "I don't have much money, and I can't get a loan from the bank." She looked back at him with as determined a gaze as he'd received from her. "But I'll pay you back. I'll work for you, or work somewhere else and make payments to you every week from my salary. I can type, or file, or do whatever somebody trains me to do. But I don't want to go to jail."

The silence that followed her words was abrupt and final, indeed like the steel doors of a prison clanging shut.

Quist continued to study her, but Lily's words were the ones echoing in his mind. *Can you really go home and forget about her? Won't you feel guilty? You'll always wonder.*

"You won't go to jail," he said at last.

"If Walker implicates me, I will."

"He's only using you to take a little of the weight off him. No prosecutor will charge you without solid evidence." He truly believed that, but he had no intention of leaving it to chance. Rising from the sofa, he reached down to take Nicki from Lily. "There's a lawyer I trust in Billings. He won't handle the case himself, but he'll give us the name of someone in New York who can."

With Lily at his side, he went to the door. There, he turned back to Jennifer, who was standing in the hall looking nearly as unsure as she had at the first.

"I'll make the calls from the hotel. We'll be staying at the Hyatt. If you want to join us there for dinner, I may have something to tell you. Say, eight?"

Jennifer nodded.

Only after they were back in the car and stuck in the rush-hour traffic did Lily turn to Quist. "What do you think?" she asked cautiously. He'd been looking dark since they'd left the house.

He shrugged.

"Is that a 'she's nice'?"

"It's a 'she's young and lost and I don't know what the hell else, because I barely spent twenty minutes with the girl.'"

"You liked her."

"I didn't spend *long* enough with her to like her."

"But you'll help her."

"A few calls. I'm making a few calls, and I'll pick up the tab, but only because I have the money and I got nothing better to do with it. And, anyway, she'll pay me back."

Lily doubted he'd make her do that, but she said nothing. Well, almost nothing. "You and Jennifer have the same nose."

There was dead silence for a minute, then a rather annoyed, "So?"

"Just making an observation."

Quist made the same observation that night at dinner.

Shortly afterward, he gave Jennifer the name, address and phone number of a top-notch lawyer in New York who was expecting to hear from her the next day. He also gave her an airline ticket, plus a check made out to the lawyer. "This will more than cover his retainer. He's to put the excess in an account for your use. I want you to stay in New York until he tells you you can leave. Keep in close touch with him, and whatever you do, don't go running off. This lawyer is your ticket to freedom from Keane."

Jennifer's gratitude was written all over her face. She looked as if she would have thrown her arms around him if he'd shown the slightest receptiveness to that. But he didn't. And though Lily, who knew how warm and physical Quist could be, could have kicked him for keeping his distance, she understood that he needed time.

For Lily, though, time was running out. She had to know where she was going, whether it would be back to Quebec or on to Quist's ranch. The issue weighed heavily on her mind when they returned to their room, and once Nicki had been put to bed, she couldn't put it off any longer.

"Quist?"

He'd just put down the phone from talking with his foreman, but his eyes had been on her the whole time. "Mmm?"

There was a different intonation to his hum. She had a strong suspicion he was thinking the same thing she was. So without preamble, she asked, "What now?"

His eyes dropped to her shoulders, then her breasts, and he invited her over with a toss of his head. Always pleased to be close to him, she rounded the bed and slipped under the arm he offered. He didn't speak, though, but put his lips against her hair.

"Quist?"

"I'm thinking."

"You have to go home."

"I know."

"Maybe I should be heading back to Quebec."

"You can't drive."

"Why not?"

"Alone in the car for that distance with Nicki, it's too much. Maybe if your wrist wasn't broken."

"My wrist is okay. It just aches once in a while. I can do most everything with the cast on."

"You shouldn't do much."

"I have to. I have to get on with my life, Quist."

He didn't say anything, but she could feel the acceleration of his pulse. Taking her face in the V of his hand, he tipped it up. "Kiss me," he ordered and took her lips hard.

She kissed him, loving the hardness for the passion it contained. He was a hard-driving man with a good heart. She wanted to be the one who gave that heart a workout. But his kiss went on, filling her senses, increasingly, to the exclusion of all else.

"Quist, wait," she whispered once, but he didn't allow her any other words. He kept her mouth busy with his own, and by the time he moved on to other parts of her body, she wasn't thinking of talk. Before long they were naked and in bed, writhing against each other in a timeless drive toward release, and when it came, it was better than it had ever been before.

Which was precisely what she'd thought the last time they'd made love, and the time before that, and the time before that.

I love you, she wanted to say, but she didn't dare. What she did say, when they'd regained their senses, pulled up the blanket and relaxed comfortably against each other was, "We have to talk, Quist."

"No need," he murmured sleepily. "You're coming to Montana. This is too good to give up."

"This…what?" she asked.

"What we have.

"What's that?"

"Something good."

"Something good in bed?"

"That, too."

She watched him closely, looked at the way his eyelids lay perfectly at rest and the way the muscles of his face were calm and the way his chest expanded with each slow, sleepy breath he took. And while she wished he was wide awake, looking her in the eye and telling her that he loved her, she had a suspicion that just then, warm and spent and unguarded as he was, he had come as close to that admission as he could.

Forty years of resistance wasn't about to topple in a few short days. Loving Quist, knowing that she wanted to be with him, Lily figured that she could give it a little longer.

CHAPTER NINE

AFTER FOUR MONTHS of living with Quist, Lily didn't regret her decision. She loved the ranch. That wasn't to say that she'd loved it from the start. It had looked big, barren and cold when she'd first seen it in January. Very much the city girl Quist had accused her of being, she was overwhelmed by the expanse of snow-covered prairie and the harshness of the hills, by the distance the ranch was from others, by the pervasive darkness of the night. More than once she pined for the noise and lights of the city.

She didn't tell Quist that. She didn't want him to think she couldn't hack it, when she knew she could. Okay, so the land was large and foreign. So she felt more comfortable inside the house and most comfortable when Quist was with her. Everything was new. She was flexible. She could adapt.

She did. As the days passed, she got used to the largeness of things. She realized that she wouldn't be swallowed up by the land if she went out for a walk with Nicki. Nor would she meet a bear. Nor would a catastrophe happen with no one around to help. If anything, *because* there were fewer people around, those people were more attentive.

The ranch house itself was a pleasure. A single-story, sprawling structure, it blended into the prairie with far more charm that she'd expected to find in Montana. Quist had been right about creature comforts. While she wouldn't have called the house plush, it had all the modern amenities she could want. And once she'd softened the rooms with things like plants, decorative baskets and wall hangings, she felt very much at home.

Yes, she loved the ranch, but mostly she loved what she did there. Her days were filled with taking care of Nicki, polishing the handsome oak furniture, baking things like cinnamon-raisin bread, fresh carrot muffins and Swedish apple pie—and her nights were filled with Quist, which was the icing on the cake.

Her wrist had healed well and was long since forgotten. With the gradual onset of spring, she thrived. Nicki thrived, too. Quist had found a pediatrician they both liked, and one glowing report after another came each month. Still a baby but looking more like a little girl each day, Nicki had the kind of sunny temperament that brought smiles to the faces of those around her, and that included the ranch hands, whom she charmed to a man.

Quist was the most charmed. He never made a big thing of it in front of Lily, but time and again she would find him in a quiet corner playing with Nicki. He always checked on her before he went to bed, and looked in on her again when he awoke at dawn. In turn, Nicki came alive when he entered the room, and when he came close, she raised her arms to him in a bid to be held.

There were times when Lily grew teary-eyed watching the two of them together. She loved Quist for adoring Nicki and loved Nicki for adoring Quist. Each blossomed under the other's attention. Their relationship was innocent and sweet.

But there were times—granted not often, because Lily did everything she could not to think about it—when she grew teary-eyed wishing the relationship were more. Though he fit the role well, Quist wasn't her husband. Nor was he Nicki's father. Lily didn't know what Nicki would

call Quist when she started to talk, or how she'd explain
his position in her life to little friends when she went off
to school. Something had to happen before then, Lily knew,
but she couldn't push the issue.

She was too happy to risk that. It sometimes frightened
her to think that if she'd stayed in Hartford a day longer,
or taken early shelter from the storm in a motel, or taken
a different road or even the same road at a different time,
she'd have missed Quist. As unlikely as any relationship
between them had seemed back then, she couldn't imagine
life without him. He filled every one of her needs. Even
after four months together, her pulses raced when he came
near. After that length of time, any critic who would have
attributed their relationship to the experience of being
snowbound together had to be silenced.

To Lily's knowledge, though, there weren't any critics.
Quist had friends and acquaintances at neighboring
ranches and in town, and they welcomed her warmly.
Several of his ranch hands went so far as to say that Quist's
disposition had taken an upswing since she'd come, and
though one part of her wondered whether they weren't
just buttering her up for the sake of the mocha-nut cake she
made, which they loved, the other part of her accepted
their compliment with pride.

There was one critic, though. Like a bad dream, she'd
thought of him from time to time since she'd come to live
with Quist. But Quist made her feel safe and protected, and
Montana was a long way from Connecticut. It wasn't
Jarrod; he had remarried and would do, she knew, everything he could to forget that Lily existed. It was Michael.
She hadn't dreamed that he would follow her.

He did just that. Late one Monday morning in the beginning of June, he showed up at the door. Unsuspecting,
she went to answer his knock. She was wearing jeans and
a shirt, and was wiping her hands of remnants of the bread

dough she'd just put in the oven. She came to an abrupt halt several steps from the screen when she saw who was there.

Her first thought was to look around for help, but she controlled the urge. "Michael," she said with cool civility.

He dipped his head in greeting. His blond hair was as perfectly groomed as always, his skin as perfectly tanned, his slacks and cotton sweater as perfectly chic. With all that perfection, he looked distinctly out of place. "Aren't you going to let me in?"

"That depends." She resumed wiping her hands on the dish towel. "What do you want?"

"To talk."

"About what?"

"What you've done with yourself in the past few months."

"I don't see why that should be of any interest to you," she said, and though she'd tried to say it evenly, something of her inner feeling must have come through. The battle lines were drawn.

Without invitation, Michael opened the screen and stepped inside. Lily countered by quickly sidestepping him, hooking the towel on the coatrack and escaping to the porch he'd just left.

"D.J.!" she bellowed at the top of her lungs. "D.J.!"

"What in the hell are you doing?" Michael cried, holding the screen door open. "I just want to talk."

She drilled him with a look. "Last time you said that, you ended up throwing things at me." She looked back at the barn in time to see a young man striding purposefully toward her. "I've learned not to make the same mistake twice," she added, then called to D.J., "Can I have your help for a minute? This man wants to talk with me, but I don't care to be alone with him."

"Sure thing, ma'am," D. J. said with a drawl and a smile. He took the two front steps in one stride, then posted himself against the porch rail.

Michael should have been humiliated, but he wasn't. Not Michael. He stared at the young man for a long minute before turning to Lily. "You're a coward."

"Uh-huh." She felt better now that D.J. was there, but that didn't mean she was calm. Her insides shook. She wished she were five ten and robust. She wished she wore armor. She wished Quist were around, but he was out in the Jeep. "So, what do you want?"

Again Michael looked at D.J., but the younger man showed no sign either of looking away or leaving. Finally he decided to ignore him, and, in a pleasant voice, asked Lily, "How have you been?"

"Just fine."

"You're seeing something of the country, I take it." When she didn't respond to that, he smiled and asked, "Do you miss the east yet?"

"Not really."

"This is…different."

"Uh-huh."

He looked off toward the barn, then the open range, then back toward the inside of the house. "A rancher's mistress. Funny, I hadn't pegged you for the mistress type."

Lily felt a momentary chill, but she shook it off. "Wasn't that what you had in mind for me back in Hartford?"

"Of course not. I wanted to marry you."

She'd never heard anything as absurd, but it didn't seem worth her breath to tell him so. "What are you here for, Michael?"

"You," he said. When she gave him a you-must-be-crazy look, he insisted, "I want you to come back with me."

"Why would I want to do that?" she asked in disbelief.

"Because you and I could be good together."

"I don't believe this," she murmured. She turned her head toward D.J. "I don't *believe* this." She glared back at

Michael. "Last time you were threatening me with all kinds of ugly things, and that was before you got violent."

"I was upset. I said things I shouldn't have."

"You certainly did, but that's not even the issue. The issue is that there's nothing between us. There's never *been* anything between us, despite what you threatened to say. Why on earth would I want to go back east with you?"

"Because this is no way to live." He shot a disparaging glance around. "Animals live on places like this. People choose more cultured surroundings."

Even aside from the fact that he'd just insulted D.J., who was within earshot, and Quist and all the others, who weren't, Lily felt personally offended. After all, she'd chosen to live on the ranch. She could have left at any time. "I think you'd better go."

"After I've come all this way to see you?"

That raised another issue, one she wanted answered out of sheer curiosity. "How did you find me?"

But Michael was looking at the approaching ribbon of dust. "Is that your rancher?"

Lily was relieved that it was. She was also relieved that D.J. didn't move. "How did you find me?"

"You wired the bank to have your account transferred here. Where's Nicole?"

The chill she felt this time wasn't so easily shaken off, and at the back of her eyes, she felt the prick of tears. "Nicole is none of your affair," she said on a note of warning.

"She's my niece."

Lily held herself still. "I have a paper that waives any claim you or your family may have on her."

"I'm saying that I care. How is she?" When Lily remained stone-faced, he said, "She was very little when I saw her last. I'll bet she's grown."

Lily refused to even acknowledge Nicki's presence,

though she was, at that moment, close by, in a wind-up swing in the kitchen.

"Come on, Lily. I'm her uncle. I'm curious."

"Nicki and I are doing just fine. Now that you know that, and now that you know I won't go back east with you, you can leave."

"You really intend to raise her here?"

Lily didn't blink. "You can leave, Michael." She didn't want him there. His presence was contaminating something that was good and pure and healthy.

"For God's sake, what kind of a life is this for a child? I mean, if you want to play the rancher's maid, that's one thing. But think of Nicole. She shouldn't have to live this way."

"Live what way?" Lily demanded, trembling now with anger and doing little to hide it.

"A bare-bones existence. This isn't life. It's just survival. Where do you go to shop around here? Where do you go to eat out? No theater? No symphony? The two of you could be spending your days at the club. Nicole could be seeing other children like her, instead of groveling with cows and dust and people who probably haven't graduated from high school."

Lily was livid. "Are you saying that a diploma is a sign of intelligence? That, Michael, is probably one of the most ignorant comments I've ever heard."

"You know what I mean."

"No, I don't. The people I've met here are open and intelligent, and when it comes to common sense, or perceptiveness, or sensitivity, they're head and shoulders above you and Jarrod—*combined*. 'I should be at the club,'" she mimicked. "I *hated* the club. When I think back to the people I met through you two, I thank God Nicki's not there. I'd rather have my daughter growing up knowing people like D.J. any day."

Michael's mouth twisted as he shot a derisive glance at the young cowhand. "Are you putting out for him, too?"

Tears gathered on her lower lids. She was rigid with fury. "Leave, Michael."

But instead of leaving, he narrowed his eyes. "Think, Lily. Think back to when you conceived Nicole and all the things you wanted for her then. This isn't for you, and it's not for her." He darted a glance at the Jeep, which had reached the driveway to the house. "And what kind of relationship do you have with that guy, anyway?" He grabbed her hand, ignoring D.J., who had remained immobile in the face of personal insults but now immediately straightened. "No wedding band. He hasn't married you. You've been living here servicing him all this time, and he hasn't married you? That's dumb, Lily. Really dumb. Oh, not on his part. I have to give him credit for that. He knows a good thing when he sees one. He's got a cook, a laundress, a housekeeper and a lover all for free. What kind of woman is going to put up with that bull?"

Lily yanked her hand back. "No bull, and I know what it looks like, because you and Jarrod gave me plenty. Everything I have here is good. I've never been happier." She heard the Jeep pull to a halt not far from the steps.

"And you think it'll last?" Michael asked, but his words were lower and coming quickly, as though he knew that he was running out of time. "You think he'll still want you in a year, or two or three? He'll tire of you. Or Nicole. Wait till she gets bigger and starts making demands. You think he's going to want you then? You'll be out in the cold, Lily. Out...in...the...cold."

"What's going on here?" Quist asked. His voice was deep and steel-edged, and his eyes were on Michael as he put a possessive arm around Lily's shoulder.

"This," Lily said shakily, "is Michael, my former brother-in-law. I told you about him. Do you remember?"

Quist certainly did. He remembered everything Lily had said and the way she'd said it. "What's he doing here?"

"He came to see how I was. But he's just leaving. Weren't you, Michael?"

The expression on Michael's perfectly tanned face suggested he was feeling thwarted, but he didn't let on to it in words. And Lily could understand why. Michael was tall, but Quist was taller. Quist was also broader and more heavily muscled, a fact that was made abundantly clear by the snug fit of his chambray shirt across his chest and the sinewy forearms that extended beyond the roll of his sleeves.

Michael recognized a formidable opponent when he saw one. Without saying a thing, he sent a final hard look at Lily. Then, exhibiting perfect posture to match his perfect attire, he walked past her, down the steps and to his car.

Quist went after him.

"Wait, Quist," Lily cautioned.

He held up a hand to reassure her, but he didn't look back. Lily watched apprehensively while he leaned low at the driver's window. She couldn't hear what he said. The distance was a little too far, his voice a little too low, the breeze a little too active in the grasses beyond the barn. The instant he straightened, Michael's car shot forward.

"I'll be goin' back to work now, ma'am," D.J. said.

Lily had momentarily forgotten his presence. At the sound of his voice, she swung a surprised look his way. "Uh, oh, sure, D.J. And thanks. Thanks for being here." Softly, just a hair above a whisper, she added, "Please forget what you heard. I don't want to upset Quist."

"Sure thing, ma'am," he said, and with a tip of his hat, he was gone.

Seconds later Quist came up the steps, but Lily was already on her way inside. Heart thudding, she made straight for the kitchen. Nicki was in the swing, just where she'd been left. Its wind-up had long since wound down, but she was perfectly content gnawing on one of the rubber teethers Lily had tied with a ribbon to the chain of the swing.

At sight of her mother, she began to gurgle and grin. Lifting her, Lily held her tightly, closed her eyes and swayed gently from side to side.

"Lily?" Quist came forward from the open archway.

"I'm okay," she breathed.

"You're shaking like a leaf. Did he threaten you again?"

"No. Seeing him was bad enough."

Babbling, Nicki began to kick against Lily's waist.

"He won't be back."

She opened her eyes. "What did you say to him?"

Quist wasn't going to tell her, because it was too crude. "Let's just say I made a little threat of my own. I think he understands that I'll carry it out if he comes near you again."

Again. Did that mean *ever* again, as in during the course of her lifetime? She couldn't ask, couldn't push.

"Hi, pumpkin," Quist said softly to Nicki. When she held out an arm, he took her gently in his. "How long was he here?" he asked Lily.

"Not long. Just a few minutes."

"Did he ask to see Nicki?"

"No. He asked how she was. That's all."

Quist wanted to know what they'd talked about, but he didn't ask. Sounding insecure, which perhaps he was, wasn't part of his image. Sounding distrustful, which perhaps had been true at one point, was no longer. He did trust Lily. He knew that her feelings for him were strong. He couldn't see her picking up and leaving him.

He figured that in her own good time, she'd tell him what Michael had said.

Unfortunately she didn't, and it would have been all right, if they'd settled back into their lives without any sign of the slightest disturbance. But Lily seemed to be quieter at times, not quite preoccupied, not quite as carefree in her silence as she'd been. It didn't happen often, but Quist was so keenly attuned to her that he noticed whenever it did.

When he asked if something was bothering her, she put on her brightest smile and assured him nothing was, and then she'd be her usual self for a while, as though she was making a concerted effort not to let him see. He began to wonder how much time she spent when he was gone, thinking about whatever it was.

A few minutes; that was all the time she'd spent with Michael, but he'd said something that lingered. Quist knew it, and the longer he wondered what it was, the more unsure he grew. The wondering was like a chisel, chipping away at the fragile base of his trust.

In his mind, the issue was a simple one. He wanted Lily to stay with him. He feared that Michael had made her a counteroffer, and while he didn't believe that she'd seriously consider accepting, knowing how she felt about Michael, he couldn't help but wonder if she was rethinking her position in his life.

He wanted to ask her, but he couldn't seem to find the words. Actually he couldn't seem to find the courage. He didn't know what he'd do if she told him that yes, she was rethinking things.

In the end the words he found surprised even him, though the time and place didn't. They'd just made love on the charcoal-gray sheets on his king-size bed. It had been a hard, fiery coupling that had carried them long and far. Their bodies were slick with sweat and exhausted. As always at times like those, Quist's guard was down.

"Marry me, Lily," he said.

Lily didn't move for a minute. Her heart, which had just settled into a relatively even beat, began to pound again. She wondered if she'd heard wrong, or if she'd imagined the words because she'd wanted to hear them so badly. Levering herself up, she looked into his face. It was damp and slumberous, but his eyes were open and though he seemed a little unbalanced, he was looking straight at her.

"Well?" he prodded.

"Uh, what—will you say that again?"

"I want you to marry me."

She was ecstatic—and frightened. Tears came to her eyes, but she willed them back. "Why?"

"Because I like the life we have together. I think it should be formalized."

That wasn't what she wanted to hear. "Why formalized?"

"I don't know. It just seems right. We're living as husband and wife. Why not make it official?"

"Is that what you really want?" she asked warily.

Quist had been hoping for a warmer reception. He wondered if his fears were founded, after all. The thought of that made him more uneasy than ever. "I want to know you won't leave."

"I won't leave."

"Then marry me."

Lily studied his face for a minute, studied the firm set of his jaw, the straight line of his mouth, the dark eyes that were more enigmatic than they'd been in a while, and though she wanted to melt into him, say yes and make him happy, her own happiness rested on knowing more. She couldn't go through life wondering whether Michael's visit had prompted the proposal. "Why now?"

"Because it's time, don't you think?" He scowled for a minute, wishing he had more patience, but when it came to matters of the heart he was too much a novice to feint and parry. Taking her face a little roughly in his hands, he said, "I'd make you a good husband. I'd make Nicki a good father. I want to have more kids, and you do, too, but I won't do that unless we're married."

Lily loved everything he was saying, still he hadn't told her what she needed to know. So she argued, "Not so long ago, you didn't like women. You weren't interested in marriage."

"I've changed."

"Just like that?"

"No, not 'just like that.'" His hands gentled around her face, thumbs picking up the long teardrops that seemed suspended at the corners of her eyes. "It's been six months, and I fought it at first. One part of me still fights—old habits die hard—but I don't want to go back to the other way of living." When she still looked skeptical, he said, "I've been good with Jennifer, haven't I?"

Lily was the first to admit that he had. He'd kept in close touch with the lawyer from New York, and Jennifer had even been west for a visit, with another one planned for the fall. While there wasn't the kind of brother-sister closeness that came from siblings sharing a past, they had a start.

"You've been very good with her," Lily said. "But that's different. She's someone you can see or not, be close to or not. You don't pick your relatives, but you do pick your wife, and if you pick her for the wrong reasons—" She sat up, effectively removing her face from his hands. Perching sideways, she drew her knees to her chest for the warmth she missed.

Quist grew cautious. "What is it, Lily?" His voice was low and slow as he studied her profile. "You're thinking something—you've been thinking something for a while now, and I've been trying to figure out what it is, but I keep coming up with zip. Tell me. I need to know."

Lily stared at the needlepoint wall hanging she'd made for the room; it was burgundy and gray to match the sheets and spread, but the gray was pale and soft, far more feminine than charcoal. It was her personal stamp on this room that was masculine in so many other respects, and it was symbolic of all she'd tried to do in his life. *It's time, don't you think?* he'd asked her. She figured he was right. If he didn't love her now, he never would. It was time to be completely forthright.

"I've been thinking about lots of things," she began. "I suppose that Michael—"

"Michael," Quist cut in. The name brought him sharply to a sitting position. "I knew it had to do with him."

"But it doesn't," she argued, eyeing him over the edge of her shoulder. "Not really. But he voiced things I'd been thinking about for a while. It's one thing when they're in your own mind, another when someone who doesn't even think the way you do says them."

Quist accepted that. Bending a knee, he propped an elbow on it and tried to look casual. "So what did he say?"

"He talked about me as your mistress. He said you had a good thing going, with someone to cook and clean and do everything else around the house. He said you'd get tired of me—"

"No *way*—" Quist began, but Lily cut him off with a hand on his arm as she twisted to face him.

"I know," she said softly. Her throat felt tight, but she pushed the words past it. "I think I knew it a long time ago, because you seemed legitimately pleased to have me here. But there was always that little question in my mind about *why* you were pleased. There was always that little question about whether it was me you liked having around, or a live-in maid, cook, lover. I didn't think about it all the time. I really didn't think about it much. I tried *never* to think about it, but that didn't work, because I've been used—and abused—once, and the hurt is still fresh. Then Michael came, and suddenly it was like he took all my little fears and put them in lights."

"But I want to marry you," Quist insisted. "*You*. Not anyone else I've known in my life. *You*. I could have hired a live-in maid, if that was what I wanted. Or a cook. Or a lover. I've got the money. But I never wanted to have anyone around. Then I met you, and things changed."

"Things."

"What I wanted."

"Why?"

"What do you mean, why?"

"Why did things change? You'd been happy before. From what you said, you were perfectly content with your life."

Quist looked off to the side. "Yeah. That's what I said."

"Weren't you?"

He looked down, thoughtful as his eyes focused unseeingly on the rumpled sheets. "I suppose I was. I had a safe life. I wasn't taking any chances on women. I used them on my terms. I protected myself." He stopped. His gaze rose to the spot where the pale flesh of Lily's hip met the wrinkled sheet. "Then I met you. You were so damned honest, it was hard not to trust you. But there was something else. For the first time in my life, I was taking care of a woman."

He raised his eyes to find that hers had flooded. When he winced, she said quickly, "It's okay. I'm okay. Go on."

He stared at her long enough to make sure that the tears were staying put. Then he shrugged. "What's to say? I enjoyed taking care of you."

"You didn't feel you were being used?"

"How could I feel that, when you resisted my help, and then you were giving me back even more than I was giving." He scowled. "Damn it, Lily, what do you want me to say? I want you here. I want to go on taking care of you. I want to go on taking care of Nicki. I want us to spend the rest of our lives together."

"You could say that you love me," she blurted out, then quickly bit her lip. She hadn't wanted to say that. It was supposed to have come from him. She was about to say something to cover the gaffe when the look of incredulity on his face stopped her.

"Of course I love you," he cried in astonishment. "Isn't that what I've been saying? Isn't it what I've been *doing* for months?"

Tears shimmered in her eyes. "You never said it. I didn't know. You never said it. I need to hear the words."

Unable to hold himself apart from her any longer, he hooked an elbow around her neck and one around her waist and pulled her to him. He ducked his head, sliding his face against her hair. "I love you, Lily." He paused. "And I need to hear them, too."

"I love you," she said, letting the tears go at last.

He was holding her so tightly that it was a miracle she could move to breathe, much less cry, but she did the latter, with the smallest, softest sobs. "I hope it's happiness," he remarked against her cheek.

"And relief." She sniffled, cried a little more, then put her hand over the wet spot she'd made on his chest. The hair was matted; she rubbed it with her fingers, feeling the strength underneath. "I was so afraid. I tried not to be. I kept telling myself that you had to feel something for me, because you were so good to me, and you seemed so happy, but there was always this niggling little doubt."

She hurried on, ignoring the hiccoughing that broke the rush of her thoughts. "Then Michael started talking about the future and what kind of life I'd have here, and it made me realize even more how good it is. It's just the kind of life I want—I love it here, it suits who I am and who I want to be, *you* suit who I am and who I want to be." She took in a trembling breath. "But then I started thinking about what would happen if I ever lost you or lost what I have here." She looked up at him with eyes that were large, still damp but true windows to her soul. "I don't want that to happen, Quist."

For a minute Quist couldn't say a word. He was wondering what he'd ever done to deserve the woman he held in his arms. She was warm and giving, honest, strong enough to support him, vulnerable enough to need his support. And she did love him. It was there in her eyes, spilling from her soul. He'd seen it before, though he'd never had the courage to call it what it was for fear of losing it, but never before had he seen it in quite such a raw state. If he'd doubted before, he no longer did. Lily's love was a part of her being. She could no more free herself from it than she could do without a heart.

That was pretty much the way he felt, he realized. A future without Lily was no future at all. She gave his life dimension, depth and color. His love for her was boundless.

"So," he said a little hoarsely, "will you marry me?"

"Oh, yes," she whispered and offered her lips for a kiss to seal the vow.

EPILOGUE

LILY COULD LOOK at him for hours, which was very much what she did during the first day of his life. She put him to her breast, but her milk hadn't come in yet, and still she found pleasure from his sucking.

Though he was sleeping quietly now, he had a strong pair of lungs. He was also long and had a shock of dark hair so like his father's that Lily grinned through her tears each time she combed it with her fingers.

He was a beautiful baby. Nicole had been beautiful, too, and still was. Inside and out. Lily was blessed.

"Anybody sleeping?" came a deep-murmured call from the door.

She looked up to see two faces peering around the door's edge. Quist was clearly making a game of it, with Nicki not quite sure she wanted to play. It was the first time she'd seen her mother since Lily had gone into labor. It was also the first time she'd been in a hospital since her own birth, and she looked apprehensive.

At the sight of them, Lily's throat went tight. But she smiled broadly, held out her free arm and wiggled her fingers in invitation. Quist brought Nicki into the room. She was clinging to his neck, pressing her cheek to his shoulder, peering at Lily as though she didn't want to, but couldn't resist.

"Hi, sweetheart," Lily finally said. "You look so pretty. Daddy put on your favorite dress?" It was lime-green gingham with grosgrain ribbon at the bodice and hem, and beneath it were white tights and tiny white strap shoes. "And he put a ribbon in your hair." Which was shoulder length, light brown and shiny. "You're my gorgeous little girl." Lily held out her arm. "Can I have a hug, gorgeous little girl?"

But Nicki tightened her arms around Quist's neck and turned her face into his shoulder.

"No hug for Mommy?" Quist asked softly. When she shook her head, he said, "Well, I want to give her one. She's my favorite big girl." He bent over and gave Lily an eloquent kiss, then sat down on the edge of the bed.

"You said *I* was your favorite big girl," came the tiny voice from his shoulder. For a three-year-old, Nicki was unusually verbal. But then, Lily mused, she was unusual in lots of ways.

Quist's eyes smiled at Lily over Nicki's head. "You're right. You are my favorite big girl. Mommy's my favorite *big* big girl." He tucked in his chin to whisper, "Want to see your brother? He's sleeping, but you can take a peek."

She shook her head and didn't look. Quist did, though. He couldn't help it, any more than he could help looking at Lily again when he was done. She was beautiful, and she was the mother of his son. On top of all the other things he loved her for, he loved her for that.

In response to the exquisite look in his eyes, Lily touched his cheek. Then she gently rubbed Nicki's arm. "I've missed you so much, Nicki. I told the doctors that I had to go home tomorrow so that I could be with my daughter."

"How are you feeling?" Quist whispered.

She grinned and nodded, looked at Nicki, looked at the baby. "Incredible. I'm feeling incredible."

"How's he doing?"

She continued to grin. "Incredible." She slipped her thumb into Nicki's loose fist. The small fingers tightened around it. "But the food here is lousy. I miss our special superburgers with bacon."

"I had one yesterday," came the high little-girl voice.

"Did you?" Lily feigned hurt. "And you didn't bring one here for me?"

"I wanted to," Nicki said, "but Daddy said we should wait and make one when you get home." She turned her head just enough so that she could peek at Lily.

"I think I can live with that," Lily decided. "What else did Daddy make for you?"

"Fluff and popcorn and Chunky bars."

"Shhhh," Quist said. "You weren't supposed to tell her that."

Nicki giggled.

Lily loved it, but she didn't let on. "Quist, that's *terrible*. Fluff and popcorn and Chunky bars?"

"Not together," he argued, as though that would excuse it.

"You're corrupting this child."

"I like fluff," Nicki said. "And popcorn. And Chunky bars. Maybe baby wants a Chunky bar." She dared a glance at the infant.

"Mm, not for a little while, sweetheart. Babies only drink milk at the beginning."

"Did I?"

"Sure, you did." Lily had had the same conversation close to a dozen times with her daughter, but she didn't mind the repetition. Babies were something totally new for Nicki.

"His eyes are closed," the little girl said.

"He's sleeping. He'll do that a whole lot."

"When can I play with him?"

"When he's awake. Would you like that?"

She looked a little dubious, still she nodded.

"Come here," Lily said, and this time when she held out her arm, Nicki went right to her. When she was snuggled close to Lily's side, she reached out and timidly touched her brother's hand.

Lily smiled at Quist, who was smiling right back at her, and there were a myriad of messages going back and forth with those smiles.

Jonathan. I like the name Jonathan. After you. I like that, too.

They say he's perfect. Thank you for giving me a perfect son.

I'm glad it was a boy. Every man should have a son.

I'm glad we waited this long. We needed the time together, and Nicki needed the time with us.

Lord, do I love you, Quist.

Ah, Lily, you're the light of my life.

And the smiles went on.

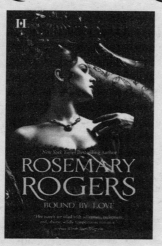

REQUEST YOUR
FREE BOOKS!

2 FREE NOVELS
FROM THE ROMANCE/SUSPENSE
COLLECTION PLUS 2 FREE GIFTS!

YES! Please send me 2 FREE novels from the Romance/Suspense Collection and my 2 FREE gifts (gifts are worth about $10). After receiving them, if I don't wish to receive any more books, I can return the shipping statement marked "cancel." If I don't cancel, I will receive 4 brand-new novels every month and be billed just $5.74 per book in the U.S. or $6.24 per book in Canada. That's a savings of at least 28% off the cover price. It's quite a bargain! Shipping and handling is just 50¢ per book.* I understand that accepting the 2 free books and gifts places me under no obligation to buy anything. I can always return a shipment and cancel at any time. Even if I never buy another book from the Reader Service, the two free books and gifts are mine to keep forever.

185 MDN EYNQ 385 MDN EYN2

Name _____ (PLEASE PRINT) _____

Address _____ Apt. # _____

City _____ State/Prov. _____ Zip/Postal Code _____

Signature (if under 18, a parent or guardian must sign)

Mail to **The Reader Service:**
IN U.S.A.: P.O. Box 1867, Buffalo, NY 14240-1867
IN CANADA: P.O. Box 609, Fort Erie, Ontario L2A 5X3

Not valid to current subscribers of the Romance Collection,
the Suspense Collection or the Romance/Suspense Collection.

Want to try two free books from another line?
Call 1-800-873-8635 or visit www.morefreebooks.com.

* Terms and prices subject to change without notice. Prices do not include applicable taxes. Sales tax applicable in N.Y. Canadian residents will be charged applicable provincial taxes and GST. Offer not valid in Quebec. This offer is limited to one order per household. All orders subject to approval. Credit or debit balances in a customer's account(s) may be offset by any other outstanding balance owed by or to the customer. Please allow 4 to 6 weeks for delivery. Offer available while quantities last.

Your Privacy: Harlequin is committed to protecting your privacy. Our Privacy Policy is available online at www.eHarlequin.com or upon request from the Reader Service. From time to time we make our lists of customers available to reputable third parties who may have a product or service of interest to you. If you would prefer we not share your name and address, please check here. ☐

BOB09

HARLEQUIN® *Romance*®

Welcome to the intensely emotional world of

MARGARET WAY

with

Cattle Baron: Nanny Needed

It's a media scandal! Flame-haired beauty
Amber Wyatt has gate-crashed her ex-fiancé's
glamorous society wedding. Groomsman
Cal McFarlane knows she's trouble, but when
Amber loses her job, the rugged cattle rancher
comes to the rescue. He needs a nanny, and
if it makes his baby nephew happy, he's
willing to play with fire....

**Available in August
wherever books are sold.**

HRI7601

BARBARA DELINSKY

77345 TRUST	___ $7.99 U.S.	___ $7.99 CAN.
66881 FULFILLMENT	___ $6.99 U.S.	___ $8.50 CAN.
66638 THE OUTSIDER	___ $5.99 U.S.	___ $6.99 CAN.

(limited quantities available)

TOTAL AMOUNT	$ _____
POSTAGE & HANDLING	$ _____
($1.00 FOR 1 BOOK, 50¢ for each additional)	
APPLICABLE TAXES*	$ _____
TOTAL PAYABLE	$ _____

(check or money order—please do not send cash)

To order, complete this form and send it, along with a check or money order for the total above, payable to HQN Books, to: **In the U.S.:** 3010 Walden Avenue, P.O. Box 9077, Buffalo, NY 14269-9077; **In Canada:** P.O. Box 636, Fort Erie, Ontario, L2A 5X3.

Name: _____
Address: _____ City: _____
State/Prov.: _____ Zip/Postal Code: _____
Account Number (if applicable): _____

075 CSAS

*New York residents remit applicable sales taxes.
*Canadian residents remit applicable GST and provincial taxes.

HQN™

We *are* romance™

www.HQNBooks.com